T0356696

LADY
KNIGHT

LADY KNIGHT

AMALIE HOWARD

JOY REVOLUTION

Text copyright © 2025 by Amalie Howard
Jacket art copyright © 2025 by Fatima Baig

All rights reserved. Published in the United States by Joy Revolution, an imprint of Random House Children's Books, a division of Penguin Random House LLC, New York.

Joy Revolution is a registered trademark and the colophon is a trademark of Penguin Random House LLC.

GetUnderlined.com

Educators and librarians, for a variety of teaching tools, visit us at RHTeachersLibrarians.com

Library of Congress Cataloging-in-Publication Data is available upon request.
ISBN 978-0-593-70506-3 (trade) — ISBN 978-0-593-70508-7 (ebook)

The text of this book is set in 11.5-point Adobe Garamond Pro.
Interior design by Megan Shortt

Printed in the United States of America
10 9 8 7 6 5 4 3 2 1
First Edition

For anyone who dares to be the exception and not the rule, never apologize for being who you are. You're more than enough.

DRAMATIS PERSONAE

LADY ZENOBIA / ZIA OSBORN
Heiress, Budding Composer, and Lady Knight

MR. RAFI NASSER
A Rakish Gentleman Painter

MISS GREER SORENSEN
Welton Student and Fellow Lady Knight

MISS LALITA VARMA
Welton Student and Fellow Lady Knight

MISS NORI KANEKO
Welton Student and Fellow Lady Knight

MISS ADA PERKINS
A Wise and Courageous Teacher

GEMMA
Lady's Maid and Keeper of Secrets

LORD KESTON OSBORN, MARQUESS OF RIDLEY
Brother to Lady Zia

LADY ELA DALVI
Friend and Future Marchioness of Ridley

VISCOUNT HOLLIS
A Grasping, Devious Peer and Rafi's uncle

DUKE & DUCHESS OF HARBRIDGE
Parents of Lady Zia and the Marquess of Ridley

MRS. PERKINS & MISS PERKINS
Owners of the Welton House School for Elegant Young Ladies

LADY PETAL JOSHI, MISS SARAH PEABODY & MISS BLYTHE DANFORTH
Students and Book Club Members at Welton

LORD BLAKE CASTLETON & LORD ANSEL CHEN
Lord Ridley's Mates

LADY ROSALIN CHEN
Lady Ela's Friend

MR. RIN KANEKO
Nori's Elder Brother

MR. KANEKO
Barrister to the Duke of Harbridge and Nori's Father

BETH
Curious Child at Little Hands Orphanage

SISTER MARY
Nun at Bellevue Chapel & Little Hands Orphanage

Alis Volat Propriis:

She flies with her own wings.

LADY
KNIGHT

CHAPTER
ONE

Strengthen the female mind by enlarging it, and there will
be an end to blind obedience.

—Mary Wollstonecraft

London, 1819

The thrill of the hunt was unimaginable. Illicit. *Dangerous.*

Never mind that we'd be the ones chased like plump, juicy rabbits, by the Bow Street Runners no less, if we got caught. Hounslow Heath was known for its crime and the newssheets had written that the authorities were cracking down.

You won't get caught. Focus on the prize.

Yes, the prize was the bounty my brother's friends carried on their way home from what I hoped had been a lucrative evening at their gentlemen's social club. And no, I would not have imagined in a million years that I would be on Great Bath Road with one of my best friends riding toward a carriage ferrying a group of gents at an hour when aristocratic young ladies should be tucked away in their bedchambers, safe and sound, like the precious darlings they were.

Thank the heavens my parents slept soundly and my lady's maid, Gemma, turned a closed eye to my capers. Because instead of sleeping, here I was . . . out of breath, heart pounding, muscles screaming in panic, and yet, so gloriously alive that I'd take this frantic race through Hounslow Heath over another day living the perfectly ordered, lackluster life of Lady Zenobia Osborn—daughter to a duke and undisputed diamond of the season.

Pah! Being a diamond of the first water was categorically overrated.

Especially for the poor twit, being *me,* who had to shoulder that heavy responsibility like a cloak made of nettles. The pressure that it bore was simply too much. Every single gaze was on me this season to find the most impeccable match . . . to be worthy of carrying such an illustrious title and show that I was the true prize.

But I wasn't some silly *prize.*

I was a person.

With a brain, feelings, and a will of her own.

On the surface, I exceeded the *ton's* requirements. One, I was pleasant enough in looks, except for the dreadful dash of freckles my governess seemed to abhor. She cautioned me daily to stay out of the sun. Not that I ever took that advice; I fed those precious little dots as much sunshine as I could—they were mine and they made me *me.* Two, I was in possession of an enormous dowry. And three, my father was an extremely formidable duke.

Furthermore, my skill at the pianoforte was unmatched, my

manners and breeding impeccable. My education was precisely adequate for a girl of my station—not that I let that stop me from listening in on my brother's lessons any chance I got. Everything else I learned after Keston went off to Eton was thanks to a well-stocked library.

Education was within one's grasp, if one cared to reach for it. Which I had always done without apology. Mathematics, philosophy, science, and other subjects like music, French, and needlepoint that were deemed acceptable for girls and taught by my governess, I devoured them all. I suspected that my parents knew that I was learned, and fortunately, they valued cleverness.

Despite my small personal rebellions, however, I was born and bred to be the perfect debutante . . . and eventually, the perfect bride to some faceless, well-heeled gentleman.

When the plain truth was I wanted more. I wanted *everything*. To write and compose my own songs someday, ones that weren't aristocracy-approved. I wanted to play them on a grand public stage. The idea of a duke's daughter being seen as a plebeian performer was scandalous in itself. While playing in the occasional music salon was appropriate since displaying one's piano skills for the purpose of attracting a husband was highly encouraged, *that* kind of *common* performance would hardly be allowed.

It was a role far beneath my station.

But I loved music, and I wanted to share my compositions with the world.

Why couldn't my parents have been happy with just one of their children being married off? My brother, the Marquess of

Ridley, had become engaged two years ago to a girl he'd been in love with his whole life and nearly lost because of his own shortsightedness. Lady Ela Dalvi was his hard-earned match, and the future Duke and Duchess of Harbridge were utterly besotted with each other.

Then again, Papa hadn't been pleased about the turn of events when his firstborn and heir practically told him to mind his own business during his rocky courtship with Ela. Defying my father's wishes would hardly go over as well for me. Girls were treated as if we were delicate china to be handled with velvet gloves and tender voices. We were only expected to sit quietly and nod and smile. To be the pinnacle of feminine perfection. Whatever that claptrap was.

This was clearly *not* my current circumstance, breaking all those rules!

No. Right now, I was living!

I narrowed my eyes as Lalita cut off the barouche, the three figures inside shouting in confusion as their vehicle pitched to a stop. Even though I was heavily shrouded in my hood, as was Lalita, a frisson of fear went through me. These targets *knew* who I was. Stealing from them wasn't exactly the right thing to do, but they were rich and wouldn't miss the money. I supposed we could have politely asked for a donation, but where was the fun in that?

"Stand and deliver, good sirs!" I shouted in a low voice while I pulled aside the coach, cocking the rifle I'd stolen from my father's collection and loosening the vowels in my speech.

In the late-night gloom, I could see bewilderment dawning on their faces as they whirled to face the business end of my empty rifle. Not that they would know that the weapon was unloaded. Lalita hefted hers as well, though her face had taken on a green hue as if she was fighting not to cast up her accounts on the ground.

Keep it together, Lalita, just a few more minutes. . . .

One of the gentlemen I didn't recognize, though something about him seemed familiar, and the second was Ansel Chen, Lady Rosalin's cousin. The third made my heart flutter and then sink to my toes. Along with Ansel, Rafi Nasser was one of my brother's best mates, and while Rafi was the *ton's* resident libertine, he was hardly obtuse. In fact, his lackadaisical personality hid an incisive mind, or so I'd observed the past few years. One mistake and I could be discovered.

That would ruin everything.

My brother was not with them, which I counted as a small mercy. I would have been a little more worried about discovery with him there, especially since it wouldn't be the first time we'd ambushed him—but my disguise was solid, thanks in part to his own fiancée, Ela, who was a master of subterfuge. Gulping past the thickening knot in my throat, I squared my shoulders and edged the horse closer.

"What is the meaning of this?" the one closest to me demanded.

"Calm down, Rin," Ansel said through his teeth. I knew the other boy looked familiar—he was the elder brother of my other best friend Nori. That made me feel better about robbing someone I didn't know. And if he was with Rafi and Keston's set, he had money to burn, and Nori would definitely approve.

"Bugger off, Ansel," he slurred. "Don't tell me what to do. What is this?"

"It's a robbery, dimwit," Lalita called out, and I nearly laughed out loud at his half-foxed expression. With any luck, they would be too deep in their cups to remember most of this. The coachman blanched and reached for his pockets. "Not you," she told him. "Just the spoiled toffs inside the carriage who can afford to lighten their purses."

Grinning at the coachman's bemused expression, I cleared my throat and threw a sack to the middle of the open conveyance, putting a little mischief in my tone. "Hands where I can see them, kind sirs. Fill the pouch, if you will. You're all much too comely to be shot tonight."

Ansel and Rin complied, though grousing all the while. Most would not put up a fight at gunpoint. My eyes widened at the bank notes, coins, rings, and pocket watches going into the bag. This would be an excellent haul.

When they were done, I let my gaze drift to Rafi, who sat sprawled lazily against the left squabs, his long arms spread wide on either side of him. One would think he was spending an indolent evening in his favorite armchair and not being robbed by armed highwaymen. Er, highway-*women*. I tried not to let myself be too affected by his presence, but Rafi was a person who commanded attention. It didn't help that he'd grown more handsome in the last year, not that I cared, of course. It was a simple observation.

Rafi Nasser always left a trail of broken hearts in his wake . . .

every girl in London wanting to be *the* girl who reformed a notorious scoundrel. Even my own brother had warned me of him, and I supposed it helped that Rafi didn't see me as anything other than his best friend's little sister. Two years ago, during Keston and Ela's courtship, he'd nipped my nascent infatuation in the bud when I'd foolishly let my feelings be known.

I am not interested in courting bratty girls. A cool, disinterested gaze had parsed my excessively frilled figure. *Especially Ridley's little sister. Go back to your schoolroom, Zia.*

I'd tucked my poor, wounded sixteen-year-old heart away and avoided him since.

That open sore of rejection didn't stop him from being unnecessarily attractive, however. Dark stubble crept over a sharp jawline, a bold nose and hooded brows making his features seem more angular in the low moonlight. Thickly lashed eyes—silvery gray in the dappled darkness—shone with something that unsettled me. I resisted the urge to check to see if my cowl was intact, shielding my features from view.

"Come now, don't be shy," I told him audaciously, fighting for poise. "Your pockets seem heavy tonight."

His eyes narrowed as he tilted his head to one side. "Who are you?"

That deep baritone of his descended over me like crushed velvet. "My identity is not important, only your valuables. But if you insist, Lady Knight, it is."

Lalita's gasp alerted me to the fact that naming any names that might lead back to us was not part of the plan. Too late now.

Rafi didn't move from his relaxed pose, a slow smirk kicking up one corner of his mouth. "How quaint . . . lady of the night, I presume?" he drawled, sarcasm dripping from his tone.

I knew I shouldn't engage, but the need to put him in his place was strong. "Knight with a *K,* as in warrior-at-arms, actually. And might I remind you that this is loaded, my lord," I said, knowing full well he wasn't titled as I hefted my rifle. "Make haste. Time and tide will wait for no man."

Something flashed across his face. He sat forward, propping his elbows on his knees, and I resisted the urge to rear back. "What's an educated young woman doing on these roads at night? Don't you know it's dangerous?"

Nerves alight, I tapped the rifle on the edge of the coach. "I *am* the danger, good sir. Now, unless you intend to test my rather excellent feminine aim, I'd advise you to stitch together those pretty lips and divest yourself of your baubles. Patience is not one of my many virtues."

The corner of that devious mouth kicked up, along with my traitorous temperature. "Pretty lips?"

"A euphemism, no more. Now stop stalling."

With that wicked smirk still firmly in place, he reached for the pouch and emptied his pockets. It must have been a lucky night at the card tables. Good for him, and even better for us. When he stretched an arm toward me, my eyes stuck on the large signet ring on his finger. It was his family ring, I knew. But any thieving highwayman worth his salt would never leave such a bounty behind.

"That's a lovely ring."

His eyes darkened. "It's a family heirloom."

"One that will fetch a nice sum."

A chuckle left his lips. "It's much too recognizable to sell, Lady Knight."

"Then perhaps I shall keep it as a memento of our meeting."

Prowling forward, I reached out to grip his fingers with my gloved left hand and grinned as I slipped it off and stowed it into the pocket of my cloak. He lurched forward to latch on to my wrist, making my pulse gallop, but a swift movement of my heel into my mount's flank broke the brief contact. "You won't get away with this," he said in a low snarl that made my already hammering pulse double.

"Already have. Do have a grand evening, your lordship," I purred, and then on impulse blew him a kiss. His nostrils flared, something flashing in those narrowed gray eyes, and for a heart-stopping moment, I wondered if it was recognition. Blowing a kiss was something the Zia he knew would never do, so it couldn't have been that. I frowned when Rafi rose off the seat as if breathing in, and I urged my horse a few more hurried steps back.

Was the rotter *sniffing* me?

I hadn't worn any scent other than daily bathwater, but still . . .

His brows drew down as I moved the stallion farther away and nodded to Lalita, who had remained in position in front of the coach. Together we drifted off the road and into the shadows. Still, I felt the press of that heated silver gaze for a full minute afterward.

"That was intense," Lalita hissed.

Before I could answer, the sound of thundering hooves over the next hill interrupted me.

"Halt! Stop in the name of the law!" someone shouted.

My heart shot into my throat. That voice definitely wasn't from Rafi or the two other boys. That was a cracking order of authority . . . as in the police. Damn and blast, of all our bloody luck! The command had sounded far enough away, but I could not be sure, so I upped my pace and urged Lalita to do the same.

"Bloody hell, who's that?" she yelled.

"Runners or local constables!" I snorted a hysterical burst of laughter through my nose. If I was captured by the Runners, I'd be the pinnacle of ruination. My father would be absolutely livid, and I'd probably be banished to a convent. Half-petrified, I laughed again.

"None of this is funny, Zia. If they catch us, they're going to lock us in jail."

"They won't snatch anyone, Lalita," I yelled back. "Come on, ride faster! We're nearly to the others. And besides, we're the Lady Knights of truth, knowledge, and justice. Nothing bad can happen to us, remember?"

Lalita, one of my close friends from school, had the gall to roll her eyes and let out a snort louder than mine. "You say that every time we're in one of these scrapes. You and these harebrained ideas are going to get us killed one day!"

"To Valhalla!" I roared.

"You are ridiculous," she said, but a wild answering grin lit her face all the same. "Stop obsessing over those Viking books about shield-maidens."

That would happen only by force. Shield-maidens were magnificent.

Panting wildly, we pushed our mounts to the brink as we darted through the gloomy, deserted fields south of Slough—thank the heavens I'd pored over a hand-drawn map for hours before choosing this particular rural area, west of Hounslow Heath. We'd left our unmarked coach near a respectable-enough coaching inn with two guards. Greer, our resident weapons expert thanks to her avid huntsman father and the last of our foursome, was armed to the teeth.

As soon as I saw the coach around the next bend of the road, I let out a sharp two-note whistle. We had practiced this before, and like a well-oiled machine, the door opened and the attached horses started moving down the street. Nori was on driving duty tonight.

A relieved grin split my face as Lalita and I dismounted, threw the reins of the borrowed horses to a frowning groom in front of the inn's stables, and ran toward our escape route. Jogging alongside each other, Lalita and I climbed in one at a time, attempting to catch our breaths as we slung ourselves back into the squabs.

Lalita wheezed, dark hair clinging to her ruddy brown cheeks. "How did I let you talk me into this?"

"You like helping people," I retorted, lungs burning, my veins mixed with excitement and relief.

"You mean *robbing* people," she muttered.

"I don't enjoy stealing, Lalita. It's a necessity." I shot her a look. "They're rich nobs who have more than enough to spare. And you know why we're doing this. To save Little Hands and Beth. To save *Welton*."

The spoils of our capers—a large stash of banknotes as well as watches and jewelry to be pawned—would be delivered to Bellevue Chapel, a church that was in danger of closing. Never mind that the money was stolen; it was for a good cause. Our school's future was in peril as well, considering it was housed in the same building as the orphanage. But the children were far more important. Little Hands was their home. Plus, the contribution included most of our own pin money.

Every little bit helped, however.

Even if we had to steal it from our peers. Well, my sibling's peers at least. We'd gotten my brother and Lord Blake Castleton, one of his other mates, the first week that we'd had the brilliant idea to fleece Keston's rich friends who wouldn't miss the coin, then Blake again because he was too easy to rob, and now Rafi, Ansel, and Rin.

Greer stared at us. "What happened?"

"Ran into some Bow Street Runners."

Her lips thinned, eyes going wide. "This far out of London?"

"They must have been scouting or in the area for something else. Word of highwaymen in this particular area is widespread."

It was true; Hounslow Heath was rife with ne'er-do-wells. Which we were not. *Mostly.*

A ripple of guilt spun through me. No matter how much I

justified it, we *were* thieves. My mama would have conniptions if she had any inkling of my criminal behavior. And my father, well, probably best not to talk about the arctic wrath of his temper. But we only took from those who were wealthy and could replace their possessions. The Lady Knight Society chose our victims very carefully. The money of our targets was much better served saving hungry orphans than being wasted at card tables or the betting track.

This was about the *greater good.*

Hauling air into my lungs, I took off my hat and tugged down the hood from the scarf that hid my nose and mouth from view, using it to wipe my sweaty face. My mountain of curls had been tamed into two braids along my scalp to fit completely under the hat, and I longed to set them free. I put a hand to my racing heart that was only now beginning to slow.

"Did you and Nori have any trouble?" I asked.

Greer shook her head. "One traveler from the inn came sniffing around, got one look at my rifle, and slunk back the way he'd come."

Greer was a tall girl, packing muscle, and when she was armed, she could be quite forbidding. Her father hailed from Norway, and she definitely had some Viking blood in her. With her blond hair and bright blue eyes, I could easily imagine her wielding an axe and a shield and running into the fray to destroy her enemies.

"Capital," I said.

"I should have gone with you," Greer said, scowling. "Lalita looks like she's about to collapse from apoplexy."

"Not apoplexy, indigestion. I shouldn't have had those extra cakes from supper," she moaned, clutching her stomach. "Fair warning: I might cast up my accounts."

Greer pulled a disgusted face. "Not on me, you won't!"

"We needed you with the coach," I said to Greer. "In case things went sour. Nori is the best driver of all of us, and you know how she is." Nori, as excellent as she was with horses, refused to touch any weapons, even unloaded ones. She was a lover, not a fighter, but we adored her and accepted all her quirks. And besides, every secret society worth its salt needed an exceptional break-out driver.

Patting the pouch of valuables, I sighed and sank into the squabs. "Miss Perkins would be proud of us."

Lalita shot me a sidelong glance. "I don't think becoming criminals was what she meant by pushing the boundaries of the expectations set for our sex." She wrinkled her nose. "Or what she'd want us to do to save her family's school."

"Nonetheless, it *is* for a good cause," I reminded her, squashing my own lingering discomfort. "Think of *Beth*. This isn't just about Welton. And let's remember what Mary Wollstonecraft essentially said—we are rational creatures and much more than our fascinating graces."

Doubt crossed Lalita's expression. "I suppose you're right."

It was my favorite concept from the treatise we'd been studying at our girls' seminary—*A Vindication of the Rights of Woman: With Strictures on Political and Moral Subjects* by Mary Wollstonecraft. The essay wasn't part of the approved curriculum for young ladies—God forbid we read anything too radical—but our teacher, Miss Perkins, was quite an anomaly herself. She was of the opinion that, as ladies, we should make up our own minds, govern our own bodies, and harness our own power through reading and education.

Such a revolutionary concept had been eye-opening . . . that we could pursue internal self-governance and break free from patriarchal norms. And so, we had. Perhaps, to Lalita's point, not exactly in the way Miss Perkins intended. But the four of us—me, Lalita, Greer, and Nori—were making a difference. We would be the change needed in our society.

That was what our friendship and our secret club, the Lady Knight Society, was about—living our best lives devoid of rules or expectations. Helping where we could, using our voices as loudly as we wanted, being true to who we were, and *not* bowing down to what a bunch of autocratic old men thought. While our society had started innocuously enough with reading dangerous books, it had evolved into a means of real action. Thus, it was an *anonymous* club. None of us wanted to be ruined and shunned, after all. Subversion required strategy.

We still had our families' reputations to worry about.

Greer was gentry and the offspring of a wealthy merchant banker and Scottish countess. I was green with envy that she'd descended from not only Vikings but also Scots—a powerful combination of warrior heritage. Nori was my father's barrister's youngest child and only daughter. With three boisterous older brothers, she was easygoing and had no rough edges to speak of. Lastly, Lalita was the daughter of the late Baronet Tenly, though she lived with her uncle and aunt, the new baronet and baronetess, who were overtly avaricious. Her mother had died in childbirth with her youngest sibling. We all expected Lalita to be married off this season to the highest bidder.

As women, wedlock was a fate we all would share, and I was determined to avoid it for as long as possible. For now, I relished these moments when my choices—no matter how questionable they might be—were mine alone . . . and *that* freedom was worth everything. Now that my brother, Keston, was betrothed, the attention on the next marvelous match in my family migrated to me. But I was *not* ready.

And the truth was I might never be.

CHAPTER TWO

Education deserves emphatically to be termed cultivation of mind, which teaches young people how to begin to think.

—MARY WOLLSTONECRAFT

While some young ladies lived for the chance to settle down with a husband, I did not. I wasn't interested in balls and ball gowns or being on display for the marriage mart. Truth was I'd grown accustomed to the simplicity of a pair of breeches, boots, a soft shirt, and a fitted coat while I'd been in Berkshire at my father's ancestral seat. Boys didn't know how good they had it. They were free to act as they liked.

Ever hear of a grand tour for ladies? The exciting, adventurous continental jaunt most young aristocratic gents enjoyed? No? Me neither.

My stomach rolled. Marriage in the aristocracy was centered around three things: shoring up fortunes, gaining a title, or building alliances.

Or, in my case, all three.

Two of the gentlemen who had offered their hands were wealthy but twice my age. Horrid! Another was an earl from a neighboring estate who could not stop sniffing and sneezing. Every time we met, I had the urge to give him my handkerchief and bring a spare. Another was a duke, which meant I would be elevated to duchess. If only he didn't smell like old cheese and sweaty stockings.

Most of the gentlemen I had met during my first season were interested in my dowry, though several of them were wealthy in their own rights. But the sole thing they had in common was how much they loved to talk about themselves. Not one of them ever asked about me, about my interests or my hopes and dreams for the future. There was not a gentleman in London I could envision myself with.

Well, maybe one . . .

I blinked, shoving away the image of my most recent quarry in his coach, like a prince on a throne with his thick dark brown hair and mocking gray eyes. I bit my lip hard. Rafi Nasser was the last gentleman I should be thinking about. Not only had we just robbed him of his belongings; he was also an arrogant cad.

And the worst kind of rake!

Like most of my brother's set, Rafi was wealthy and eligible, and he knew it. Heir to his uncle's viscountcy, he was also the stepson of a powerful Qājār shah and had more money than Midas. His mother, a striking Persian widow who had remarried and returned to the place of her birth, made sure her son's personal coffers were always brimming.

It didn't help matters that Rafi was as gorgeous as his mother, was charming to a fault, and had a flirtatious, wicked smile that made my heart flutter, even when it wasn't directed at me.

Which was never.

Though he'd crushed my fledgling infatuation, there was a tiny part of me that would always wonder whether we might have had any future together. But that was a useless fantasy because Rafi Nasser was a heartless rake who'd made his withering opinion about my affections quite clear. Huffing an irritated breath and pushing the unwelcome rumination from my brain, I turned my attention to Greer, who announced we were nearly back to Mayfair.

When we arrived at the mews attached to my family's ducal residence in Grosvenor Square, Nori deftly detached the horses and led them back into the stables while we went into the small carriage house. As capable as any groom, she would take her time seeing to their needs.

After greeting Gemma, my lady's maid, whose displeasure was obvious in her pinched expression, I made sure the curtains were drawn. Gemma was not fond of my escapades, but by now she'd become a reluctant accomplice, at least for the children's sake. We would both be in huge trouble if my nighttime adventures came to light. "You can go to bed, Gemma. We will be fine, I promise."

Her sidelong glance was skeptical, but she bobbed. "Very well, my lady."

She took her leave, and I lit a lamp in the cottage that we had redecorated to be a comfortable and welcoming refuge. It had originally been meant for me to use as a musical studio for practice since the music room in the main house was too close to my father's study. In the country, at our ducal seat, I had an entire wing to myself. Here, my beloved Viennese fortepiano stood neglected in the corner, and I felt a twang of guilt. I hadn't been practicing of late, more interested in the activities of our secret society.

We had all divested ourselves of our exterior trappings when Nori came in flushed and smelling of horsehair and leather. "Well, that was a bit of an adventure," she pronounced, running a hand through her short mop of pin-straight black hair. "Perhaps we shouldn't venture so far into that dodgy area of Hounslow Heath. We're lucky we didn't run into more trouble or that the horses didn't get hurt. That coaching stop is notorious for bandits."

"We're quite safe and sound," I pointed out. "And we're so very nearly to our goal of raising the three hundred pounds we need for Sister Mary."

Her midnight gaze narrowed. "Barely. Were those Runners I saw on your heels?"

"Yes," I said, wrinkling my brow. "They can't have known who we were, however. We could have been anyone. It was just bad timing." I retrieved the pouch from my coat pocket and hefted it before passing it to Greer. "Rin was there in the carriage tonight," I told Nori.

She looked surprised. "My Rin? As in my brother who is supposed to be on his grand tour?" I nodded, squashing my burst of envy as Nori rolled her eyes. "He must be back. Hope you fleeced him good."

"I did. He was in his cups, but it looked like they'd all done well at the tables."

"That was too close," Lalita said.

"How much did we get?" I asked Greer as she rifled through the contents of the bag.

"One ring, three pocket watches, one snuff tin, a gold cross, and about twenty-two quid."

Two rings, if one counted the one stashed securely in my pocket.

"See? Worth it," I maintained.

Nori nodded. "I'll get the jewelry and tin to the pawn-broker's."

When I'd first suggested the idea for us to help the church and orphanage in distress à la Robin Hood, the other three girls had been aghast, until I'd explained that we wouldn't be in any real danger, considering our targets would be my brother's friends. And it would save Beth. That had been the clincher. Beth was a seven-year-old orphan whom we all adored, whose mother had died from consumption, and who had been taken in by Sister Mary, a nun at Bellevue Chapel. If the Little Hands orphanage, which adjoined Welton and the church, closed, Beth and the rest of the children would have nowhere to go. While I desperately wanted to safeguard Beth and Little Hands, the Welton House School for Elegant Young Ladies was also part of the same tenement and was sublet from the church by the owners, the three Perkins sisters. Thus, the finishing school would also be at risk of closing.

The owner of the land intended to sell the three attached buildings on the property block to Viscount Hollis, who'd convert Bellevue into one of the largest gaming hells in London. Its location between Mayfair and Covent Garden was prime. Or at least, that was what I'd overheard Sister Mary say. It didn't help that the struggling chapel had been defaulting on its loans for months and was being chased by creditors.

Swallowing my lingering disquiet, I glanced up, eyeing each of my best friends in turn. "One more score, and we'll have enough. We've come this far, and we can't stop now. The children, our classmates, even the parishioners—they're all depending on us. Sister Mary said the church will lose everything if they can't pay their quarterly lease. We can't let that happen."

Greer pinned her lips but gave a terse nod of her blond head. Of our small group of friends, she was always the easiest to convince. After a while, Nori cleared her throat and rubbed her chin with a soft murmur of agreement. Lalita gulped down her biscuit, looking like she was going to swoon again. "Zia . . . we nearly got arrested. By *Runners*."

"Don't worry," I said, and shoved down the feelings of worry and guilt dueling in the pit of my stomach. "I know just who to target next. We won't get arrested, I promise."

"Who?" she asked, eyes wary.

"Viscount Hollis."

Greer let out a low whistle. "Rafi Nasser's uncle?"

I swallowed, wondering if I was being uncharacteristically foolish. Given our evening, I should stay far away from that particular gentleman or any of his family. Something about the way he'd stared at me had troubled my mind. Then again, that had probably been nerves. Besides, this would have nothing to do with Rafi. . . . It had to do with his odious uncle, who deserved to be fleeced for such a worthy cause.

It was he, after all, who had designs on Bellevue for his atrocious gaming hell.

Certainly, my friends and I could find other reputable finishing schools to attend. But *he* was the monster who wanted to oust innocent orphans!

"The viscount goes to the Danforth's gambling hell every Saturday and spends a fortune. You know he's behind this plan, so he should have to pay. Next weekend, we'll do it fast and dirty. He won't even know what hit him, and no one will be the wiser. Trust me."

My heart gave a wild thump as if in protest of what, deep down, I secretly hoped.

That despite the risk, I'd cross paths with Rafi again.

The Welton House School for Elegant Young Ladies, a prestigious and exclusive seminary for gifted young women, only had room for twenty students at a time. The girls ranged from fourteen to eighteen in age. I suppose I was the twenty-first, thanks to a very generous donation to the school from the Duke of Harbridge. Not that Papa had been pleased about that in the least—

daughters of dukes usually did not attend finishing schools. They had governesses and private tutors, and like my brother, I'd had multiples of both.

However, Nori, whom I'd known since her father worked for mine, attended the school. And then I'd met Greer at a country house party in Reading two years ago, and she'd been so rapt with her arts-and-music teacher that I'd become obsessed with attending. My father had immediately said no, but Mama, who was a little more progressive in her thinking thanks to her own broad West Indian upbringing, had been adamant that instruction with other young ladies from other backgrounds would be good for me. It helped that the school had an excellent music program, considering the youngest Perkins sister was a virtuoso who played six instruments.

I smirked. People in the *ton* might think that men were in control, but powerful women always had agency in a world that, historically, wasn't conducive to equality. My mother was the perfect example of that fact. Not only was she beautiful with her lustrous deep bronze skin, immaculate style, and charming elegance, she was as smart as a whip. Growing up, I'd seen her handle Papa's rigidity and reserve with a clever acuity to be admired.

You can catch more flies with honey than vinegar, love, she'd often said to me. *Pick your battles wisely because there isn't a moment in our lives where we women are not fighting for something. Your choices are the only thing within* your *control.*

And so, Papa had reluctantly conceded to her indisputable logic, and I was allowed to attend as a day student two or three times a week for a few subjects, including musical composition, while we were in town and Parliament was in session. I counted my blessings. There was simply no chance he would have agreed for me to board with the other girls who shared rooms there. I still had my duke-approved governess and tutors, which mollified him somewhat.

Thank goodness Welton House wasn't terribly far from Mayfair, but it was worth every minute of the cramped carriage ride. When the weather became nicer, perhaps I could ride, accompanied by a groom and my chaperone. But for the moment, being driven back and forth was a condition of my father's, and one he would not budge on.

Right now, I sat with Lalita, Greer, Nori, and three other girls in the classroom waiting patiently for our favorite language, music, and arts teacher to arrive. Miss Perkins was the youngest of the three sisters who ran the school and part of the whole reason I'd fallen in love with Welton. Apart from her musical genius, her outlook on life was unlike anything I'd ever encountered. She lived fearlessly and unapologetically. She wasn't demure, and she wasn't soft-spoken. She wasn't subservient or invisible.

No, Miss Perkins was vivacious, impetuous, and opinionated.

Despite being the offspring of an impoverished baron and forced to work because of her family's reduced circumstances, she had chosen to live on her own terms over marrying a man to secure her position. Working as a governess, among other things, she had traveled all over the Continent and to the Far East, following her passions for art, music, and culture. Given her range, particularly with music, when she'd returned to England, her sisters had offered her a place at the seminary.

She taught things that no one else did, at least not to impressionable young ladies. She encouraged us to form our small book club, filled with selections *we* chose, and she allowed us to read books that weren't part of the approved curriculum. As required, we read Shakespeare and studied French, Italian, and Latin; played music; and critiqued art. But every term, we also chose a book that high society would not approve of and read that in secret. In fact, the text we read and discussed last was *A Vindication of the Rights of Woman.* Her older sisters would *not* approve.

Nor would our parents and guardians. . . .

After a few minutes, Miss Perkins entered the room and locked the door. Her auburn hair was barely contained in a haphazard bun, loose pieces flying everywhere, but her green eyes sparkled with humor and knowledge. Freckles more plentiful than mine were scattered over her face, giving her a very gamine appearance, despite her being in her mid-to-late twenties.

These book club sessions were clandestine for good reason, and we were all very careful to be discreet when we met to discuss contemporary literature. In addition to my three best friends, there was Lady Petal Joshi, a slightly older girl of Indian descent and the daughter of a marquess, along with Miss Sarah Peabody, the pale-complexioned, well-heeled daughter of a doctor. The last, Miss Blythe Danforth, was a shy, soft-spoken brunette whose father owned a popular gaming hell. Despite her background and common origins—and the fact that my father would have apoplexy if he knew who her people were—I liked her. Her shyness hid a bright mind and a sly sense of humor.

"Good afternoon, ladies," Miss Perkins greeted us with a wide smile as she propped herself upon her desk without care for propriety.

I grinned as light blue stockings peeped out from the tops of her worn ankle boots. In this room, we were all encouraged to be ourselves. Greer and I were the only ones of the group who had taken to wearing blue stockings beneath our garments like Miss Perkins. It was a nod to the Bluestocking society of old, which had championed literature, arts, education, and intellectual conversation. Supposedly, they had gotten their name when one of the founders invited a new member to come in his everyday blue stockings. A few of the society's original female founders, like Elizabeth Montagu and Hannah More, had been writers themselves, fighting the patriarchy via the power of the pen.

We had read their works in our clandestine book club, too.

"Good afternoon, Miss Perkins," everyone replied.

"So here we are, nearly to the end of this rather lengthy and provocative treatise by Wollstonecraft. What are your thoughts thus far? Any new thoughts since our class last week?"

I wrinkled my nose, not wanting to admit that I'd already devoured the whole essay in no time at all. Once I'd started, I hadn't been able to stop. Mary Wollstonecraft had been ahead of her time and her opinions about women's rights were eye-opening and empowering.

Greer raised her hand. "I agree with Wollstonecraft's disdain of the idea that 'every woman is at heart a rake.' Choosing a husband isn't about passion."

"A witty rake might be exciting, but that won't last," Sarah interjected with a nod.

"And how would you know?" Nori said under her breath, though everyone heard.

Sarah canted her strawberry blond head, glaring at Nori. "If a match is based on that alone, there's nothing for the couple to fall back on as life progresses. Rakes are a trap. As the author says, 'Common passions are excited by common qualities.'"

"That's a sweeping generalization," I remarked. "Shared interests could develop as well, and not all men considered rakes are lost causes or lacking in character and wit."

"Says the one of us with the most privilege, who can choose from the crème de la crème of suitors," she shot back. "Some of us do not have the luxury of love or being able to refuse a half dozen offers. You're so conceited, Zia."

I bristled at the unexpected attack. I was well aware of my advantages, and I did not take them lightly, but for her to assume that I had it any easier in this particular matter was vexing. Or to call out the fact that I had said no to the gentlemen offering marriage with whom I hadn't had a rapport. I wasn't about to throw the rest of my life away by wedding someone I didn't at least esteem. That didn't make me . . . conceited.

"Ignore her," Nori whispered, but I still balled my fingers in my lap.

Sarah wasn't finished. "And besides, what of your brother's

mate Mr. Nasser? He's a rake through and through who dallies shamelessly with older women, I've heard. Are you suggesting that I am mistaken in my opinions and that such a man would make a good husband? If so, perhaps I should ask my father to reconsider his suit."

At the mere mention of his name, my stomach jolted, then dove to my feet. Rafi had expressed an interest in courting *her*? Since *when*? An ugly stab of jealousy took me by surprise, and I tried desperately to keep my face blank. I had no claim over him. Beyond the fraught bit of tension the other night, Rafi paid no attention to me. Clearly, however, he had noticed Sarah. That knowledge was gutting.

Miss Perkins clapped her hands, drawing our collective attention. "Ladies, while impassioned discussion is appreciated, let's keep it to the themes in this work. What are your thoughts on the author's opinions that early teachings impact later decisions?"

"I suppose that's accurate," Nori said loudly, attempting to ease the tension. "If we are taught that a certain way of thinking is natural, then by default, we will gravitate toward certain behaviors. Information leads action. Horses are trained to trot, to canter, and to jump. As awful as the comparison is, women are treated the same by men." She paused for a moment, her forehead wrinkling in thought. "We are taught how to think and act from infancy. Any choices we make in life will be limited by what we are allowed to know of it."

Miss Perkins smiled. "Excellent deduction, Miss Kaneko. And that is why we are here. To form our own opinions based on the information at our fingertips. A well-read girl has an army at her disposal."

"Knowledge is power," Blythe chimed in softly.

Miss Perkins's smile widened. "Yes, but not on its own. *Action* is power. Anyone can glean knowledge. It's what you do with it, and it's the choice to act, that makes it explosive. Knowledge is simply tinder; action is the flame. Remember that."

CHAPTER
THREE

Women are told from their infancy, and taught by the example of their mothers, that a little knowledge of human weakness, justly termed cunning, softness of temper, OUTWARD obedience, and a scrupulous attention to a puerile kind of propriety, will obtain for them the protection of man; and should they be beautiful, everything else is needless.

—MARY WOLLSTONECRAFT

The most interesting—and most exhausting—thing about the London season was undoubtedly the balls and parties. They were incessant, sometimes two or three in a night, and the whole point was for any unmarried person to see and to be seen.

Beauty, breeding, and wealth were revered.

The diamond of the first water often embodied all of those. I should know—I was chosen last year after my presentation at court. God rest Queen Charlotte's soul, though by all accounts, the ball would carry on in her memory. Despite the charm I had to employ to be the season's diamond, I'd come to resent the unwanted mantle, along with all its heavy, unrealistic expectations—that the diamond would make the most exceptional match, that every young lady should aspire to be so beautiful and perfect. But little did they know, my efforts were devoted to avoiding *any* kind of match.

Even during the months leading up to the spring season when Parliament was in session the week after Easter, country parties abounded, with the goal of creating possible matches before the real frenzy of the marriage mart began in late April. Hence, this ball at Lady Rosalin's parents' home in Mayfair to celebrate the start of the season was crowded.

I stared at the beautiful Asian girl, best friend to my future sister-in-law, Lady Ela. She had become so much more confident in the past two years. Rosalin used to be the favorite victim of a notorious bully who had hoodwinked the whole *ton,* and she had fought her way out of that girl's shadow with Ela's help. No one missed the social-climbing Poppy Landers, least of all me. She had been toxic and obsessed with my brother and was the reason I kept my circle of friends small and tight. Trust was a rare commodity in our world, especially with most of the debutantes desperate to become an Original or the next queen bee. The competition was, undoubtedly, cutthroat.

"Lady Zenobia," an amused voice said. "How interesting you look tonight. That contraption has you resembling . . . a giant meringue tart."

I peered up at my older sibling and forced down a bark

of laughter. Keston wasn't wrong in his comparison. "Begone with you, Brother. Don't you have a soon-to-be marchioness to annoy?" Until our father died and passed on the ducal title to his male heir, Keston went by the Marquess of Ridley. In a few short months—*finally*, given the delay from the yearlong mourning period when our grandfather passed—he and Ela would marry, and she'd receive her own courtesy title of marchioness.

Keston smirked. "I almost didn't believe Ela when she said you could barely get out of the carriage and through the entrance doors. I gather you're determined to be the coal of the season instead of its diamond?"

"I haven't the slightest idea of what you mean," I replied with a dismissive toss of my head.

"No? Then why are you hiding out in this cramped little nook instead of dancing like the rest of your friends and charming the masses?"

Keston, the rotter, knew me far too well. Smoothing the scowl from my brow, I glanced to where Lalita and Greer appeared to be having the time of their lives in a rousing quadrille. Though neither of them had my particular problem. Greer had been engaged since infancy, but that didn't stop her from living on her terms. And Lalita . . . well, an excellent marriage was needed thanks to her grasping aunt and uncle who craved social elevation. She had two younger sisters, who would only benefit if she made a splendid match, so she was more open to the idea of being courted than I was. Then again, I did not have the burden of younger siblings.

Keston shook his head with a laugh and glanced around the narrow space. "How did you even get in here? I assume a bust or statue might have been in this alcove at one point?"

"Persistence," I said. "And I needed a break."

Lady Rosalin had had a horrified look on her face upon first glance but was much too polite to comment about my appearance. Her mother had simply lifted her brows in surprise. Thank heavens my own parents had another event to attend. Otherwise, I would not have been allowed to leave the house dressed as ghastly as I was.

A giggle escaped my lips. "If you continue to annoy me, Kes, I will be sure to save this for your wedding. Wouldn't *that* be the talk of the town?"

"You wouldn't dare!" he said but laughed. "You love Ela too much."

He was right. I did adore my future sister-in-law.

Tossing my head, I smoothed the rather execrable ensemble I had chosen. The pale cream color complemented my bronze curls and deep golden-brown skin as most shades did, but that was as good as it got. Layers upon layers of tulle doubled the space I normally occupied, and its unflattering shape meant that I did indeed favor a stiff-peaked dessert. One made with salt instead of sugar.

I grinned. Knowing three of my rejected suitors from last season fully intended to renew their suits, I'd made sure to make myself as unpalatable as possible.

My fellow Lady Knights had cackled when I'd modeled the gown and told them my plan to shock and disgust, Greer snorting so hard that she'd toppled over. Nori had befittingly dubbed me the Queen of the Meringue Monsters. The gown had seemed like such a great idea at the time, but it would be a lie if I didn't admit I had regrets. This eyesore was as hot as an oven, and I was roasting. I opened my fan and waved it like I was on fire.

"Hullo, Zia," Ela said, joining my brother, her hazel eyes wide with horror.

"Don't say a word," I warned, fanning harder. "Clearly, I did not think this through well enough." My scowl reappeared as I took in Ela's two-piece silk gown in a gorgeous Indian style that bared the tiniest sliver of her stomach. I gritted my teeth in absolute envy. *My* stomach was currently drowning under perspiration and excessive beading.

"Very well. I'll keep my opinions to myself," she said, hiding her grin. "Your face is alarmingly red. Are you all right?"

"Yes." Drops of sweat rolled down my spine. "Did the temperature just go up a million degrees?"

"It is warm in here," she said, and squinted at the balcony doors on the other side of the room. "More people have arrived. Perhaps we should escape to the terrace? Though I'm not certain you'll be able to fit through the doors." She eyed the width of my dress more closely. "How many petticoats are you wearing?"

"Five."

"Good God, Zia!" She burst into giggles. "Well, no one can call you incapable of committing. Although, is the idea of an engagement truly so bad?"

"You know I don't wish to wed," I said. "At least, not right now. I want to experience the world before I'm handed off like chattel to the highest bidder."

"It doesn't have to be like that. Your brother hardly treats *me* like chattel." Her mouth curled in a sardonic tilt, and her eyes sparkled. "He knows exactly what would happen if he did. My alter ego would make a reappearance, and he'd regret ever speaking."

"Luckily, I treasure both versions of you," Keston said with a charming wink that made me roll my eyes.

Everyone in London knew the story of Lady Ela returning two years ago in disguise as a wealthy heiress to take down her former best friend turned nemesis, who'd had designs upon my brother and ruling the *ton*. I'd always seen through Poppy's machinations, and while Ela's revenge plan had almost cost her everything—her friends, her social standing, and a second chance with Keston—it was wonderful to see them en route to a happily ever after. I supposed love wasn't *so* bad.

Then again, *my* heart hadn't been on the line.

No, my heart was in a lockbox, currently suffocating to death under fifty layers of tulle.

That reminded me of my current circumstance. Until the dancing set was completed, I was trapped in this furnace of an alcove.

In a normal dress, I might have been able to slip by unnoticed along the periphery of the ballroom floor. But if I attempted to do that in this unsightly gown, the result would be that of a bowling ball cleaving through bowling pins.

"Kes, go fetch your sister a large glass of water," Ela said, eyeing me and taking out her own fan and flicking it rapidly in my direction.

I shot her a grateful smile. "Thank you."

"A pitcher if you can manage it," she added as Keston kissed her cheek in an overt display of affection that would have ordinarily made me gag, but I was much too hot to cast judgment on their nauseatingly sweet love affair.

After he left, Ela's serious gaze met mine. "This will be your second season. You do realize that all eyes will be upon you and any match you make? It doesn't matter what you wear. In fact, I bet that half the young ladies here will be commissioning dresses like yours from their modistes within the week. Their mamas will all think it's some new fashionable style by the trendsetting, beautiful Lady Zenobia Osborn, last season's diamond."

"Ugh. I should leave before that happens."

Every girl here should be smuggled a copy of *A Vindication of the Rights of Woman*. Women didn't have to cater to the rules set by men to compete to be the most beautiful, the most elegant, and the most sumptuously dressed. But the late Queen Charlotte had uplifted that archaic way of thinking by pitting us young women against each other every single season when we'd had to be presented at court. We were born and bred to not think for ourselves, to never question the status quo, to never set one foot out of line.

"Honestly, all of this is exhausting, isn't it?" I muttered. "This constant performance as if we're nothing but brainless dolls in pretty ball gowns. I'm sick of it. Life would be so much simpler if I were the daughter of a shoe cobbler."

Ela bumped my hip with hers. "I know what it's like to have little money to your name. Your challenges would be different but still present. Whether you're the daughter of a merchant or marquess, you are expected to marry and not be a burden to your family. If you lived modestly, you might be forced to work less-than-favorable jobs."

"I'm not afraid of work," I said.

Ela had the audacity to snort. "Zia, you've never worked a day in your life. When I was at Hinley, I scrubbed chamber pots whenever I went against the Price sisters, who taught lessons at the school, which was often." I wrinkled my nose. Ela had been sent away to a seminary in northern England when Poppy had fabricated a story that Ela had been compromised by a local boy, thus ruining her reputation. I'd never believed Poppy. But in our world, a man's word was everything. And that boy, the vicar's nephew, had lied through his teeth that Ela's virtue had been taken.

"I could do it," I said stubbornly. I was made of stern stuff, surely, but perhaps a test was in order. The Lady Knights could volunteer to help at the orphanage. That should even out our moral ledger a bit. Then again, it might take more than a few freshly washed chamber pots to even out the handful of robberies we were pulling off to keep the school open.

Suddenly, I spotted Keston returning—thank heavens—with an enormous pitcher of water. Relief sluiced through me, but then I noticed the gentleman walking behind him and groaned. My irritation doubled. Rafi appeared much too debonair for words in raven-black attire. He might have been an arrogant cad, but he wore a suit of formal togs like he was born for them. Tall, athletic, and lean, he commanded attention. My brother drew stares, too, but Keston was off the market. Rafi was not, and everyone with a working pulse knew it.

I could *look*. No one had to know.

His dark hair was swept back from his brow and fell in silky waves to his shoulders. It wasn't de rigueur to have long hair, but Rafi did not care. His nose was long but that only complemented his high cheekbones and square jaw, along with his pair of full, perpetually quirked lips. My pulse sped up quite ridiculously.

Rafi greeted Ela, and his odd spell on me was broken. The heat must have been getting to my good sense because mooning after *this* particular gentleman was a recipe for the worst kind of heartbreak. Dragging my eyes away, I accepted the glass Keston gave me and gulped thirstily like a person left in the desert too long. When that was empty, he poured a second glass, which went the indecorous way of the first. I knew I mirrored a gluttonous boor, but the sweet, sweet coolness gave me relief.

"Slow down, Sister," Keston warned. "You'll have a coughing fit." He turned to his fiancée. "Now that I've officially saved this damsel in self-imposed distress, would you reward me with a dance?"

Ela shot me a dubious look after a pointed stare to Rafi, but I shooed her away. She shouldn't have to suffer for my choices, and I could survive a few minutes with London's favorite rake. I fastidiously ignored him to pour myself a third glass while my body temperature desperately attempted to regulate. I forced myself to take small sips. He made a humming sound, and with an internal sigh, I glanced out of the corners of my eyes to find a much-too-delighted Rafi. I knew that whatever came out of his mouth was going to aggravate the spit out of me.

"Say your piece before you choke on your hubris," I muttered.

That silver-gray gaze sparkled with unholy glee as he surveyed me from head to toe. Ela had once described his eyes as dark gray, but those mercurial irises could never be so prosaic. I braced myself when said eyes widened with false shock. "Dear God, Lady Zenobia, is that *you*? I did not recognize you," he said, slapping a palm to his chest. I scowled at the Thespian performance. He bloody well knew it was me. "Did you tumble into a vat of egg-white icing, perhaps?"

"Mr. Nasser," I replied, and inclined my head as politely as I could, though my fingers itched to toss the rest of my drink into his face. But that would be a fruitless waste of perfectly refreshing water. "Clever as always. However do you keep that wit of yours so impressively sharp?"

His eyes danced with mischief at my reply. I wanted to kick myself. A reaction was always what he strove for, especially if it led to trouble. The man thrived on drama. "I am committed to perfection. I would ask you to dance, but I'd be too afraid of being smothered to death."

"What a pity," I murmured. "You could use a good smothering."

"Why, Zia," he said in a low voice that scraped over my senses and stepped alarmingly close even with my many layers. "I'm wounded. One would think you didn't hold me in any esteem at all." That voice deepened to a rasp. "Unless, of course, smothering by skirt is what you intend."

I flushed and put a few inches' distance between us until I was jammed up against a wall. "You are a cad. Go torment some other girl. You've already made your opinions of me clear. Keston's silly little sister, was it?"

"I don't remember calling you *silly*, but be that as it may, I like tormenting you," he said. "You're astonishingly delightful to bait."

I bristled and clamped my lips together, knowing he was goading me yet again. God, how I longed to laud our latest heist over his arrogant head! Instead, I chose silence as a deterrent. It worked for a minute or two, and then, because this was Rafi, he leaned in much too close for comfort. So close that I could smell sandalwood and fresh rain. It was a unique combination, but one I'd always associated with him, and one that never failed to make my heart trip over itself like a buffoon.

"What on earth are you doing?" I demanded, unable to move, trapped as I was by the alcove wall and arguably the most infuriating male on the planet.

"You smell like orange blossoms."

I froze. Every single thought fled my brain as my eyes flicked down to the left hand that would be missing its signet ring beneath its glove. The ring, currently burning a hole in my skin at the end of the chain around my neck, felt heavy. I'd kept the dratted thing out of some perverse sense of triumph at besting the oh-so-cocky Rafi Nasser, who had callously rejected me, like a secret victory token. In truth, I had no idea why I'd worn the ring tonight. Maybe it served as a reminder that I was more than Zia the diamond. I was Zia the rebel.

Or perhaps you simply wanted to wear his ring like a calf-eyed fool.

I ignored that voice. Not that he would guess what lay under my bodice, but just as I'd associated a fragrance with him, perhaps he was doing the same. "It's a common scent," I said in a neutral tone. "Like rose water."

"Is it? You're the only female of my acquaintance who favors it, so not as common as you think."

I racked my brain and pointed to our gorgeous hostess, who was dancing past. "I believe Lady Rosalin wears it, as does my acquaintance Miss Lalita Varma. So perhaps you're not nearly as observant as you think."

He didn't even respond to the jibe, his piercing, stormy stare narrowed, likely trying to determine if I could be the bandit he'd encountered in Hounslow Heath. For once, I was thankful for the layers shrouding me, making it difficult to associate this girl with the one on horseback. But it would take more than that to head him off. I had to play the part of the insipid, spoiled heiress—one he could never associate with a fearless robber.

"Heavens, have you ever seen a crush like this? Finding a husband amongst this crowd will be as simple as falling off a log." I simpered and peered up at him through my lashes. "Or a wife, in your case," I added, and smiled when I saw the slightest flinch of his shoulders. "In fact, a little bird told me that you are intending to court someone this season."

His cockiness disappeared as dark eyebrows crashed together, a muscle leaping in his cheek. For a moment, I missed seeing the ever-present smirk. "I am not."

"Oh? So, Miss Sarah Peabody is mistaken?" I couldn't help my frown. Was he lying? Or had Sarah fibbed to get under my skin? It was likely the latter. "She said you were."

"I have no idea who that is," he growled, then shook his head. "Unless it is yet another scheme of my uncle's. But I do not intend to court anyone, least of all anyone handpicked by him. Please excuse me, Lady Zenobia."

Satisfied, I watched as he strode across the ballroom to where his uncle stood in conversation near the refreshments room. A swift exchange of words followed before Rafi stormed off to the foyer. A part of me—a foolish besotted part that needed to be quashed—instantly mourned his absence, and I fought the senseless urge to run after him, huge dress be damned. But I knew he would not welcome it.

And I had enough sense to not go where I wasn't wanted.

I shivered. Rafi Nasser was like lightning . . . a burst of elemental energy sizzling through the air, signaling the arrival of a devastating storm. One that had the power to raze everything in its way, leaving nothing but ruin.

So why on earth did I feel the urge to throw myself directly into his path?

CHAPTER FOUR

My own sex, I hope, will excuse me, if I treat them like rational creatures, instead of flattering their fascinating graces, and viewing them as if they were in a state of perpetual childhood, unable to stand alone.

—MARY WOLLSTONECRAFT

"Ladies," Miss Perkins said in a cheery voice, carrying a stack of books in her arms. "I have something very special for you."

Perking up with the other girls, I sat forward in my seat, wondering what she could possibly have chosen for us to discuss next. Perhaps it would be a gothic romance novel, one that we were expressly forbidden to read. Novels, for the most part, were seen by men as useless diversions for women. Even the works of Jane Austen were considered provocative, frivolous, and irrelevant.

Having read both *Pride and Prejudice* as well as *Emma* last year in our special book club, I vehemently disagreed with that assessment. Austen's commentary of social customs and values was unerringly precise, especially her satirical views on class, status, and wealth. In class discussions, each of us found something of ourselves in the Bennet sisters. They were intelligent, resourceful, and brave . . . seeking much the same things we were—agency, independence, purpose. Emma, despite her proclivities, was not afraid to be herself. Lizzie Bennet, even more so.

But what I loved most about both novels was the central premise of love. Deep down, like those heroines, I desperately wanted someone who could see me. To see that I wasn't some brainless high-society heiress . . . to appreciate that I wanted to compose music, to travel and see the world. Someone who could accept *me* for me.

I focused my attention back on Miss Perkins, who was handing out the red-bound volumes she'd brought with her. When Greer received hers, she let out an uncharacteristic squeak and started practically vibrating with excitement. Curious, I took in the title as the book landed on my desk and felt my own face break into an enormous grin.

It was *Frankenstein; or, The Modern Prometheus.*

This had been Greer's secret book club request several months ago but had been bypassed until now. The *Times* had deemed the book inappropriate for the delicate, undeveloped minds of precious young ladies. I'd instantly wanted to read it but had been waiting for some of the furor to die down.

The incendiary novel had been anonymously published only at the start of last year, and no one knew the identity of the author. People had speculated, of course, when the sensational horror story flew off shelves in bookshops and raced around drawing rooms. The reigning guess was the poet Percy Shelley, considering that the book had been dedicated to William Godwin, his father-in-law and a political writer he highly esteemed.

A few had even conjectured it was Austen trying her hand at another genre, which I could not fathom. She wrote about social satire and romance, not horror and murder. Others had insisted it must be a man since the story itself was so disturbingly graphic. As if only a man could be so creatively macabre. If I had to guess, I would venture to say that it was Ann Radcliffe, who was known for her gothic fiction with supernatural elements.

Miss Perkins perched on her desk and surveyed the room. "Thank you to Miss Sorensen for suggesting this title last autumn. After much thought, I believe collectively you might be ready for this, especially after our last author, Mary Wollstonecraft." She let out a breath, a small crease marring her brow. "However, it was a rather difficult decision, given the monstrous and disquieting subject matter, which is why I took so long. I understand if anyone here chooses to abstain from reading this book, no explanations required."

We all glanced at each other, and while a few faces wore uncertain expressions, no one spoke up. The whole point of the book club was to broaden our minds with subjects the men in our society considered unsuitable. And for gently bred young ladies, this book pushed all the limits. Nori and Sarah seemed as enthusiastic as Greer and I, though Lalita, Petal, and Blythe were decidedly less so.

Petal raised a tentative hand. "Is it frightening, Miss Perkins?"

"Parts of it are, yes," she replied with a thoughtful expression. "It does include explicit murder scenes, and the description of the monster itself might be alarming to some. You are not under any obligation to read, Lady Petal. As you know, book club is purely voluntary. You may rejoin for our next selection."

Petal shook her head hard as if the fear of missing out was much greater than the fear of the material. "No, I want to try."

"Very well." Miss Perkins cleared her throat and went on, "I agreed to read this novel for our next discussion for several reasons, but the primary one is that it was penned by a young woman who was a mere eighteen years old at the time of writing." Dead silence resounded. "The author was close to all of you in age, if you can imagine such a thing."

A handful of gasps echoed through the room as my mouth fell open, and my gaze instantly narrowed in disbelief, not at the fact that the author was near our age, but that Miss Perkins was actually aware of the author's identity. "I beg your pardon, but are you saying that you *know* who wrote this book?"

Smiling, Miss Perkins canted her head. "I do know, but you must promise to keep it a secret." Her gaze spanned the room to meet each of our eyes. "Some authors choose to publish their works anonymously for their own personal reasons, and we must honor that choice. I trust that all of you can keep one more secret, considering we are here to discuss . . . provocative literature."

Nori chuckled while Greer let out an impatient noise with a vehement nod. "You have my word," Greer volunteered instantly.

"And mine," I replied, quickly followed by the agreement of the others.

Miss Perkins tucked a loose tendril of hair behind her ears. "As you already know, Lord Byron is my third cousin, once removed."

More nods ensued. I still found it astonishing that *our* Miss Perkins was distantly related to one of the most prolific poets of our generation. Greer had been in absolute histrionics to learn that both our teacher and the baron had Scottish roots like her, despite the fact that Aberdeen and her native Edinburgh were a hundred miles apart. *Scots are Scots,* she'd claimed.

"Three years ago in Switzerland, my cousin was joined by three other writers at his residence in Geneva, and they had a competition of sorts to write the best ghost story." She pointed to the books in our laps. "*Frankenstein; or, The Modern Prometheus* was born out of this competition."

Sarah squealed and nearly swooned out of her seat—everyone knew she was massively infatuated with Byron, not so much for his poetry as for his looks. In fact, I suspected she'd only joined the book club because she'd wanted to toady to Miss Perkins with some obscure hope that she might one day meet the poet. He was handsome, sure, but gossip churned that he was an irrepressible rake. Not my type, thank you very much.

But isn't it exactly your type?

I steadfastly ignored that vexing inner voice as well as the accompanying vision of playful dappled-gray eyes in a tawny-brown face.

"Who was it?" Sarah whisper-shouted. "Please do tell, Miss Perkins. Lord Byron has such exquisite taste."

I suppressed my groan as Greer and I exchanged a look, but

we were too interested in the revelation to bother with Sarah. Miss Perkins beamed. "The author is Mary Shelley."

"The daughter of Mary Wollstonecraft?" Nori put in with round eyes that reflected nearly everyone else in the room. My mouth fell open. The woman in question did not frequent my social circles, but I'd seen her once or twice in passing.

Miss Perkins bobbed her head. "The very same."

With some skepticism, I wrinkled my brow. "Why wouldn't she want to admit that she was the author after it became so successful? Sir Walter Scott lauded it, saying that it displayed 'uncommon powers of poetic imagination.'"

"Given the restrictions placed on our sex, I imagine that it must have been to protect her children," Miss Perkins replied with a shrug. "And perhaps, too, she feared society's reception to a degree. The works of female writers are often trivialized and dismissed, but one of such an unexpectedly violent nature would have drawn more attention than usual. She also had her critics, particularly with more conservative members of society. Many think the story is disgusting, absurd, and immoral."

"How did you get all these copies?" I asked Miss Perkins, tracing a finger over the spine. "I heard only five hundred were printed, and they're long gone."

"My cousin was generous enough to send me his own volumes, and I found two others at circulating libraries. So please be careful as they must be returned when we're done."

I suppressed a flicker of disappointment at that. I would have loved to add the novel to my own precious, private collection.

Nori flipped through the pages and let out a low whistle. "I cannot believe she wrote this at our age! I can barely write a sonnet, much less an entire novel."

I shot her a grin. "Yes, but I bet Mrs. Shelley doesn't know a thing about horses. We all have our gifts."

Greer snorted with an impish look. "Well, except for you, Zia."

I gaped in false affront. "Take that back, you wretch. I am an organizer. An excellent organizer. I *organize*."

"Let's not forget, she's also a first-rate pianist," Lalita said loyally.

With a triumphant bellow, I pointed at her. "What she said!"

Miss Perkins stood and clapped her hands for us to settle down. "Ladies! Now seems like a good time to adjourn for the week. Begin reading, and we will meet again next week. I truly look forward to hearing your thoughts." She paused with her usual reminder at the door. "Don't forget, discretion is key. I would not want these novels found and confiscated."

Greer had come up with the ingenious idea of covering our secret books in brown paper, which had saved us more than once from prying eyes, but it wasn't foolproof. We always had to be extra careful, especially with our reputations as well as Miss Perkins's future on the line.

Knowledge was a perilous pursuit, but certainly worth the price.

Saturday evening and the timing of our next heist arrived all too quickly. Rolling my tight shoulder muscles, I pulled my hat low and dragged the neckcloth up over my chin, my heart racing in my chest. While we usually kept our criminal jaunts to the outskirts of London, where none of us would be recognized, this was new. The gaming hell, Danforth's Den, was in the West End and belonged to Blythe's father. I pushed that fact out of my head.

There was little chance that our classmate Blythe Danforth would be out at this time of night. She would likely be at home or at a social function, no doubt where my friends and I *should* be. Not hiding in a narrow, grimy backstreet in Piccadilly across from a building that reeked of urine. But this was it—the only chance to get a sizable chunk, if not all, of the money we needed and to hinder our nemesis's plans.

Not only did Viscount Hollis intend to demolish Bellevue and Little Hands, but he was also a smarmy, cruel old man who treated his servants atrociously, not to mention his own nephew. He'd threatened to cut Rafi off when he'd learned that his heir was interested in painting. The old bigot had acted as though such a hobby was less than manly, though he'd remarked slyly that it was probably expected of a boy of Rafi's less-than-blue blood.

Rumor had it that he'd hated the fact that his younger brother had wed a Persian woman, and Viscount Hollis was known for his terrible, derogatory opinions about her heritage. It continually astounded me how small-minded people in the aristocracy were. One would think that as part of such a modern society, we would have come to appreciate the value of a diverse spectrum of citizens. But no, people of all walks were careful to hide their real prejudices. I found it ironic that the woman the viscount so reviled was now the wife of an eastern sovereign.

"Any sign of him?" Greer whispered at my back.

"Not yet," I said, tapping the empty pistol I'd pilfered from Keston on my knee. Not that he would notice. He was much too busy with wedding preparations to know that I'd been in his rooms and picked the lock on his chest. I'd put the pistol back later, of course, but the smaller weapon was much less obvious than my usual rifle.

We waited a long while for the viscount to emerge from the gaming hell. After several hours, I toyed with the idea of going inside, but even though we were dressed as young men, our disguises weren't infallible, and if we met up with any danger, we would be exposed in a strange place with no known escape routes. But as the minutes ticked by, I grew more and more restless. We *needed* this score. We had to come up with the funds to stave off Bellevue's creditors and buy ourselves more time. Worst case, the building would be auctioned off to the very man we planned to rob.

"Are you certain Hollis arrived and went inside?" I whispered to Greer.

She squinted. "Yes. I saw him, and his carriage is still over there. He hasn't left."

Then he must have simply been passed out inside. With the amount of liquor that went hand in hand with gambling, that was highly probable. Or maybe he was spending time with a woman. I wasn't naïve to the fact that more salacious things than gambling happened in such clubs. In that case, we would have no choice but to wait.

"We should go inside," Greer suggested. "If he's sotted, we have a better chance of divesting him of any winnings in there than we do out here."

"It's too dangerous," I said with a shake of my head. Restlessness skittered over me, though, along with the unpleasant thought of remaining in this dank, smelly alleyway for much longer. "Even if it wasn't, how would we get in? It's membership only, and neither of us is dressed in evening wear."

A smirk curled Greer's lips. "The good thing about Danforth's is that they care more about coin than station, but since we don't have any money, there's a servants' entrance just over there. We can sneak in, then split up to cover more ground. We'll be quick. And if you're worried about Lalita and Nori, don't be. Sometimes plans have to be adjusted on the spur of the moment to account for irregularities."

Disquiet swirled, but neither option—waiting here for heaven knew how long nor entering a notorious gaming hell—made me feel confident. We were safer outside by a sliver of a margin, and I was just about to say so when slurring male voices drifted down the alley, getting louder. My stomach lurched.

"Zia," Greer said softly with wide eyes. "We need to move."

"Fine, we go in, but only for half an hour, that's it," I said. "After that, we reconvene out here."

"Got it."

Our disguises would hold up so long as no one got too

close and we stuck to the shadows. With care, we would not be revealed as female, or worse, recognized. I'd learned these tricks of deception from Ela, who had fooled everyone in the *ton* into thinking she was someone else for nearly an entire season.

We checked each other carefully in silence, retying the neck-cloths meant as masks to serve as loose cravats. Greer had no trouble passing as a young man. With her height and angular features, along with the false mustaches she had secured for us, she could easily pass for a working-class man. With the clothes I'd purloined from Keston, I resembled a young dandy.

Thankfully, as Greer had pointed out, unlike some of the more elite gentlemen's clubs, Danforth's welcomed all. I took a deep breath, and we crossed the street, keeping to the cover of darkness to avoid the men at the other end and angling around the club to the back. A few workers were hooting and throwing dice at the end of the alley, and fortunately, the door was propped open with a small brick.

Greer stopped near the side where a pile of crates was stacked and handed me one. "Hold this over your shoulder and act like you're meant to be delivering this. Follow my lead."

Confidence was half the battle in deception, and Greer stalked in there like she was on a mission. "Delivery for the director," she said in a deep tone to the hard-faced man standing near one of the inner doors. My brows rose.

The man narrowed his eyes. "Delivery of what?"

"How should I know?" Greer groused. "Take it up with him, but if you would prefer to keep management waiting, I'd much rather leave these with you. No skin off my back."

He practically quailed and waved us past. Seeing such a big man react so strongly made a cold shiver coast down my spine.

"Who's the director?" I asked Greer in a low whisper as we strode down the corridor to where music and voices rose.

She whispered back, "He watches the play in the gaming room to make sure no one gets out of hand, and supposedly, he's ruthless."

I frowned. "How do you know that?"

"Blythe told me he cut a man's fingers off once for cheating."

I blanched. Suddenly, venturing into this gaming hell didn't seem like a great idea. Following Greer's lead, I put the crate down once we were out of sight of the doorman and inhaled to calm my nerves. "I'll take the gaming room and then upstairs," I told Greer. "You check the dining and billiards rooms in the back. Half an hour, understood? No matter what."

She nodded and left. I was on my own for the next thirty minutes. My stomach roiled, but I threw my shoulders back with the arrogance of a young buck with money and acted like I belonged there. My hat was low enough to obscure my hair and eyes, and I flattened my lips. They were much too plump to not draw attention, and the last thing I needed was to fend off some overzealous drunken goose.

Not wanting to waste time, I plowed through the crowd between the faro and hazard tables, searching for the viscount. I passed card tables with men playing whist and vingt-et-un, making absurd wagers that had my eyes going wide. I never understood gambling, or the fact that men could risk entire fortunes on a hand of cards, the races, or even something as asinine as making a wager in a betting book that someone might be wedlocked before another.

Precipitously, my heart stopped as I caught sight of a familiar face only a few chairs away. Rafi's ring at the end of the chain around my neck warmed, or perhaps that was just my skin now uncomfortably hot. As if he were caught at the end of a tether, his spine straightened as he parsed around the room, a slight frown on his brow. Gracious, had Rafi *seen* me? Gasping, I ducked behind a column and peered at him, idly holding a set of cards, the long fingers of his free hand drumming on the tabletop.

Why was he here? Was he keeping an eye on his uncle? Or worse, was he with my brother? Dear God, I hoped not. I scanned the rest of the table, but there was no sign of Keston. Rafi surveyed the room again, that hooded gaze fixated on something, and I ducked out of sight. My pulse rate doubled, but I forced myself to relax. I had to find his uncle, not get waylaid!

After confirming the viscount wasn't on the gaming floor, I scurried up the stairs and peeked into the open sitting rooms. Growing more discouraged by the moment, in the second-to-last salon, I spotted my target lounging in an armchair, asleep. What were the odds? But I didn't question serendipity and tiptoed closer. I wasn't adept at thievery. Luckily, his coin purse was halfway out of his coat pocket. Very slowly, I reached for it, tugging it loose and wincing at the soft clink.

A tight breath left my lungs as the purse fell into my palm, and then my eyes caught on the gaudy diamond stickpin winking in the folds of the viscount's cravat with a gem that was as big as a quail egg. Should I? The salon remained empty, but it might not be for long. A quick glance at his open mouth and closed eyelids shored up my courage. Sod it—he deserved to be fleeced! Ever so cautiously, I slid the pin free of the fabric. A loud snore made me freeze in place, but he didn't awaken. Not wanting to tempt fate, I pocketed the items and hastened down the stairs.

Now to check that Rafi was still where I'd left him.

Breathing hard, I counted to ten and peeked around the column, only to discover that his seat was empty. Damn and blast! Where had he gone? I turned and crashed into a broad chest with an *oomph.* Before I could regain my wits, a strong grip had my elbow and steered me to a quieter corner. I blinked and peered up from beneath the brim of my hat to a pair of gray eyes that were sparking with anger.

"Zia," Rafi seethed. "What the devil are you doing here?"

I wrenched out of his grip, a dozen lies on my tongue. "How did you know it was me?"

"Your hair," he said in a growl as his gaze canvassed me. Words failed me as I glared at the offending spiral that had sprung free of its hold and tucked it back up. "What is on your face, and why are you wearing men's clothing?" he continued, his eyes narrowing in displeasure. "What are you up to? Good God, Zia, don't you know what kind of trouble you've put yourself in? Are you here alone?"

I glared at him, his uncle's possessions burning a hole in my pockets. "Which of those would you like me to answer first, or shall we keep a running tally of why Rafi Nasser thinks it's his job to monitor my whereabouts or my person?"

"Does Keston know you're here? Does Harbridge?" he demanded. No, they didn't because both my brother and father would lock me away for life if they did. "You are reckless, Zia, taking such risks with your bloody reputation at stake. Honestly, what were you thinking?"

My jaw clenched at his curt tone. "It's none of your business."

Fury and something else burned in those gleaming gray irises, and I felt my heart skip a tiny beat. Rafi had never truly paid attention to me, but he was certainly doing so now. I couldn't decide if I liked it or not. Having that lupine gaze fixed on me made me feel like a hare being stalked. Suppressing a shiver, I exhaled and considered my options. I had to get out of here somehow.

Opportunity arose when a groggy Viscount Hollis came stumbling down the steps toward us, and I caught sight of a wide-eyed Greer before she jerked her head toward the exit. The viscount teetered into his nephew with a drunken greeting that might have been an insult before slumping against him, and while Rafi attempted to steady his uncle, I turned and slipped through the crowd to catch up with Greer.

Dimly, I heard Rafi's voice yelling something and then caught sight of the man who had let us through. His face screamed bloody murder. Greer glanced over her shoulder and froze at the burly lads heading our way. We were trapped.

"Quick, this way!" a soft voice said, and my heart leaped at the sight of a familiar face two doors down a narrow corridor. Blythe! It wasn't like we had much choice at the moment. I glanced at Greer, and we both nodded. The door snapped shut, but Blythe held up a candle. "I don't even want to know what capers you two are up to."

"Do you live here?" I asked curiously as we followed her down a level, smelling the scents of a bustling kitchen.

"My father has apartments on the upper levels of the club," she said over her shoulder. "When my mother is ill, sometimes I visit, though I'm forbidden to come downstairs for obvious reasons. It was lucky that I forgot my books in his study."

"How did you know it was us?" Greer asked.

"I see your face practically every day at Welton, Greer," she said with a laugh. "And, well, I am deeply jealous of Zia's curls— I'd recognize those bronze, gold, and brown spirals anywhere, even with those horrid mustaches."

Blythe led us to a small scullery that had a door leading outside. "Thank you," I told her when she held it open with a conspiratorial smile. "We owe you."

Hot on Greer's heels, I dashed down the street and high-tailed toward the main square, only relaxing when we were in a hackney. That had been much too close. If it hadn't been for Blythe, who knew what might have happened? Would Rafi have made me go with him? Outed me to my father? Would he still? Alarm took hold in my chest.

"I got the viscount's purse, but Rafi was there, too," I blurted.

Greer's blue eyes widened comically. "Did he recognize you?"

"Yes."

"That's bad, Zia. Really bad. What did you tell him?"

I bit my lip and groaned. "Nothing, but he's not the type to let things go. He didn't see you, so I could say I was curious as to what a gambling den looked like. Or I was visiting Blythe. I'll handle him, I promise."

"How?" She shot me a skeptical glance, and I bristled.

"Don't worry about that. I'll take care of it."

First, I'd have to figure out what Rafi wanted . . . and then, I'd have to come up with a way to bargain for his silence.

CHAPTER
FIVE

Women, considered not only as moral, but rational creatures, ought to endeavour to acquire human virtues (or
perfections) by the same means as men, instead of being
educated like a fanciful kind of half being.

—MARY WOLLSTONECRAFT

Sitting in the Welton classroom, I flipped through the pages of
my copy of *Frankenstein,* barely heeding Miss Perkins's instruction for us to find the scene we'd last read.

It was difficult to focus on discussing *Frankenstein,* with my
apprehensions boiling over what had happened with Blythe. At
Danforth's, she could have turned us in or exposed us, but she'd
chosen to help Greer and me. That had to count for something.
I wasn't a suspicious person by nature, but I wasn't naïve, either.
I'd seen far too many girls our age throwing each other under
carriage wheels . . . over a boy, new friends, or power and influence. In truth, I was accustomed to being used by others as a

means to get closer to my illustrious mother and father or, when Keston had been unattached, to get into his good graces.

No one in the *ton* did anything without a motive.

What was *Blythe's*?

I centered my focus on Miss Perkins, who was in the middle of writing the major themes of the novel on the chalkboard. I was still inspired by the fact that the author of such a gripping, horrifying tale was a young woman my age. Mary Shelley did not cave to the restrictions placed on our sex by society, nor had she felt inferior to the Eton- and Harrow-educated male writers of her acquaintance, like her husband or Lord Byron. On the contrary, she'd written a story that had been hers to tell in all its gruesome glory. Though the authorship was anonymous, for valid reasons, the pride I felt in my chest for a fellow young woman defying convention filled me up. The members of our secret book club weren't the only ones attempting to break free from gilded cages.

We were at the forefront of a quiet but fierce revolution.

An educated mind—an *enlightened* mind—was a thing to be esteemed. Women were just as capable as men in thinking, creating, reasoning, and philosophizing. Our brains were fertile lands in desperate need of cultivation. In *Strictures on the Modern System of Female Education,* Hannah More, another writer I admired, likened the human mind to soil, which had to be properly tilled, depending on its composition, for the best possible result. Why should we have our God-given gifts quelled? As Miss Perkins always said, ignorance wasn't bliss; it was and would always be a woman's curse.

Said sharer of wisdom stared at each of us in turn after she'd finished writing on the chalkboard.

FRANKENSTEIN; OR, THE MODERN PROMETHEUS
Prevailing themes and motifs
Creator —→ Creation

Conception —→ Animation

Life   Death

"Before we begin," Miss Perkins said, "might I inquire, Lady Petal, if you are comfortable pressing forward with the material? I know you had expressed concerns about the subject matter last week."

Petal blushed when all eyes landed on her, her discomfort evident. "I believe I can persevere," she said after a moment of hesitation, though her voice wobbled.

"Very well," Miss Perkins said. "But do let me know if at any point you are put off."

"I will," Petal said.

Sarah raised her hand. "Miss Perkins, are you certain this wasn't written by Lord Byron or even Shelley? It seems rather absurd for an eighteen-year-old girl to pen something so indecorous."

"How is it indecorous?" Greer shot back. "Even so, isn't that why we are here? To read and discuss things that others have decided are too vulgar for our precious female sensibilities?" She narrowed her eyes. "And why does a story of this kind have to be written by a man anyway? Our brains are not childlike, infantile organs. Mrs. Shelley is as capable as any of her male counterparts."

Sarah tossed her head. "I just think that such profane subjects are better suited to male temperaments."

"Is that true of your dear Lord Byron?" Greer scoffed. "I thought he was the epitome of charm and chivalry."

"That's a gross generalization," I said, glancing over my shoulder to see Sarah's fair skin heating to crimson at Greer's scornful tone. "Controversial ideas and profanity aren't limited to sex. We must question the status quo. I, for one, think it's admirable that Mrs. Shelley is the author."

"Anyone else agree with Miss Peabody?" Miss Perkins asked, and as expected, Petal's hand flew up. A few seconds later, so did Lalita's. I raised my eyebrows, but everyone was entitled to their own opinions.

"Fair enough," Miss Perkins said. "All views are valid, though I must echo Lady Zenobia's mission to question societal structures built in the shadow of the patriarchy. We are, after all, here to expand our minds, and I encourage you to be open." She cleared her throat and pointed to the chalkboard. "Moving on. In this novel, we have a creator and his creation, and everything that lies between its conception and earthly animation. What other themes do you see at play here other than those of life and death?"

"Family," Blythe volunteered first, surprising everyone. "Part of the reason the monster went down the path he did was because he felt so alone. He had no one. And he even says that was what made him a murderer."

"Well done," Miss Perkins said before adding that to the chalkboard.

"What about ambition and power?" Sarah asked. "Dr. Frankenstein broke the natural order of things to create his ungodly creature after his mother's death, simply because he was obsessed with life, creation, and resuscitating the dead. He wanted to play God."

"Good!" Miss Perkins said as Sarah preened. I wanted to roll my eyes. It was no secret that she was obsessed with both power and ambition and would do anything to elevate her station in the *ton*. "Any others, girls?"

"Revenge?" Lalita ventured hesitantly. "The monster is innocent at first, but when he is spurned, mistreated, and abandoned, he becomes angry and wants vengeance."

"Wonderful, Miss Varma." With a pleased expression, Miss Perkins wrote that on the board as well.

I lifted my hand, but Nori beat me to it. "The definition of monstrosity. Is the monster monstrous for being who he is? Or is Victor Frankenstein more so for having created him?" She tapped a thoughtful finger to her chin. "Furthermore, as Lalita noted, the monster when he is awakened is innocent, but then he is shaped by the monstrous things he encounters and hears from humans. He *becomes* a monster and a killer by virtue of external factors, so that's a matter of nurture, not nature. And also, is his maker even more monstrous for abandoning him when he is the one responsible for giving him life in the first place?"

Miss Perkins nodded. "Very insightful, Miss Kaneko. Do you think the monster could have had compassion and empathy if he'd been treated with such?"

"Absolutely," she said. "Biological nature and environmental influences are both factors in the growth of any individual. The creature was molded by his circumstances and surroundings."

Miss Perkins gave a firm nod. "So then, was Frankenstein's creation a human turned into a monster?"

Petal snorted. "The thing was always a monster. It was never human, so how could it be expected to learn human behavior and mannerisms?"

"But did he not live and experience the same pains we do?" Miss Perkins pressed.

"An amalgamation of many men does not make one man. A human can be a monster, but a monster cannot be human," Lalita said.

"I agree. It was an abomination, a killer, which meant it was going to behave as such. A dog doesn't know it's anything other than a dog," Petal added, nodding at Lalita.

I frowned. "That's a narrow way of thinking of life. A dog is a dog, yes, but said animal isn't born vicious, unless it has been grossly mistreated," I countered. "And by your definition, as a woman, I will always be constrained to the preconceived notions of my sex—always considered lesser. Ergo, I must fit into this box labeled *female* that has been constructed by a male hand. I should not want to study mathematics. I should not want to fence or ride astride. I should not write gruesome gothic tales. I should not speak or do anything out of turn or be anything that fathers and husbands do not deem appropriate. That inherent bias weakens any power I might have."

Miss Perkins offered me an encouraging smile. "Lady Zenobia has a point here on prejudice. We've read Wollstonecraft, Mary Shelley's mother, and her views on women being seen as fully realized humans and not diverting half creatures solely dedicated to the existence of men. If I, as a woman, were given the educational tools to better myself, treated with empathy, and placed on even footing as my male counterparts, would that impact who I became?"

"Yes!" Greer and I said at the same time.

"No, wait. It's not the same thing," Petal argued sullenly. "None of us is a perverse, pieced-together, immoral creature."

Greer laughed. "So, a monster can't be taught? You're here, aren't you?"

"Take that back, you beast!" Petal screeched so loudly that my ears rang.

"Girls, please." Miss Perkins threw a worried stare to the door, and sure enough, not a handful of minutes later, heavy footsteps came marching down the hall. We instantly quieted, including a purple-faced Petal. Our books went under cushions and were tucked between skirts.

An urgent look from the teacher had us sobering before a hard rap on the door came, and it opened to display the most senior Perkins sister . . . and the strictest one. Her reddish hair was scraped back into such a severe bun that her face appeared gaunt. The coloring and physical resemblance between the sisters was clear, but that was as far as their likeness went. If Miss Perkins was unconventional and progressive, her eldest sister was the polar opposite. She was focused on piety, modesty, and intense religious instruction. Thank goodness I wasn't boarding here. Greer and the others had told me chilling stories of her lessons.

"What is going on here, Ada?" Mrs. Perkins asked with narrowed eyes, surveying the room. "I heard quite unladylike screaming. Young ladies do *not* raise their voices." I swallowed down the instant urge to bellow at the top of my voice, just to prove her wrong. Our voices were meant to be heard, even Petal's. "You are not scheduled for a lesson."

"Remedial instruction, Sister," Miss Perkins replied, lifting her worn copy of a conduct manual—*The Mirror of Graces* by a Lady of Distinction. "On etiquette."

I almost snorted aloud. That particular manual was another useless piece on how to ensnare a husband.

Mrs. Perkins's eyes narrowed. "And the noise?"

"Lady Petal was quite overcome when a monstrous spider crawled over her desk, Mrs. Perkins," Greer said, her face the picture of innocence. At Petal's glare and Greer's emphasis on *monstrous,* I bit back a bubble of laughter and ducked my head. I was under the elder Perkins sister's power to bar me from her school. Or worse, force me to endure hours of devout instruction to calm my overzealous humors.

"Where is said creature?" Mrs. Perkins asked suspiciously.

"Miss Sorensen kindly relocated it through the window, Mrs. Perkins," I said ever so sweetly with a graceful cant of my chin. I did not require *The Mirror of Graces* to know how to turn on the charm or employ the clipped politesse of my station. I had been bred to be a peeress from birth. "The creature was a surprise to us all, though we will endeavor to instruct Lady Petal that there is naught to fear. A spider, after all, is only a spider, not bearing any malicious intent, unless threatened."

Nori covered her chortle with a cough, while Miss Perkins's eyes glinted with a spark of humor.

Mrs. Perkins's hard gaze softened, most likely because of my father's generous donation to her institution rather than my impeccable conduct. "Well, then. Thank you, Lady Zenobia and Miss Sorensen," she said at the door. "Lady Petal, do remember that a spider is a precious creature of God's making." She sent a dismissive glance to her sister. "Carry on."

The minute her footsteps faded, nearly everyone erupted into smothered giggles. Petal wore an infuriated glower, which sent Greer and me into stronger fits of laughter.

"I believe that's enough tempting fate for today," Miss Perkins said, her own lips twitching. "See you at our next class. Until then, remember, *Alis volat propriis.* Do try to spread yours once or twice."

I grinned. *She flies with her own wings* had to be the best adage of all time.

Because we, women, were born to soar . . . and I intended to see the sun.

CHAPTER SIX

I am fully persuaded that we should hear of none of these infantine airs, if girls were allowed to take sufficient exercise, and not confined in close rooms till their muscles are relaxed, and their powers of digestion destroyed.

—MARY WOLLSTONECRAFT

An urgent meeting of the Lady Knights was to take place in the gardens at Welton House after chapel and right before our scheduled book club, and my mood was somber. As I walked toward the meeting point, a voice calling my name had me turning around. "Hullo, Zia!"

"Hullo, Beth!" I smiled and waved at Beth as she walked with Sister Mary outside the orphanage, helping to tend to the meager vegetable garden. Thick ivy crept up the walls, hiding the age of the stone, but the edges of the roof were crumbling in places. The cracking shingles were in dire need of repair, and even the large windows were nearly opaque with grime. The nuns were spread thin as it was, but this was home to many like

Beth. The little girl raced over to the small hedge that divided us, pigtails bouncing and small face alight.

"When will you come read to me?" she asked excitedly. "I want *The History of Little Goody Two-Shoes* again." That nursery book was a favorite with the children, especially Beth, since its heroine Margery was also an orphan. For a seven-year-old, Beth was remarkably resilient, saying that as long as she had a sturdy pair of shoes, she could be happy. It had nearly broken my heart.

"Soon, Beth. I promise! It's Greer's turn next and then it will be mine." Reading to the children was part of our charitable duty as deemed by the eldest Perkins sister, and it was one I greatly enjoyed. I glanced up, hearing the nun calling for her. "Now go finish your chores before we both get into trouble with Sister Mary the dragon."

Beth giggled, blew me a kiss, and raced obediently back to the smiling nun. The brief burst of happiness at seeing the adorable little girl was short-lived as my worries for the fate of the orphanage weighed upon me. A nasty bout of croup had strained the coffers, and on top of everything, the roof was now leaking and in need of repair. Even with the added contribution from our nemesis, Viscount Hollis, we were falling short by a goodly amount since the diamond stickpin had turned out to be made of paste and was worthless. None of us had any extra pin money to spare.

Things appeared dire for Little Hands unless we could come up with a viable plan. I greeted my best friends in the small grove near an old ornamental pond and took the only open spot on the bench.

"So, I have an idea to make up the rest of the money," Nori began softly. "But you're not going to like it."

Lalita frowned. "Is it dangerous? Can we get hurt?"

"Yes, and also probably yes," she replied, gnawing on her bottom lip. She tucked the flyaway wisps of her sleek black hair behind her ears. "There's a secret race that happens every season between Eton, Harrow, and Westminster on Rotten Row, quite unoriginally called Midnight Row. But what can I say? Boys have no imagination."

Lalita gasped, her voice a squeak. "You want us to attend a horse race? At midnight? Surely not!"

"There's some lighting there, I believe. It will definitely be dangerous because the path is shadowed and also can be made treacherous by the weather." Nori drew in a breath. "The boys will give no quarter. But here's the best part. The winning pot will more than cover the rest of what we need to save Welton and then some."

"Racing in the dark sounds like a terrible idea," Lalita muttered.

Rotten Row was about eighty feet wide and covered over a mile of ground. I'd ridden it many times, though I'd never raced on the thing at night. I narrowed my gaze in thought. "Can anyone enter? How does it work? It's just a free-for-all, start to finish?"

Nori shrugged. "It's complicated, and I only know because my brother was one of the founders." Nori's brother Rin was as horse-obsessed as she was, so it was no surprise that he was involved. He was a few years older than us and ran with a very fast set. "Each school is allowed four teams of three, but there are also extra slots open to any other teams with invitations. I can get that from Rin. He owes me a favor."

"Are girls allowed?" Greer asked, curious.

Nori shook her head. "Not officially, so we will have to be in disguise just to be safe, but we'll use the dim lighting to our advantage. Also, there are no sidesaddles, so you have to know how to ride astride. In the first stretch, one of the three riders must race to the end. Out of sixteen, only ten riders will be able to advance their team to the second race. If someone from your team is at the bottom of the ranking, the entire team is eliminated. So, the goal is to be aggressive and quick. The first length is the worst because the field is so crowded. After the second stretch, which goes from the far end of Rotten Row back to the start, only five teams will move on to round three, which is the final race." Her face twisted.

"What is that expression?" I asked.

"Since it's the last race, there might be obstacles," Nori said. My stomach dipped, but I was accustomed to jumping over fallen branches and short hedgerows in the country.

Greer frowned. "What if all four teams from one school are in the top five?"

"It isn't fair, but it has happened before. The race is vicious, with all kinds of tricks and underhanded ploys. Sometimes one of the teams for a school will sacrifice its position or take out the competition for their top team to make it through." My eyes went wide at that.

"How much is the contribution?" I asked, blood racing.

"I think it's still ten pounds per rider, so thirty per team," Nori said. "But sometimes the boys add in extra. A couple of years ago, I think Rin said it was near four hundred quid. So, if we win, that will be more than enough to cover the three hundred pounds we need for Bellevue and Little Hands."

I bit my lip. We would have to dip into the money we'd already collected for the entry fee of thirty pounds. It was a big gamble. If we won, that money could make all the difference. But if we lost, we would be much worse off than we were now. And that wasn't the only problem. We needed three capable riders and horses of fine racing stock.

Nori cleared her throat like she'd read my mind. "I can get the horses, and I would be one of the racers."

Considering I'd had horse-riding lessons since I could walk, I was a capable rider and could handle being astride. In fact, I preferred it, even though society frowned upon young ladies sitting in such an indecorous position, despite the fact that incorrectly fitted sidesaddles could be dangerous for the horses as well as painful for some riders. I'd learned that tidbit from Nori.

"Me too," I said. "I can ride."

"Don't look at me," Greer said, hands spread wide. "I couldn't race a horse to save my life. Give me a curricle or a phaeton and I'm your girl."

I glanced over at Lalita, who was shaking her head, her face paling at the expectant expression on mine. She was our only choice. "I cannot. After the last time when we were chased by the Runners, I fear my constitution may not be able to handle mounting a horse. Besides, I would only slow us down."

My heart sank. "Lalita, please. We need you."

"Don't ask me to do this, Zia," she said, her voice wobbling.

Despair overcame me. One sliver of hope, and it was snatched away. But as disappointing as her response was, I'd never force Lalita to do something that she wasn't comfortable with. We were all about empowering one another, not diminishing.

"I can do it," a soft voice said, and we all whirled around.

"Blythe." We'd been so engrossed in our conversation that we hadn't even heard someone approaching.

"I didn't mean to eavesdrop, but I saw you and Greer and wanted to see how you were both doing after what happened at Danforth's the other week." She gnawed her lip and wrung her hands as we remained silent.

My brain whirled as my stomach churned uneasily. How much had she heard? We couldn't risk word of our nocturnal activities getting out, and Blythe, as nice as she was, wasn't someone in our circle of trust. "You can do what exactly?" Nori asked, a suspicious look on her face.

"Race," she said in a small voice. "I mean, I'm a capable rider, and I've always been around horses. . . ." She trailed off, seeming uncertain, and swallowed. "My uncle is Old Dick Tattersall, the grandson of Old Tatt. My cousins are Richard and George Tattersall."

"As in the horse auctioneers? Those Tattersalls?" Nori asked, though her suspicion had lessened, and her eyes went wide in awe. Tattersall's was *the* auction house for prime horse stock in London, open every Sunday between twelve and two in Hyde Park.

"Yes," Blythe said.

Lalita wrinkled her nose. "Why would you want to help us? You could get into trouble."

"Why not?" she countered, walking closer. "Sounds like you need a third, and I'm quite fond of racing."

"What's in it for you?" Greer questioned.

Blythe peered down and then inhaled as if searching for courage. "Friendship, I suppose," she said quietly. "I don't have many friends at Welton. My father has high hopes for me to learn the niceties and accomplishments of a proper young lady, but it hasn't been easy." She drew in another deep breath. "Some people aren't very welcoming to commoners, but well, you lot seem different." She smiled shyly at Greer and me. "Honestly, I'd never expected to see anyone in high society in disguise at Danforth's."

"Thanks for the rescue, by the way," I said. "You saved our hides."

"What were you doing there?" she asked.

Greer and I glanced at each other. "It was a dare," Greer said quickly. "Sometimes we dare each other to do things that most young ladies might not do . . . like this race, for instance."

Blythe's eyes narrowed slightly, and for a second, I worried that she saw right through Greer's fib, but then she burst into a snort. "So audacious, I love it."

"Not so nice when you're almost caught and escape by the skin of your teeth," I said. "Luckily, we had the help of a new friend."

The grin completely transformed her face, making her pale green eyes glow. She was a comely girl, but I'd rarely ever seen her smile. Even in our book club discussions, she was clever in her remarks when solicited but mostly preferred to observe.

"We plan to donate the winnings," I said, after glancing at the others and receiving their inaudible affirmations in turn. Lalita took the longest, but eventually she nodded with a soft sigh. Given her reticence to ride, Blythe was our only option. And saving the orphanage was the most important thing, even if it meant risking Blythe finding out that we did a lot more than just race. Stealing was a crime that could land us in Newgate Prison.

Greer gave a decisive nod. "You have to give us your solemn vow never to speak a word of this to anyone. Our reputations would be ruined; yours as well."

"You have it."

Though I was nervous, Blythe deserved a chance. And we required her help to have any shot at winning the Midnight Row pot. It was quid pro quo. Whatever happened, we would go from there—I could drive myself up the wall for hours worrying about a betrayal that hadn't yet happened and might never . . . or I could give Blythe the benefit of the doubt.

She wasn't an official Lady Knight, but that didn't mean she *couldn't* be.

A thoroughly illegal horse race down Rotten Row at midnight had to be the epitome of folly. My vexing conscience was ever swift to supply the warning, but nothing—not even fear—could take away from the thrill that scuttled down my spine. Hundreds of lamps along the row's edges had been ignited, bringing in more light than we expected. We would have to be extra careful to avoid being recognized. Me especially. Conscious of the tight braids beneath my hat and what had happened at Danforth's, I dragged a finger around my nape to make sure that not a strand was loose and secured my face covering.

There was a slight chill in the air, despite the pleasant days, but fortunately, we had dressed for the occasion in warm coats and lined breeches. We stood in a loose circle on the periphery of the milling crowd of people and horses, watching with apprehension as Nori presented Rin's letter of invitation to the gentlemen who seemed to be in charge.

I'd been surprised when Rin had conceded, considering this whole race could land any of us in hot water and also completely demolish our reputations should our identities be compromised, but Nori's brother had always been a radical thinker and had always treated his younger sister as though she stood on equal footing with him. Not unlike Keston with me, though he would hardly approve of this. Nori had said Rin had laughed when she'd asked for the invitation and instructed her to uphold the Kaneko name by raising absolute hell.

From a distance, I recognized a handful of the boys who attended Eton. A towering, familiar silhouette caught my attention at the edge of the melee, and my heart stilled. For a moment, I wondered if it was Rafi, but shook my head. There was absolutely no reason for him to be at *this* race at *this* time. Sure, he'd gone to Eton, but I'd never heard my brother or any of his other mates ever mention Midnight Row. And a younger me had been prone to eavesdropping.

I huffed a laugh. Just because Keston hadn't mentioned this particular race, it didn't mean that Rafi wouldn't have participated. He'd always been the wildest of them all with many other friends outside the quartet I knew.

"Riders," a deep voice intoned. "Ten minutes."

Glancing at Nori, I rolled my shoulders to ease the stiffness. Blythe was already at the other end to race the second lap, and I would bring up the rear in the final stretch. We'd taken her at her word with her skill, and Nori said that any offspring of a Tattersall had been born with the riding gene. Besides, anyone would be better than Lalita, or worse, Greer.

"Damn my hide!" Nori swore.

I peered at her. "What is it?"

"Rin is here," she said, scowling and pointing to a tall boy I recognized from our last highwayman heist, who was getting his horse into position. "My brother promised he wouldn't race tonight. What the devil is he *doing*?"

"Nori, focus," I said vehemently. "We can do this. We have to do this. It doesn't matter who's racing or what they throw at us in the last race."

Going serious, she huffed and nodded. "You're right."

I stuck my foot in the stirrup and pulled myself into Ares's saddle, feeling the stallion paw the earth beneath me. I kept my grip firm on the reins and patted his glossy brown neck. Ares was Nori's, but I'd ridden him before. He was temperamental but fast. Unfortunately, unruly crowds made him skittish, so I was hoping he'd keep calm until we rode out. Nearly three dozen riders and horses, not counting the excited spectators currently making wagers, were making *me* nervous. Hence our position at the edge of the throng.

"Don't get crowded on the rail, and aim for the middle of the pack as soon as the whistle blows," Nori warned. "Remember: There are no rules, so be careful."

I sucked in a bracing breath and nodded. Our standing as one of the four outsider teams gave us the worst placement nearest the rail. Once the horses bunched together, it would become a death trap if we didn't attempt to gain some speed at the whistle. I'd seen enough sanctioned horse races to know. This was a deviously vicious event, but I couldn't help being gleeful. Young ladies would never be allowed to race, at least not openly, and I wanted to teach these arrogant lads a lesson.

"Two minutes," the voice said. "First-lap riders, take your places."

Whoops and hollers filled the air; the chaotic energy coursing through everyone was infectious. Despite girls not being allowed to race, there were a few in the crowd. They could watch and cheer but could not participate. I fought an eye roll at the injustice. I caught sight of Greer on the sidelines, and she held her fist high. She mouthed the words *Lady Knights,* and I let the chant settle in my brain. The Knights made our own rules.

"How much is the pot?" I asked Nori.

Nori's eyes brightened. "Five hundred or thereabouts."

Five hundred pounds. No wonder the excitement was high. That was a fortune—not that any of the boys actually needed the money like we did—funds that would not only satisfy the lease for the church but feed, safeguard, and clothe children like Beth for years.

I watched as Nori got into third place from the rail, shouting something foul to her older brother, her body small in comparison to the other riders. But her size was an advantage in these kinds of races. Less body weight for a capable horseman—or horsewoman, in this case—meant a faster speed. Nori would make the top ten. She was brilliant on a horse, but then again, these boys were without scruples.

The whistle made Ares whinny and rear upward, and I used my knees to get him back into position, squinting as clods of dirt rained through the air. I lost sight of Nori in my attempt to bring my horse under control. Plumes of steam rose from his nostrils. I was certain Ares could sense my nerves. Horses were intuitive like that, so I forced myself to calm. If I couldn't get myself together, then the race would be lost before it even began.

I was so focused on keeping myself and Ares settled for the last race that I didn't see another horse and rider approach until they were practically on top of me. Ares neighed and reared up again, and I scowled, ready to give a piece of my mind to the intrusive rider.

"Why don't you watch where you—" I broke off as my eyes collided with a familiar gray pair and gulped. Of course, it had to be him. "What are you doing here?"

"What am *I* doing here? I should ask you the same thing," Rafi said, lips pressed thin, his handsome face tight with irritation. I suppressed my desire to squirm at the intensity of that hard, silver stare upon me. There was no warmth in his expression, but then I bristled and reminded myself that what I did was categorically none of his business.

My chin jutted. "Why? Because I'm a woman?"

"No, you daft girl," he ground out. "You could get hurt. Seriously hurt. These lads are ruthless. People have broken bones in this race. They won't care if you're female."

"And how will they know?" I tossed back in a low, furious voice. "Are you going to tell them who I am? Will you expose me?"

"Have I done so yet?" He blew out a breath, his own horse prancing impatiently. "Zia, be reasonable."

Frowning, I stared at him, his particular choice of words sparking a rebellious flame inside me. If I'd had even one smidgen of self-doubt about racing, it would have been extinguished by those damnable words. *Be reasonable.* As if my brain was beyond any capacity to make decisions relating to the well-being of my own person. I was more competent on a horse than most of the gents at this race.

My frown deepened. "Did you know I'd be here?"

The edges of those high cheekbones flushed, and for a moment I wished it weren't so dark. I could swear that Rafi was embarrassed. "Rin told me that his fearless fiend of a sister was planning to crash the race, and he wanted to see what she was up to. Considering you're as thick as thieves with her, it wasn't hard to put together that *you* might be one of the trio. Color me not surprised in the least."

A raucous round of cheering erupted from the other end of the track. The top ten must have been announced at the far end of Rotten Row. I hoped to the high heaven that we were still in the running. Anything could happen on a racetrack at night— a horse could become lame, a rider could fall or be thrown, a contender could be edged out at the last moment. I wasn't counting my chickens until I saw Nori for myself. If we'd made it to the next round, she would be cantering back shortly, and Blythe would be getting ready for the second race.

"So, what? You came to stop me?" I asked, glaring at Rafi and lifting a cool brow.

"Can anyone prevent you from doing anything once you get an idea in your head, my lady? You have always been extraordinarily headstrong," he said with a long-suffering stare, though something soft in his voice hinted at fondness as if it was a quality he was resigned to admire. "If you intend on following through with this foolhardy plan, I came here to make sure you finish the race in one piece."

"And how would you do that? By wrapping me in wool?"

"Don't tempt me," he replied in a low growl. "If anything happened to you, I—" He cleared his throat and glanced away. "Your brother would never forgive me."

Stunned, I peered up at him, but he wouldn't meet my gaze, and for a moment, I pondered what he'd been about to say before he'd broken off. Was *Rafi* worried about *me*? No, he was simply looking out for his best mate's little sister. He had to be doing this out of loyalty to Keston.

"Is there anything I can say to change your mind?" Rafi asked.

"No."

Just then, Nori cantered through the riders on the side of the track, her face bursting with victory. "Third place! We're in for the next race!" Her gaze flicked to Rafi as she pulled alongside me and balked in instant recognition. "Mr. Nasser, I didn't think you deigned to race Midnight Row anymore. Let me guess, you're riding with my no-good, two-faced Janus of a brother tonight?"

He canted his head and sighed. "I am."

"What!" I blurted. "No."

"Afraid, Firefly?" His lip curled as my brain faltered over the peculiar nickname. Was he being facetious? "Good, you should be. I've won this race more times than any other aside from Rin, and I'm a legacy," he said arrogantly. "Watch. Once the whistle blows, Blake will be tearing down the path with an easy lead."

"Wait—Blake is here, too?"

But his reply was lost in the wind as a distant whistle echoed through the night, and the sound of thundering hooves and muted shouts reached us. Heart pounding, I dismounted from Ares and secured him in a quiet corner under a tree. I tunneled my way into a gap in the crowd where I could see the track. I'd told Nori to focus, and here I was unraveling like a spool of thread at the thought of being pitted against Rafi and Blake, both excellent equestrians.

When the first of the riders came into view at the half-mile marker with a substantial lead, I nearly groaned aloud. Lord Blake Castleton. As usual, he was grinning insufferably and waving to the crowd like a grandstanding showman instead of a jockey in the middle of a race. Arguably, Blake was the most entertaining of my brother's friends, but right now I wanted to punch him. This was a game to him, whereas for us, it was the future of our school and an orphanage full of destitute children. We *had* to win.

But my enthusiasm waned when I counted the next four horses in the lead, and Blythe was nowhere in sight. Her mount was russet brown, but in the guttering light, all the steeds' coats looked the same, like mottled charcoal. I squinted at the riders, wondering if I'd missed her, which was easy to do.

"Do you see Blythe?" I shouted urgently over my shoulder to Nori, who had joined me on foot.

Her dismal expression mirrored mine. "No. Yes, I think . . . is that her . . . ?" But her voice trailed off as we both counted up to seven. There was still no sign of our teammate. Had something happened? Had she fallen or missed the whistle?

Suddenly a horse broke from the pack, heading out on the outside, and my smile widened. "I see her."

Her body was crouched low over her horse, her gallop so seamless that she and the stallion could be one creature. She ate up the yards, passing one rider, then another and another. Blythe only had to make the top five to qualify, but the determination on her face was clear.

"Good heavens, she's incredible!" Nori crowed.

The distance between Blake and Blythe narrowed, and I could see him glance over his shoulder with surprise. He might lose in the last lengths, if he wasn't careful.

"Go, B!" Nori roared at the top of her lungs, and I joined her, keeping my own voice pitched deep.

"Which team is that?" someone shouted to the right of me.

"One of the alternates," another person answered.

Rafi bumped my arm. I'd forgotten he was here in all the excitement, and he, too, had joined Nori and me at the edge of the rail. "That rider's seat is skilled," he remarked, and lowered his voice. "Who is it?"

"None of your deuced business," I replied, my smile so wide I could barely contain it.

Blythe remained in pursuit of Blake, and she'd clearly bided her time, knowing that her horse had the speed and stamina to bypass all the other challengers. A mile and a quarter wasn't long, but a smart jockey knew when to push his mount. Or *her* mount, in this case. The two leaders were nearly to the finish line when Blythe's hat flew off, and the gasps tore through the crowd as the waist-length coils of her hair unfurled.

My stomach sank—we were done for.

CHAPTER
SEVEN

In fact, if we revert to history, we shall find that the women who have distinguished themselves have neither been the most beautiful nor the most gentle of their sex.

—Mary Wollstonecraft

"Is that . . . a *girl*?" someone roared.

"She can't be here!"

"Disqualify her!"

My stomach dipped in dismay at that, and by the time Blythe crossed the finish line a hair behind Blake, the crowd was in a full-on furor, calling for her disqualification on account of her sex. A horrified Blythe dismounted, face apologetic, but losing her hat wasn't her fault, and she'd taken second place fair and square.

"Nice work," I told her. "You almost had Blake."

The redhead in question dismounted and joined us to congratulate Blythe. Unlike the other gentlemen, who were behaving like we'd infiltrated their secret club—which, to be fair, we had—Blake was all smiles. He didn't care that Blythe was female, only that she'd been an excellent contender. "Well done! You nearly bested me."

Blake grinned at Nori and then his eyes landed on me. Drat, I should have ducked my head, but it was much too late. His smile stuttered as his mouth fell open, gaze darting to Rafi, who only gave a small warning shake of his head. Not that Blake ever listened to anyone. "Z, does Kes know you're here?"

I glared at him, prepared to defend my choices, but was saved when the organizers of the race closed ranks on us as the chants for ineligibility continued. "We had an invitation," Nori said before they could get a word in, and yanked off her own hat and face scarf. More shouts ensued. "One's sex shouldn't undermine one's skill."

"This is a gentleman's sport," said a tall boy with a tight scowl. "And clearly you were aware of that, or you would not have hidden your identities."

Not wanting everyone to discover that a marquess's sister dared to race, I lowered my head and kept my brim low. Rafi must have seen because he nudged closer, his big frame helping to keep me hidden. Nori had an excuse in her brother. But I was a lady . . . with a duke for a father, who was feared for good reason.

Nori's scowl rivaled the boy's. "It's easier to ride in breeches, you jackanapes." She pointed at her bosom, the telltale rise and fall of her chest obvious beneath her coat. "I'm not at fault if you don't have a pair of working eyes to deduce that these are indeed breasts."

Smothered laughter rippled through the group. The boy's lip curled into an ugly sneer. "Now, see here—"

Blake clapped him on the back. "Calm down, mate. It's only a race. Don't allow the bruised egos of the losers get your under-garments in a twist. Let's see how they do in the final race." There was some agreement in the gathering, though still mostly murmurs of dissent.

"The rules are the rules," the unpleasant one insisted. "No women."

Nori stepped forward, fist raised. "My brother—"

"Is not in charge," the boy cut in coldly.

An incredulous laugh ripped from her. "Rin *invented* this race, you clod-head. Half the people here know I'm his sister. Or are you just completely oblivious and blinded by your own conceit? Rin, where are you?" she shouted.

Blake cleared his throat. "He's, er, being congratulated for winning the first leg." I bit back a snort; that could mean any number of scandalous things because Rin had an even worse reputation with the ladies than Rafi did.

Brows drawing down, our spoilsport folded his arms and clenched his jaw. With some alarm, I could see that this was going to go nowhere fast, but to my utter surprise, Rafi lifted a gloved hand, stopping the sputtering boy in his tracks. "There are no rules to say that females may not participate in Midnight Row. It is rare, true, but not prohibited. Mr. Kaneko would say the same, but clearly, he is otherwise occupied at the moment."

"Mr. Nasser," one of the other gentlemen said, his tone nearly reverent. My eyes rounded, recalling that he had called himself a legacy. Nori had said that Rin was one of the original founders. Was Rafi one, too?

The argumentative boy jutted his chin. "They should be ruled out."

"No," Rafi said curtly, his stare cutting the disputer down like the honed edge of a blade. "They ride. Or do *you* wish to be barred from future events?"

The boy's mouth snapped shut as he glowered with sullen hostility. A slew of muttering rose up in the wake of Rafi's threat.

"Will women be able to race now?"

"Are these the new rules?"

"Is it the beginning of the end? This is a man's world."

I almost rolled my eyes at the last statement. Blythe had just proved beyond a shadow of a doubt that she was better than most of the male riders here.

A solemn Rafi eyed me when the group dispersed after a pointed glare on his part. He leaned in. "What's the real reason you're doing this?"

I hesitated. Should I tell him the truth? It wasn't like I had anything to lose or be ashamed of. "We need the funds."

His eyes widened in surprise. "*You* need funds? Doesn't your father give you ample pin money?" He held my gaze as my expression fell, lips pressing thin. "What do you need it for anyway? A new gown? Trinkets?"

For some reason those sarcastic words felt like knives stabbing through me. Of course, he would assume that. He was no different from any other gentleman in London who imagined fashion and frippery were all women dreamed about. Not that there was anything wrong with fashion—I adored a beautiful gown myself—but there was a huge difference between wants and needs. A dress was a want; saving Beth and Little Hands was a need.

I lifted my chin. "No. And even if it was, that would be none of your concern, would it?"

"Tell me what it is for, then."

Gritting my teeth, I swallowed, wanting to defend myself and my principles but unwilling to risk exposure of the Lady Knights, considering our actions involved robbing *him*. "I can't tell you, but it's for a good cause, I promise you."

His face serious, he stared at me long and hard, his gaze probing as if he could see right into my head. After a handful of fraught moments, I wasn't sure if he'd gotten what he wanted, but he nodded once and left to get his horse. I was equally relieved and perturbed at the cool dismissal, but then again, I'd never pretended to know how that boy's mind worked.

Once he had mounted his gray stallion, Rafi gave a signal to a man holding the whistle.

"Riders, take your places," the starter called out.

I turned to retrieve Ares and mounted. I shot Rafi a quiet glance, but he was focused on getting into place at the starting line. For an instant, I wondered what was going through his head. Why did he stand up for me? He could have easily agreed with the others and ended our hopes—and my participation in the last race—then and there.

A mix of curiosity and gratitude shot through me, though I pressed it down.

Rafi didn't do anything for anyone else. He pleased himself. This had to be his underhanded way of showing me that I was out of my element. That I should be in a salon somewhere, playing a pianoforte and singing like a well-behaved girl. Was that what he intended? To prove the Lady Knights didn't belong here? I tossed my head. Well, too bad.

Any knight worth her salt would never concede without a fight.

Guiding Ares forward, I took my place at the end of the row with the other four riders and assessed my competition. Two of the remaining teams were from Eton, one from Harrow. Rafi and I were the last two of the five, a legacy team and an alternate team. I caught sight of Nori, Blythe, and Greer, and they were all screaming. The noise filtered to a dull roar, and all I could hear was the blood rushing between my ears.

Then the whistle blew, and the race was off. Ares's muscular body launched forward, and I crouched into position, the night air billowing against my body. My competition and I were neck and neck, and though I knew what to expect, I was completely unprepared when the rider to my left veered into my flank, forcing me to divert. A cruel grin split his face.

"Go back to the bedchamber where you belong," he shouted.

Fury filled me along with the urge to sink to his level and retaliate, but I'd win by beating him soundly. And fairly. The line of riders grew more staggered as Ares pulled forward, his powerful body gaining precious inches with each breath. As we crossed the halfway marker, I could see the finish line in the distance, my peripherals on Rafi only a length or two ahead and the two Eton boys on either side of me. It seemed like Rafi was directing the pace, but why would he? Unless he was waiting to see what the other riders might do. . . .

It didn't occur to me that I was in trouble until the two Eton boys started crowding me, right before I caught sight of the pole three feet off the ground, stretching across the track. Lanterns had been lit, thankfully, so the barrier was very visible, but I would need enough speed to jump it.

"Back off, you cads!" I screamed, but they just leered and pressed closer. At this pace, I wouldn't be able to jump safely without injury to me or the horse, and though I desperately wanted to win, I couldn't put Ares in harm's way.

Making my decision, I slowed more, but the monsters slowed with me, and ice filled my veins. They *wanted* to hurt me . . . likely as some perverse form of punishment for daring to enter their bigoted little race. If I could not slow down, I would have to go faster. I nudged my heels into Ares's ribs and loosened the length of the reins. "Go, boy!"

The slack was enough for Ares to burst past the two horses containing him, and then we were flying. Rafi was still ahead, and I watched him vault with effortless ease. I sensed the other three trying desperately to catch up as our lead broadened. My lungs squeezed in my chest as I fought to keep breathing. My thighs burned and my muscles screamed with the effort of staying in the saddle, but I could see the finish line.

"Just a little more, Ares." I grunted as we reached the hurdle. "We can do it. Jump, boy!"

Going against the customary habit for riders to lean back

mid-leap and lead the horse to land on four legs or the back legs, I shoved out of my saddle and put my weight forward on the stirrups, moving with the stallion's natural gait. Ares and I soared over the pole like poetry in motion, landing on his forelegs and eating up the yards.

In the next few breathless heartbeats, Rafi and I were abreast of one another, our horses nearly in sync, and I met that piercing stare that held a kind of wondrous admiration. Everything around us disappeared but those few seconds of connection. I let out an exhilarated laugh as a genuine grin full of fondness curved his lips, completely transforming his face to something I'd never seen before. Something directed in its entirety at *me*.

Suddenly, I felt like Icarus, only this boy was the sun.

Rafi's smirk made my knees wobble; Rafi like *this* made every bone in my body feel like sun-warmed honey. Even if I lost—which wasn't going to happen—I would remember this moment and that unguarded, tender expression for the rest of my life.

On the heels of that smile, his eyes glowed with awe and approval, and he offered me the slightest cant of his head as if I had proved my mettle. Perhaps it was my imagination, but in that same breath, I sensed rather than saw his mount marginally slow. But it was much too quick for me to put any stock in it. Rafi wasn't the sort to willfully lose.

Focusing on the rest of the race, I crouched low and gave the last stretch everything I had. I wasn't entirely certain that we were going to win, despite my earlier affirmation, but by God, I could only give it my best. With a burst of fortitude, I sucked in a breath and pressed my knees down, the small impetus just enough for Ares and I to soar over the finish line . . . by a nose.

Dear heavens, we had won!

My pulse had yet to calm as I slowed Ares to a trotting pace, making sure to cool him down properly and let his heated blood circulate. "Good boy," I told him, patting his sweaty neck. "You did it. Thank you, thank you, *thank you.*"

"Are you thanking your horse?"

Rafi trotted up next to me, his brown face glistening with sweat and his dark hair blown back over his brow, the shoulder-length strands tangled from the wind. At some point, like Blythe, he'd lost his hat. He looked deliciously windblown. I ignored the sudden heat in my own blood and put it down to me needing to cool off just like Ares.

"He was as much a part of the win as I was," I said.

His mouth twitched. "Well done, both of you, then. That jump was something!"

"Thank you." Suddenly suspicious of what I'd felt in the last seconds of the race, I studied him with narrowed eyes as we cantered easily down the path. "I'm certain you had the lead, but you let me pull ahead there at the end. Why?"

His face was unreadable. "I didn't let you do anything. The faster equestrian won."

"Rafi."

His lip curled, something like satisfaction lighting those mercurial eyes. "I like it when you say my name."

"I beg your pardon," I replied, flustered considering that the small liberty was typically used only in my head. He had never actually given me leave to address him so informally by his first name. That was reserved for family, close friends, and . . . intimate persons. My cheeks warmed. "I mean, Mr. Nasser."

"No, I much prefer the former," he said, lip curling at the corner. I had to keep my jaw from gaping at the low, smoky tone of his voice. Rafi Nasser had never turned that voice or those eyes on me in such a way. I'd seen him do it many a time at many a ball to many other young ladies, however. No wonder they all tumbled like bowling pins.

When had he stopped seeing me as anything but Keston's troublesome younger sister?

No good could come from the answer to that question.

I steeled my spine and stopped myself from dissolving into an ignominious swoon. That would *not* do at all. When I stared at him, calm as the breeze, he sighed and patted his horse. "Again, I didn't *let* you win, my lady. You triumphed on your own merit. I'd ridden Thunder earlier this morning, and he was on his last legs." He ducked his chin with a sidelong glance at me. "Besides, you are in dire need of the funds, are you not . . . for your charitable good cause?"

"Yes," I said softly. I could see the curiosity in his gaze, but he didn't press further, which I appreciated.

He reached over and gripped Ares's reins, his gloved fingers so close to mine that I could feel the heat radiating off him. My breath fizzled as he leaned closer. "Don't put yourself in danger like this again. I mean it."

And that was how a tender moment got crushed like an ant encountering a giant bootheel. He was back to being Rafi the rotter, all arrogance and high-handedness. I reared away, jerking his hand from its hold. "Don't tell me what to do."

"I will if it's for your own good," he said mildly.

"How would *you* know what's good for me?" I spluttered with indignation, though my traitorous heart quivered.

His brows rose as he sat back on his horse and folded his arms. "Because I know you. If there's trouble, you will undoubtedly find it. Or it will find you. Someone has to save you from yourself."

"And you volunteered for the position?" I demanded. "The hero on the white horse galloping in to rescue the damsel in distress?"

"Make no bones about it, you're as much a damsel as I am a hero, Firefly."

"My name is Zia." Scowling at the unwelcome warmth the nickname elicited, considering it was the second time he'd used it, I cleared my throat and stared straight ahead. "Will you tell my brother?"

He pondered the question, those silver eyes glinting. I didn't like the suddenly calculating look in them. "No, but you owe me."

Relief was instantly followed by outrage. How dare he make this transactional? "Owe you for what?"

His dark chuckle made my insides catapult as he picked up his pace and glanced back at me over his shoulder. "For keeping your secrets, of course. And you will tell me what that money is for, my lady. Maybe not today, but you will."

He reached toward me, a reply frozen on my lips as he went

to tuck a tiny curl that had escaped my hat back into hiding and pull the brim down. He was much too close for comfort . . . the sandalwood-and-rain scent of his heated skin dizzying my confused senses.

"I won't," I said, but my voice was much too breathy for my liking. Tugging on the reins, I turned away and directed Ares to the right of Rotten Row, where Nori, Greer, and Blythe were shouting and waving in complete delight.

"You did it, Zia!"

I grinned back, tired but exhilarated, and shoved Rafi Nasser to the back of my head. "We did it. Team effort. Let's get our winnings to Sister Mary."

In hindsight, it had been a miracle that my identity hadn't been discovered by the public. That would have been a debacle that I might not have been able to come back from. I could imagine the headlines now: LADY Z CAUGHT IN SCANDALOUS RACE WITH UNMARRIED GENTLEMEN AT MIDNIGHT! My full name would not be printed, but everyone would know. Gossip in the *ton* was literally food for survival . . . and anything involving my family was especially juicy. During Keston and Ela's rocky courtship, the newspapers once accused poor Ela of going on a scourge of terror across all London!

The hounds would have had a field day with me.

But no matter, it was already done, and we had amassed

enough money for the rent to save Bellevue and Little Hands, at least for now. We had bribed my young coachman Brennan for his silence with enough coin, considering he was the one who usually ferried us to the pawnbroker's in St. Giles, a seedy area of town, when we needed to pawn jewelry from our heists, but it helped that he was also completely smitten with Lalita.

Greer shot her a teasing look after we'd all climbed in and she'd finished giving him instructions. "He's categorically besotted with you."

To my surprise, a violent blush seeped into Lalita's cheekbones. If I didn't know better, I would say that Brennan's unrequited infatuation might not be so one-sided, but a coachman would never do for a girl of her station, and certainly not with her aunt and uncle's lofty ambitions for an aristocratic, *rich* match. "I have no idea what you're talking about."

"Don't you?" Greer quipped, then made kissing noises.

The glare on Lalita's face could have scorched the inside of the carriage. "I think you should concern yourself with your own affairs," she snapped. "Not everyone has been betrothed from birth, free from the obligation to put themselves on display every season for the sake of everyone else but themselves."

The outburst startled us. She'd never given any indication that she was opposed to finding a husband. Greer had Lars, her epistolary fiancé whom she'd been engaged to since birth, Nori was not being pressured to marry, and I had the power to pick my future spouse. Or would, at least, until my father put his foot down, and then I'd be in the same boat as Lalita.

"I'm sorry," Lalita said, and burst into tears. "My uncle has decided to choose a husband for me. I feel so powerless. And Brennan, well, I do like him, but he's just a coachman."

I bit my lip. Instead of saying anything, we hugged our friend close. Sometimes no words were better than meaningless ones.

The rest of the ride from my home to Bellevue was quick, and by the time we arrived, Lalita had stopped crying. We tightened our plain cloaks and entered through the church at the front before proceeding down the narrow hallways to the attached orphanage.

Sister Mary greeted us, her lined face drawn, though she pushed a dim smile to her face as she led us to her small office. "Friends, it is wonderful to see you. Have you come for a visit? The children have missed you." She gave a fond sniff. "Beth, especially, now that she is well again."

"Where is our girl?" Nori asked.

"Last I checked, she was outsmarting everyone at chess."

I chuckled. Beth was by far our favorite. We usually spent quite a bit of time at Little Hands, though of late we had stayed away while the croup had run its course. One of the many rules of Welton was each young lady's contribution to charity, so we helped distribute food to the needy every week, but we enjoyed taking turns reading to the children the most.

Once we were in the privacy of the room, I pushed the money into Sister Mary's fingers. "We collected this for you. It should be enough to tide you over for a good while, including the rent and care for Beth and the other children."

Her eyes watered, a slew of emotions taking over her face as she studied the contents of the pouch in dazed shock. "How did you do this?"

"Will it be enough, or are we too late?" Nori asked nervously.

So far, Sister Mary and the other sisters had been able to scrape by each quarter, but this time had been difficult since the property owner who wished to sell to Viscount Hollis kept illegally increasing the amount of the lease.

"You're just in time," she said, tears brimming. "And it's more than enough. Bless you, children, bless you."

This right here, *this* was what our efforts were about. Seeing the joy on Sister Mary's face was worth every second of pressure and the risk of getting caught. Our ways might have been unorthodox and illegal, especially the thievery bit, but every human being deserved to be fed, healthy, and housed.

"Can we read to the children today, Sister?" I asked. "We have some time to spare and would love to help."

Her smile was everything. "They would love that."

As we filed down a narrow corridor and entered the spartan nursery, Beth's small face lit up from where she was now playing with a well-worn puzzle. "Zia! Greer, Lalita, Nori! I missed you!"

I knelt and opened my arms. "Missed you, too, Honey B."

She giggled as she snuggled in. "That's not my name, Zia."

"But your name does start with *B*, doesn't it?" I said, despairing at the feel of her ribs beneath my fingers. "And you're as sweet as honey, so Honey B it is."

"Then you're Honey Z," she said brightly.

Nori dropped to my side. "More like Salty Z," she said, and hoisted the little girl from my lap and proceeded to tickle her. "My turn!"

After that, it was a swarm as the other little children rushed toward us for their cuddles and tickles. The room was filled with childish laughter that lifted my soul. God, the hope and delight on their faces, even in their misfortune, poor health, and poverty, wrenched at my heartstrings. Where would they go if Viscount Hollis took over this place? Other orphanages in London were already overflowing. This was their home.

The school was our home away from home. And the church was a safe haven for many others. We couldn't let this place get demolished.

We simply *couldn't*!

CHAPTER EIGHT

Taught from infancy that beauty is woman's sceptre, the mind shapes itself to the body, and roaming round its gilt cage, only seeks to adorn its prison.

—Mary Wollstonecraft

Luncheon at Welton today had been taken in the garden on account of the unexpectedly lovely spring weather. Earlier that morning, I'd had a music class in which Miss Perkins had encouraged me to keep expressing my own personal style, and I was inspired. Toying with the strings and the sounds wasn't the norm, but it fascinated me. I had experimented with bits of rubber, paper, and metal on the pianoforte strings, and the results had been incredible.

I was still thinking about my next piece when Nori said, "I think we should induct Blythe into the Lady Knights." We sat on curved benches eating our meals in the sun. She and I were paired up, as were Greer and Lalita.

Greer glanced up. "I agree."

Biting into my cucumber-and-cold-chicken sandwich, I nodded. "She really came through for us with the race. We wouldn't have been able to give Sister Mary the money she needed."

"And when we were at Danforth's, too," Greer added. "She didn't have to help get us out, either."

Lalita let out a nervous exhale. "Do we trust her, though? We all have a lot to lose if our . . . activities are made public knowledge. Trust has to be earned."

The four of us had built strong bonds of friendship, but that didn't mean we couldn't or shouldn't include others. I understood the fear, however. One loose thread could unravel the whole thing, and all of us had too much to lose. "It has to be a unanimous decision," I said.

"Yes, for me," Nori said quickly.

"Me too." That was from Greer.

Lalita chewed her nail. "Can we trial her? It was only the one race, which was dangerous, but still not unlawful like the other thing we do. I don't want to be imprisoned because of someone's loose lips. I have enough to deal with having my uncle breathing down my neck this season."

She had a point. "That's a good compromise," I said, and the other two agreed.

After lunch, we filed into the reading salon and took our seats. We weren't late, but everyone else was already there, including Sarah, Petal, and Blythe. Even Miss Perkins was present, which was unusual. She was always late. Our teacher looked like she had something up her sleeve, and I sat forward in my seat with eager expectation.

Miss Perkins cleared her throat. "We have nearly completed our discussion of *Frankenstein,* and the final project to wrap up this book will be done in pairs." Excitement filled me, and some of the girls started eagerly chattering. "The pairs will be chosen at random by me."

Groans and complaints met that pronouncement.

"Miss Perkins," Sarah whined. "Can't we pick our own partners? Surely it would be better for everyone that way?"

For once, we were on the same page, only because if for some reason we got saddled together, I might actually die. I didn't dislike Sarah, but I did feel that a lot of her behavior was performative. She only said and did things that would make her look best in any situation, not out of the goodness of her heart. That didn't make her a bad person; it just meant that we'd likely butt heads.

"There are seven of us," Greer pointed out, glancing around the room. "The pairings will be uneven."

Miss Perkins smiled. "Someone will have the misfortune of being paired with me. Now, before we get into the project ideas and unions, I wish to have one more discussion. In the novel, Victor tells Robert that knowledge can lead to 'destruction and infallible misery.' What are our thoughts on this?"

Nori raised her hand, and Miss Perkins allowed her the floor. "I suppose it depends on how the knowledge is employed. Misery is a consequence of its misuse."

I gave a thoughtful nod. "I don't believe it all leads to destruction. Knowledge is information used by a person to grow and create. If it is used to cause harm, then yes, it can lead to one's downfall. But knowledge should be about becoming better than we are, not worse."

"Victor Frankenstein thought he was advancing himself by creating his creature," Miss Perkins pointed out. "In his mind, that made him a better scientist. So, who defines what is better? Why does his experimentation make him a nefarious person?"

"Maybe because he tampered with the laws of humanity without all the facts?" Nori suggested. "He knew the basics, but he wasn't equipped to handle his creation. That's hubris."

Blythe's hand shot up, her face animated. Perhaps our influence was having a positive effect on her shyness. "The fact that he created the creature isn't what makes him nefarious; it's the actions he takes afterward by abandoning it. The creature could have been good had it been taught how to love."

"Dr. Frankenstein's behavior to abandon it wasn't unethical," Lalita objected. "A doctor can use laudanum to treat or to kill. Too much, and it's poison. He has a moral responsibility to other people, who might be hurt by his choices and actions. Knowledge can be used to help or cause damage. In this case, the latter result was obvious. He just couldn't see that."

"Why was it obvious?" Blythe asked.

Lalita scowled as if she didn't expect the rebuttal. "The creation was unnatural. Against nature and God. Only He can bring life into the world."

"She's right," Petal agreed vehemently. "No good can come of piecing something broken together. Besides, who could love something that looked like that?"

Nori swung around with narrowed eyes. "Re-creating something new from a broken thing isn't always ugly or useless. The Japanese art of kintsugi involves the repair of cracked pottery with gold, and the result is often quite stunningly exquisite art. Even the deepest of scars can be beautiful."

Petal scoffed. "Your comparison is hardly fair. A monster is not a tea bowl."

"Outstanding observation, Miss Kaneko," Miss Perkins said, ignoring Petal's outburst, her gaze landing on the rest of us. "So, let's consider this. Do appearance and beauty make something more lovable? Could you love a snake or a rat?"

"Snakes are beautiful," Greer said.

"Disgusting!" Sarah said, shuddering. "No, I could never love either of them."

I shrugged. "For me, both have value. Snakes hunt rodents. Rats get rid of waste. They are natural parts of a healthy environment. I'm not quite sure I would be able to love them, though I do not judge those who do."

"What about people?" Miss Perkins asked. "Does beauty impact how they are treated?"

That had an easy answer. Beauty was revered in the *ton*. Beautiful people were surely given more attention, more access. However, external beauty did not always mean that a person was kind or good. A pretty face could hide a rotten heart, as I knew only too well, having been in the same circle as Poppy Landers, who had tried to destroy Ela twice.

But the truth was that loveliness of one's disposition opened many doors, particularly for women, to make a good match—the single goal of our existence. Beauty was worth much more than our brains, especially when it elevated the social status of the men we were with, while intelligence could be considered a threat to a man's own position. And intelligence from a woman whose beauty could not uplift a man was the ultimate offense.

Truthfully, I'd much rather be praised for being smart.

"Of course, it does," I said. "But ideals of worth are different all over the world. England is not the epicenter of civilization. In other countries, like India and Russia, women like Rani Ahilyabai Holkar and Catherine the Great were celebrated for their intelligence and their physical aptitude, not just their appearance. In fact, Catherine was no great beauty herself."

Miss Perkins cleared her throat. "And who is to decide whether that last bit is true, Lady Zenobia? Beauty is subjective, is it not?"

I felt my cheeks warm at her challenge, but she had a point. I nodded. "You're right. It is."

Greer stuck her hand in the air. "And comeliness can be varied by culture, too. Hair color, skin color, eyebrow shape, lip fullness, head coverings, forehead shape and size, nose length, the list is endless, and the preferences are vast."

"Beauty is bought by judgment of the eye," Nori added with the slightest peek at Blythe, which I wouldn't have caught if I hadn't been looking directly at her. "Everyone's tastes are different."

Sarah curled one of her sleek reddish-blond locks around her fingers and simpered. "There's nothing wrong with being pretty, if you ask me."

"Of course not. But what is *deemed* as such is being questioned," I pointed out, beating Greer to the punch, though from the glare on her face, she would have been much harsher in her reply.

Sarah had probably been told from birth how perfect she was. She was a beautiful girl, there was no doubt, with her fine features, glossy hair, and smooth, rosy complexion. But there was something to be said for a person becoming less attractive the more one got to know them. Vanity was beauty's downfall. My favorite author—though Mary Shelley was fast becoming a favorite—Jane Austen had written that "vanity working on a weak head produces every sort of mischief."

I added, "A kind heart should matter more than any surface appearance. I'd much rather be plain and astute than pretty and witless."

"So says the diamond of the season, regaled as beautiful and oh so witty," Petal muttered as Sarah let out a loud scoff.

My spine tightened. "I didn't campaign for the title!"

"And yet your perceived beauty and privilege have earned you the most coveted spot in our set," Sarah said.

Swallowing hard, I paused. *Had* I taken stock of my own advantages? The truth stung, but I wouldn't deny credit where it was due. "Fair point, Miss Peabody."

She smirked. "The monster could have had the kindest heart in the world, and it would not have mattered," Sarah went on. "Fear of the unnatural is a powerful emotion. If a snake approached you, would you pet it and whisper how pretty it was, or would you flee? Instinct is innate."

"Someone with an interest in snakes might," I replied.

"But would you?"

I refused to be baited. "We are not only talking about me, now, are we?"

Miss Perkins slid off her table and clapped. "Excellent discourse, all of you. So, can beauty be a sharper tool than knowledge? Are both things equally dangerous? Or is one more lethal than the other?"

"Any tool can be lethal if used with malicious intent," Nori said with a shrug. "If every romantic poet is to be believed, beauty is a fierce weapon that can certainly lead a man to war. Think of Helen of Troy or even Sita in the *Ramayana*. Both women were abducted, which was followed by war, and claims of infidelity." She exhaled. "And one could argue that what we are doing here, gaining knowledge beyond the realms of what is acceptable for our sex, is dangerous as well."

Miss Perkins's eyes glinted. "In what way?"

"Both women are examples of how power can be wielded." Nori tapped her temple. "It is no secret that society wants us biddable and obedient, but we have our own minds. A woman with a book can be just as deadly as one with a coquettish smile."

Our secret book club could not bring upon a war, but we could certainly disrupt the aristocracy with our words and progressive thinking.

"Well put, Miss Kaneko." Miss Perkins pulled a pocket watch on a chain from her skirts. "Before we run out of time and you get reprimanded for being late to chapel this evening, let me assign the final project." I reached for my notebook and pencil as she passed between our seats. "Each pair must create something, either a new creation or one composed of existing parts. Anything goes as long as it is original, and upon presentation"—she smiled widely—"or *animation,* your peers must all be prepared to discuss whether it lived or failed."

"Capital," Greer said, blue eyes wide with anticipation.

Our teacher smiled and consulted a small sheet of parchment. "And now for the pairs. Miss Sorensen, you are with Lady Petal." The joyful expression on Greer's face morphed to pure horror. "And before you argue, my decisions are final. Miss Danforth, you are with Miss Kaneko, and Miss Peabody is with Miss Varma." Her warm gaze met mine. "That means you're with me, Lady Zenobia, unless you have any objections."

I'd suspected that I might be the lone man out, considering I was the only day student in the group. The others would be able to work on their projects more often. I didn't mind. I adored Miss Perkins, and she'd always been enthusiastic about my music. Maybe I could do something with that for the project. "None at all, Miss Perkins."

When classes were dismissed, I decided to head back to my home in Grosvenor Square. I did not have to go to chapel with the others, which I know rankled Mrs. Perkins, but my father's donation made her keep those opinions to herself. Some days I went, as I found theology quite interesting, but today my father had summoned me.

My nerves thinned as the carriage approached our family's

residence, and I pulled myself together. This conversation would undoubtedly be about my suitors, and he would make some ultimatum about my duty. I did not relish fighting with my father. We were much too similar in temperament to ever see eye to eye. I did not have my mother's patient and wise disposition, though I had inherited her passionate nature. Combine that with my father's intractability, and the outcome was an impulsive, hardheaded young woman.

I was under no illusions as to my place in society, but I wanted to *live* . . . even if it was only for a few months, on my own terms. I wanted to follow my heart and my dreams. I wanted to make my own choices instead of adhering to the ones that had been made for me since birth. I was on the cusp of being tied to a fate that wasn't of my choosing. My father might have allowed Keston to yank on the leash of duty, but I would never be so lucky.

I murmured my thanks to Brennan, the coachman, as I descended the carriage and climbed the steps with leaden feet. Our very efficient butler opened the front door with a smart bow. I swear in all my eighteen years I had never seen that man crack a smile. He took great pride in his position and did not suffer any fools, including my brother and me, who had tried many a time to break that stoic facade.

"Lady Zenobia," he intoned. "His Grace is in his study."

"Thank you, Forsythe," I said, handing him my cloak, bonnet, and gloves. "Did he say he wanted to see me right away?"

"Posthaste, my lady."

My father's schedule was always *posthaste.* A perverse part of me wanted to keep him waiting, so I strolled leisurely up to my bedchamber and refreshed myself before wandering to the music room. I knew I was acting like the spoiled child my father often accused me of being, but my small personal rebellions were too satisfying to relinquish so easily.

I ran my fingers over the polished keys of the grand pianoforte. It wasn't like the square one in my carriage house—no, this one was a priceless piece with rich rosewood, gold inlays, and custom engravings. Though I was always encouraged to play Bach and Mozart, my willfulness seemed to stretch to my music. The piece I played was one of my own original compositions, one I'd worked on weeks ago with Miss Perkins. Considering the proximity of the music room to my father's study, I knew he would hear it.

Unlike the elegant, harmonious progressions of the classical masters, this piece was experimental and sharp, and fluctuated between tender and thunderous. The complexity of the dissonant notes reflected my contrary mood and the despair currently flooding my spirit. And now, buoyed by my teacher's encouragement, I reached inside and plucked the strings harder to change up the sound. It would irritate my father to no end. He called such music *common*.

"Dearest," a lilting voice said, and I glanced up to see my mother at the entrance to the music room. "I did not know you were here. Weren't you supposed to be at Welton?"

My fingers didn't stop the chord progression, flying over the keys with practiced form, the bass repetitive and harsh. "I was summoned," I said, and scowled. "By His Majesty."

"Don't be impertinent," my mother said, walking into the

room. As always, the duchess was impeccably put together, in a cream-and-saffron-yellow dress that made her rich brown skin glow. Inky braids were wound around her head in a series of intricate clusters, the style framing her face like a crown. My mother wore her beauty with effortless ease, but the gleam of intelligence in those dark eyes made everyone in her presence think twice about underestimating her.

My fingers faltered. "I'm sorry, Mama. I'm just—"

She folded her elegant body onto a nearby sofa. "I know. Continue, please. Is this a new piece? I haven't heard you play in an age."

"Papa hates it," I said sullenly, hitting two notes in constant repetition on my left hand and discordant chords on my right.

"Music is expression, my girl, and yours is evocative and powerful." Her caring gaze met mine. "Never let anyone, including your father, impact your voice."

"He's impossible," I said as I finished the piece on a dramatic crescendo. "I cannot abide by all his intolerable rules."

"Your father only wants what is best for you, Zenobia," she said softly. "And I've taught you how to find your own way within the parameters of what is expected of ladies of our station, haven't I?"

"I'm not you," I whispered. I wasn't even a quarter of how extraordinary she was.

"No, dearest, you're *you,* and there's no one better to tell your story."

I moved from the piano bench and sat beside her, resting my

head on her side. "Were you happy when Grandfather arranged your match with Papa?"

A chuckle emerged from her. "Not at first. We were strangers. He was arrogant and high-handed and presumed he could tell me the opinions I ought to have. I divested him of that notion rather quickly." Her arm slid over my shoulders, pulling me into her. That was one thing about my mother—she could be dressed in the fanciest of ball gowns and that would never stop her from holding us close any chance she had. "I rather loathed him, actually."

"Telling tales about me again, Duchess?" my father said from the doorway.

"Always," Mama said as she crooked a finger for the duke to join us. It never ceased to astound me how different he was around her. My father was a rigid man, but his edges softened whenever she was near. If only every conversation I had with him could be with my mother present.

"Forsythe said you had returned," he said, his cool blue gaze flicking to me after he pressed a kiss to my mother's brow. To my surprise, he sat on my other side, sandwiching me between them as they had when I was a small child. Those were simpler times, when my wishes did not clash with his, when obedience took little effort. I'd always wanted to please them . . . until I didn't.

The moment of peaceful nostalgia was much too fleeting as my father cleared his throat. "We must discuss the matter of suitors."

"Alexander," Mama warned. "Let it rest."

"She must marry, Sanaa." His stare cut to hers above me as they exchanged a prolonged look that I didn't care to decipher. "This is her second season. I've tried to be patient and to be progressive in that I've let her have the time to choose someone pleasing to her, but at the end of the day, she has to be settled."

My mother must have seen my ferocious expression. She placed a hand on my father's arm. "Darling, these things can take time. It is only her second season."

"A second, then a third or a fourth? And what then?" A muscle in his jaw flexed as he sighed. "I've been lenient. I've accommodated your wishes. What other father in the peerage allows his daughter such freedoms? We have to face the reality that marriage is your noble duty, Zenobia. One cannot escape one's fate." He scrubbed a palm over his face. "I shall permit you this one last season, but if you haven't found someone by the end of it, I will select a husband for you. Is that understood?"

I rose, all warmth gone as coldness seeped through my veins. "As you wish, Your Grace. Your demands are more than clear."

"Zenobia . . . ," my mother said.

"No, Mama. I understand that *duty* comes before all, that I am nothing but a commodity, and that my happiness pales in comparison to preserving aristocratic bloodlines."

Fists balled, I bit my lip so hard the taste of copper pennies flooded my mouth as I swallowed past the enormous knot in my throat, trying desperately not to burst into sobs. I didn't wait to hear what more either of them had to say and swept from the room.

CHAPTER NINE

Meanwhile, strength of body and mind are sacrificed to libertine notions of beauty, to the desire of establishing themselves, the only way women can rise in the world—by marriage.

—MARY WOLLSTONECRAFT

With a loud groan, I glanced up at the overcast sky from my quiet spot in the gardens at Osborn House. I was surrounded by crumpled sheets of parchment, the puckered spheres like little grenades of incompetence. Who knew that writing an acrostic verse to express my feelings about *Frankenstein* would be such an impossible feat? The poem was meant to go in tandem with the musical piece I was composing.

My emotions veered from rage to melancholy to bitterness to absolute loathing . . . not for the monster, who was a murderer, but for the circumstances that had driven him there. Perhaps every gentleman embodied Dr. Frankenstein, and the twisted monster that threatened and plagued humanity was a metaphor for society. Or perhaps women were the metaphorical monsters, unable to act or think for ourselves, stitched together by a social hierarchy built on the whims of men. The message from a young woman to her sex was that we were all just cobbled together. Half beings, as Mary Shelley's own mother had once said.

My thoughts churned. Did not the themes of the novel parallel womanhood? Loss of innocence, the ambition of men, injustice, fate versus free will . . . The similarities were rife.

Gritting my teeth, I threw another sheet to the grassy patch of ground to join its brethren and nearly snapped my quill in half in frustration.

"What did that poor sheet of paper ever do to you?" a deep voice drawled, making me nearly leap out of my seat in fright.

I turned, heart racing. "Mr. Nasser, what are you doing here?"

"I accompanied Ridley," he said, using my brother's courtesy title. "The duke wanted to see him about a bill in Parliament before we headed to White's for a luncheon."

White's was a gentlemen-only social club, yet another institution that placed their members on unearned pedestals, simply for the sake of being male. "What bill in Parliament?"

"Something to do with British currency and the gold standard."

I shook my head. One day, a bill would be passed about a woman's right to have a voice in her own future, and I would scream my delight to the high heavens. Rafi strolled to the table and picked up my novel. "A little light reading?"

Snatching it from his fingers, I glowered. "None of your

business." When he stooped to swipe up one of the discarded parchments, I blushed and rose to grab it, but he held it high out of my reach. "Give that back, you busybody!"

"What's this, then?" he said, unrolling it, fending me off with one hand as I attempted to climb him like the gnarly tree he was. "'*F* is for fighting to be seen and heard, *R* is for revenge, though it may sound absurd. *A* is for the apathy that consumes my heart, *N* is for never feeling . . .'" He trailed off as my ears burned with humiliation. Clearly, I would hardly receive any accolades for being a poet. "Never feeling what?"

"I don't know yet."

He peered down at me, curiosity alight in his gray gaze. "What is this for, Firefly?"

"A school project if you must know. Now give it back." I shot him my most scathing glare. "And once again, do not call me Firefly."

Still fending me off with one hand, he nodded to the other balls of paper littering the grass. "The muse isn't striking, I gather."

"Aren't you observant?" I snapped. "Hand it over, Rafi. I mean it."

"Or what?" A slow, playful smirk that caused a host of butterflies to erupt in the pit of my stomach bloomed over his face. Gracious, that wicked curl of his lip could sway the most modest of ladies to temptation. Was it directed at *me,* or was it just Rafi being Rafi?

"Or I'll . . . I'll . . . ," I growled through my teeth. "I'll kick you in the shins!"

"Perhaps I should call you Hornet instead of Firefly," he teased, reaching out to tug on one of my spirals that had sprung loose from its pins. "I should have known that a girl who trounces her competition in a horse race, sneaks into gaming hells, and reads about monsters would be vicious."

Those gray eyes that glinted silver in the sunshine peered down at me, making me lose focus for a second. Or perhaps it was the curl that he idly caressed between his fingers that made my breath falter. Goodness, how had we gotten so close? Barely a handful of inches separated us, likely from my futile efforts to retrieve my dreadful poem. The press of his gaze felt as tangible as touch, and I sucked in a shallow breath. I could feel the heat of his body and smell the woodsy warmth of his skin. The combination wreaked havoc on my scattered senses.

Each inhale made the rise of my bosom nearly touch his lapels. And with his fingers tangled in my hair, anyone could look outside one of the windows of the manse and form an indelicate opinion. For some reason, I couldn't bring myself to care. "Why do you call me Firefly?"

Smudges of red lit his cheekbones, and for a moment, I thought he wasn't going to answer, but then he canted his head to study the tight coil of hair that he still held. "You always reminded me of a fierce little beacon. Small but mighty." He chuckled quietly to himself. "No matter how angry I was or how lost I felt, I'd look at you and see that light shining, then ground myself."

Speechless, I stared at him as my blood warmed. "Oh."

"You haven't lost that spark, and I hope you never do."

The flush on his cheeks deepened as he abruptly let go of me and took a small step back as if he hadn't meant to say any of that. The confident, swaggering Rafi was nowhere to be seen, and I found this side of him to be unexpectedly sweet. He ran a palm over his dark hair and then stuffed his free hand into his trouser pocket, looking adorably awkward. Who knew a gent with a reputation for being a shameless rake had such a warm sponge cake center?

"That's rather poetic for you," I told him, for lack of something clever to say. Those mercurial eyes met mine and held them.

"Yes, well, I mostly call you that because you are a pest," he added in a cooler, mocking tone that did not fool me. It was as though he'd reminded himself of our usual rapport. "Some fireflies are predacious. They poison their enemies."

Hiding my smile at his prevarication, I cocked my head. "So, I'm a vicious, poisonous beacon? Isn't that a contradiction? Touch me and die?" I snatched the parchment out of his other hand while he wasn't paying attention and stuck it into the pocket of my dress. "One could argue that some lovely things are worth getting pricked for. A rose isn't a rose without its thorns."

"A rose won't kill you. I meant beautiful but *deadly,* like the oleander flower, so fragrant and delicate, and yet it can cause convulsions. Or the golden dart frog, which secretes a toxin that will stop a man's heart."

I blinked, my own heart in danger of stopping. *He thinks I'm beautiful?*

He also thinks you're deadly, you ninny.

Clearly, I could not quite read Rafi or trust myself around him. At times, he was brotherly in a domineeringly protective way, as he'd been during the race, and other times . . . when he stared at me like I was the spark in his darkness, my heart teetered on a precipice that shouldn't be breached. It would be so easy to fall for his charm. But many a girl, including my nemesis Sarah, had dashed herself on the rocks that were Rafi Nasser.

I refused to be another casualty, even if his earlier words had been sincere.

In truth, *he* was the beautiful danger.

"Trust me, my father wishes I were more boring and less willful," I said glumly, and crouched to gather the rest of the discarded papers. "It would make his life much easier. If I were obedient and dutiful as a lady should be, perhaps I could be the perfect daughter."

"Perfection is a myth," Rafi replied softly. "We are forced to meet unreachable expectations, and any dreams we might have become ancillary."

"Even yours?" I asked, looking up, curious at the bitter notes in his voice.

A muscle flexed in his jaw. "Yes. Mine, too."

I desperately wanted him to confide in me, but a few moments of camaraderie did not make us bosom friends. I knew Rafi had always wanted to be a painter, but his uncle had threatened that if he didn't focus on more masculine pursuits, whatever those were, he would be disinherited. The man was stuck in the Dark Ages if he thought painting wasn't a worthwhile endeavor. Tell that to Botticelli, Rubens, and Da Vinci. Rafi wasn't in need of money, however. He could quite easily leave and pursue those artist's hopes of his.

"Hey, Nasser! Where've you gone?" my brother yelled, and Rafi and I both jumped apart another foot as if we were on the cusp of being caught in a ruinous embrace. People in the *ton* had been marched to the altar for less. I was here without a chaperone, after all, even if it was in my own garden.

Keston rounded the bend on the path, and he grinned when he saw me, though his smile wilted when it fell on Rafi, who now thankfully stood a respectable distance away. "Mother said you were out here, but I didn't expect to find the two of you together. Honestly, I'm surprised not to have to break up a brawl or at least clean up some bloodshed."

My cheeks heated. "We're not that bad, Kes."

He let out a scoffing sound as his eyes took in my novel and papers. "Father surely doesn't know you're reading that. Unless you're planning on giving him apoplexy, that is. *Frankenstein*'s not exactly ladylike reading material."

"And what exactly is? Lessons on etiquette? Needlepoint design? Tutu decoration?" I shot back, earning a shocked snort covered up with a cough from Rafi.

My brother halted with a wary expression at my glower. "Never mind. Read what you want."

"Thank you." Choked laughter came from Rafi's direction. "Where's Ela?" I asked. "Is she with you?"

"She's consoling Lady Rosalin," Keston said with an exaggerated sigh. "Blake's courting someone new, so she's in a funk."

I liked Rosalin, but she tended to fall in love every month, which was usually at the root of her problems. She was infatu-ated with Blake, with whom she'd supposedly shared a kiss once, forever ago, but Blake was a free spirit who wasn't ready to settle down. Everyone could see it but Rosalin, unfortunately. Ela was far more patient than me. I was much too busy carving out space for myself and guarding the minuscule freedom that I had to worry about boys.

My gaze slid to Rafi and just as quickly fell away.

He and Keston strolled toward the residence, but after a few steps, Rafi slowed and looked over his shoulder. "Your verse has promise," he said, slanting a half smile my way. "Don't be so hard on yourself, Firefly. Just write from your heart."

The West End of London was dirty and terrifying most days, and infinitely worse at night. Especially on underground fight-ing nights, with hundreds of unwashed bodies bellowing wagers at the top of their lungs and furiously exchanging money in a cramped tavern. The place, aptly named the Hog's Head, took on its own monstrous personality.

A woman with an enormous mug of ale nearly crashed into us. "Watch it, pigeons!"

I blinked. Did she just call us weak people who were prime to be swindled? *Good.* That meant our disguises were working. We'd gone even further as to put over our chins false facial hair that Greer had somehow gotten from a local theater. It was much more convincing than a flimsy mustache!

"This is wild," she said with a grin plastered on her face. She looked good as a boy, the blond beard making her look rugged and mean. The piecemeal clothing we had filched from my brother's armoire and the stubble on our faces helped to sell the story, but her spine was too straight. Too proud to mimic commoners of these parts. And she was big, so she didn't exactly blend into the grimy background.

"Slouch more," I whispered to her. I did the same, the band I'd bound across my chest pulling tightly and making it hard to breathe. That was a small price to pay for not being outed as female. I caught sight of a well-heeled man observing us from one corner, but he just as quickly strolled away when he saw me looking. I shook off my nerves—no one knew us. We were pushing the boundaries of acceptability by being here, which was part of the thrill, wasn't it? The knife-edge of discovery hovering over our heads.

Coming to the Hog's Head had been Greer's idea. The Lady Knights weren't only devoted to engaging in charitable endeavors and reading dangerous books. We'd initially formed the club as a means of breaking the control held over us. Rules were meant to be broken. Safely, of course. Every month, we each took turns to pick one thing to try—an outing or an interest—to which we might normally not have access.

Most weren't hazardous. Lalita had voted for us to try her uncle's cigars, which had been revoltingly disgusting. I didn't even know why gentlemen chose to sit in clouds of foul-smelling smoke after dinner. On my first selection, I had opted for us to learn archery. That one had taken some finesse to find someone to teach us in secret, but I'd wheedled Blake into doing it. We'd even had a contest at the end. Lalita had won by a stretch, much to everyone's surprise. She confided that when her father had been alive, he'd taught her the sport in India, but she missed him too much to go into further detail.

Nori's first choice had been to have a breeching ceremony, which was peculiar to say the least, but she insisted her brothers had each done it, going from children's dress to knee-length fitted pants. "It is a milestone for young boys," she'd explained. I didn't pretend to understand why she felt it was so imperative—it was important to *her,* and that was all that mattered.

Getting four pairs of breeches sewn by Mama's modiste with our measurements had been surprisingly easy since no questions had been asked. Then again, she wasn't paid to be nosy, so that was a blessing. We had all discarded our dresses and stays to wear them, followed by a feast to commemorate the occasion, and exchanged gifts. In hindsight, it had been pleasantly liberating. For my next choice, I was planning to make us all attend a performance in Covent Garden. The newly launched Adelphi Theatre was putting on a concert featuring music from all around the world.

"We really should not be here," Lalita said under her breath as we pressed deeper into the cramped space, and I glanced at her. "What if we get caught?"

She'd become a bundle of nerves in the past few weeks. For her, this was a countdown on finding an appropriate husband to appease her uncle and aunt. She could not risk scaring away suitors or upsetting her guardians.

"Keep your head down, and we won't," Nori told her. "Let Greer have her fun, and then we can go."

We were only here as curious spectators. I'd heard my brother and his mates discussing the outcomes of bare-knuckle boxing before, and Greer's father used to be a prizefighter himself until he met Greer's mother and became a successful merchant banker.

Greer's blue eyes were bright. "This is amazing!" She turned to speak to the man at her side, and before we knew it, she was handing coins over and he was writing the sum in a small notebook.

"What are you doing?" Lalita hissed.

She let out a snort. "Wagering, what does it look like? I'm betting on the underdog. Odds are twenty to one."

An enormous man, one we had noticed at the entrance and who could be the director of the place, stopped beside us. We all froze, trying to look as inconspicuous as possible. His attention landed on Greer. "You're a sturdy lad," he said, checking her over like one would a horse at auction. "You look like you could throw a punch, or at least take one. We let amateurs fight. Any interest in a round or two?"

Greer's eyes practically bugged out of her skull with excitement. "In the ring?" she said, deepening her voice to a gruff rumble and remembering to flub her proper diction. "Who with?"

"That young lad over there."

Glancing up, I followed Greer's gaze to where he'd pointed. A boy around our age who seemed fit and strong was stretching out his limbs. At first glimpse, it seemed like Greer had a lot of muscle on him. But still . . . that didn't mean they were evenly matched.

I nudged her arm. "Are you sure you want to do this, Gre . . . Gregor?"

"Why not? I'll wipe the floor with that tosser," she replied with a grin. "Bet on me, will you?"

Lalita let out a noise of distress as Greer went off with the man, leaving us alone. "What if she gets hurt? Those boys are vicious."

Nori shrugged. "So is Greer."

When the thinner of the two boys fighting smacked a right hook into his opponent's cheek, a splatter of blood went flying across the ground . . . along with what looked like a tooth. Lalita gasped, and I could tell she was holding it together by a thread.

I squeezed her shoulder. "Greer was taught by her papa."

My words did little to reassure her, and the crowd went wild when the smaller boy was declared the winner. I caught Greer's eyes over the crowd, and she winked. She'd bet a quid, and with twenty-to-one odds, that was a cool twenty pounds. I dug into my pockets for the coin I'd brought with me and approached the man she'd spoken to before with the book.

"What are the odds for the next match?" I asked him in a deep, gravelly voice.

"They've gone up now since the win last round," he said gruffly. "Thirty to one in favor of Jimmy Fleetfoot versus"—he consulted the penciled-in entry on the corner of his sheet—"Gregor the Viking."

I almost laughed aloud at that. Greer would love her fighting name. Deuce it, I was jealous. "Two on Gregor the Viking to win."

Nori shuffled up beside me. "What are the odds for a knock-out?"

The man consulted his book again. "Fifty to one, sixty in the first round."

"A quid from me, then," she said. "First round."

His eyes widened, but he sniffed dismissively as if our loss would be his gain. Which it very well might be. They were both bold wagers, given the terrible odds stacked against Greer. "Good luck."

I was sure that we would need it, but I believed in my friend. When the whistle blew, and "Gregor" was announced, the jeers of the crowd were loud. Nori, who wouldn't hurt a fly despite her saucy temper, looked like she was going to punch the man next to us right in the face. Greer's opponent, Jimmy Fleetfoot, was obviously a crowd favorite, because when his name was called, the roar was thunderous. Nerves took hold of my belly as the starting gong sounded.

Jimmy was indeed swift on his feet, but I could see Greer studying his movements. Her father had taught her that any fighter's style was evident in the first few minutes of a round—their choices told a story of whether they were aggressive, passive, or some combination of the two. Taking a few deflected hits was worth the wait.

My heart climbed into my throat as Greer did just that, a fast fist glancing off her shoulder, followed by three sneaky jabs to her torso as he danced around her. Lalita squeaked when Greer sucked in air and shrugged off the punches. But her eyes were still full of glee. She ducked and weaved for the next few hits, and I could see the triumphant expression on her opponent's face as if his win were a foregone conclusion.

"Viking . . . more like milksop!" someone shouted, kicking off a fresh round of insults and catcalls.

"Are you going to fight, lad, or stand there all day and let him beat on you?" a man near to us asked.

"Wait for it, you bastard," I heard Nori say under her breath.

Lalita frowned. "Wait for what? Why *isn't* she fighting back?"

"Watch," I said. I caught the exact moment when Greer coiled her body into action, her large form deceptively agile as she sidestepped an incoming uppercut on footwork that mimicked that of the first minute. She bobbed as her opponent came toward her for a torso hit, and she grinned, her right fist going back almost to her ear before she let it fly.

The punch was so fast and so hard that poor Jimmy Fleetfoot went down like a sack of moldy potatoes and didn't move. He was out like a candle flame. There was dead silence in the room as Greer threw a fist into the air, after she'd made sure that he wasn't getting up anytime soon, and then everyone was shouting and screaming.

"Hell, yes!" Nori screamed. "I told you!"

While we waited for Greer, who was currently being swarmed by eager spectators, we went to collect our winnings. Not a bad haul, thanks to Greer.

"Friend of yours?" the bookkeeper asked as he handed us the money.

"Sure is," Nori said.

The man who had offered Greer the round accompanied her back to us. He stared at us in turn with a wide grin on his scary features. He'd bet heavily on Greer, too, and had made a small fortune. "Next up is the blade rounds. Any takers here?"

My stomach gave a lurch. Out of our group, I was the best with an épée—I'd learned at the same time as Keston, who had educated me after each of his lessons with his fencing instructor—but I also didn't want to get impaled and bleed out in the middle of Seven Dials. "Why does a place like this have fencing? It's a boxing club."

He laughed and gestured with his arm. "Look around, lad. Some of you rich nobs like to come to this neck of the woods, and I like to make easy money." His lips curled into a sneer as he considered us part of that group. In our borrowed clothes, we could be young gents out on the prowl. "Where do you lot go to school? Eton? Harrow? In fact, I'd wager right now that at least one of you little dandies is good with a sword as part of your fancy classes?"

I didn't answer him but cleared my throat. "What are the rules?"

"First to draw blood wins."

My friends watched me with wide eyes as I considered my odds of coming out of this without bleeding. Fight to first blood could be quick. It could also be longer, depending on the skill of the duelists.

"Does anyone ever die?" Greer asked.

The man took much too long to answer, and his lie was as

smooth as honey. "Not in a very long while." He surveyed me, opened his notebook, and lifted his pencil. "Don't worry, it will be a fair match with one of your own. What's your name?"

"Knight," I said, watching as he wrote down *Mr. Night* in his little book and not having the wherewithal to correct him.

"Z—" Lalita broke off and balked at the fact that she'd nearly used my real name. She coughed loudly to cover it up. "Are you truly considering this? It's daft."

"It's all in good fun," I said, and rolled my shoulders.

I was given a rusty-looking épée at the entrance to the ring and debated my chances of not just getting skewered but being poisoned by these unpolished blades. In for a penny, in for a pound, as they said. I followed the burly man to the middle area, trying not to stare at the red patches staining the ground.

"Welcome all!" the director thundered. "I have a special treat for you. A match to first blood between Mr. Night and anyone here who issues a challenge."

His words rang in my ears. Wait, *what*? I thought he'd already scouted an opponent who matched me physically. I sent a horrified look to my friends, questioning my life choices, when a deep, growly voice floated through the crowd. "I accept."

CHAPTER TEN

For only by the jostlings of equality can we form a just opinion of ourselves.

—Mary Wollstonecraft

Oh, damn and blast.

I was *so* going to be trounced. That didn't even sound like a boy . . . it'd sounded like a man. A grown man with probably more facial hair than the sparse beard I sported, and most likely a big, skilled, ham-faced giant of a brute who would carve me from chin to navel without blinking an eye. My breaths shortened to shallow pants as the crowd parted to let through my adversary, but I couldn't see with the gaslit lamps shining into the ring and obscuring my vision. Even when I squinted, I could only detect movements and shadows.

My palms were slick with sweat on the hilt of the thin sword. I glanced to where Greer, Nori, and Lalita stood, registering the identical expressions on their faces with a frown. They looked . . . aghast. Dread filled me. Oh, dear God, was he huge?

Did he look like he was going to cut me into tiny pieces? All of a sudden, it felt like I had bitten off more than I could chew. But only when he came to the edge of the ring did I feel my heart sink to the very soles of my feet, and the dread in my stomach turned into full-blown panic.

Rafi.

And by his expression, he *knew* it was me. The recognition—and fury—were both written all over him as he prowled toward me in the ring. Someone handed him an épée of his own, and he swung it lazily to one side in a practiced hand. Oh, dear heavens. I could not possibly be pitted against him in a duel. I barely heard the round of cheering that reached the rafters. All I could see was him.

The director asked for his name and Rafi hissed a reply through his teeth. A shiver wound through me. Goodness, he was *irate.*

"Night versus Nasser," the man roared. "Place your bets, my friends. Don't underestimate the small one. First blood wins." He left the ring, and that same starting gong echoed through the space. Everything fell away but the man facing me.

"What are you doing here?" I asked as Rafi and I circled each other. He didn't answer, only quirked a thick, dark brow, his mouth pulled into an unforgiving, flat line. He thrust his weapon toward me, and I automatically parried with a block. It wasn't an aggressive strike, but the quickness of it made me catch my breath.

It couldn't be a coincidence that he was here . . . or had

volunteered to duel. What were the chances that on yet another Lady Knight outing he would be in the same place at the same time as us? Suspicion bled through my panic. A thought occurred to me, and I felt my brows slam together. "Did you follow us here?" I demanded.

A muscle pulsed in his jaw as that dark silver gaze bored into mine. "What do you think? That this rathole is a place I would willingly frequent? I've had someone making sure you were safe since Midnight Row . . . whenever I could not." My stomach warmed for no reason at all, but then Rafi's slitted stare took in the space full of churlish, bellowing spectators. "This is beyond reckless, even for you."

Warm feelings dashed, I resented the disparaging way Rafi addressed me as if he had any right to judge my actions. I wasn't his to defend or protect, even if he was doing it out of some pitiful obligation to my brother. I didn't want his overbearing opinions smothering me. "It's harmless fun, Mr. Nasser," I bit out, echoing my earlier sentiment.

"Harmless?" he snapped, sword thrusting in a ruthless lunge.

On the defensive, I reared back, feet dancing out of his path as I spun and swung to meet his blade. My weapon crashed into his, the force reverberating up my arm, but I relished the strength of the strike. I followed with another series of upward slashes, forcing him back. Those gray eyes widened as his anger was swapped with the sudden need to focus. I let the smile curl my lips.

Oh, yes, I *wanted* first blood.

"Didn't think I could fence?" I taunted, launching another round of flashy, rapid thrusts. "You should recognize the style. After all, my brother hands you your pride every time you spar, doesn't he?"

"Ridley taught you?"

I winked. "The pen can be mightier than the sword, but only if the latter isn't in a woman's grip."

His lips twitched. "Cocky."

"I know my skill."

Setting my teeth, I lunged toward him, and the next handful of minutes were a fraught sequence of attacking and retreating as our blades collided over and over. Rafi was competent, but I could sense that he was holding back to be gentlemanly and didn't want to hurt me. It was an advantage I would not ignore. It wasn't *my* fault that his misplaced chivalry didn't belong in this ring. I had wanted to teach him a lesson by toying with him, but I was finished playing around. And besides, the sweat on my face was loosening the glue that held my beard in place.

With a sly grin, I whirled and flicked my épée with a flourish, performing for the crowd as I lifted my left hand and beckoned Rafi forward. It was a cheeky move, one that had the mob roaring with approval. Thunderous shouts met my ears, and I caught sight of my friends' slack-jawed expressions. I supposed they hadn't ever seen me fence before.

Not one to be cowed by my showmanship, Rafi arched an amused brow and went on the attack. I held him off easily and then went in close so that he could not swing his weapon. The position meant that I couldn't, either, but I wasn't there for a strike; I was there to goad. "You always underestimate me, Mr. Nasser."

"I'm seeing that," he said. "You're very good."

Those gray eyes glinted with a flash of something other than amusement. Admiration? Awe? Both pleased me more than they should. My stare dropped to his mouth, and my knees gave an unnatural wobble. His usual crooked smirk conspicuously absent, his lips were full and soft. I wanted to surge to my tiptoes and see how they tasted.

Where the devil had *that* thought come from? I didn't want to *taste* him. I didn't want to do anything of the sort! Cheeks burning, I dragged my eyes away before I did something reckless . . . like kiss him in a room full of strangers, and then possibly lose the facial hair that was hanging on by a thread. But Rafi loomed closer, crowding me with his towering height as if he could sense my momentary weakness and sought to take advantage.

My pulse hummed. I *wanted* him to take advantage . . . to fling me over his shoulder and ferry me away as though I were an unruly shield-maiden in need of a firm hand. Oh, good gracious, Mary Wollstonecraft would turn in her grave if she could read my mind. I had to cut back on the penny Viking romances. A hysterical giggle ripped from my throat just as I threw my elbow to catch Rafi in the stomach, flicked my épée high, and swiveled out of the almost-embrace, nearly losing my footing in the process.

"Something funny, Mr. Night?" Rafi asked in a thickened voice, and then frowned as if something strange had occurred to him, but his attention snapped to me when I lunged toward him. The harsh clash of metal followed as we renewed our dance for a handful of ferocious seconds.

I narrowed my eyes. What had he been thinking then? Had he wanted to kiss me, too?

Enough, Zia.

"I just find it comical that you think you can best me," I boasted.

His steps quickened, forcing me into an indefensible position against the ropes. "See? You're good, but you're not that good."

"I beg to differ, sir." I grinned and pointed the tip of my weapon with a cool lift of my chin. "You've lost, and you don't even realize it. You really should get some medical attention for that cut."

His brows drew together as he slowed and lifted his fingertips to the side of his neck. When they came away wet and red, disbelief ran through his expression. "When? How?"

I could see him running through the entire match in his head, trying to find the exact moment when I'd bested him and earned first blood. He let out a huff as he did and answered his own question. "When you elbowed me in the belly," he deduced. "Tricky. Good thing we aren't in a proper gentlemen's club, or you would face disqualification with that move."

Scoffing, I gave a mocking bow that was worthy of the royal court. "Make no mistake, I could trounce you soundly there, too." I winked. "Too bad you don't allow women. Men's pride would take a necessary beating. Perhaps I should fashion a

Trojan horse, infiltrate your manly fortress, and raze all bias to the ground."

A low laugh left him. "With you at its helm, I don't doubt in the least that you could."

"And the winner is Mr. Night!" the director announced. Rafi canted his head in rueful acquiescence as the crowd went absolutely feral.

Once more, the underdog had triumphed. We both gave courteous bows to each other, and I felt something slide against my neck but paid it no mind. I was too busy gloating at the win and waving at the crowd to notice Rafi's suddenly thunderous expression as his eyes fastened to my waistcoat. Following his gaze, I glanced down and felt the blood drain from my body at the sight of the gold chain that had shifted loose and its make-shift pendant . . . his signet ring.

Fool, fool, fool.

"Where did you get that?" he asked.

A dozen suppositions ran through his gaze, and it would not be long before he came to the right one. In utter panic, I dropped the épée, turned, and ran.

"Wait!" he thundered over the noise of the crowd, but the knowledge in his voice made the hairs on my nape stand.

When I reached my friends, they tried to embrace me for the win but stopped at the look on my face. "We need to go. *Now.*"

Greer balked. "What? Why? We still need to collect our winnings."

"Leave them," I gasped, winded at the effort of pushing

through so many bodies, my heart racing at the thought of Rafi catching up and demanding answers. Ones that weren't a simple matter of sneaking into a gaming hell or participating in illegal horse racing or dressing in disguise at a boys' club. We'd *stolen* from him. I'd taken his family heirloom, and though I'd vowed to find a way to return it with him none the wiser, I simply hadn't done it. The small piece of him had become too precious to give up.

And now my silly desire would be my downfall.

Our downfall. I wasn't alone in my crimes.

"I'll get our earnings. Bellevue could always use the money to buy books for the children, or we could donate it to other orphanages," Nori said with a determined look. "You go on ahead. I'll find my own way home."

I glanced over my shoulder, but Rafi wasn't in sight. "Are you certain?"

"Yes," she said. "We earned this fair and square."

"Very well, be safe!"

But as rotten luck would have it, as we tried to head for the exit, chaos exploded as a team of Runners infiltrated the place. People shouted and ran in all directions. Dozens of bodies shoved at me in an uncontrollable river, and I found myself separated from Greer and Lalita as the throng bore me away. Greer's dismayed expression crashed into mine, and I sent her a reassuring glance, despite my own screaming distress.

"I'll meet you outside," I shouted, hoping she could hear over the din. "Outside! Find Brennan!" When she nodded, I let out a breath of relief.

Thankfully—as small as those thanks were—in the melee, Rafi was nowhere to be seen. Escaping capture by the Runners was the goal now. Shoving and swimming through the sea of unwashed bodies, I felt my poor beard finally give up the ghost. But everyone was in too much of an uproar to pay attention to me.

Keeping my head down, I moved forward with dogged resolve. I caught sight of the director running toward what might be a back exit. Instinct made me follow. The Runners were likely at the front, though that didn't stop the horde from pushing in that direction. With each step, I gained ground toward where the man had disappeared. Escape was so close! With a last burst of strength, I pushed through the tide and screamed with joy. A joy that fizzled as quickly as it had erupted.

"Going somewhere?" Rafi drawled.

My heart dropped to my toes. How did he keep finding me so fast? Perhaps I could feign my way out of being in possession of his property. After all, he had no idea how I could have come upon the ring. I could have purchased it at a pawnbroker's shop or found it in the street. The lie was flimsy at best, but I didn't only have my own skin to protect.

I swallowed the lump in my throat. "I need to get to my friends. Nori got separated from us. I have to find her. Can you help me? And then I promise I will answer your questions."

He cocked his head, studying me like he would a dangerous sample under a microscope. "The man I hired to follow you is with them. He'll put the three of them in your coach before more Runners arrive," he said. "Don't worry, they are safe and will be on their way home."

Despite my own predicament, I exhaled gratefully, my breath seizing when he caught hold of my elbow and steered me down the narrow hallway to what was indeed a rear exit into an alley. "You and I, however, are going to have a little chat."

"Rafi, I have to get home," I said in a wobbly voice, not entirely unwilling to use his given name or even tears to get my way. The advancement of female rights would not save my friends in this moment.

"I'll see you there," he said. "*After* we talk."

He gripped my arm firmly as we emerged on a street parallel to the one we'd entered earlier, and he hurried us toward a plain dark carriage. I faltered, considering whether I could make a run for it. Seven Dials was a warren of narrow streets that someone could easily vanish in. I was fast, I could do it. But despair sank in as I considered the consequences if I did.

This wasn't a safe part of London, and a necessary part of my disguise had been lost. Without facial hair, I couldn't hide the very delicate slope of my jaw or the plumpness of my lips. If my hat went, my hair would be a dead giveaway. No good could come of me fleeing . . . not *here* in a den of thieves and criminals. I was between a rock and a hard place, and facing Rafi's certain wrath was hardly the better of the two choices.

Botheration, I couldn't do it. I *couldn't* get in a coach with him.

I half turned before that grip on my arm tightened, his voice slicing between us. "Don't even think about it, Zia."

He practically lifted and bodily tossed me into the carriage before climbing in behind me and instructing the coachman to take us the long way to Mayfair. Cramming myself back onto the velvet squabs of the bench, I saw him take the space opposite and lean forward with his elbows propped on his knees. His gaze bore through the fabric of my waistcoat, the ring burning a hole in my chest through my shirt. "Where did you get the ring?" he demanded in a low, curt tone, not wasting a single second.

"It's Keston's," I blurted, and faked a confused look.

"Is that so?" he asked, leaning back with a contemplative expression. I nodded. "Why did you run when I saw it? Surely your *brother's* ring would not cause such a panic?"

"I . . ." My brain went blank. My fingers curled into my breeches and dug into my thighs. His gaze followed the movement, and a sharp exhale left him. In horror, I realized that the sitting position had made my coat ride up and pulled the fabric of my breeches tight against my legs, exposing their length and shape. But I was a fool if I thought that that would be enough to distract Rafi.

His jaw tightened as he lifted that saturnine stare to mine once more. "Speak."

Inspiration hit. "I didn't leave because of the ring. I saw the Runners," I blurted out. "Anyone would. I couldn't exactly risk being discovered."

"Show me the ring, Zia," he said after a long moment.

I clutched a hand to my chest. "I cannot. That's personal."

"Why? Ridley is my friend. He would not care if I had a look at it. What are you hiding?" Rafi's voice lowered to a taunting rasp that arrowed to places on my body that should not be mentioned in proper company. "Is it a lover's?"

"How dare you?" I snapped, wide-eyed at the insult. "And besides, even if it were, that's none of your deuced business."

As if some invisible line had been crossed, he canted his head, eyes flashing with irritation. He crossed one booted foot over his knee, the epitome of relaxed elegance, though I knew that he was more of a cobra waiting to strike than a gentleman who would entertain my ladylike foibles. "We can ride around London all night, if that is your wish."

"My parents think I'm at a musicale with Lady Ela," I said. "They will worry."

He nodded. "That they will."

My bluster seeping away, I could see by the stubborn set of his jaw that he would do exactly what he threatened with no thought to those consequences. Not even propriety could save me now . . . not that there was any room in this situation for decorum.

Rafi leaned forward. "You either show it to me yourself, or I take it off you. Your choice, my lady."

I gasped in unfeigned outrage, though something delicious unwound through me at the wicked promise spoken in his whisper. "You wouldn't!"

"I would. Don't test me, Firefly."

A mortifying heat scorched my cheeks as my heart thundered behind my rib cage. "My name is Zia, you lout!"

His lip curled in that hateful smirk. "Not Mr. Night? Or should I say Lady Night?"

Silence detonated between us as the impact of those last two words settled like ash in the wake of a lethal explosion. I froze as unbelieving silver eyes crashed into mine, searching for answers that he thought were absurd. Preposterous, even.

"Fine," I said in desperation, reaching up to unfasten the clasp. "Take it. I don't know what you even care. It's a silly man's ring one of the maids found in the billiards room. The way you're behaving, it's like you think it's yours or something."

Rafi didn't even blink as the necklace and ring ended up on his lap. His eyes remained on mine like he was a predator with a fascinating prey in his sights. The image of a motionless cobra returned to my brain, and I gulped.

"Lady. Knight." The two words were soft, though they sank into me like lead shot. I flinched at the impact. "*Knight* with a *K*. Bloody hell." His nostrils flared as he inhaled, and I instinctively leaned back. "It was *you* that evening in Hounslow Heath."

If I could have thrown myself from the carriage without risk of death, I would have. "I don't know what you're talking about," I said stubbornly.

"It was the name you gave that night as you stole our belongings at gunpoint." He lifted the ring that was still warm from my body and clasped it in a large, tight fist. "You took this from me, and you smelled like orange blossoms."

I clamped my lips shut. I knew that fragrance would return like a vengeful phantom insistent on my destruction. I'd stopped using the oils in my bath as a paranoid precaution, but perhaps Rafi had noticed my scent a long time ago, which made my efforts moot. A slow, irrational warmth dissipated through me.

When had he noticed my scent? *Why* had he remembered such an intimate part of me?

"What were you thinking, Zia?" he snarled. "I know it was you, don't even try to pretend or prevaricate." He snapped his teeth in frustration as those hard eyes canvassed me from head to toe, a muscle drumming wildly in his cheek. "I should have recognized you! But why would the daughter of a duke be out on a notorious highwayman route in the middle of the night? Stealing from people with a rifle, of all things!"

My eyes shot skyward at his histrionics. "Don't get your smallclothes into a bunch."

"My smallclothes . . . ," he sputtered, his handsome face going ruddy with aggravation. That jaw of his flattened into a stiff, uncompromising line, making his cheekbones stand out as he glowered at me. Heavens, even in the throes of vexation, those exquisitely sharp features took on a mesmerizing cast. Inky tousled hair tumbled around his face from our run through the streets, and my fingers itched to put those silky tendrils to rights. Rafi Nasser was gorgeous at the best of times, but like *this* . . . so wondrously unraveled, he took my breath away.

"How could you be so rash? Have you not a single sensible thought for your own safety?" He pinched the bridge of his nose between his thumb and forefinger, long eyelashes dipping down to cast shadows on his face in the guttering lamplight of the coach. An irritated growl broke from him. "Devil take it, Zia, you make me want to . . . tear my bloody hair out!"

Silver irises glittered, his upper lip ferocious off white teeth in a snarl. He resembled a wild, savage wolf whose den had been trespassed upon. A wolf that didn't know whether to mark its territory or snatch me up for dinner. At that, a throb pulsed deep in my chest. Too hot for comfort, I threw off my hat and yanked off the crudely tied cravat around my neck.

"Is this a *joke* to you?" he demanded, glaring at me, and for once, my instincts took note of the fact that the gentleman sitting opposite who did not find my harmless antics amusing in the least was nearing the end of his rope.

"The rifle was empty, for heaven's sake, I lied," I grumbled with a long-suffering sigh as the coach came to a shuddering stop at our destination in Mayfair. With the safety of my home in sights and steps away, I lifted my chin, moving to open the coach door. "You are overreacting. I'm alive and well, aren't I?"

I nearly shrieked when he pitched forward, trapping me, his eyes narrowed and the rich scent of him crowding my nostrils as if I didn't have enough sensory overload to deal with already. One arm was braced on the top of the bench, the other against the side of the carriage. "And what if someone had pulled a pistol on you? How would you have defended yourself with an empty weapon? Did you think about that?"

"Well, they didn't," I said mulishly. "*You* didn't."

I saw the exact moment that Rafi lost the brittle hold on his temper, those pretty eyes promising retribution as a low feral sound rumbled in his chest. Every hair on my body stood on end in the cramped space of that coach with him looming over me like a vengeful god. He was close enough to kiss.

"You are . . . *argh*, I cannot . . ."

In helpless supplication, like a silly, silly moth, I leaned forward. I wet my lips, his words faltering at my all-too-obvious invitation. With a groan, he hesitated the scantest of moments before his mouth swooped down, crashing into mine.

CHAPTER ELEVEN

In fact, it is a farce to call any being virtuous whose virtues
do not result from the exercise of its own reason.
—MARY WOLLSTONECRAFT

Sweet baby cherubs on high. Rafi. Nasser. Was. *Kissing.* Me.

Rafi Nasser, who didn't like me. Who saw me like a sister.
Who pushed me away.

Suddenly, every reasonable thought reduced itself to absolute
nonsense in my brain at the purposeful movement of his lips.
The soft pressure of his mouth belied the wildness of the storm
that had been swirling in his eyes, and even on the cusp of being
provoked beyond reason, his touch was excruciatingly gentle. I
could only focus on his full lips moving tenderly against mine
in a kiss so sweet that my toes curled in my boots and my very
capable brain dissolved to mindless fluff.

I'd experienced one or two quick pecks in the past—even an
experimental and rather interesting one with Nori—but nothing compared to this feeling of being completely unraveled from

head to toe from the one simple touch. My heart pounded like a drum behind my ribs as his mouth slanted over mine, parting ever so slightly. When the tip of his tongue swiped against my bottom lip, the taste of him exploded across my heated senses.

Mint, cloves, and something uniquely him, crisp but warm like the delightful rain and sandalwood scent currently enveloping me. Desperate for more, I gasped, one arm reaching up to grasp his neck and hold him firmly in place as though the kiss were at risk of being taken away. Groaning into my mouth, he obliged with a muffled laugh at my boldness, his left palm shifting to cup my chin and angle my face to where he wanted it. And then we were both lost to sensation as the kiss deepened and heightened . . . as he took control and kissed me as if I were the air he needed to live.

Me.

Heaven help me, I couldn't get enough.

After what seemed like an eternity of exploration, he broke the embrace and drew back, breathing hard. His lips were red as I imagined mine must be, and I pressed a single fingertip to their trembling, tingling contours. His gaze darkened, and his body tilted forward as if compelled by an unseen force before he shoved himself back a safe enough distance away.

Swearing a low oath, he scrubbed a hand through his hair. "This was a mistake."

I frowned at him, euphoria crushed by despair. "No, I—"

"You should go," he said thickly. "It's late."

Flummoxed, I stared at him for several moments, but he would not meet my eyes. I had never imagined Rafi of all people to be such a coward. With a deep inhale, I squared my chin and retrieved my hat from where it had been jostled to the floor of the carriage. I'd never been the kind of girl to beg for anything, even something as trifling as an explanation, so I exited the coach without another word.

I slipped around to my carriage house in the back of the residence, and after sponging off and changing into a loose dress, I sat at the small desk tucked away in the corner. My chest felt like it was ten times too tight. Rafi's kiss and his horrid response to it had ignited something inside me—a desperate need to do *something* . . . to give voice to the questions warring and writhing within me like a nest of little serpents.

Why had he kissed me?

Why had he spurned me?

Would he expose my secret?

I felt untethered, my emotions soaring high and crashing low. I wanted to scream my frustration to the skies, but that would not be wise at this late hour, lest the entire staff of the manse, including my very protective family, come running.

In a way, I felt like Dr. Frankenstein, frantic to expel some monstrous creation.

I shuffled through the papers sitting on my desk and read through my last effort on the acrostic verse that had stumped me.

Just write from your heart. Rafi's parting words of advice after he'd read my attempt flicked through my head.

I picked up the quill and dipped it into the ink pot. Studying what I'd already written, I scratched out *apathy* and changed it to *anger*.

F is for fighting to be seen and heard,

R is for revenge, though it may sound absurd.

A is for the ~~apathy~~ anger that consumes my heart,

N is for never feeling so broken and twisted apart.

K is for the kiss that you carved onto my soul . . .

E is for everything you now withhold.

N is for the noxiousness that tethers me to life,

S is for the savage storm and the bitterness of strife.

T is for time stretching out, endless and alone,

E is for my enemy, which you have become.

I is for the insufferable longing I withstand . . .

N is for the nightmare wrought by cruel hand.

I gave a humorless scoff at the last. Being discovered by Rafi was a nightmare in itself. I never should have worn that silly ring. What had I been thinking? That it was some kind of keepsake, some cherished memento of our escapades? It had only been the harbinger of my doom, and I'd brought it upon myself.

Fingers flecked with ink, I reached for another sheet of paper.

O is for the oasis of darkness that fills me,

R is for realizing that I deserve better, you see.

I exhaled. The truth was, we as humans were conditioned to receive what others deigned to give, not what we were worthy of.

T is for terror that I will rain down in spades,

H is for the horror no one can evade,

E is for the emptiness my blood does pervade . . .

My fingers hovered over the page, my emotions whittled down to a peculiar hollowness. Poetry in its simplest state, like music, was a form of catharsis, and the words flowed like a healing balm. My poem was a stitched-together construct—an amalgamation of chaos—and though I was no Lord Byron, the words were mine, even if raw and unpolished.

M is for the monster who is finally free.

O is for the utter obliteration of empathy.

D is for death, destruction, and dire consequence,

E is for the end of all, of me, of gentle conscience.

R is for the reason that slips my mind,

N is for nihilism that will burst in kind.

Despite my conflicting feelings about Rafi, he was right. The words had come after all; they had fountained from me, like a song taking form. I'd only had to connect with how I could see myself on the page. How my father's expectations and the weight of duty continued to influence both my choices and my actions. How trapped I felt by default of my sex and my station. How powerless I was to so many external forces that had nothing to do with what I truly wanted. Like the monster, we were shaped by nature and nurture in equal measure.

Prometheus was the last word in the novel's title. The letters taunted and teased, all of the creature's hurts and despair—all of my hurts and wishes—yearning to get out. Yearning for birth. I'd liberate us both.

P is for pain.

R is for rejection.

O is for obscenity.

M is for mayhem . . .

E is for the evil is that evil does,

T is for the tragedy of never knowing love.

H is for the fallow heart that weeps for you,

E is for the echo of despair and everlasting virtue.

U is for the us I shall now never know,

S is for my shame and my forever silent sorrow.

With a sigh, I slumped back into the chair, dimly noticing the pinkish pale streaks of dawn appearing through the window. Restlessness still churned in my veins as if the sparks inside me had ignited into a full-blown inferno. The acrostic verse screamed to be translated into musical notes. Taking the parchment with me, I rose; stretched the stiffness out of my muscles, sore from being hunched over my desk; and made my way to the pianoforte. I tested each key, pressing the ivory bars softly in turn. Like the words, the music flowed as my fingers skimmed over the keyboard.

Heavy with hope and brought low by despair, the discordant notes echoed the turmoil the creature had faced and the disastrous consequences of Dr. Frankenstein's actions. Every few measures, I would write down the musical notes in pencil for the upper and lower staffs. The arrangement was consistent with the types of sounds I'd been exploring lately—all dissonant and sharp with furious crescendos juxtaposed with tender adagios.

By the time I was finished with the musical composition, I was finally bone weary.

With an enormous yawn, I dragged myself through the main house to my bedchamber, the bustling sounds of the servants preparing for the day indistinct to my tired ears. Gemma would have guessed that I was probably in the carriage house. When the proverbial muse struck, one could only succumb. I discarded my dress and climbed into bed.

Too bad I'd forgotten exactly which day it was.

"Lady Zia. Wake up, Lady Zia," a voice said, a hand shaking me gently and then more firmly when I groaned and hid my face under a pillow.

"Go away, Gemma," I grumbled. "I want to sleep."

She let out an exasperated huff as if she'd been trying to wake me for a while. "The duke is commanding your presence in the breakfasting room and said he is expecting you posthaste. He is in a *mood.*"

I groaned loudly as that sank in. Whenever my father was in a terrible mood, his commands were meant to be obeyed. He was a good man, one made even better by his duchess, but that cold temper of his was legendary for a reason. I'd inherited mine from my mother, whose West Indian temper was truly as fiery as the Scotch bonnet island peppers she so loved. When Papa was irritated, everyone steered clear. And now I'd been summoned into the vortex of frost.

I knew what it would be about, of course. The bone of contention between us: my future marriage. We were well underway in the season, and I was sure he wanted to make his ultimatum clear . . . as if it weren't as clear as crystal already. I burrowed under my blankets, but there was no escaping Gemma. Or my father.

"My lady! You must get up."

"Must I?" I whined.

"It's Sunday breakfast, my lady," Gemma said, and I blinked in confusion before flying up so briskly that my brain spun. Today was *Sunday?*

Sunday breakfast was the one tradition my mother cherished, and being late was frowned upon by my father, who insisted— rightly so—on keeping his duchess pleased. Stuffing the heels of my palms into my sticky eyelids, I rose, stretched, and grouchily performed my morning ablutions. Goodness, I felt so groggy, my brain blessedly quiet, but I suppose I had put it through a rigorous marathon until the early hours.

Even after splashing and sponging my face and body from the water in the bowl on the dresser, I couldn't summon the energy to move quickly enough. When Gemma made an impatient noise, knowing each minute was precious, I stepped into the stays and gown that she had removed from the armoire. After she fastened the ties, I pinched my cheeks to put some color in them while she removed my curls from the silk sleep bonnet and worked my hair with some specially made pomade, so it stayed healthy and shiny.

She deftly fashioned it into a loose chignon held together by a jeweled comb, leaving a few loose spirals to frame my face, which was ghostly, with dark circles congregating under my eyes from the lack of a proper sleep and the late night. My thousand and one freckles stood out in harsh contrast from my golden-brown skin, and I scowled at them. Some days, they were the bane of my existence, especially when they looked like whole constellations.

Rafi likes them.

I didn't care one whit what that sneaky, controlling rogue thought about me.

Gemma held up the rouge pot to paint my cheeks and lips, and I shook my head. I didn't need to look fancy for my father, only presentable. Besides, there would be no one at breakfast other than my parents, my brother, and Ela, unless they had made their excuses, though missing Sunday breakfast was rare.

In fact, I hoped desperately that they were there, at least to draw some of the duke's attention away from me.

By the time I trudged downstairs on leaden feet, I was ready to return to my bedchamber and pretend to have taken ill, but the only people to suffer my father's overbearing moods were the servants, and if I could help thwart his irritation, then I would. No one deserved the fallout from my choices, least of all the people who were employed here.

Two maids scurried out of the breakfasting room, their faces ashen, and my stomach dipped unsteadily. Gemma hadn't been wrong. Everyone seemed to be treading on eggshells. I nodded to the two footmen standing at attention outside the doors, and even their mouths were drawn tight.

Smoothing my skirts, I entered the room, a false but bright smile fixed firmly in place. Two footmen and the maid serving my father blocked the other end of the table, but I attempted to conceal my relief when I spotted my mother, my brother, and Ela. The fates weren't so cruel, after all. In my overly fatigued state, I was sure to say something rash, especially if my father brought up betrothals again. Ela and Keston would be excellent diversions.

"Good morning, Papa, Mama," I said, and walked sedately toward the empty place setting.

"Good morning, Zenobia," the duchess said with a fond smile while my father speared me with a glance and grunted. That was better than nothing, I supposed.

"Keston, Ela, how wonderful to see you both!" I greeted my brother and his fiancée with so much enthusiasm that they both stared at me with raised brows. Ela hid her smile behind her palm, even as my father's vexed stare snapped toward me.

Too much.

My stomach rumbled as the delicious scents of steaming cocoa, spicy tomatoes and saltfish, curried chickpeas, creamed eggs, and roasted bacon rushed into my nostrils. Perhaps this summons was a blessing in disguise. My mouth watered. . . . I hadn't realized how famished I was. Perhaps a good meal would help.

As expected, my weariness made my emotions much too transparent for comfort. This was made even more apparent when I rounded one of the footmen serving my father to see none other than Rafi Nasser gracing me with that nauseating smirk.

For a weak second, the vain part of me wished I had let Gemma put on the rouge or a dash of rose lip stain, but why was I even thinking of impressing him, of all people? I should have been more worried that he was going to expose my secret in front of everyone! Was that why he was in my home?

"What are you doing here?" I demanded, making his smirk widen and my mother release a chastising sound.

"Lady Zenobia," he said, that rich molasses voice doing things it shouldn't at this hour. I thought of honeyed kisses and smothered sounds of pleasure. "You are such a vision of loveliness this morning."

Was it just me, or did everyone else at the table hear the sly condescension in his voice as if he'd meant exactly the opposite, an insult couched in a false compliment? Any thoughts of honey slipped away. Honey? More like vinegar. *Sour* vinegar. The sourest!

I sniffed with disdain. "Mr. Nasser, what a *delightful* surprise, although this is usually a *family* breakfast." I hoped my exaggerated emphasis would match his own skillfully cutting mockery, but to my annoyance, amusement danced in that gray gaze, lighting those mercurial irises to a shining silver. Gracious, I was much too unprepared for any of his games . . . or his gorgeous eyes. Or wondering whether they'd gone silver when we'd kissed.

Oh, stop, for mercy's sake.

"I invited him," my brother said, watching me with a narrowed gaze as if he could see right through me to my scandalous secrets. "Is that a problem? I know you two have been at odds and ends for years, but Rafi is my best mate."

Yes, his best mate who had *kissed* me!

I bet my brother wouldn't be so fond of Rafi if he knew. Sometimes, Keston's friends did join us for meals, but this wasn't just any friend. This was a gentleman whose lips had touched mine, who had witnessed my capers . . . who knew far too much about me for his presence here to be spontaneous. No, he was here to torture me. But for what? What nefarious plans was he hiding behind that stupidly handsome visage?

"You're late," the duke said in a clipped voice when I waited for the footman to pull out my chair.

"Apologies, Papa, I overslept," I said, taking the empty place to my mother's right, opposite Keston and Ela. I glowered.

"And why is that?" my father asked.

Rafi the rotter, whose brows had risen with expectant curiosity as if daring me to tell the truth. I swallowed hard. There was no way I could admit that I'd been at an underground fighting club betting money with petty thieves and, even worse, *participating*.

Ignoring the persistent press of my father's gaze, I kept my face serene. "I was working on a project for Miss Perkins at Welton and didn't notice how late the hour had grown."

Instantly, I knew I'd made a silly mistake in bringing up the Welton House when his frown deepened and his mouth flattened in abject displeasure. I wanted to kick myself. Had seeing Rafi rattled me so completely that my thoughts were so unguarded? I clamped my mouth shut lest I let something more untoward slip, but it was too late.

The mention of Welton was a spark to unlit tinder, and all I could do was brace.

CHAPTER TWELVE

Nature in everything demands respect, and those who violate her laws seldom violate them with impunity.

—MARY WOLLSTONECRAFT

The duke set down his fork, putting that icy-blue gaze on me. "You should be focused on considering an appropriate match for the season instead of gallivanting about with girls lower than your station and listening to wild ideas quite unsuitable for a duke's daughter."

"Wild ideas?" I blurted, despite the risk of fanning the fires. Clearly my tongue hadn't received the message that we weren't allowing any kind of speech today. "Is it so wild to think that a woman should receive an education beyond what should please her future husband? Even Mama studied astronomy and mathematics."

"With a tutor," my father said in a mild tone that was at extreme odds with the layers of ice in his blue eyes. "Not at some foolish finishing school with grandiose ideas."

"Well, it's not like a woman can attend Cambridge or Oxford." My mouth firmed as I bristled. "Besides, I *like* Welton."

"People are talking," he noted.

When I opened my mouth to reply that I didn't care what any bigoted old fools in the *ton* thought, my mother beat me to it. Her dark brown gaze flicked to her husband. "Who is talking?" she asked in a soft voice that made everyone sit a bit straighter.

It took quite a lot or certain incendiary topics to get a rise out of my mother, but people gossiping about her family was at the top of the list. We often drew enough scrutiny thanks to my father's powerful position as a duke and his very vocal duchess who made no bones about fighting for women's and human rights. As a family, we were well aware of our privilege. My mother had always upheld that those who could help *should* help, and those who were able should always fight for the weaker and downtrodden.

"Sir Richard," Papa responded eventually, catching my attention anew as my mother arched a cool brow. "The new Baronet Tenly," he added in explanation when her nose wrinkled with a lack of recognition.

I, however, instantly perked up at the mention of Lalita's uncle. I didn't care about the men in the *ton* and their asinine opinions in general, but Tenly was a different story. What was *he* saying? And could his opinions be why Lalita was so cagey all of a sudden? The happy girl who'd been so enthusiastic about the Lady Knights last year had been recently replaced by an uncharacteristic fusspot who questioned everything our small secret society stood for.

I tried to bite back the question burning my lips, hoping my father would continue, but I could not help myself. "What is he saying?" I blurted, drawing my mother's curious stare as well as everyone else's, including Rafi's. Clearly, I hadn't hidden the urgency of my words.

The duke slanted an impatient glance at me. "That the teacher is unfit to shape the minds of genteel young ladies. Her ideas and methods are . . . concerning."

"*Unfit?*" I sputtered. "Concerning how? And besides, how would Sir Richard even know what shapes a woman's mind? The man is a fossil from the Dark Ages who believes that women should be seen and not heard, should wait upon a husband hand and foot, should be completely subservient, and should be sold to bolster his personal status in society." My eyes burned and my fingers curled inward into fists and dug into my palms at the utter unfairness that a man's selfish command could take away all hope from a woman. From one of my best friends, to boot.

The entire room went dead silent at my outburst.

"Zenobia!" the duke demanded. "What has gotten into you?"

Fists balled, I swallowed, trying to keep my rioting emotions at bay. "Not *what,* Papa. *Who.* Miss Ada Perkins. Mary Shelley. Hannah More. Mary Wollstonecraft. Lady Ela Dalvi. The Duchess of Harbridge." I sucked in a shallow, painful breath, hoarse from my tirade. "They've gotten into me."

My gaze slid to my mother, whose face was unreadable though her eyes shone with something like pride. She canted her head in acknowledgment, though she remained silent, ceding the space to me. She believed in advocating for oneself but would step in if necessary. I glanced over at Ela, gauging her reaction, but she wore an unguarded, fierce look of admiration that slid over me like a warm, comforting blanket.

We, women, had to stick together. Power lay in solidarity.

Even though I didn't want it to, my gaze flicked to Rafi, too, expecting to see a disdainful expression that I had obliterated decorum at my father's own table. Instead, I saw interest. Interest and wonder. I didn't let either of those things affect me too much.

Well, I tried at least.

The duke's gaze threatened to skewer me, however. "Is this the daughter we've raised? To shout over the dining table? To argue in polite company? Perhaps Sir Richard has a point about this Perkins woman, one that I've been slow to recognize. One I must investigate myself."

"Investigate for what?" I replied now that the gauntlet had been thrown, despite the flicker of alarm curling in my belly. Sir Richard might not be commanding enough to shut down a school, but my father would be. His sway and influence were far-reaching.

"For the untoward corruption of young, delicate minds," he said, and I barely held back from letting out a disparaging snort. The duke was still my father, and I would not disrespect him even if I disagreed with his prehistoric views about female fragility. "Tenly believes we must protect our daughters from the philosophies and teachings of uncultured heathens."

I laughed. "Miss Perkins might be a tad unconventional, Papa, but she is not a *heathen*. You say that as though she's going to come with an army bearing pitchforks to unseat the aristocracy. To lead a rebellion against your precious patriarchy, which would keep my fragile, useless sex coddled and swaddled so that we can hardly breathe to form any opinions."

"Zia." That soft warning came from my mother, and I bit my lip at my nickname, sensing that I might have gone a step too far. Even Keston was watching our father carefully. Not that Papa would ever lay a finger on me, but words could hurt as much as strikes. The duke was stuck in his ways, especially having been brought up swathed in the privilege and influence of a birthright that came with being male, wealthy, and titled. He had changed since marrying my mother, but Rome hadn't been built in a day, as the saying went.

Inhaling deeply, I bent my head in contrition. "Apologies, Papa. I only feel very strongly about my purpose in society. I'm more than what has been expected of girls of highborn birth in the past." I cleared my throat. "You and Mama have always told Keston and me that we should never be held back by mediocrity. Keston has followed his heart, and we all know he will make an exceptional duke when the time comes. Is it wrong to want more than what high society expects of me?"

A muscle leaped in my father's jaw, but when his eyes met mine, the ice had been tempered with some degree of understanding. "No, it's not wrong, my dear." A rare smile cracked his austere features as he peered over at my mother, who wore a similar look of affectionate forbearance. "I suppose I should not be surprised. You have your mother's intelligence and ambition, along with my intractability and resolve. An explosive combination."

I knew my father too well not to expect that more was coming.

He signaled for the footman to bring him a refreshed coffee. "But there's a huge difference between teaching approved literature and disseminating inciting or misleading information that may have terrible consequences."

It was on the tip of my tongue to argue which men got to decide what literature was "approved," but the quiet warning in my mother's eyes stopped me. If there was one thing my mother excelled at, it was getting what she wanted with minimal resistance. It wasn't just about using honey, it was also about *when* to use it. And right now, even though the duke was somewhat placated, pushing him could have a much worse outcome . . . for me, anyway.

"I understand, Papa." Tamping down my agitated feelings, I took a bite of my now-cold toast, turned to my brother and Ela, and forced myself to change the subject. "How go the wedding plans?"

"Well enough, I suppose," Ela said with a wide smile as my brother stared adoringly at her. "The license has been obtained, the banns finally posted, and I'm being fitted for the dress. You must come soon so that you can be measured as well since you're one of my bridal attendants. The dresses will be so lovely!"

I'd been honored when Ela had asked me to be a bridesmaid. There were a few others, including Lady Rosalin and Ela's friends from Hinley, the seminary she'd attended for three years. Her mentor and guardian, Lady Felicity, the Countess de Ros, was going to act in the stead of Ela's late family. Church, as she was affectionately called, was both elder sister and mother to Ela and loved her as if they were of the same blood. It also turned out that the countess and my parents had apparently known each other for years before she'd vanished from London. She owned the school in Cumbria that Ela had been sent to. That story was one of the most interesting things I'd ever heard, how she and Ela had both saved each other.

Love took so many forms.

"I can't wait to see," I said.

"You will love them, I promise! Truly, the colors are to *die* for!"

Suddenly, I frowned as a thought occurred to me, and I narrowed my eyes at her looking much too innocent, those hazel eyes sparking with mischief. "Wait. You're not going to make me wear some atrocity, are you?"

"Why of course!" Ela pronounced with a straight face. "Seven pounds of mustard-yellow tulle have been ordered for each of you, and enormous bonnets with feathers dyed to match."

"Don't forget the faux fruit," my odious brother put in, unable to hide his smile.

"Ah yes," Ela said dreamily. "Grapes and cherries galore."

"I pray that you are jesting. Your face is entirely too serious."

"The dress you wore to Rosalin's season-opening ball inspired me."

My expression at the recollection of that off-white monstrosity must have been obvious, because Rafi chuckled. Ela turned her amused stare on him.

"Oh, don't you think you're getting away, Sir Bridesman.

You will be dressed in matching tails and trousers in a gorgeous shade of olive green." She sighed. "Green is such a marvelously versatile color, is it not?"

"No," he spluttered, and for once, we were united in absolute horror.

I shook my head. "Sunshine yellow. Buttercup yellow. Even butterscotch yellow is preferable to mustard. That just looks like cat's spew. And *olive* green? You might as well call it goose-shit green."

"Zenobia," my mother chided, though there was no heat in it.

Ela burst into laughter. "Do tell us how you really feel, Zia."

Her laughter was contagious, and even my father broke into a terse smile.

"You are a rotten wench," I told her, and then reached across to give her a sideways hug. "But I would endure the abysmal yellow cat's spew just for you."

Ela chortled. "I know. Don't worry, we are all in a lovely champagne color. My dress will be adorned with marigolds to honor my mother, and the bridesmaids will wear ones embroidered with chaconia to honor your mother." I blinked. The chaconia was a scarlet flower only native to Mama's island of birth. I met my mother's eyes, and they were brimming with tears. She hadn't known.

"Oh, my dears," she said, pressing a hand to her breast. "How thoughtful and lovely."

Keston threw his hands into the air and waved her off. "Don't look at me! It was all Ela's idea. I would never have come up with something so unique." He jerked his chin at Rafi. "As it is, because I have no imagination whatsoever, the bridesmen shall be wearing black with white cravats and ruby stickpins to match the ladies." He grinned fondly at Ela. "But all the credit must go to my beautiful future marchioness."

"Thank you, good sir." Ela beamed up at my brother, and even I could feel the warmth emanating from her.

The way my brother looked at her like she was his whole world made my heart swell. Even my father was regarding them with a softness that resembled affection. Out of the corner of my eye, I saw him reach for my mother's hand, and that act alone was one of the few that made me adore my father, even when he was being fractious and hard-bitten, which was 95 percent of the time. And especially when it came to my future.

My eyes slid to Rafi, who hadn't said a word. We didn't have a history as Ela and Keston did, only recent interactions. And a secret, scorching kiss that he had clearly already put from his mind. The ambivalence rubbed . . . and not in a good way.

"Mr. Nasser, you're awfully quiet," I said, not knowing why I was poking the beast. Or perhaps I did. I wanted him to be rattled as much as I was. "Cat got your tongue?"

"Sometimes it pays to listen, Lady Zenobia," he said. "Observation is a fond pastime of mine, one I find offers great insight into things."

I kept my expression neutral. "Like what?"

"Think about a mouse in a maze. If given its freedom, where would it go?"

With a frown, I studied him, but he was perfectly serious.

Could he be in his cups this early in the morning? I glanced around the table. Ela and Keston were in low conversation with each other as were my parents. No one was paying any attention to us. "I don't understand."

"The mouse is free to go anywhere as long as it's inside the maze," Rafi said, and then I realized what he was talking about. The mouse was me. The maze was . . . social expectation. He'd taken my earlier conversation with my father and created this strange metaphor. Not that I was a mouse. I was the furthest thing from it.

"But what if the mouse loathes the maze?" I said. "Because the maze is restrictive and tedious, and everything the mouse has ever seen before day in and day out. Shouldn't the mouse be granted its escape if the maze was somehow bested? If there was a loophole the mouse found."

Appreciation shone in his hooded gray gaze. "So, what then does the mouse want?"

I stared at him and shrugged. "What does any creature want? Freedom to choose their own path, even when those choices might have unforeseen consequences."

Like someone catching said mouse in action.

That last part was left unsaid, but the meaning was real, stretching between us like a sticky web between two warring spiders. "The mouse isn't foolish," I added.

"No one said it was," came his cool reply.

Suddenly, I became aware of two pairs of eyes watching our heated volley across the table. Thankfully, my parents were still in deep conversation. The last course had long been cleared, but

I'd barely noticed, so engrossed I'd been in the intense debate with Rafi. The servants brought in dessert, usually my favorite part of a meal. But I barely took notice of the mouthwatering soursop cream ice . . . a real treat considering how expensive and difficult ice was to keep in most households. And the soursop itself was not a fruit native to English shores.

"What are you two talking about?" Ela asked, her eyes absolutely full of interest as they swung back and forth between Rafi and me. Gracious, I didn't need her to read anything into this, and I knew she would because Ela was annoyingly perceptive. She'd learned to read people quite well when she'd returned to London, even ones who were valiantly hiding things. I kept my face blank, a polite half smile visible and my fingers busy fiddling with my spoon.

This was it. This was the moment when he would expose me, give me up to my family because he, too, thought I should be controlled and kept within the maze. Rafi and I stared at each other, the passing seconds burdened with tension, and I wiped my sweating palms against my skirts. Would he?

"Philosophy," Rafi said, and I exhaled audibly.

"One of my favorite subjects," Ela said, taking a bite of her dessert, but I could see she was hardly convinced that there wasn't more to our debate.

At the same time, Keston let out a sound of boredom. "Not mine, and my brain is in need of a long rest."

"What was the discussion?" Ela asked.

"We were discussing mice in a maze," I said, knowing she wouldn't let it go. "To which Mr. Nasser contended that unless there was a dearth of cheese, the mice would not care for anything."

She looked disappointed. "Oh."

"And other mice for company, don't forget," Rafi added with a sidelong wink when Ela was paying attention to her bowl. I stared at him. What did *that* mean? That misery loved company? That he'd expose my friends? That he was going to hold my secrets over my head forever?

"Don't let your treat melt," he said, gray eyes catching mine. "It's your favorite."

But it was only after I'd cleared my dish of the creamy, sweet, tangy, icy goodness that I realized what he'd said—this flavor of cream ice *was* my favorite. How had he known?

Or better yet, *why* would he have known that tiny fact? About me?

CHAPTER THIRTEEN

Men and women must be educated, in a great degree, by the
opinions and manners of the society they live in.

—Mary Wollstonecraft

My decision to follow Rafi in secret wasn't made in haste. In
fact, I'd pondered it deeply for a week . . . seven days of treading
lightly and wondering if and when the bootheel of Rafi Nasser
would crush me. He was doing it on purpose, I knew. The cad
seemed to enjoy keeping me on edge for his own twisted pleasure, and I'd had enough of it. Plus, he had started this game,
after all, by having someone follow me in the first place.

The time had come to give him a dose of his own medicine.

Dressed in my favorite ensemble with a hat pulled low and
my curls tucked away, I'd trailed him all the way to Covent Garden. I stayed in the hackney I'd flagged down, having paid the
coachman a handsome sum to follow Rafi's carriage at a careful distance. For some reason, I hadn't wanted to use Brennan,
despite his loyalty. This felt too personal. We'd just passed the

Covent Garden Theatre on Bow Street, which was quite crowded for the evening hour, and I kept a sharp eye on Rafi's coach.

When the carriage slowed and Rafi descended from inside, I frowned at the name of the tavern into which he'd disappeared. The Blue Dahlia Tavern. It was opposite the Drury Lane Theatre and boasted quite an ill repute that even *I* had heard of. Or rather, Nori had heard it, thanks to her loquacious and dissolute brothers, and filled us in.

I glanced down at my nondescript clothing—black breeches, dark shirt, plain coat, and a low-brimmed hat. My disguise might hold up in there, but one misplaced tug of my hat in a boisterous room of drunkards and my identity could be at risk. My bronze curls weren't tightly secured underneath it. I gritted my teeth. I'd have to come back another time. I had just resigned myself to doing just that when Rafi emerged and reentered the carriage. Only, he wasn't alone. He'd collected something—or rather, a female someone—and resumed his journey.

Knocking on the roof for the coachman to follow, I tried to ignore the spike of jealousy in my gut. I'd no right to any sort of possessiveness when it came to that particular gentleman. . . . My only goal here was to find any leverage on him since he knew of my secret identity. That was the *sole* reason for my interest.

Rafi was a notorious rake with a fast reputation. I knew better than to expect a leopard to change his spots, and I could hardly expect him to do so just because we'd shared one unexpected—and unexpectedly fiery—embrace. Lots of girls had probably enjoyed his kisses. Disgruntled, I let out a hiss and focused on where we were headed next. It turned out that his destination wasn't far. This area seemed to be less rowdy than the one we'd left, though it was still indisputably London's West End.

When Rafi descended the carriage steps, assisting his companion—who wore a crimson dress that was so snug in the bodice I wasn't certain she was able to breathe—my jaw tightened, but I shoved whatever *that* feeling was far away. I had no time to be captious, or any right to be. She looked lovely, to be fair.

I paid the coachman, who bit the coin before pocketing it, and told him I'd have another for him if he waited. He studied me with narrowed eyes, assessing me for truth. I stared back at him. As if I would cheat the old codger, but this wasn't exactly Mayfair. He finally nodded.

Keeping to the shadows, I followed Rafi and the woman at a discreet distance to a tiny square that included several buildings. He walked to a small structure with large, indistinct windows that seemed like a storefront, though it also appeared to be part of a residential building, considering the many windows above. *Odd.*

Did Rafi *live* here? But he lived in Mayfair in a very expensive residence a stone's throw from mine. Suddenly, I felt confused and discomfited. *Should* I be following him? If this was indeed another residence, then I was invading his private affairs. Shoving down my discomfort, I firmed my shoulders. So what? He'd invaded my privacy first by interfering in my business.

This was war . . . and war meant trespassing boundaries. With renewed purpose, I waited a few minutes and then crossed the street, keeping my head low. I didn't know what I would find, but if I waited long enough, I might catch him in some compromising position. One that I could use as collateral to make sure he kept my secret.

"You can do this," I told myself in a low whisper right before I crept under the window and released a breath. I'd waited long enough for some propriety to be observed, though I hardly knew what that constituted in this instance. Rafi was alone with a beautiful woman. I wasn't *that* sheltered to not know what went on between men and women behind closed doors.

Counting to ten while quashing all my guilty doubts, I stood up and peeked in. The glass was scratched and dirty, and it took my eyes a while to adjust, but what I saw was not what I had braced myself to see. I mean . . . the woman was scandalously undressed to her chemise and stockings while reclining on a chaise longue, but Rafi stood behind an easel where another woman in a plain blue dress was instructing him on some shading with a small brush. I had a clear view of the easel, and even through a scuffed window, Rafi's talent was obvious.

He was *painting*?

I'd known this was his passion, but it was common knowledge in the *ton* that his uncle had forbidden him to continue with such an "unpalatable, reductive" hobby. I stood there like a Peeping Tom and watched as the woman I assumed was an instructor moved away to adjust the model. Mesmerized by Rafi's deft brushstrokes, the golden-brown paint highlighting the texture of the woman's bare legs on the canvas, I felt the breath catch in my throat in complete awe.

Heavens, he was so good! I had not expected him to be. Like everyone else, I thought he only dabbled, but Rafi had real talent.

His color and textures reminded me of Titian, an Italian Renaissance painter from the sixteenth century. The detail in his work was compelling, the lines of the model so fluid that he could have been a master painter himself. I was no art connoisseur, but I'd been to enough galleries with my mother to appreciate true skill.

And Rafi had it in spades.

My brain jumped back to the conversation we'd had at breakfast about mice in mazes, and for a sharp heartbeat, I wondered if Rafi had also been speaking about himself. He was caught in the same pattern that I was . . . desperate to find a way out by any means necessary and yet bound to our respective duties. He as a viscount's heir, and me as a duke's daughter.

I wanted to write and compose, to be allowed to have my own views, for my desires to *matter*.

And so did he.

I hadn't realized that I was standing there like a frozen statue until a passerby, one who smelled like he'd drowned in a vat of gin, bumped into me, sending me careening into the window. The loud bang had three pairs of eyes peering up, one startling silver-gray pair in particular.

I didn't wait to see whether he'd recognized me. I whirled and ran across the street to the waiting carriage, letting the door slam behind me as I caught my breath. The last thing I saw through the small carriage window was Rafi's irate face as he scoured the streets. I slumped down against the squabs though I knew he couldn't see me. Well, it was finished now.

And I knew his secret.

The fan in my hand was doing nothing to move the stale, hot air in the crowded ballroom. And even when I fanned harder, all I got was the stench of French oils and perfumes pervading the air. Hadn't these people ever heard of a bath? Perfumes weren't soap! But tell that to half of the overfed, overindulged aristocracy.

Mama had insisted I attend this ball, hosted by the Countess de Ros, Ela's guardian and my mother's cherished friend, and I knew that the directive had come from my father, who was relentless in his desire for me to choose a husband.

"One would think he wanted to get rid of me," I'd grumbled earlier to my mother when we were climbing into our coach.

"He only wants to see you settled and cared for, Zenobia," she'd replied. "It's only what every father hopes for."

"What about my happiness?" I'd shot back. "Doesn't that count for anything?"

Her brows had risen. "What do you dream of, then?"

"I don't know. Anything but this!" I'd said, unable to articulate my feelings and only seeing the looming trap of wedlock in front of me. "He doesn't care about me being happy. He'd rather see me saddled with some old goat for posterity. To check some imagined action on a list so that it makes him feel like he has accomplished something."

Mama had taken hold of my hands, her dark eyes kind but serious. "I know you're upset, but complaining and grumbling will get you nowhere. Think about what it is you want. I've taught you this. In our lives, particularly as women, there is never a straight path, but that doesn't mean the destination is unreachable." She'd tapped my temple. "You simply have to use that powerful mind in that pretty head of yours and put it to work."

"But he'll give me no choice," I'd replied in a small voice. "No matter how much I quarrel with him or try to come up with another solution. It's pointless. I've thought this through, Mama!"

That keen gaze had glittered with a cunning intelligence. "Have you?"

Her words had sunk in during the carriage ride over. There had to be a way to get what I wanted in a manner that would satisfy my father . . . and my duty.

Muttering a curse as I stood near a potted fern that I hoped hid me, I groaned under my breath. I was counting the minutes until I could leave. Balls used to be fun, until they'd become a means to an end. A why-don't-you-get-married-already kind of end. Mutinously, I pressed my lips together. I would have to be dragged to an altar kicking and screaming. And then I laughed at my hollow posturing. I'd never embarrass my family so publicly. It was the whole reason I was so worried about Rafi exposing me. Nothing I did could come back to my parents. Or my brother.

My eyes instantly darted to where Keston and Ela were dancing at the center of the ballroom, mooning at each other. With a sigh that might have been envy and a sip of my warm punch, I caught sight of Lalita dancing with some gentleman with a shock of white hair, who looked like he wasn't long for a crypt.

Good God, was she truly considering him? But then I noticed Sir Richard and his wife looking on with fervent, pleased eyes on the other side of the ballroom, and my heart sank. No doubt the man had to be titled. It was despicable that they'd use their own niece to elevate themselves.

Marriage was a transaction. I *knew* that. But it didn't mean that I had to like it.

I wasn't in need of a title, but I knew that my father would expect an appropriate match for someone of my station. Suddenly, I had the urge to run off with a footman and board the first ship bound to anywhere but England. No matter the wild fantasy, I could never do that. Duty was much too ingrained in the very marrow of my being. I tugged at the heavily embroidered bodice with its many dozens of seed pearls and cursed again.

"Such language isn't quite ladylike, Lady Zia," a low, butterscotch-rich voice chided, making my heart skip a treacherous beat.

I glowered, too hot to turn. "Go away, Mr. Nasser, or you'll get a blistering you won't soon recover from."

I could almost feel his lip kicking up into that smirk. "Promise?"

My head swiveled. "What do you want?"

"A dance."

"My dance card is full," I said in the haughtiest voice I could manage.

"No, it's not," he said from behind me, that deep voice of his doing unnatural things, making my skin tighten and my breath hitch. Had it gotten ten degrees hotter, or was it just me?

"You make up the names to avoid dancing with anyone you don't know or like."

I sputtered. How on earth could he know that? Was I so transparent?

Abruptly, I turned and was faced with Rafi Nasser in all his effortless elegance. With his height and athletic form draped in raven-black evening clothes, he was beyond gorgeous, the crisp white cravat heightening the warm light brown tones of his skin. His dark hair was brushed back from his face, the curling ends of the silky mass just touching his collar. His cheeks were clean-shaven, that hard jaw sharp enough to cut glass, and his eyes glittered like pools of mercury. Words failed me as I forced myself to breathe.

Could I stomach being that close to him?

Being *held* by him?

"No, thank you," I clipped. "I don't wish to waltz."

His gaze brightened, the playfulness intensifying. "Why not? Afraid, Firefly?"

I bristled, probably just as he'd intended. With Rafi, everything was calculated, and I was certain this was, too. But I had some power now; we were even in the manipulation stakes. "You cannot trick me into agreeing, Mr. Nasser."

"Fine, where's the duke?" he said, glancing over his shoulder. "I'm not above persuasion. I'm sure he will have something to say about his daughter's late-night proclivities."

Was he trying to *strong-arm* me into dancing?

"And I'm sure your uncle will have something to say about your secret studio!" I shot back.

Surprise lit his eyes. Drat and blast. He *hadn't* known it was me, and now I'd gone and let the cat out of the bag too soon.

He slid his hands into his pockets and smiled, leaning in so only I could hear, his warm breath brushing my ear. "Naughty of you to spy, Zia. Ah, but who has more to lose? A girl with a supposedly unimpeachable reputation . . . or a young man with a belittled, pathetic little hobby?"

I wanted to blurt out that his art was hardly a hobby and certainly the furthest thing from pathetic from what I'd seen, but Rafi was the enemy here. I didn't need to shore up that enormous ego of his. Gritting my teeth, I glared mulishly at him. "Perhaps you're right. I'll just find Viscount Hollis and inform him of his nephew's whereabouts and how he's arrogantly disobeying his edict."

A muscle flexed to life in that lean jaw, and I had to contain my own rush of victory, but it didn't last long. "What will it be, Zia?" he said in a soft, velvety voice that didn't fool me in the least. "Will you leave me standing here like a sad wallflower, or shall I drop to one knee and beg for your favor?"

He wouldn't, the wretch! The gossip would be untenable. But his eyes gleamed in devious challenge, and I realized that of course he would . . . just to prove his point. We glowered at each other in a battle of wills until, finally, I let out an airy laugh as if he was so far beneath me I couldn't even see him.

"Fine, have your dance if you're going to be such a brat about it," I said. "Can't have the uncatchable Rafi Nasser seem like he's begging for scraps on his knees, can we?"

"That mouth of yours will get you into trouble," he said,

but he extended his arm like the gentleman he pretended to be. Underneath all those good looks and charm was a thorough rogue to the bone.

"Were you trouble the other night?" I shot back, and his gaze darkened. The double-edged innuendo was clearly a mistake . . . as suddenly, all I could think about was our ill-fated kiss.

And then we were on the floor, the strains of music beginning. Rafi's right hand slid around my back while my left hand rested on his shoulder, and we clasped hands. A foot of space separated us and yet it felt like an inch . . . and dwindling. I could not swallow a single sip of air.

"Breathe, Zia," he whispered, and at his words, the sudden rush of air into my lungs made me gasp.

"What?" I panted.

"You were turning blue," he said, moving me gently into the first turn, much more gently than I deserved after our little spat. "Why were you holding your breath? Should I assume that I smell dreadful, and you were trying to save yourself?"

I shook my head at his small joke, still trying to regulate my breathing. Could I admit that I was afraid of what dancing with him would mean? That everyone, and I mean *everyone* in the room, was looking at us? Some girls with envy, others with anger as though I'd stolen something from them that was never theirs to begin with. I could empathize—it was how I'd felt when he'd been with the woman in the scarlet dress in Covent Garden.

"I didn't eat any supper," I lied, and focused on not tripping over my own feet, or his. Usually, I was a graceful dancer, but all my skills, it seemed, had completely deserted me.

We remained quiet for the next few one-two-three beats of music, and I felt my body flowing and ebbing with his as if we'd waltzed together a thousand times. So many guests weren't even hiding the fact that they were ogling us, and the gossip would be flying about the ballroom by now. Rafi was very eligible, but he certainly wasn't the type to waltz. At least, I'd never seen him with anyone. We'd danced together a time or two before, but never *this* dance, which was scandalous by any standards, given how close the partners stood. Twelve inches wasn't much distance at all, and the press of his fingers at my back felt so . . . intimate.

"This is the first time we have waltzed," I said.

I could feel his stare, but I kept my gaze on the diamond stickpin winking from his cravat. "Yes."

"Why did you want to?"

"Because I've always wanted to," he said softly, and I nearly stumbled to an undignified halt in the middle of the dancers. "You can't deny there's something between us, Firefly," he said as we turned and clasped arms into a sideways circle. That time, I really did stumble, and it was only by his quick reaction that he saved me from falling onto my behind in an indecorous heap and being the laughingstock of the season. I was completely stuck on the second part of Rafi's confession. I gaped at him even as my pulse tripped. This had to be some elaborate trick.

"Yes, years of bickering." It was the only reply I could manage.

"And friendship," he said when I'd found my feet again, though proper brain function was taking longer to return the more he spoke. I glanced up at him. His face remained neutral as if all he had on his mind was this dance. I realized that was for everyone else watching us. I frowned. How much of Rafi was this mask of insouciance he wore? It was second nature to him, whereas I was certain that my every emotion remained transparent to all.

"You don't even like me," I bit out. "You've *said* that in no uncertain terms. That I was nothing more than the bratty sister of your best mate."

"Two years ago." A muscle flexed in his jaw. "And things change. People change."

Evidently, my mind was too baffled to function—I'd somehow blinked and ended up in an alternate reality where Rafi Nasser was insinuating that he'd caught feelings. For *me.* When the music ended, he drew me out onto the balcony. I went without protest, considering I was still in shock. A spontaneous kiss was one thing, but I did not want to get my heart trampled upon.

I caught sight of some of the stares and knew that tongues would be wagging, but at least there were other people out here taking in the air. We wouldn't descend into the gardens, where couples often disappeared for a tryst. That would be beyond scandalous, though a part of me was deeply curious about what happened behind all those hedgerows.

What happens in the arbor stays in the arbor. I stifled a giggle. Clearly my brain had not caught up with good sense. I coughed politely.

"Mr. Nasser—"

Rafi turned to face me. "Before you push me away, hear me out. I want my uncle off my back as much as you want your father off yours. We can help each other."

"By pretending to court?" I asked.

"Who said it'd be a pretense?" he countered, and my heart fluttered. "We would simply be getting to know one another, as we have been."

I lifted a brow. "Whereupon I act out, and you follow and try to talk me out of it?"

Rafi grinned, the smile crinkling his eyes. "Naturally."

My amusement guttered. "What about Keston? He won't like it."

"This isn't about him," Rafi insisted.

True. But I knew my brother, and he was aware of his best friend's rakish exploits. Keston would be furious if he got wind of the courtship. Still, I mulled over the idea. My mother's words chose to come back to me at that moment. Had I truly exhausted all the options? Because this was an option I hadn't considered . . . being courted by someone I could be marginally fond of.

Fine. More than fond.

As if he could sense my almost capitulation, Rafi took hold of my hands. "Give me a chance, Zia, that's all I ask."

CHAPTER FOURTEEN

Let us eat, drink, and love, for tomorrow we die.

—MARY WOLLSTONECRAFT

My heart fluttered like a wild hummingbird caught behind my rib cage as my gaze settled on him while that patient, intense gaze of his remained on me. I should have been ecstatic, but according to my brother, Rafi was emphatically averse to anything resembling commitment, and yet here he was, asking for a chance to court me. I didn't want to get hurt by being naïve. Any girl who went into a relationship trying to change a person was doomed to failure.

But he'd said that things had already changed. Was I foolish to believe him?

He was known in the *ton* as an unapologetic rogue, and I was the studious only daughter of a duke.

He was two years older, and I was his best friend's little sister.

We didn't suit, but our first kiss had spoken volumes.

"Are you angry that I followed you?" I asked bluntly. "Is this you trying to keep me close so that I keep your secret? That I caught you painting in your studio?"

"Painting?" We both jumped at the interruption. "What studio?" Spittle flew from Viscount Hollis's mouth, his face enraged.

Rafi went pale, his fists curling at his sides, and all I wanted to do was widen my stance and defend him against this despicable toad of a man.

"Viscount Hollis, how lovely to see you," I said in my most angelic voice. "Art is a particular hobby of mine, and well, my papa, the *Duke of Harbridge,*"—I cringed internally at the emphasis—"has always been one to indulge me. Mr. Nasser was just informing me of a studio he used to go to."

I saw the viscount frown. "Painting is not—"

I could see where he was going, and I immediately nodded in fervent agreement, cutting him off mid-sentence. "It's certainly not something anyone can do, considering the greats like *Michelangelo* and *Rembrandt.*" I was laying it on thickly, but the man's skull had to be as dense as rock. Would he even know who they were?

He grunted. "I suppose."

"Harbridge would be *most* appreciative that your nephew was so kind to me." My father would be nothing of the sort, but it wasn't as though the viscount could confront my father, considering they weren't acquainted. It would be an egregious faux pas for him to approach the duke without proper introduction. I might resent and loathe them, but the stringent rules of high society could be useful when one was in a pinch.

We both watched as he turned on his heel without another

word and disappeared into the melee. My lip curled in distaste. "Why does he dislike you so much?" I asked.

"He hates my mother's ancestry." Rafi gestured to his person. "And by default, mine. He also begrudges the fact that his title will be mine someday, while I resent the promise I made to my mother to honor my father's line by accepting the viscountcy."

"He is truly appalling," I murmured, and shook my head. "What a bigot! Honestly, he was one of our most deserving heists." For a moment, I forgot who I was talking to, until Rafi started chuckling.

"You *robbed* him?" he asked, and then his eyes went round with delayed realization. "At Danforth's when you came downstairs. He claimed his diamond stickpin was missing."

My cheeks went hot. "Ah . . . no? Never seen a stickpin in my life." I had to bite my tongue from retorting that the diamond was fake.

"Save your fibs, Firefly." Rafi shook his head when I tried to look innocent and failed miserably, and then curiosity lit his gaze. "I am not cross about it, but are you going to tell me why you followed me the other day?"

"Are you going to tell me how you know my favorite flavor of cream ice?" I countered.

"You're quite vocal when you like something," he replied without prevarication, brows rising. "And I notice things. Now answer my question."

A guilty flush heated my cheeks. "I wanted to know your secrets for once."

"And?"

"From the little I saw, you're quite good," I said, peering up at him, watching the moonlight play over his sharp features. Lines of shadow and light cut into his face, making him have a stitched-together, eerie appearance. I wondered if I looked the same.

"You think so? That I'm . . . good?"

Splotches of ruddy color filled his cheekbones. Was the great Rafi Nasser actually blushing at my compliment? Surely, he must have some idea of his own skill? His painting made me think of my music—the creation that was unique to us and born of our own minds. Creative vision was a gift and not one to be squandered. Then again, if someone was consistently belittled for their passion as Rafi had been, self-doubt and insecurity might be second nature.

"I do," I told him sincerely.

When Rafi offered me his arm to go back into the ballroom, it felt like the world as I knew it had monumentally shifted. I felt the press of every single pair of eyes boring into us as though there were an enormous sign above our heads that proclaimed we were now a couple. Perhaps I was the only one who thought a connection between us was untoward. Or not, as Sarah Peabody practically gored me with daggers in her eyes when we strolled past.

My fingers convulsed on his arm as he steered me once more to the ballroom floor instead of toward the refreshments room where my friends were, right into the thick of things. "What are we doing?" I asked.

His lip curled, the Rafi everyone knew back onstage. "Dancing."

"Again?"

His hand slid down my arm in a deliberate stroke that had my head reeling. "I've heard that three times is enough to declare one's intentions, so we better give the gossips something to chew on." I exhaled in a huff; he wasn't wrong.

"Very well." We were *doing* this. Really doing this.

Rafi's finger tipped my chin up. "Stop overthinking it."

"I'm not," I fibbed. My brain was whirling like a children's top. "Everyone's watching."

"Let them." He smirked with his brows raised. "Now act as if you like me."

I almost burst into laughter. "I do like you when you're not being an overbearing, bigheaded cad who thinks he's God's gift to the female population."

"Can you blame perfection?"

"Such arrogance." Snorting, I stared at him and shook my head. When the music started, he guided me into the first steps. I had a sneaking suspicion he'd reverted to his flirtatious default in order to distract me. My body was stiff, my spine snapped straight, and I forced myself to relax. "I'm going to regret this, aren't I?"

"Rafi Nasser and regret don't exist in the same sentence."

"Oh, dear God." I giggled. "Tell me you did not just refer to yourself in the third person, for mercy's sake!"

"Alas, Mr. Nasser will not be taking any other questions at this time."

By the time we twirled into the next measure, horrified

laughter bubbling in my throat at his deadpan expression, I forgot all about being nervous or worrying about who was watching.

Miss Perkins always insisted that our last gathering for the spring school term be one part education and one part celebration before most of us committed to the season in earnest. The school remained open year-round, of course, but any progeny of peers, like Petal and I, as well as wealthy gentry like Lalita, Nori, and Sarah, were expected to be on pretty display, all in the hopes of catching a husband.

Blythe was the only one on the fringes of polite society, considering her father's status as a lowborn gaming hell owner. Though he had more money than half the aristocracy put together, he lacked the proper breeding that the patronesses of the *ton* required for entry into their illustrious ranks. By default, Blythe did, too, despite the fact that her grace and faultless manners outshone most of the people in our set. She'd confided that, like me, she'd had governesses growing up and was instructed to death on etiquette as well as dancing, playing the harp, and needlepoint. Her father also had lofty dreams for her.

Did Blythe even *want* a rich, titled husband? A grin curved my lips as I caught one of the furtive, heated looks she and Nori exchanged while walking arm in arm behind me. Perhaps not. I was happy for them. Nori was one of my dearest friends, and she deserved to find someone who was as obsessed with horses as she was. I'd made the mistake of getting in the middle of a very frenetic discussion regarding champion bloodlines. I did worry that their relationship was growing a tad too fast, but who was I to judge? I was now practically engaged.

In a matter of days following the ball and the third dance we'd outrageously had, the gossip rags had gone wild with speculation over Rafi Nasser finally being off the marriage mart. This morning's headline in the *Times* was particularly on the nose, leaving little room for speculation.

HAS THE UNCATCHABLE MR. N FINALLY BEEN CAUGHT? HAS THE TON'S FAVORITE RAKE BEEN SHINED BY LAST SEASON'S DIAMOND?

As we neared the schoolroom, I decided to broach the subject instead of tiptoeing around it. I wasn't worried that my friends would question my choices, especially since they were already well aware of my father's unreasonable demands for me to marry.

"Did any of you see the newssheets this morning?" I asked, stopping just before entering the west end of the building.

"You mean that scandalous piece about you and Rafi?" Greer teased.

I blushed. "That's the one."

"Is it true?" Nori asked.

I nodded, cheeks warming as she clapped me on the back with a loud whoop. "Then I'm happy for you, Zia!" she said as Greer beamed her agreement and Blythe shot me a small smile.

They sauntered into the building, Greer waggling her blond brows the way past and whispering, "I knew it."

Lalita, however, paused on the stoop. She observed me

quizzically and asked, "Why the sudden change of heart? I thought you didn't like him."

"It's not that sudden," I replied. "We're just getting better acquainted, that's all. I think maybe he might not be so bad."

Her gaze turned curious. "Rafi the *Rake*?"

The slightest measure of censure underscored her tone, and I bristled at the overt judgment. It was on the tip of my tongue to tell her to mind her own business, but it wasn't as though she was wrong. I'd thought the same about Rafi until recently. He had a fast reputation. She just wasn't privy to the real Rafi, the one I was only now getting to know.

Forcing a grin to my face, I tossed my head and gestured for her to follow the others. "Let's just say I'm keeping an open mind. Everyone deserves a second chance, don't they?"

"What did Lord Ridley say of your pairing?" she asked.

My brother didn't have an opinion because I hadn't exactly told him, though he probably would have seen the *Times* by now, and if he hadn't, no doubt Ela had. "He's fine with it," I lied. "Rafi's his best mate."

Knowing me as well as she did, Lalita shot me a skeptical look, but thankfully she didn't press the issue. I followed her into the classroom and took my seat. This wasn't Keston's life . . . it was mine.

"Ladies," Miss Perkins said moments later when we were all settled. "I'm excited to see what each of you have come up with." Her eyes met mine. "I am particularly eager for yours, Lady Zia." With my hectic social schedule, we had only been able to meet once, and she'd been fascinated with my idea.

I smiled. "*Hear* mine, you mean." With that, the others also looked at me.

Miss Perkins gestured to the pianoforte in the corner of the room, but I shook my head. "Would it be acceptable if I went last?"

"Of course," she said.

I knew Greer and Petal had been working on a toy built from scratch. I watched mesmerized as my talented friend showed off the miniature stage she and Petal had built, and the performance they enacted with the hand-painted paper scenes, each sliding across a grooved wooden base. "Our creation was this children's toy theater," Petal explained. "Miss Sorensen and I had our challenges with the construction of the set, and the story ideas, but we think our creation works."

Per Miss Perkins's instructions, the rest of us had to judge whether their experiment was a success or a failure. I gave them an enthusiastic nod. It was exceedingly original, and the "show" that they put on was a snippet of the scene where the monster was brought to life.

"Well done," Miss Perkins said, and the rest of us clapped.

Next up was Lalita and Sarah. I hadn't envied Lalita being paired with someone like Sarah, but to my surprise, she hadn't said anything much about the partnership. I sat up eagerly as they carried a tray between them to the middle of the room. They had baked a creature that represented Shelley's description of Frankenstein's monster, with dark-veined sponge batter and cleverly placed flowing black ribbons for hair! It was a genius idea and played to Lalita's baking strengths.

"Our idea for the creation was this cake," she explained. "But

Sarah came up with a little something extra." She bumped the girl's shoulder playfully, and I frowned. Since when had they become so friendly? Had I been so wrapped up in my own life that I hadn't noticed? I shook it off—they were a team for this project—civility had to be enacted. "We each added ingredients, and well, it's a surprise." Lifting a knife, Sarah cut into the cake, severing the monster's legs, arms, torso, and head. Then she cut those into six parts, one for each of the rest of us, including Miss Perkins. "Go on, taste," Sarah said with an evil glint in her eyes. "Start at the legs."

Tentatively, we each took a piece. It tasted like normal sweet cake, and Lalita's were especially delicious. I ate the rest of mine with relish. Next up were the arms. My face twisted as the taste of salt overwhelmed me. It wasn't bad, just unpleasant. Greer smacked her lips and pronounced it was good. We reached for the torso, and this time, I had to spit out the morsel, stomach curling at the overly sour lemon taste. Saliva filled my mouth, and I swallowed. One could only imagine what the head would entail. With trepidation, I bit into the tiniest crumb, expecting the worst. Bitterness coated my tongue as the overpowering taste of coffee crushed my senses.

"We put different tastes into each part," Lalita said. "The sweetness was a sign of the creature's first steps and innocence. The arms were when his self-doubt crept in, and the knowledge that he was different."

She glanced at Sarah to continue. The girl nodded, pointing to the parts. "The torso represents how much his heart soured, and the bitterness of the head coincides with how bitter and hostile he became by the end."

My jaw dropped. Their idea was absolutely brilliant. I clapped loudly, proud of my friend who had created something so deeply insightful.

Miss Perkins's smile was wide. "I am proud of both of you, but particularly you, Miss Varma. I know you became a little concerned about the reading material."

She had? That was news to me. Had I been too preoccupied to notice? Why wouldn't she have said something? Lalita blushed as she and Sarah retook their seats. I leaned over to squeeze her shoulder. "Incredible effort," I told her, and she grinned happily.

Nori and Blythe followed. "I'm afraid ours isn't as good as theirs, but we tried our best," Nori said as they carried what appeared to be some kind of metal sculpture to the center of the room. I stared curiously at the horse, or at least what resembled a horse—no surprise there considering their mutual love for the animals—impressed by the interconnected parts. "Ours is this piece, which is composed of different metals," Blythe said shyly, and I saw Nori give her a reassuring nod. "We used iron, silver, copper, and paste as the varied facets of our monster. Each metal has its own properties, some harder and some softer, but we wanted to focus on the visual patchwork effect."

She exhaled, and Nori stepped in. "Most of the creature's limbs are iron, indicating its physical strength, and its body is copper and silver while its brain and heart are made of paste, demonstrating its weakest points."

"It's a work of art," Miss Perkins commented thoughtfully. "Well done, girls."

Though the thing was horrifying, with cameo pendants for eyes, something about it was admittedly mesmerizing. It was beautiful in a mismatched-hide kind of way, the colors merging in a metallic tapestry, even if those weird makeshift eyes were terribly off-putting. Beauty, no matter how small, could be found in something considered ugly on the surface, but perhaps that was part of the whole point of this exercise.

As Nori and Blythe went back to their seats, I sucked in a nervous breath. My project was very different in that it was a musical composition that went with an acrostic poem as opposed to something tangible as the rest of them had done. Since it was technically a performance, perhaps I needed to include a little ambience. Thank goodness it was a little overcast outside. I stood and closed the drapes, making the room instantly somber and gloomy.

Smoothing my damp palms on my skirts, I drew the three pieces of parchment from my pocket and handed one to Miss Perkins. "If I may beg your assistance to read, while I play." I had messengered a final copy of the poem along with my intentions for the musical composition a few days before, so she knew what to expect. She'd offered a few small notes on the poem.

I watched her face as she scanned it anew, her eyes rounding with each line, a small smile playing over her lips. Green eyes lifted to mine, approval in them. "This is good, Lady Zenobia. Truly thoughtful work."

"Thank you." My cheeks warmed at the praise. I didn't need

the written poem since I'd memorized it, but I set the second piece of parchment with the sheet music on the stand. "My creation is a bit different," I said to the other girls. "I made mine into a piano score."

"Go, maestro!" Greer let out an enthusiastic whistle, and I grinned at my friend.

With a theatrical bow, I walked over to the pianoforte, but before I sat, I opened the lid to expose the strings. Taking the extra piece of parchment, I rested it on the middle set of strings and then secured a nut and bolt on the lower end. This was either going to be amazing or a dismal failure. Taking my seat, I rested my hands gently over the keys and breathed in a calming breath. I glanced at the teacher. "I'll give you the signal."

I didn't wait before my fingers broke into the opening chords of the overture. The placement of the parchment made the strings vibrate differently when they were struck by the hammer. The expositional notes were fierce and powerful, telling the story of a man who had played God and given life to something beyond natural imaginings. When the tempo changed and went to a slower, more lyrical movement, it was to symbolize the birth of an innocent creature, one charmed by wonder.

As the progression softened, I nodded at Miss Perkins.

Then she began to read my poem aloud, her voice pitched perfectly to match the tones of the music, underscoring the creature's growing despair. I played the abrupt harmonic shifts with each line, softness juxtaposed with discordant notes, made even more so by the metal on the bass E-flat string. By the time Miss Perkins reached the second section of the acrostic poem—*or* and

The—the music had devolved into a rhythmic, melancholy pulsing, like a heartbeat . . . one that grew stronger and louder, driven by a dark compulsion.

The next part was echoed by a more turbulent theme, the brutal chord progressions flying from my fingers in cascading and rapid arpeggio, building, building, and building in more complex variations to something unsustainable . . . for the monster to finally break.

The G major chords became discordant with each forceful line, and the last was soft, a single repeating note the only sound in the room, giving the word *mayhem* its own distinctive gravitas. It signaled the entrance of the last theme in my piece. This was undoubtedly the softest, most regretful and tragic part of my composition. The ending was the swan song of a creature who had lost everything and all hope, and the music reflected that journey in a flowing, rich, transformational harmony, heightening the contrast of the creature's chaotic emotions in the previous theme. The adagio was tender and heartfelt, a delicate treatment of the rhythms and harmonies, as it reduced to a melancholy finale.

And one of profound, everlasting regret.

There wasn't a sound in the room when I finished playing, my fingers lifting off the keys, before it exploded into applause and screams. The latter were mostly from Greer and Nori, but everyone seemed staggered, wearing the same stunned expressions. I bit my lip shyly and stood. *This* was the music I wanted to compose. Raw, discordant, and real.

Unfortunately, it was also unprecedented and unconventional.

Which made it . . . unsuitable.

Miss Perkins had wonder and awe in her eyes. "I have never in all my years heard anything like that. What was the distortion on the strings? Intentional, correct?"

"Thank you, and yes," I said, cheeks going hot with equal amounts embarrassment and pride as I retook my seat. "It's a new technique to temporarily modify the sounds."

"That was amazing," Greer shouted. "I knew you were good, but honestly, Zia, that gave me goose pimples!"

Nori nodded, eyes glistening. "I was crying there toward the end. The music felt so sad and so sorrowful, like he'd just given up because there was nothing left for him but pain." She pressed a hand to her chest. "It could be the score of a gothic opera."

I blushed. It was hardly as good as all that.

"I found it peculiar." To no one's surprise, that was Sarah, and her minion Petal was vigorously on her side, but what really shocked me was Lalita's infinitesimal nod of agreement. *That* struck like an arrow to the heart.

CHAPTER FIFTEEN

We never do anything well, unless we love it for its own sake.

—Mary Wollstonecraft

The horse whinnied and nearly unseated me because I was much too distracted.

I could barely concentrate on the heist at hand. The Lady Knights were down a person because Lalita had bowed out claiming sudden illness, which was suspicious, but I'd have to think about that later. Blythe had stepped up in a Lady Knight trial by fire, though she had remained at the meeting point with Nori, and while she knew that what we were doing toed the line of respectability—Greer had told her that we were spying on someone—I was certain Blythe suspected there might be more to the story.

We *were* spying on someone . . . the vile viscount who had the power to destroy Bellevue, Little Hands, and Welton. Sister Mary had confided that their next quarterly payment for the lease had tripled, which was astronomical. The portion that the Perkins sisters contributed for Welton would increase as well, and I was guessing they could not afford it, either.

I was certain such an increase had to be against the law somehow, but the nun said the paperwork on the building allowed it. I'd had half a mind to show it to Mama, but I needed more proof first. If we could prove that Viscount Hollis was behind the unlawful rent hikes, perhaps we could have a leg to stand on.

"Maybe he's not going out tonight," Greer said, rubbing at her nose. "Or he's already out and we missed him."

I let out a breath. "I think we should go in there."

"Into his house?" Greer whispered, eyes rounding.

"I'm tired of waiting," I said. Besides, Rafi wasn't at home with his uncle. He was out with Keston, Blake, and Ansel. It was the perfect time to do some snooping. I inhaled a full breath. "You wait here. If I'm not back in thirty minutes, fetch Rafi. He's at White's with my brother. He'll know what to do."

Greer shot me a worried look. "Zia, I don't like this, especially you going in there alone."

"I can always pretend I was trying to find Rafi," I said with a jovial toss of my head that hid my nerves. "A ruined reputation is better than being tossed into jail, no?"

"This is no time for jokes!"

"Who's joking? The church, Little Hands, and Welton are in trouble." My fingers fisted the reins when the horse shifted nervously beneath me, as if sensing my emotions.

"I don't like it," she repeated stubbornly.

I dismounted. "Thirty minutes. I promise I'll be careful."

Before she could protest, I hurried away. My body was trembling with apprehension as I crossed the street from the park where we had hidden. The residence was dark but for the glow of soft light on the ground floor, which meant that most of the servants might already be abed. A tiny voice inside warned that unlawfully entering someone's home was very different from robbing my brother's friends, but I shrugged it off as I slunk around the side. Maybe a kitchen door would be unlocked.

But before I could move, a voice filtered through an open window farther back, and I froze to flatten myself against the wall. It was nasally and very recognizable. Damn and blast, the viscount was at home! My heart raced at the fact, at how close I could have come to being caught red-handed. Then my ears pricked up at the sound of "Bellevue" and "Welton," and despite the urge to flee, I crept closer.

"I don't care that those pesky women are making trouble, Atkins," the viscount growled. "I need them out and that tenement condemned."

Atkins? Who was that? What pesky women? I was sure I'd heard him say *Welton* a few seconds earlier. Was he talking about Sister Mary or the Perkins sisters? I pressed closer, sucking in a sharp breath when my boot snapped a twig, but when no one stuck their head out the window to investigate, I exhaled.

"The church hasn't defaulted on their payments yet. Out of the blue, they were able to settle their accounts. And the women managing Welton are protecting their school," the man called Atkins replied. Pride filled me at that—we had achieved something monumental. "They have influential parents and donors on their side. Frankly, it looks bad that you're trying to demolish a church, Hollis."

"This deal will be lucrative for all of us. The gaming hell cannot fall through, and the banks won't wait." The viscount swore viciously, making me flinch. "If that boy won't come to heel with his inheritance, we need to move quicker. Just get them out, no matter what it takes."

"We have to abide by the law here," Atkins said. "They're not defaulting on payments as you expected. You have no grounds."

A sound like a fist slamming into a piece of furniture ensued. "Then we have to find a way to make them. Anything to get them out! I swear, hysteria is brewing in that school. The youngest of the sisters is the loudest and vilest. She needs to know her place!"

I stifled a grin and silently pumped my fist in solidarity with Miss Perkins, who I knew would do everything to fight for Welton and her students. Though I wanted to learn more, I didn't dare risk staying any longer, and I scurried back to where Greer was waiting across the way.

"What happened?" she asked me.

"Hollis was at home," I panted, trying to catch my breath.

"Did he see you?" Greer asked in horror, her stare instantly tracking me for injury.

I shook my head and mounted my waiting horse. "No, I overheard him talking to someone called Atkins about how frustrated he is because Sister Mary paid her bills. He's furious."

"What does that mean?" Greer asked.

I grinned. "That our plan is working."

Rafi stood in front of an easel with a painting that he was putting the finishing touches on. In the past week and a half, his studio in Covent Garden had become a secret rendezvous for both of us, even though it was risky. Gemma accompanied me for propriety's sake, but she usually sat in the front parlor doing needlework. There was also a pianoforte so I could practice my music, and I enjoyed watching him paint.

I was burning to ask whether he knew about his uncle's gaming hell plans for the Welton property . . . and what the viscount had meant about Rafi not coming to heel with his inheritance. I knew Rafi was wealthy from his mother, and from what I'd overheard, it sounded like if the banks ultimately decided not to fund Hollis's gaming project, Rafi would become his coin purse. But Rafi wouldn't kick out a bunch of orphans and destroy a school for the sake of his birthright, would he?

Then again, capitalist logic was a monster in itself. And to be fair, he'd promised his mother. . . .

"What made you decide to become an artist?" I asked instead, biting into a pear that sat on a table beside me, the very one he was painting. "Did you wake up one day and think, that looks like fun!"

"No, not exactly." He glanced up and scrubbed a thumb over

his chin, leaving a streak of white paint behind. "I was visiting my mother and her new husband, and the art in the palace was like nothing I'd ever seen before. The colors were so vibrant, the textures so realistic. I would spend hours in the gallery, seeing something different each time." He shrugged. "I wanted to produce something like that, and my mother was permitted by the shah to indulge me with lessons from the royal artist."

"What was it like," I asked, curious about his eastern family. "Meeting and getting to know your stepfather? Do you have brothers and sisters?"

"A brief acknowledgment and dismissal can hardly constitute getting to know him. I have over one hundred stepsiblings." At my look, he sighed. "In addition to his four wives, including my mother, he also has hundreds of concubines. I'm my mother's only child, however."

"Good gracious, he must have been busy." My eyes widened. "And exhausted."

Rafi stared at me before bursting into laughter, his eyes sparkling. I joined him, nearly choking on my pear as I convulsed with chortles. When we'd calmed, he peered at me over the top of the canvas, his eyes drawn to the half-eaten pear. "I did not give you leave to eat my chosen subject, my lady."

Grinning audaciously, I took another bite, feeling juice run down my chin as well as the press of his stare tracking the movement before I wiped it with my sleeve like an absolute boor. That was another thing I loved about being here in Rafi's studio. There were no rules, no disparaging stares, no judgment. "You were done with it, and I was hungry," I said. "May I see the final product?"

He lifted the canvas and flipped it. The painting was so lifelike it looked like it was popping off the background. Various hues of green and chartreuse shimmered off the pear's skin, making my mouth water even though I held the actual subject in my palm, but it was so real that I could have reached out and plucked it off the page. I could almost taste it. That was a testament to the artist that his work was so evocative.

Rafi's talent was astounding, but his arrogance was not, so I schooled my features into a neutral expression. "It's satisfactory," I told him with a sniff.

His jaw dropped in fake outrage. "You're a hard one to please," he said, and shook his head with a grin as he replaced the canvas, knowing I was teasing him. I never gave him my true opinions, though sometimes I could not hide my awe at his talent. He was that good . . . and he knew it. "*Satisfactory,* she says. What on earth must I do to earn your heartfelt favor, my lady? Paint something comparable to Michelangelo's *The Creation of Adam*? Bleed onto my canvas? How shall I astound you?"

"You could paint me," I blurted before I could stop myself, cheeks on fire at my boldness, but it was out there now, landing with the subtlety of a bomb. "Like that girl you had in here a fortnight ago."

Rafi went still, eyes fastened to me. "That would not be proper," he said quickly, resuming his brushstrokes, though the painting was already perfect in my opinion. He was a bit of a perfectionist when it came to his art, as though getting it right was deeply personal. It was yet another anomaly. The Rafi everyone saw didn't care about anything, or at least, he pretended not to.

"Why?" I demanded.

His brows rose. "You are a lady, Zia. Some rules are simply unbreakable. Your reputation is important."

I scoffed. "As if me being here, *alone, unmarried,* and practically *unchaperoned* in your presence isn't ruinous enough. That ship has long sailed, Mr. Nasser." I wasn't jesting— notwithstanding Gemma's presence, if we were to be caught, my reputation would suffer. And the ensuing gossip would fuel the *ton* for the entire season!

"Rafi," he murmured, reminding me of our agreement to be less formal with each other when we were outside the public eye. That intense gray stare lifted once more, pinning me like a butterfly against the velvet back of the chaise that I was propped upon. "I don't think you know what you're asking. You do realize she was disrobed."

My mouth dried as I picked at a piece of imaginary lint from my skirts. "I am aware. Perhaps not as en déshabillé as she was, but I wish to be"—I cleared my throat—"your subject."

The words felt racier than I'd meant them and made me squirm in my seat, but I refused to drop my gaze. I was not this forward when it came to getting what I wanted, but I desperately desired him to paint me. Like the pear, I wanted to see myself through *his* eyes. I was inordinately and suddenly obsessed with the idea of Rafi as the creator and me as the creation.

It was untoward, of course, what I was asking, but I was sick of everything being perfectly mapped out for me, including the marriage I was supposed to be securing. The intimacy of it was much too appealing to be eclipsed by something as pedestrian as decorum. I supposed it was a form of reinvention—portraiture through the artist's eyes. Or perhaps it was that the press of those very eyes on me made me extraordinarily unsteady.

"I want you to," I said firmly. "Paint me, unless of course *you* are too worried about propriety." Rafi didn't answer my jab, but he did switch out canvases for a fresh one. I panicked when he prowled toward me, my breath catching in my throat, pulse flying high. I instantly lost my bluster. "Wait. I didn't mean right *now*!"

"No time like the present." His voice was taunting as though he expected me to retract my request, payback for suggesting he might be caught up with modesty. That slightly cocky beat of challenge had my spine stiffening. "Do you want to change your mind?"

"No," I said in a breathy voice when he stopped short of the chaise longue.

"May I adjust you?" he asked politely as if he were asking me for a dance, but this wasn't a simple dance or even a waltz. This was rather much more intimate. Scandalous, truly. I should have been clutching my imaginary pearls. And yet, I'd never felt more alive. Skin prickling, my breaths went shallow as I gave a tiny nod. "I need words, Zia."

"Yes," I practically squeaked.

His eyes did not leave mine as his hand descended, and I sucked in a sharp breath. He touched my knee, and it was all I could do to stop from bursting into flames at the point of contact even through layers of silk. "Legs, here." He seemed completely unbothered, squinting critically as I did as he'd ordered. "Shoes and stockings off, I think. Is that acceptable?" The rasp in his voice had my blood rushing through my veins as though he wasn't as unaffected as he seemed.

Thankfully, he didn't intend to perform the task for me, or I might have expired on the spot. The idea of him watching me was enough to give a girl conniptions. Not enough to stop, however. Boldly, I kicked off my shoes one by one, but not so brazenly, I dropped my stare. Reaching down with trembling fingers, I loosened the ribbons above my knees and quickly rolled down the stockings, pulling them off before arranging my skirts back into position.

When I finally managed to meet his eyes, his cheekbones were flushed a dull red, and I couldn't help myself even though I'd learned that taunting Rafi never went unanswered. "You're blushing, sir. Were you this embarrassed with the other model?"

That smirk appeared for a half second. "She wasn't you. My best friend's bratty little sister."

The tingles that followed the first part of his reply disappeared immediately with the second. Keston would bloody murder me. Murder us both. Which was why I'd been avoiding him like the plague. Ela had let slip that she'd conveniently lost the newssheets from that day—for which I was grateful—but had told me in no uncertain terms that Rafi and I needed to come clean to Keston before he found out. I pushed the thought of my brother from my mind. This had nothing to do with him, and everything to do with me. Being here was *my* choice. Asking Rafi to paint me was *my* choice. Undressing was *my* choice.

"She was a woman, no?" I pointed out, feigning nonchalance with an idle sweep of my palm. "The subject of the flesh is the same. I hardly see how one bodily form or another matters to an artist's eye." I was shamelessly fishing for more. I knew my reasons, but what were *his*?

His scent overwhelmed me when he reached up to loosen the pins holding my hair in place, the copious bronze and brown-gold spirals falling every which way. The ends curled and caught around his fingertips as if they never wanted to let go. In that moment, I knew how they felt. Sliding his fingers through the tight ringlets, he tucked several tendrils away over my shoulders, his stare dropping to my lips for an infinitesimal moment.

"I didn't kiss her, did I?" he said softly.

Ah. The *kiss*. The pivotal moment that had led us both here. Led *me* here. The heartbeats stretched out, each one louder than the last, as I slowly exhaled, my eyes clashing wildly with his. How could gray be so hypnotic? We were so close I could see the silver shards in his irises and the hint of blue at the center. But that wasn't what kept me immobile. One inch more and our lips would rediscover each other.

"Did you like it?" I blurted. "The kiss?" And then I wanted to kick myself for sounding so desperate.

His lips quirked. "What do you think?"

"You haven't mentioned it until now," I said. "Maybe it was the worst kiss you've ever had, and you blocked it from your mind. Maybe you kiss so many girls that you forgot."

"Hardly." Soft laughter left him, his sweet-scented breath gusting over my chin. "I tried to block it from my mind, but only because I couldn't stop thinking about repeating it."

"Oh." I could barely control the flush that rolled through me at the unexpected confession. He wanted to kiss me again?

A finger lifted to brush my cheek. "These freckles are an artist's dream."

I stifled the burst of pleasure at his touch, unconsciously leaning in for more, but then he sat back on his haunches, the sudden loss of him disorienting for a sharp second. I cleared my desert-dry throat and moistened my lips, ignoring the way his gaze darted there. "Is this pose sufficient?" I asked, bringing us back to our task in case I did something absurd like fall off the chaise into his lap and crash my lips to his, giving us what we both clearly craved.

Stop! Focus! None of that!

He sourced a cushion from another chair and directed me to sit up before he placed it at my back. "Prop your back knee up and bring your hem up just to your ankles on your other leg," he said. "One arm up over your head and the other holding the pear to your mouth."

He moved back to the easel, concentration written on his face. "Eyes on me," he said. "Chin slightly up and to the left. Just so. Display that long neck of yours."

"Is it a good neck?" I nearly groaned out loud.

"A very good one, in fact," he replied. "Very sketchable. Very paintable. Very long." He coughed.

Given the number of *very*s in that response, perhaps he was as edgy as I was. Still, the compliment warmed me. He liked my neck. He'd thought about kissing me again. I heard the rasp of pencil over paper as he sketched the outline, and I didn't dare move a muscle.

He let out a sound of amusement after a few minutes when I had an unbearable itch on my arm that was growing by the second and was certain I was sweating from holding it together. "You can relax a bit. I've already drawn the basics."

I scrubbed at the infernal itch. How did artists' models sit for so long? It was definitely a lot harder than it appeared. Perhaps one could meditate. Though my nature was much too impatient for that. And all I could think about was kissing . . . and the fact that he'd thought about it, too.

"What's next?" I asked to distract myself. He'd explained his painting process before, but I wanted him to talk so that I wasn't forced to fill the silence with more nonsense.

"I start with a couple of initial drawings in pencil to get the pose right and then a larger one when I'm satisfied. Then I'll paint a warm sepia imprimatura hue over the sketch. After that, I'll add a color wash and the individual paint colors in the first go."

"And what do I do in the meantime?"

He glanced up as he made wide passes over the canvas, presumably with the sepia hue thing. "Sit there and look pretty."

"You are armed with compliments today."

He stilled, eyes tracking the exposed skin and a muscle flexing to life in his cheek, but kept his voice light. "I thought I'd made it known that I shall throw my lot in with the other witless sycophants. Your beauty outshines the sun. Your smile makes the heavens weep. You are a gift to everyone around you. Your charm is a bounty upon which poets—"

"Stop, stop, that is enough, truly," I said with a giggle at his grandiose statements.

He smirked. "But I'm not finished, oh Diamond."

"Please, I beg of you, desist." I snorted. "Stick with painting."

Our amusement faded as I lay back on the chaise. While Rafi kept working with the occasional glance in my direction, I stared at the ceiling. There was a mural painted upon it, one of wide green meadows and bucolic rolling hills. It looked idyllic and peaceful. I wondered if Rafi had painted it, but the paint was too faded to be recent. It wasn't quite his style, either, the colors much too flat and untextured.

"Do you own this place?" I asked.

"I lease it from a friend," he said. "A mentor of sorts. Why do you ask?"

"I was pondering who painted that mural."

His eyes flicked up. "Not me. It's a little bland for my tastes, though I suppose pastel landscapes are the rage these days." I much preferred the unapologetic boldness of his art. "I enjoy the use of color, as you can tell. Perhaps a smidge too liberally as the owner of this place says."

I wondered whether his mentor was the older artist I'd seen instructing him in this very room. It was incongruous, really, how much common ground we had between us. He, too, sought instruction from someone who might not be approved by the *ton* and who viewed the world with discerning eyes. I wanted to escape via my music, and he pursued the same via his art. We were both pretending to be people we were not in public, living in skins that didn't quite fit as they should.

"Rafi," I asked, peeking at him. "If you could be anyone else living anywhere in this world but here, where would you be?"

"It's probably a cliché, but I'd be a painter in Paris," he said without hesitation. "Montmartre, specifically. You?"

"Perhaps Venice or Vienna," I said softly. "Or even Paris as well. I'm fascinated with the French musicians of the Baroque period. I'd play my music in theaters in front of hundreds."

He smiled. "Wouldn't it be grand if we journeyed to Paris?"

I kept my mouth shut, imagining the two of us living our best lives and following our dreams in peace, without the weight of expectation and duty hanging over our heads. Other images ensued, memories of that kiss that made my skin heat and my body warm, followed by fantasies of us living together as a true couple that made my breath hitch.

Racy thoughts aside, what would life with Rafi be like, if he was in his element? Seeing him like this all the time? Unguarded. *Happy.* Would I be the same? I couldn't quite envision myself as simply Zia the musician as opposed to Lady Zenobia, duke's daughter and society heiress, but it was a dream worth savoring for a few seconds.

"Who is your favorite musician?" Rafi asked, drawing me out of my reveries.

I thought for a moment. "Vivaldi, probably, which is why I said Venice or Vienna. He was born in Italy but died in Austria.

His music is so wild and arresting, you can't help but feel like you're being caught up in the middle of a fierce thunderstorm. The way he viewed the world was unique. He's best known for the violin, and also the cello as a solo instrument, but I like transcribing his compositions to the piano."

Rafi's lip was caught between his teeth in concentration, but he glanced over at me. "I've heard you play. You're undoubtedly talented, but even that is ambitious. His transitions are absurdly fast, I mean," he added when he saw that he'd caused affront. "Not that it's ambitious for *you*. Just in general." He closed his eyes. "I'm bungling my words."

"Don't worry about it," I said, wondering if he would think the same if he heard me play in my own singular style or if he would be like everyone else, wanting the overly ornamental and overdone compositions of current musicians. My ambition when it came to music had no boundaries.

"You should play," he said.

I frowned and sat up from my reclining position. "What about the painting?"

"I've practically memorized all of you," he explained, and then flushed as if he hadn't meant to admit that. My heart skipped a slow beat when our gazes collided. "I mean I have what I need to finish," he said, and pointed at the instrument. "Now go. Perhaps it will add more dimension to my piece. I've always said art and music go hand in hand. Both forms of expression filtered through the hands of the creator."

He waggled his fingers around his brush for emphasis, while I clenched mine in my lap.

"I can't," I said. "I don't have music with me."

"I've seen you play without sheet music before. What about the Vivaldi transposition you were mentioning before? Come on, Firefly, don't leave me in suspense." He eyed me with just enough provocative arrogance to have my spine straightening. "Or was I right in saying how ambitious it was?"

It was uncanny how he knew exactly how to get a rise out of me. In truth, my competitive streak would probably be my downfall one day. But not today. With a huff, I stood and walked over to the covered instrument and gently unveiled it. My breath caught. It was a gorgeous walnut Conrad Graf fortepiano, per the paper label above the keys. I recognized it instantly because we had one at our home in Berkshire and in my studio. What would something like this be doing here?

Pianists like Beethoven and Schubert played on Graf's instruments. I ran my fingers lovingly over the black and white keys. The piano was expensive and well loved, but if it had been sitting in disuse, it would not be playable. I pressed the C note, and it rang clear. Then I played the chord, which did the same. The notes fell over me like sunshine.

"Do you have a screw or two around here?" I asked Rafi, looking over my shoulder. "And might I have a piece of paper?"

He frowned. "Whatever for?"

Oh, he was in for the full musical extravaganza of Zia Osborn. I'd only ever kept my playing traditional for fear of what others might think. "You'll see. Now, hand them over."

Although skeptical, he dug into a nearby box to provide

two mismatched screws before tearing a piece of paper from a sketch pad and handing it to me. I made my way over to him and perused his desk to see if there was anything else I could use. The thing about this special style was that it never sounded the same. The shape and weight of the items used were different each time, and that impacted how they interacted with the piano strings. And it took patience and preparation. But Rafi painted in silence while I got the pianoforte ready.

I could sense his curiosity, but he was more than familiar with the creative process. In fact, I'd watched him cycle through some truly bizarre actions—like stretching and calisthenics—before facing the easel. Creative types were peculiar. Once I was satisfied that the instrument was prepared, I sat on the stool and ran my fingers through a quick exercise before breaking into an arrangement of Vivaldi's *Four Seasons* "Summer."

Each time the hammer hit the lower register strings that had the screws attached to them, it rang with an unusual discordance one would never expect from a piano. It was undoubtedly an interruption, but it did something special to the piece, adding an element of menace to the already-sharp melody. On the upper register, the weight of the paper was less obvious, but it still added a layer of subtle complexity.

I could feel Rafi's eyes on me when I stood and used the end of one of his paintbrushes to span some of the strings as one would a guitar, then continued the measure smoothly. When I was finished, I was afraid to look at him.

Slow clapping made me turn. "Consider me corrected," he said. "That was like nothing I have ever heard before."

"Is that good?" I asked, covering up the instrument and returning to the chaise.

"Zia," he said, awe written all over him. "Like you, it was one of a kind."

CHAPTER
SIXTEEN

The mind will ever be unstable that has only prejudices to
rest on, and the current will run with destructive fury when
there are no barriers to break its force.

—MARY WOLLSTONECRAFT

Scanning the guests at the ball as Rafi and I danced again, I saw
my father's pleased expression. Viscount Hollis was also present,
and the sight of him made my blood boil. I wanted to kick the
man in the shins for suppressing his nephew's innate and incom-
parable talent.

Rafi had finished the painting of me, and true to form, I
had been shocked at the beauty, texture, and depth of the final
composition. I could hardly believe that I was the same girl lying
back on that chaise longue. He had captured my soul, it seemed,
from the dreamy expression in my eyes to the stubborn tilt of my
chin, and the relaxed nature of my limbs, as though every inch of
them had felt safe to be slack and soft. Even the half-eaten pear
had taken on a life of its own, the white insides gently discoloring

as if my attention had been stolen elsewhere by something much more enticing. It was incongruous to me that a painter could glean so much, but Rafi had, and for the first time in a very long time, I felt seen.

"What are you thinking?" Rafi asked. "I can see the gears in that brain of yours running a mile a minute."

"Just how terrible a painter you are and what a categorical waste of time that sitting was," I teased. His eyes lit with gray fire, that sultry smirk tipping one side of his lips upward.

"So hard to please."

I lifted a cool brow. "Only for some. There's a secret, you see, to win my eternal affections."

"And what is that?" he asked and twirled me with effortless grace before bringing me back into his body with a quick, breathless snap. "Being an excellent dance partner?"

For a heightened moment, every part of my front had brushed every part of his before settling the requisite distance apart. Or perhaps that had been Rafi. One glance at him staring at me with a wicked expression confirmed my suspicions. He'd done that on purpose!

Not that I was complaining.

Any excuse to touch him seemed to be my desire these days. And it seemed as though he enjoyed it as much as I did. Being with Rafi was a delicious kind of torture. I saw glimpses of his true self while he painted, and yet I'd only scratched the surface. I wanted to decode the mystery that was Rafi Nasser, peel him apart layer by intricate layer until all his secrets were mine.

"No," I told him, relishing the flex of his fingers at my waist and the five heated points of contact. "But I will admit that it's definitely an advantage."

"Someone who laughs at your jokes, then?"

"I am rather funny." I wrinkled my nose as we crossed forearms and spun around each other. "But no. Try again."

He let out a sigh. "I give up. This is much too difficult."

"One simple challenge and he folds like a wheat stalk in the wind. One small trial of the mind and he concedes at the smallest resistance. No stamina at all."

"Must you be so vexing?" he demanded, though there was no heat in his voice, only lighthearted amusement. "And, Firefly, make no bones about it, I have stamina."

My blood heating at the riposte, I pursed my lips. "You know, I've heard talk about you, all boasts and so very little action."

A bark of wicked laughter left him, and I felt almost giddy with delight, despite being much too audacious with my innuendo. "Is that a fact?" His hands punctuated those words with a tightened grip on my waist, pulling me indecently closer into his hips.

"You are abominable, sir," I said with mild outrage as I breathlessly reinstated the requisite twelve inches between us, though inside I was slowly incinerating.

"What?" he asked with mock innocence, but I was rather used to that too-guileless expression of his that promised untold mischief.

I glowered at him. "You know exactly what. My brother is here somewhere."

On the next turn, I caught sight of Ela exiting the refreshments room, and she stopped in her tracks to stare before glancing behind her, presumably for her fiancé. My stomach swooped uneasily. Rafi and I were playing with fire by not telling him, and we weren't exactly subtle with multiple dances. While my parents might be accepting of our courtship, Keston was an unknown.

He was protective of me, even with his mates. That was part of the reason I was reluctant to tell him. I didn't want to come between him and Rafi, but I also didn't want him to forbid us from seeing each other. I refused to choose.

"We should talk to Keston," I said with a gulp.

Rafi nodded. "I think so, too."

It bothered me the way people saw Rafi, even my brother. Though I'd witnessed his shameless flirting myself in the past, I couldn't think back to the last time he'd actively solicited the attention of other ladies. At least, not since . . . me.

"Tell me something," I asked him. "Why the pretense to always be someone you're not? Or make people believe you're one way?"

That mask of his immediately descended, his playfulness vanishing. "Who says it's false?"

"I do," I replied, staring him down.

"Very well, be relentlessly annoying," he said. "It's quite easy. People don't expect much from you other than a laugh and a good time."

"But you're so much more than that."

"I'm glad you think so, Miss I-Must-Fix-Everyone, but I like my life the way it is." Something about the way he said it made me look up at him. *Really* look at him, past that ever-present smirk, past the sardonic expression, past the cavalier lilt in his voice.

"Do you, though? Do you like hiding what you love? Who you truly are?" I whispered. "Rafi, you're so talented. People would love your art, if you only cared to let them see. Isn't that what art is about? Sharing it with others?"

He eyed me, brow arching. "Is that what you're doing? Sharing your music?"

"That's different."

"It's really not."

Rafi wasn't wrong; I was just not ready. My music was intensely personal. Daughters of dukes weren't composers, at least not in England. Only a few years ago, I'd read about a German princess, Amalie of Saxony, who composed operas to Italian libretti, and she had given me hope. But my kind of music was beyond what was considered acceptable, even for nonaristocratic male composers. It was too different . . . too bold.

I'd let Rafi hear it because he'd shared his passion with me. I'd shared it with Miss Perkins and the other girls because there was a circle of understood trust, especially given the nature of Miss Perkins's unconventional instruction.

But everyone else? The *ton*? My *papa*?

No, thank you.

I cleared my throat as the last strains of music ended. "Fine, your point is valid. Escort me to my friends, if you please."

"Tell me what the secret to your affection is first."

I should have known he wouldn't let that go so easily. Raising my brows at the overt command in his tone, I whirled out of his arms and glanced over my shoulder as I strolled insouciantly away. "If you truly want to know, I've no doubt you'll discover it on your own. You're a determined fellow. Thank you for the dance, Mr. Nasser."

My heart unexpectedly buoyant, I walked over to where Lalita and Greer stood. "Well, that looked cozy," the latter said with a lascivious smile. "So, things are progressing between the two of you?"

Lalita wrinkled her nose with a perplexed expression. "I still can't see it. Rafi Nasser, the worst rogue in London, settling down?"

"He's not like that," I said too quickly, making both of their inquisitive stares converge on me. They didn't know him . . . or that the whole rake thing was a performance. It was easy to keep people at arm's length and from probing too deeply when they thought you a frivolous, charming scoundrel. "Where's Nori?" I asked.

"She's dancing with Blythe," Greer replied. "Those two have been as thick as thieves, like you and Mr. Nasser. The Lady Knights are falling apart," she grumbled theatrically. "We haven't attempted a proper heist in weeks or done anything to horrify and smash the patriarchy."

"We are not falling apart," I said, though guilt sluiced through me at the fact that apart from the failed incident at Viscount Hollis's residence, I'd been spending more time with Rafi and neglecting my friends. Or the Lady Knights.

"I heard that Bellevue is going up for auction in a month,"

Lalita said. "The whole building block, including Little Hands and Welton."

I gasped in shock. "Since when?"

Greer growled through her teeth. "Since the piece-of-horseshit owner realized that Sister Mary was suddenly able to pay their bills and he wasn't going to oust them naturally for the sale. So he raised the rent by an exorbitant amount and initiated legal proceedings to get a writ of possession."

I frowned. "What's that?"

Lalita's face tightened. "According to Nori, her father said it's a legal document that would give the landowner rights to the property."

My stomach dipped. I recalled the conversation I'd overheard under Viscount Hollis's window. Was that what Atkins had done? Had he and the viscount made some sort of legal threat while convincing the owner to increase the rent to make it unaffordable? They had no grounds for eviction, but clearly, they'd found a loophole.

"Can he do that?" I asked.

"No idea," Greer said.

God, an auction! We would never be able to pull together the kind of money required to buy an entire property housing a school, church, and attached orphanage. I racked my brain, trying to come up with a solution, but nothing came to mind. Nothing short of robbing a bank. But that was a far step from pilfering our friends' bottomless pockets or fleecing a selfish, undeserving peer to serve the poor.

Could Rafi help us? He was wealthy enough to buy it single-handedly, but why would he? It wasn't his problem. Maybe there was a way we could get our friends together and collectively come up with a solution. But we'd need a plan soon, or everything we'd risked life and limb for would be in vain.

"I bet Sarah could help," Lalita said, and I swung around, convinced I'd heard her incorrectly.

"Sarah . . . Peabody?" Greer scoffed as I pierced Lalita with a sharp frown.

Her brown cheeks went ruddy while she chewed her lip, avoiding both our stares. A sour feeling spread in my stomach. "I might have told her about the Lady Knights and what we fight for."

"Lalita!" Greer and I said in unison.

"What?" she said defensively. "She wants to be a part of it. Aren't we always saying that the more help we have, the better it is?" Her expression went mutinous. "And besides, why does Nori get to have Blythe, but I can't have Sarah? Everyone's paired off but me. It's not fair."

"No one *has* anyone, Lalita, and we're hardly paired off," Greer said with a sniff. "Nori and Blythe are, well, that's not any of our business. But we have always been in this together. Blythe saved our skins at the gaming hell. She saw us and chose to help us at risk to her own safety and reputation. She didn't have to do that. She could have left Zia and me high and dry, and then where would we be?"

"Sarah can be trusted!" Lalita insisted. "You don't know her."

I couldn't control the slight sneer that distorted my lips, though my heart ached as if I'd been punched right in the chest.

I kept my fingers balled into fists so I didn't rub at the intangible bruise there. "And you do?"

Brown eyes bored into mine, my friend's face falling like she, too, could feel whatever the widening gap between us was. "I do now. More than you do anyway."

Ouch. My mother had always told me that I couldn't control other people's actions; I could only control my own. I would not take responsibility for Lalita's choices, but I could acknowledge that I'd been too wrapped up in other things to notice that my friend had been pulling away.

"Lalita, you know that we have to make collective decisions when it comes to the Lady Knights," I said carefully. "You were the one who wanted to trial Blythe in the first place, and she only volunteered for the last outing because you were unwell." I tried not to let my skepticism regarding her purported illness show. "It puts everyone in danger if what we are doing gets out. People would not understand."

Her lips set into a recalcitrant line. "I told you. Sarah's on our side."

"Sarah Peabody doesn't care about anyone but herself," Greer said. "Or she pretends that she does so everyone thinks she's a pious little do-gooder, when the truth is, she'd never stick her neck out for anyone. When put to the test, her word is weak. If it had been her instead of Blythe, we would have been up the creek without a paddle."

Lalita's face crumbled, but she jutted her chin. "You don't know that."

Greer didn't. *I* didn't. But there was a saying that if a person showed you who they were, it would be in your best interests to believe them. Sarah Peabody hadn't earned my trust, and she might have convinced Lalita that her heart was in the right place, but my friend had always been too quick to believe in the best of people. Her soft heart would always be her undoing, but it was also one of the things I loved about her.

"Fine," I said gently. "We'll discuss it with Nori and figure it out."

Greer's expression read as incredulous, but the relief on Lalita's face hit me hard. Worry and guilt twined within me. *Had* the fact that I'd been focused on my own problems pushed Lalita in Sarah's direction? I hadn't forced her to make that choice, but that didn't mean I was entirely blameless. Friendship took effort and communication, and if either of those two failed, someone was bound to get hurt.

A few days later, we'd planned to meet in my carriage house to discuss the very matter and take a vote as to Sarah's presence in the Lady Knights. My gut still churned at the thought of trusting her, but now the cat was well and truly out of the bag. If we didn't let her in, we ran the risk of her ratting us out, and if we did, well then, we would be putting our trust—and reputations—into the hands of someone who hadn't earned it.

"Good God," I heard my father thunder just as I was making my way through the house to the back entrance. "What is the world coming to these days when young ladies disgrace themselves in such a vulgar manner? I knew that bloody school was a mistake!"

At the word *school,* my ears perked up, and I softly reversed my careful footsteps to the cracked door of my father's study. Frowning, I peeked through the narrow sliver to see my parents studying the newssheets spread over his desk. My father's mouth was pulled into a flat line, his blond brows drawn together, and my mother's normally brown complexion was a pale, sallow hue. That alone was enough to make my stomach churn.

"Alexander, you don't know that it's the school," she murmured, but her face belied her calm words. "It simply says that it's a teacher in question."

"One bad apple spoils—" he began, but she cut him off.

"Does not mean anything. The only way we can get to the bottom of it is to ask our daughter."

Was Miss Perkins in trouble? My breath hitched, and I made to move away so I wasn't in their immediate crosshairs but froze as my father's palm slammed onto the surface of the desk. "Zenobia will not be exposed to a"—he glanced down at the papers—"'hysterical nervous condition and an imbalance of humors, causing young women to abandon all decorum.' That's what the reporters are calling it—*hysteria.*"

I blinked. Viscount Hollis had used the same term when I'd eavesdropped on his conversation beneath his window. I knew what hysteria was, or at least that it was what the doctors named anything resembling bad, irrational behavior by girls, especially by well-heeled young women, who they claimed sought attention. I rolled my eyes. It was that kind of backward thinking that had led to the Lady Knights in the first place—a silent and secret but active protest of sorts against the idea that girls were somehow more fragile or less resilient than boys.

"It's hardly hysteria," my mother was saying.

My father let out a scoff. "Then what on earth would cause Hollis to make such a claim? It's preposterous, is what it is. Fathers need to take a firm hand with their daughters."

"Do they?" The duchess's tone was mild, but her irritation was clear. "We have always encouraged ours to be an independent thinker. I would hardly expect Zenobia to be some prosaic copy of every other demure, obedient highborn girl." She paused. "After all, you certainly did not marry one."

A faint protest emerged before silence cut him off, followed by the rustling of clothing, and I strained to hear before belatedly realizing what the sudden quiet meant. My father was not a demonstrative man by nature, but I had caught my parents in more than one embrace over my childhood. Mama was his opposite, as hot as he was cold, and frequently had him loosening that rigid spine of his. Dear God, were they . . . *kissing*? I fought back a gag—*who needs to see that?*—and backed away from the study.

I'd get my hands on those newssheets somehow.

I'd known that Viscount Hollis had to be involved. What had he done to poor Miss Perkins? Was he also trying to smear or discredit her?

I hurried through the kitchens to the mews outside and snagged my ever-loyal coachman. "Brennan, I need you to go to Viscount Hollis's residence and deliver an urgent message to Mr. Nasser that I'm requesting his presence at once." I leaned in. "Only Mr. Nasser, you understand." When the boy nodded, I exhaled. "If he's not there, check at White's, but it is imperative that you find him."

"Will do, milady," Brennan said with a bob.

"And if you happen to see today's newssheets in the servants' quarters, will you bring them to me?"

He nodded. "Yes, milady."

The slimy feeling in my belly spread like an oil slick on a wet surface as I hurried to the carriage house where my three friends would hopefully be waiting. None of this boded well for the future of Welton. With the unfortunate timing of Lalita's confidence in Sarah, I found it hard to believe that this wouldn't come back on us somehow. The Lady Knights would be accused of hysteria.

Turned out I didn't have to ask Brennan to find today's newssheets because Greer, her face uncharacteristically ashen, held a neatly rolled bundle when I burst through the carriage house door. "Welton," she announced, hoisting it up, "is royally fluffed."

Nori snorted from where she sat slumped on a chair near the window. "I think you mean another *f* word."

I glanced around the small space, but it was just the three of us. "Where's Lalita?"

"Not here yet," Greer said, and I could hear the note of misgiving in her voice. Was that another sign? The fact that Lalita wasn't here? But before I could dwell on it any further, the door swung open and there she stood, her expression placid as though she wasn't aware of what was happening.

"What's wrong?" she asked, staring at us in turn.

Greer's eyebrows rose. "You haven't seen the newssheets?"

"No," she said with a shake of her head as she removed her cloak. "I slept poorly and did not awaken as early as I normally do. What scandal has happened this time?"

"The newssheets are calling Miss Perkins a heretic, spreading hysteria among us girls," Nori drawled from the corner. "Know anything about that, Lalita?" I sent a glare Nori's way. There was no proof that Lalita was involved or had any role in what had been reported. She was innocent until proven guilty.

"Why would I?" she asked with a frown, amusement fading as she took a few seconds to read the somberness pervading the room.

"Apparently," Greer said, shaking the newspapers, "Miss Perkins is being accused of hysteria, and people, led by Viscount Hollis, are pushing to shut Welton down because the school's students are acting out in indecorous ways."

"What?" Lalita's eyes rounded in genuine shock that couldn't be feigned. I knew my friend, and she wasn't *that* great of an actress.

Greer opened up the newssheets over the table. My eyes caught on the word *hysteria* in bold caps in the headlines, and I fought the urge to roll them—trust some male reporter to start a furor that young ladies of the *ton* were going wild. I scanned the article, which seemed to be written to generate its own hysteria.

Viscount Hollis was, and I quote, "extremely concerned with what was being taught to society's next generation of young ladies." Pah, he was full of hot air . . . hot, gassy air. All that ogre cared about was removing Welton as an obstacle to his plans for razing the buildings for his gaming hell. My stomach fell at the paragraph that claimed a student at Welton had mentioned the existence of a secret, rather untoward book club under Miss Perkins.

Damnation. My fingers clenched at the betrayal. Who would have done such a thing?

"So, if it wasn't any of us who talked to the reporters, then who was it? Do you think it could have been Blythe?" I asked, glancing at Nori.

Nori flew up, her creamy cheeks red with affront. "No, she would never betray us, even if she's not officially one of the Lady Knights yet."

"What about Sarah?" Greer demanded with a vicious glance to Lalita. "She knew about us, didn't she?"

Lalita shook her head. "She wouldn't do that, either."

"And you know her so well?" Nori shot back.

"I do, actually," Lalita ground out in rancor.

"Then can you prove she kept our secret?" Greer asked.

Lalita's mouth fell open. "How would *I* know if Sarah said anything? She promised she wouldn't. And besides, there's no mention of the Lady Knights in the article, only a nameless book club. What about Petal? It could have been her, too." She glared at us in turn. "If you're going to accuse me of something, then do it."

A still-furious Nori pointed at her. "We would be bloody brainless not to make the connection. Sarah Peabody hates us, and Zia in particular."

"Are you calling me stupid?" Lalita demanded, though her voice shook as if she was on the verge of tears.

"If the shoe fits," Nori snapped, fists curling as she stomped closer.

I lifted my hands and got in between them. "Enough! Arguing amongst ourselves serves no purpose, nor does pointing fingers. So, stop this right now. It's not helping." I cleared my throat. "I sent Brennan to fetch Rafi. He helped us that night at the underground fighting club, remember? Perhaps he'll be able to shed some more light on this, and who his uncle's sources are, and then we will address it in a rational, levelheaded fashion."

Because despite society's attempts to pigeonhole us, that was what we were: lucid, sensible, and clever. We would not fall into the trap of preconceived notions, and by God, we would not become the bedeviled, *hysterical* creatures society expected of us.

And we would save Miss Perkins, Beth, and our school, no matter what.

CHAPTER SEVENTEEN

The man who had some virtue whilst he was struggling for
a crown, often becomes a voluptuous tyrant when it graces
his brow.

—Mary Wollstonecraft

Rafi waited until the next afternoon to finally call at my residence. To say the least, seeing him, tousled with that smirk firmly in place, allowed me to inhale the first full breath I'd taken in a day. Thankfully, my father had been busy in Parliament, so he hadn't summoned me, nor had he made any decrees about my future at Welton, despite the fiasco.

Greer, Lalita, Nori, and I were on tenterhooks, but nothing new had been printed in the newssheets—or at least nothing incriminating the Lady Knights. Or perhaps the reporters were waiting to whet the appetites of those waiting for more. The discomfiting sensation in my stomach persisted, however, and I'd tossed and turned throughout night, imagining all sorts of unpleasant scenarios, including being sent away in disgrace as

Ela had once been. Ruination was rarely survivable. Ela had done it, but the odds that all four of us would were next to none.

Once Rafi and I were ensconced in the library—with the doors open, of course, and my lady's maid, Gemma, standing just outside, though she was quite unhappy to do so—I wasted no time in throwing myself into his arms. It was unseemly of me, but I did not care.

"Where were you?" I muttered into his chest, inhaling his scent with a deep sigh before pulling back to punch him in the arm.

He scrubbed a palm over his face. "I am sorry I didn't send word. I saw the newssheets and I spent the entire day trying to figure out what my uncle was up to and what he'd reported to the *Times*. It makes no sense that he would go after a church or a school."

Did Rafi not know? Glancing up at him, I let out a harsh breath. "Rafi, did your uncle ever ask you about going in with him on a venture to build a gaming hell?"

His eyes widened but he nodded slowly. "Yes, a while ago, but the financials did not make sense to me, so I told him it would be a money pit. How do you know about that?"

"The property he intends to buy is where the church is, and the orphanage," I explained. "Where my school is. It's all the same plot of land." I chewed on my lip, choosing my words. "I know you asked me once, and I couldn't tell you, but the money we . . . took was for the orphans, Rafi, to try to save the church from defaulting on their payments. And we were successful! But Lalita said it was going up for auction soon." There was no judgment on his face, only concern. "I think your uncle is purposefully discrediting Miss Perkins because the school is complicating the sale."

"That sounds like something he would do," Rafi said dispassionately. "Welton has a decent reputation, so he has to destroy that first."

"Not many know about our . . . capers or can tie them back to Welton. You, Blythe Danforth, and Sarah Peabody. I trust Sarah the least. Apparently, she has left London with her parents, which is highly suspicious."

I pulled him over to the sofa and sat, gesturing for him to do the same. Though we were both in plain view of Gemma, I shimmied closer to him, wanting to take some comfort in his presence, but reluctant to be too bold. Our hands were nearly touching on the cushion.

"Are you well?" he asked softly. "I'm truly sorry I didn't come sooner."

"I was so worried your uncle had done something, locked you away or forbidden you from seeing me and catching my so-called hysteria."

Thick eyebrows rose over surprised gray eyes. "Nothing could keep me from you, certainly not him."

Heavens, that *voice*. Like smoke and sun-warmed honey. The edge of his smallest finger grazed mine, the point of contact blisteringly hot between us. Where were his gloves? I wondered dimly. Not that I was complaining, far from it. Tingles raced through my blood, firing through my chest and the pit of my stomach, and when he slid his finger alongside mine, the touch was deliberate and provocative in the extreme. Heat whirled through me like a cyclone as my lungs emptied of air, each second of prolonged touch fanning the flames.

"Rafi. What are you doing?" I mumbled, each sip of oxygen a herculean undertaking.

His voice was a rasp. "Nothing. I—"

He cut off with a gulp undulating the lean, bronzed column of his throat, but from the look in his eyes, it was obvious he had something to say. *That* look said that he'd been about to express something monumental.

His fingers were bolder now, sliding maddeningly against mine. It made me entirely too breathless, as if our furtive, forbidden touches might be discovered at any moment. As if my maid would see us and end the delicious torment, but our hands were well and truly hidden between us. Rafi tilted his chin, and I could feel the waft of his breath on my face. It would be so easy to turn my head and close the few short inches between us, my lady's maid be damned. Then my lips could be on his.

My mouth dried with want, every nerve in my body screaming for me to give in, and I fought from squirming in my seat as my muscles tightened with a beating, overwhelming need for more. He twisted his wrist and the backs of his knuckles feathered over mine. It felt illicit, that surreptitious encounter of bare skin upon skin. Everything drilled down to that sublime connection—our heartbeats, our breaths, our mutual desire—and I was enflamed.

I cleared my throat, fighting for clarity in a fog of yearning.

"If, for some reason, word gets out about our escapades, my father will be furious. Even if the Lady Knights were doing it for a good cause, the scandal will be interminable." Feelings instantly cooled, I chewed on the inside of my cheek, worry swamping me. "The timing is strange, especially with your uncle's involvement."

As if sensing my apprehensions going haywire, his fingers moved to slide in between mine, clasping our hot palms together. My breath hitched at the boldness of the action, my gaze darting to the door where my maid was standing. She was focused on the hallway and not on us. My pulse streamed when Rafi squeezed.

He undid me more than any other boy I'd ever met, and while I trusted him, he was also a distraction. I had to stay focused on what was in the wings for the Lady Knights because it wasn't just me at risk of being exposed. . . . If Sarah was behind the article, as I suspected, we would be in a lot of trouble. Forming the whole group had been my idea, so I was responsible.

I could not afford to make mistakes, not now, when our reputations were in danger of being sullied. With effort, I disentangled my fingers from Rafi's, not meeting his eyes, though I could feel his surprise. But I couldn't formulate a logical thought when I was around him, much less when he was touching me.

I stood and walked a few paces away to the bookshelf, thankfully feeling my temperature cool with each step. "What's next?" I asked over my shoulder, proud that my voice was firm. "When you spoke to your uncle, did he mention the Lady Knights?" I asked.

He shook his head. "Not that I heard, but he claimed to have seen letters from the parents of students who weren't happy about the book club."

"Which ones? Did he say?"

"No, but he could be lying. We both know in our world, a peer's word is worth more than any actual proof." Rafi leaned back and placed his arms along the top of the sofa, crossing one booted foot over the opposite knee. He looked like a pasha sitting there, indolent, arrogant, and so gorgeous that my brain gave an indelicate stutter. Why did I get up and walk away again?

Right. Yes, of course. The Lady Knights. Our predicament. Tarnished reputations. Possible incarceration. Expulsion from the echelons of high society. Utter and unequivocal ruination. The warmth in my veins slivered to ice.

"He will stop at nothing to get what he wants," Rafi went on. "Even if it means ruining the livelihood of three pious women, eliminating a school, and displacing dozens of orphans."

"How can he get away with this?" I mused. "Claiming it's hysteria will only cause chaos among the *ton*. Miss Perkins is quite lucid, I assure you."

Rafi leaned forward. "Unfortunately, gossip is a very easy way to sow discontent. Scream that young women are excitable, irrational, and uncontrolled, and every aristocratic male will be up in arms. It doesn't help our cause that it's one of the most commonly diagnosed disorders of our time."

My heart tripped at the way he'd said *our* cause. "It's ridiculous."

His face was solemn. "I don't disagree, but many doctors have used such a diagnosis to commit women to asylums."

The breath rushed out of me as my entire body slumped in cold, horrendous realization. Oh my God, was that what Viscount Hollis intended? To incarcerate Miss Perkins in a mental asylum? I couldn't even imagine the horror of such a thing!

We had to get to Welton.

But of course, we were much too late.

It was a complete witch hunt by the time Rafi had us driven to Welton in his carriage, only to learn that the Perkins sisters weren't there. My brother's coach rolled to a stop behind ours outside the school, and I exhaled a sigh of relief at the sight of him and Ela. I'd sent Brennan to find them, and I was grateful for their presence, even though I'd kept them at a distance lately because of what was going on between Rafi and me.

When one of the servants explained that the missus and her sisters had been taken to Justice Hall in the Old Bailey, I frowned, at a complete loss for words. The Old Bailey? Why on earth would three teachers be taken to a public courthouse that normally dealt with criminal cases like assault and murder? Did the viscount intend to commit all three Perkins sisters on false charges? It seemed preposterous, and yet, I'd seen for myself how the word of a man could be taken for law. Poor Ela's reputation had been ruined just by virtue of a dishonest boy.

As far as I knew, one could not simply turn up to the court-house and demand to be heard, but it would not surprise me if the viscount had contacts in the Old Bailey. It seemed rather extreme, but given what we knew of him and what Rafi had corroborated, Hollis was ruthless. He'd be out to get what he wanted . . . and would employ any means to do so, even if it meant destroying innocent women.

"Let's go," my brother said, sharing a dark look with Rafi. "This will become a spectacle, if your uncle has anything to do with it. Mark my words." Keston glanced at my faithful Brennan, who had accompanied his driver, and beckoned him. "Take one of the horses here and fetch Their Graces the Duke and Duchess of Harbridge at once. My parents are at home and will come. Tell them the Marquess of Ridley requires their assistance posthaste at the Old Bailey and to summon the family barrister. Explain as best as you can."

The suggestion did not sit well with me, considering my father's chilly opinions of the situation, but we could not take on an enraged Viscount Hollis alone. I could only pray that our mother would be able to accompany our father—at least she was a voice of reason.

"Keston," I began, staring at my brother, worried. "He's not going to like this." I swallowed. "The scandal of it, especially."

He nodded. "I know, but he's one of the most powerful peers in England, and he might be a harsh man, but he's just. He will know what to do."

"He hates Welton," I insisted. "This is a bad idea."

Keston shrugged. "It's the only one we have. Unless your

secret suitor has a better one?" He shot us a baleful glare. "Did you think I wouldn't find out?"

Rafi sighed. "Mate."

"Not now, Kes," Ela said, rubbing his arm, for which I was grateful.

"Let's get over to the courthouse," I said, heading for Rafi's carriage.

Utter pandemonium reigned in the street as we arrived at the Justice Hall at the Old Bailey, which sat northwest of Saint Paul's Cathedral and was built beside the ominous brick walls of Newgate Prison. Now, there was a place I didn't wish to ever see the inside of. Though the courthouse had been rebuilt long ago and walls were in place to keep the public out, that didn't mean they could not get in. One could pay a fee to be a spectator in the gallery for cases.

I could already feel the stares flocking to my person as well as my brother's, Rafi's, and Ela's as we swept through the halls. Recognition would be quick to follow, especially considering our well-tailored clothes. We were curiosities as well as potential targets of both thieves outside and journalists inside.

Once we were inside the courthouse, we exchanged heavy glances as the Perkins sisters appeared momentarily before disappearing with several grim-looking gentlemen, one of whom was Viscount Hollis. His hawkish face was wreathed in disgust and disdain, his eyes hard and merciless. He caught sight of his nephew standing beside us and his expression hardened.

"Rafi, you should go," I told him softly. "Don't worry about me. Keston is here."

Instead of agreeing, he pressed closer to my side, his tall frame a solid comfort. "No. I'm not leaving you here to fend him off alone. Either of you."

He'd included my brother at the end for show, but Keston was more than capable of looking after himself, and Ela was here, too.

"Who are those men?" I asked.

"The sheriff and John Atkins," Keston answered.

I gasped. That was the name of the man I'd overheard! "Who is he? Atkins?"

"The Lord Mayor of London," my brother replied.

Oh. That information did not bode well, considering his scheming with the viscount. I glanced at Rafi. "Does your uncle know him?"

"Unfortunately, yes. They knew each other as lads in Kent, and Atkins used to be a shipping merchant with whom my uncle had a very prosperous arrangement. He owned several shipyards on the Thames."

My heart sank. Powerful men would stop at nothing to protect their interests, even at the expense of others. And powerful men allied together were even worse. If Viscount Hollis wanted to bring down Welton on such flimsy charges, he might succeed. And I still didn't know if the Lady Knights would play a part in this debacle.

We stopped in a hallway to wait for my parents, not knowing what we were walking into and not wanting to expose ourselves without them. My anxiety deepened as the minutes went by. Would my father come? He was deeply committed to family, but he hadn't liked Welton from the start, and while he was somewhat progressive in his views, he was still a stickler for propriety and reputation. And he *loathed* scandal with a passion. I feared that we were all about to become embroiled in one no matter how hard we tried to avoid it.

Voices drifted from a side door leading to the courtroom, and I could not help overhearing the current case that was being tried. From what I could gather, the case was about a young man who had been convicted of stealing. My eyes widened when I heard the evidence being presented, and then my stomach dropped. He was being tried for taking a bloody *handkerchief*? I waited breathlessly for the verdict and felt ill when I heard it. The plaintiff was fourteen years old and sentenced to being transported for life.

"Dear God," I whispered. "A handkerchief. Where is he being transported to?"

"Australia most likely," Rafi said grimly.

That was on the other side of the world. Oceans away! Would that happen to me? To Greer, Nori, and Lalita if our crimes under the Lady Knights were discovered? Would we be sentenced to transportation? Or *worse*? Our crimes were much worse than lifting a piece of fabric—we'd stolen hundreds of pounds. It would not matter that our victims had been our family and friends. They would not care that we had delivered all the money to the destitute and starving, and being the daughters of gentry and the peerage would not save us in the eyes of the law.

Panic bubbled up into my throat, and I felt myself breaking out into a sweat.

The next case began, and the sick feeling in my belly only

grew. Before the court stood a woman accused of breaking and entering into a private residence and stealing ten rings and five brooches. It was much too close to what we had stolen—albeit we didn't enter someone's home—but still, the crime was near enough. My breath shortened to shallow pants as I strained to listen to the woman's defense. She claimed someone had dropped the items, and she'd only retrieved them.

Laughter followed, and I waited with bated breath. Would they be lenient because of her sex? Foreboding drummed through my bones. Transportation would be the least of her punishment unless she was found not guilty. Hope was a strange thing when fear was so pervasive that you could barely think beyond it. And still . . . I hoped for her sake. She was only nineteen, not much older than the boy who had gone before.

My knees buckled at the sentence—death.

"Rafi," I bleated in a suffocated whisper. I did not care who was watching—my brother, his fiancée, no one—I grasped his hand, leaned into him, and buried my face into his chest.

"That won't happen," he whispered. Scandal and ruination were the least of my concerns as reality sank in at the cost of my actions. The truth of the Lady Knights could still come out, and if proven guilty, we could be sentenced to *die*.

"What's the matter with her?" I heard my brother ask.

"The verdicts we overheard just then, I suspect," Rafi answered.

"The law is harsh," Keston said.

I clenched my teeth and straightened, my eyes burning with unshed tears. "She stole, but did any of the men in there stop to ask what might have driven her to such a desperate thing? She is just a girl, for God's sake, with her whole life ahead of her."

Keston's eyes narrowed with interest. "You're rather distraught over the fate of a stranger."

"Have you no compassion, Brother?" I asked in a whisper. The Lady Knights had stolen money from him, too. Would his opinion change if he suspected that I was involved? Or if he knew of the intention behind the theft? "The boy before is a child who stole a piece of fabric. That girl is between us in age."

"I suppose they could have been more lenient." He observed me, gaze falling to the hand that remained interlocked with Rafi's, which I instantly released, my cheeks burning.

Ela's stare snapped to mine, and I pinned my lips between my teeth. She wouldn't even have to ask. My feelings were written all over me, and any woman in love would recognize the affliction in another. The sudden realization made my breath stutter and goose bumps break out over my arms. Dear God . . . was I *in love* with Rafi?

No, *no*.

This was simply the usual minor infatuation that had simmered constantly for weeks. Wasn't it? When had I started thinking of Rafi as my rock rather than a pretty face to drool over? When had contentment at the pleasure of his company overcome the feelings of impossible yearning I'd always associated with him? Of course, like any hot-blooded girl, I'd fantasized about a future with him, but now that we'd shared our secrets, our hopes, and our dreams, a future felt . . . tangible. It was no longer merely a semi-besotted fantasy.

Rafi wasn't perfect, but neither was I.

Keston lowered his voice, eyebrows slashing together in sudden brutal understanding. "Exactly how serious is this courtship?"

"We—" Rafi began, but was interrupted by the arrival of my parents.

Thank God. I did not want to have to explain that I was smitten with his best friend, the same man he'd once called a libertine. Neither Ela nor Keston was naïve, but I had more pressing things to worry about. Namely the thunderous expression on the Duke of Harbridge's face as he closed the distance between us.

"What the *devil* is going on here?"

CHAPTER EIGHTEEN

But what a weak barrier is truth when it stands in the way
of an hypothesis!

—Mary Wollstonecraft

The scene in the Lord Mayor of the City of London's private
parlor could have been reflective of a refined, sedate social call in
the middle of Mayfair, though the tensions ran dangerously hot
beneath all the forced politesse. It was because of the arrival of
my father, I knew. The duke's authority made spines snap tight
and chins lower in deference, but it was the presence of the deceptively reserved Duchess of Harbridge at his side that made
dispositions instantly be checked.

Pride sluiced through me. My mother was a force to be reck-
oned with, and everyone in this room knew it, even the Lord
Mayor himself, whose admiration was evident. If there was a
woman who held more sway in her little finger over any man
than a queen of England, it was my mother. Together, my parents

were formidable, but would that might and influence be enough if the truth somehow came out?

That their daughter was nothing but a lowly thief, no matter her motivations?

My stomach roiled, and I could taste the bile in the back of my throat.

Our family barrister and Nori's father, Mr. Kaneko, took his place beside my parents, and the temperature cooled further. I gulped and clasped my hands in front of me, lest I reach for Rafi again in front of others who would not be as discreet as Keston and Ela. I focused on the Perkins sisters, who sat on a sofa in a neat row at the other end. The older sisters looked like mirror images of each other, with pinched lips and wan complexions. Miss Perkins, however, still wore her usual calm expression, eyes twinkling with wit and intelligence. She did not seem put out to be here, but I still felt a frisson of guilt.

The duke cleared his throat. "Explain," he commanded in a stern tone to Viscount Hollis. The distaste on my father's face for the man was well hidden, but I still saw it.

"Your Grace," Mr. Atkins interjected, finding his voice and perhaps being insulted that *he* hadn't been asked to explain the situation in his own chambers. "The viscount brings grave accusations against the Welton House School for Elegant Young Ladies, ahem"—a pompous sneer distorted his lips—"for spreading the malady of hysteria."

Instantly, my dislike for the man tripled, both for the sneer, as if it were a crime to have women make a foothold for themselves in a male-dominated world, as well as his accusatory and unfounded words that would no doubt get the attention they sought. Gasps of horror filled the room. There was nothing like the word *hysteria* to provoke fear in the hearts of weak-minded men. Or women, I amended, as my gaze landed on the two older Perkins sisters.

"We've done no such thing!" the eldest protested. "We provide education in gentility, manners, needlework, drawing, music, and religion. I assure you, sirs, our students are pious, *proper* young ladies."

I took the temperature of the room. The men were frowning, their expressions hard and dour. Any misstep in duties, behavior, or modesty by a female in their eyes was a sign of a mental condition that could see a woman locked in an asylum without much cause. Being emotional was a violation. Having an opinion was an offense. Seeking equal treatment was a downright crime. But all of that was blamed upon a woman's courses and her biological susceptibilities. Hysteria was also known as the "daughter's disease." As if intelligence or self-esteem were an illness. A snort left me, and my father's glacial blue eyes rested upon me for a moment.

"That school is a disgrace and should be shut down at once," Viscount Hollis said loudly. "These women must be questioned and charged for taking such risks with our daughters."

Several of the men including the Lord Mayor and the sheriff had daughters. Presumably ones attending finishing school. Sure enough, their faces reflected their disdain.

"Do you have any proof of this other than hearsay?" my mother asked calmly. The viscount's beady gaze slid to her as if she were a gnat who shouldn't have spoken—his biases were very clear in that one look—but he would not dare offend my father.

"My own fair judgment is proof enough, Your Grace," he said in an oily voice. "As an upstanding member of society, it's my duty to call out a danger to our precious children."

I wanted to vomit at his supercilious tone. "Because you attended Welton or have a daughter who is a student there?" I remarked, drawing attention from all corners that I suddenly wished I hadn't.

"Are you condoning such behavior, Lady Zenobia?" Viscount Hollis asked like a cobra about to strike. The tone of his voice suggested that I had some vested interest here, or perhaps I carried some guilt myself—which I did, but my deepest secrets did not have anything to do with his witch hunt. I would do whatever it took to protect my friends, should anything come to light about our now-regrettable activities. "Don't *you* attend Welton? It is rather . . . curious that you're here. As if you might have something to hide. Some involvement perhaps? It could be that you, too, have been caught by hysteria."

"Have a care, sir," my father said, his voice like pure ice. "Your accusations are in execrable taste, and I'll caution you to mind your tongue. My daughter does not attend Welton as a student. She's interested in particular lessons."

"And what are those, might I ask?" That question came from Mr. Atkins. It was a clever one, if Viscount Hollis's expression was any signal. I could see the interest swirling through their gazes. What kind of instruction would the daughter of a duke require at a finishing school? Unquestionably, she would have had her own tutors and governesses. I was already accomplished, having already come out to society.

"Music. And literature," Miss Perkins answered.

Mr. Atkins pounced. "What kind of literature?"

She hiked her chin, and for once, I wished my teacher wasn't so outspoken. With men like these, prodding their thin-skinned pride was a disaster in the making, but I knew without a doubt that it was what she would do. "Shakespeare. Austen. Wollstonecraft."

"You see?" Hollis roared triumphantly.

The Lord Mayor sputtered. "*Wollstonecraft?* That woman is a vicious harpy with unconventional, dangerous views that go against our great institution. And her daughter is no better with the company that she keeps."

"Poets like Byron?" Miss Perkins replied.

"Political activists!" he said and slammed his hand down on the table before staring at the other two sisters. "What kind of school are you running here?"

"I beg your pardon, Lord Mayor, we had no idea . . . ," the eldest Perkins spluttered in outrage, turning to glare at her youngest sister.

"I was right," Viscount Hollis finished in satisfaction. "Did you know about this, Harbridge? That they're purposefully infecting their young minds with such devilish propaganda?"

My mother lifted a cool hand. "Exactly what is the crime being discussed here?" she asked. "One of reading? Regardless of whether those writers are political, surely we can judge for ourselves what is right and what is wrong. On that note, Mr. Atkins, we all do questionable things from time to time, don't we? When it comes to the matter of opinions, integrity, and even *property,* one could say. You, as well, Viscount Hollis."

Damn. I grinned. My mother was literally a take-no-prisoners goddess. She might have been vague, but everyone here knew what she was alluding to. They were all hypocrites, comfortable on their high horses and with their protected positions, and yet they saw no issue with dehumanizing actual people. Then again, these men viewed their wives as property.

"I beg your pardon?" the viscount demanded, his expression sour as though he'd sucked a particularly bitter lemon.

The duchess smiled gently . . . though anyone with eyes could see that that soft smile had teeth. "I'm simply stating that no one is free of judgment, are we? And we all strive for the best versions of ourselves, or at least, I hope we do. But I digress. If anyone should have a problem with the literature our children consume, it should be the duke and myself. Not you, Parliament, or anyone here. Or are you insinuating that we are incapable of minding our own house?"

Mr. Atkins went beet red. "Of course not, Your Grace, but we must be diligent. In truth, we have already received a serious complaint about this school and the materials discussed."

Here it was. My heart wavered in my chest. Who would—

"A Mr. and Mrs. Peabody have withdrawn their daughter from Welton House on the grounds of discussion about a gothic horror being unsuitable for their daughter's gentle nature."

My jaw ached from grinding it. I knew it had to be her!

"What book are you referring to?" my father demanded.

"Frankenstein; or, The Modern Prometheus," Mr. Atkins read off a sheet on the table. "An absolutely reprehensible piece of claptrap. Viscount Hollis is correct to be concerned. We can all see what's happening here. Hysteria is the least of our fears if our young women's good virtues are exposed to such violent delusions." I almost snorted. What did reading a gothic novel have to do with a girl's virtue? The two were hardly related, and yet, these men were all nodding like they'd solved the worst kind of crime. He scowled at the Perkins sisters. "Have you anything to say for yourselves?"

"We had no knowledge of this, Mr. Atkins," Mrs. Perkins said with pursed lips. The sisters stood and sneered down at the youngest Perkins. "I assure you we are as horrified as you are. Our sister is a disgrace, and we shall cast her out at once. We implore you to charge her with whatever punishment you deem fit."

"No!" I shouted. "It's not her fault. I do not suffer from any such affliction, nor am I in danger of losing my virtue. Miss Perkins deserves no punishment."

"Zia," Rafi warned quietly.

"Ah, yes, the prodigal daughter speaks again," the odious viscount drawled. "One who frequents gambling hells in secret."

What? How did he know that? My brain was racing. Both my parents' eyes were fastened to me, and I could feel the shock in my father's gaze. He might not care what I read, but he would certainly care about my whereabouts, especially to a gambling den.

"Zenobia?" he asked.

Lie, Zia, lie.

But when I opened my mouth, a heartfelt denial wasn't the thing to emerge. The cocktail of emotions that barreled through me left no room for anything but truth, the words emerging like acid. "Papa, I can explain."

The room erupted with exclamations of "See! It's hysteria! Without a doubt!" "The daughter of a duke being so scandalous!" "A diamond of the season? More like a lump of coal."

Viscount Hollis bared his teeth in triumph. "Nephew, you were at Danforth's. Tell me, do you recognize the girl who stands beside you? I do recall being fleeced of my belongings that evening. And didn't you say you lost your ring as well?"

Rafi bristled beside me, but his voice was mild. "We both know that you were in your cups, Uncle. As was I, admittedly, after a rowdy night at the tables. As far as my ring"—he lifted his palm and removed his glove—"it is quite safe on my finger. I won't lie to support whatever vendetta you wish to pursue here."

"You sodding ingrate!" the viscount spat. "How dare you?"

Ignoring his relative, Rafi turned to the Lord Mayor and to my parents. "Mr. Atkins, Your Graces, it is true that Lady Zia was at Danforth's."

My heart sank as my father's eyes went glacial, and the disappointment in my mother's was too much to bear. What was Rafi *doing,* outing me like this? Had I imagined that he'd even cared about me, or had that been a lie all along?

"What the hell were you thinking?" Keston hissed.

Rafi canted his head, his gaze sliding to my brother's for a brief but meaningful second. "Regrettably, it was all part of a dare, tasteless though it might have been in hindsight."

"You took my daughter to a gaming hell?" my father seethed.

My mouth dried as my gaze flew up to Rafi's, but the only sign of emotion was the muscle that flexed in his jaw.

He nodded.

"This is what I was worried about, Zia. My friend doesn't know when to take life seriously," Keston seethed, his expression hard.

Rafi stiffened, but this was my mess. But before I could open my mouth to tell the truth, Mr. Atkins rapped his knuckles on the table. "That is all well and good. But aside from the secret book club, let's discuss this *other* secret society. What are they called? Yes, these Lady Knights. Are they a vigilante group started at that school by that very so-called teacher? What say you, Miss Perkins? Do you deny encouraging these impressionable young girls to act out?"

Oh, dear God.

My blood chilled to ice in my veins as every eye in the room converged on Miss Perkins, including those of her own sisters, who had already cast her aside like she was the plague. This was going to be a bloodbath with my poor teacher sacrificed for the sake of these men's ruffled pride, misplaced sense of propriety, and greed.

Miss Perkins stood, head high. "I would not call it *acting out*, Mr. Atkins. I simply advocate a way for them to express themselves within a society that tells women that we cannot do anything but simper and sigh or wait to be plucked from boredom by a handsome suitor . . . or left to wither on the vine like unproductive fruit. I am proud of my girls for being so daring."

Viscount Hollis's eyes narrowed. "So, you admit it, then? That you purposefully coerced your charges with your political indoctrination? You wanted them to be . . . *productive*?"

I blinked. He made the last word sound like it was something inherently evil . . . as though she were shaping us to be disruptors. No, Miss Perkins only wanted us to think for ourselves, to step outside the box meant to cage us in. To live authentically. But now the pitchforks were out, and a scapegoat was in sight. Someone had to pay for being so bold as to challenge the status quo.

"Learning *is* political, my lord," Miss Perkins said firmly, unaffected by the viscount's tirade. I could see my mother's interest sharpen as she studied the other woman as though her unflappable courage was admirable. Would my mother intervene? Stop the viscount from whatever personal vendetta he seemed to be on? Nip this whole thing in the bud before any attempt at weeding out the truth became lost in scandal and hearsay?

"Zenobia," my father demanded. "Is this true? Were you involved in these Lady Knights?"

"Yes, but it's not what you think" escaped my lips before I could kick myself for sounding like an imbecile and compounding my own guilt in seven heedless words. Explain what? That the Lady Knights were indeed a proud product of Welton? That I had robbed people, including the viscount, his nephew, *and* my own brother? That I should be on the other side of this parlor wall being tried like a lowly criminal in the courtroom? I swallowed, my throat thickening.

"Zia?" my mother said, but her expression was not condemnatory.

"We . . . no, I mean, it was just me . . . nobody else. I wanted change," I stammered. "The church couldn't pay their lease, and there was an orphanage that needed money for clothes and food. It wasn't all bad, because we only needed to get to three hundred pounds to pay off that debt, and we managed it. Welton is the best thing that ever happened to me." I glanced at my teacher. "Or at least Miss Perkins was."

But my redirection was too late as astonishment bled through the room. Oh, dear God, I was bungling this completely. That was the thing when something became more interesting than the truth. Highborn girls gone wild with hysteria was far more provocative than any precious orphanage in need of saving.

My father appeared to be on the verge of apoplexy, a vein throbbing in his forehead. "You are saying you were part of this *gang*? And don't try to convince me that you acted alone."

"Papa, I . . ." But there was nothing I could say to stop the hurt and betrayal from blooming over his face. I wasn't only part of the Lady Knights. I had *led* them into this, and now here we were. I deserved whatever would come my way.

"It's not a gang, Your Grace," a familiar voice said softly from behind us.

Footsteps echoed through the large but already crowded parlor. With effort, I turned in slow motion, my mouth dropping open in surprise. Why had Greer come? She and the others should not be in this room. I would take the fall, not them. "Greer, no."

"Hysteria!" Viscount Hollis sneered.

"No, my lord. Not at all," Greer said, pulling herself to her full height as Nori, Blythe, and Lalita joined her, the last trying and failing to seem brave. Nori met her father's eyes with her head held high. "Quite the contrary. We were all of perfectly sound mind." Her proud, fierce gaze flicked to me. "But we cannot let an innocent person be blamed and castigated for our choices; not our teacher . . . and certainly not our friend."

I felt my eyes well with tears. God, I was so lucky to have her—*them*—in my corner. They didn't have to do this. They had so much more to lose than me, and yet they had shown up.

"Miss Perkins is not at fault here," I said, turning my beseeching stare to my father. "The whole thing was my idea. She's innocent."

"*Innocent?*" The viscount let out an actual growl. "No matter how much you try to sugarcoat it, *she* is the source of the corruption. The school must be shut down at once!"

"Actions must be taken," the sheriff burst out as everyone stared at the teacher in question. "Someone must be held accountable. We cannot have our young women running around willy-nilly and being encouraged to do God knows what. Vigilantes, you say? Preposterous!" He shook his head in abject disgust.

"It's not like that," I protested, but they did not want to hear any more, the noise in the room rising as they bellowed, poor Miss Perkins firmly in their vicious sights. It would be seconds before the bailiff would be called at this rate. And it would be

Miss Perkins in that trial room, fighting for her life. "You can't do this! She has not done what you're accusing her of!" But my voice went unheard in the melee. Even her sisters threw their own flesh and blood to the wolves, desperate to extricate themselves from blame.

My mother clapped her hands loudly, commanding attention, her mouth pulled into a tight line. "I have heard enough, and so has our family barrister, the Right Honorable Mr. Kaneko. We are leaving, and Miss Perkins will accompany us."

"Your Grace," a purple-faced Mr. Atkins sputtered. "This is highly untoward. This woman has been accused of causing controversy."

Mr. Kaneko stepped forward. "Unless you have empirical evidence that Miss Perkins or these girls were involved in a crime against the viscount's person, or you are certain beyond a shade of any doubt that she is the instigator of an unqualified diagnosis of hysteria, I'm afraid you have nothing but conjecture." He smiled at Nori before he turned to a seething Viscount Hollis. "You may certainly file your grievances, but it will not be this evening, sir."

"This is absurd!" the viscount fumed.

My mother sniffed. "Absurd or not, Viscount Hollis, you may take your accusations up another day, but right now I am taking my family home." The words alone were harmless, but the underlying meaning was not. The Duchess of Harbridge was not a woman to be crossed. She could ruin lives with a cut direct. One word in aristocratic circles, and he would be *persona non grata* and ousted from high society.

"Nephew, with me," Viscount Hollis said with a sharp jerk of his head.

Rafi's spine locked, and he deliberately reached for my hand in front of everyone present. "No, Uncle. I'm with her."

The viscount sneered, gaze sliding to me. "You're siding with this scapegrace and her mouthy mother?"

My father let out a growl, body practically vibrating with rage. "Be very careful, Hollis. That is my wife and daughter you're denigrating. I might be a duke, but I'm not above planting a facer." He turned his acerbic stare to Rafi, his gaze dropping to our linked palms, fire flashing in his gaze. "And *you*. Gaming hells? What's next? Brothels? If you know what's good for you, you'll stay a far step from my daughter."

I gasped as Rafi went rigid. "Papa, wait. You can't!"

My father's jaw locked. "I can, and I will."

CHAPTER
NINETEEN

The man who can be contented to live with a pretty useful companion without a mind . . . has never felt the calm satisfaction that refreshes the parched heart . . . of being beloved by one who could understand him.

—MARY WOLLSTONECRAFT

One might imagine it was a funeral, given all the somber gazes in my father's library. Perhaps it was—the certain demise of Lady Zenobia Osborn. The thunderous expression on the duke's face as he paced a hole in the carpet was responsible for half of it, and nothing seemed to be able to appease him, not even my mother's calming influence. We were waiting for Keston, who had taken a hackney to see Miss Perkins safely home. My friends had followed them in Rafi's carriage, and I'd promised to check in with them later. If I survived, that was. . . . I'd ridden in silence with Ela and my parents, and you could have heard a pin drop in the carriage.

After what seemed like an eternity, when I heard voices in the foyer, I ran out.

"How did it go?" I blurted when I saw my brother removing his outer trappings and handing them to Forsythe. His broad frame blocked the door for a moment, and my heart sank as I took in that he was alone. I'd hoped to see Rafi, too, but certainly, no one would dare disobey the Duke of Harbridge.

Cursing softly as his gloves fell, Keston bent, and the object of my affections appeared behind him. Relief mixed with alarm as I drank Rafi in, wanting nothing more than to hurl myself into his arms, despite my father's decree that he should stay away. Worry won out over the initial burst of joy as he, too, removed his cloak and hat. Goodness, I was happy to see him, but did he intend to stay? Papa was on a rampage and most definitely needed time to calm down.

"Miss Perkins?" I asked again as Keston approached.

"She was as well as could be expected."

I studied his grim expression. "And how was that? Her sisters might cast her out with nothing."

The boys shared a look. "She's safe, though they did."

"Beasts!" I said feelingly, and then my body went cold with apprehension as the consequences sank in. "What will happen to her? She lives at Welton. She'll have nowhere to go. How can she be safe if she's homeless?"

"She has somewhere to stay," Rafi said, walking toward me, gray eyes warm.

"But she has no other family." I blinked in confusion.

Keston clapped his friend on the back to keep him from moving closer to me. "I offered for her to stay here, but she's at his place in Covent Garden until things settle or she finds rooms of her own."

My heart categorically melted. This *boy*. The studio was his most private space in the world, and he'd given it up to help a veritable stranger.

"Where is everyone?" Keston asked, and I jerked a thumb over my shoulder.

"Library."

I waited for Keston to head in that direction, but he wasn't budging. He stared at me, his brown eyes unwavering. "In the Lord Mayor's parlor, they spoke of a vigilante group called the Lady Knights, and Rafi mentioned the name Lady Knight some months ago, from someone who robbed him. The funny thing is, something very similar happened to me by a group of women." He paused, that narrowed gaze pinning me. "You wouldn't happen to know anything about that, would you, Sister dear?"

My face flamed as I gaped like a fish out of water. "Yes! I'm sorry I took money from you to feed hungry orphans!" I blurted, and scrubbed a palm over my cheeks. "Kes, please. We can talk about how awful I am later. Just let me have a few moments with Rafi without Papa running him off."

His gaze hardened at the informal address. *"Rafi?"*

"He's my friend, too," I said softly, knowing Rafi was much more than that. Keston looked like he had a lot more to say—after his declaration at the Old Bailey—but with a frustrated grunt, he turned on his heel and marched out of the foyer.

"Ten minutes, Zia," he tossed over his shoulder.

That would have to be enough. I turned to Rafi, my pulse humming frantically like butterfly wings under my skin. "Why did you come back after what my father said?"

"I told you before, Zia. Nothing and no one can keep me from you." A hand lifted to wrap around the end of one of my curls as he gently tugged, a slight smile curving those perfect lips. "Not even the fearsome Duke of Harbridge."

It was endearingly brave, but my father made grown men quake. "He's furious, Rafi. If he sees you, I don't know what he'll do."

His fingers cupped my chin. "I'll just have to take my chances."

"Why would you do that?"

"You know why."

For the second time in a handful of minutes, I was struck speechless both by his words and that soft, *soft* look in his eyes as they drifted over my person with tenderness. My heart stretched to bursting, and my lungs shriveled as everything shrank down to just the two of us. What was he saying? Why was he looking at me like that? Could it be what I was imagining, or was it something else?

"Tell me," I whispered.

"For such a smart girl, Firefly, I'm shocked you haven't figured it out." With a laugh at my instant huff of indignation, Rafi reached for my hand and brought it between us as he stepped closer. He was so close that if I took a deep enough breath, my chest would brush his. Heat spilled through me at the thought, and parts of me pulled deliciously tight as unbearable tingles raced over my skin.

We were in the middle of the foyer with people like Forsythe and footmen milling about, out of sight for the moment but definitely there. Our servants were discreet, but we were being reckless out in the open even if he was simply holding my hand. But if Rafi kept staring at me like I was the most precious thing he'd ever seen . . . as though he wanted to immortalize every inch of me on a canvas in his head, I could not be expected to be responsible for my actions. Not when every sensible thought seemed to be draining from my brain.

"You are decidedly the most infuriating girl on the planet," he said softly, lifting my knuckles to his lips and pressing the lightest of kisses to them. My breath hitched, pure want barreling through me on a wave. Storm-bright gray eyes lifted to mine, swirling with so many emotions I could barely begin to decipher what each meant—trepidation, fear, fondness, desire—the same cocktail currently making my brain a hopeless mess. The touch was so delicately chaste, and yet the desire in his turbulent gaze was anything but. No, that stare glinted with exactly what he wanted to do to me. I locked my knees to keep them from buckling.

"I am?" I said, and licked my dry lips.

He nodded with another soft kiss, though that intense gaze dipped to my mouth and darkened before capturing mine once more. "And the most incorrigible, intractable, and heedless person, and yet, I would not change a single hair on your head. In truth, you have beguiled me, Lady Zenobia Osborn."

"I must say, Mr. Nasser, you have impeccably dreadful

timing," I croaked as his lips continued to trace a path of sensuous destruction over my scorching skin. "Because I'm certain I am about to be sent to a convent for all eternity."

"Then I shall scale the walls and rescue you."

I laughed dizzily, not even bothering to retort that any woman worth her salt would be able to rescue herself. Sometimes, it was nice that someone else cared enough to do it for you. "Who would have thought you were such a romantic?"

"I suppose I have a painter's heart. Buried though it is under all these magnificent layers of my splendid self," he said with an insouciant wink.

"That arrogance will be your undoing one day, sir."

He arched a brow. "So, you don't think I'm magnificent?"

I thought he was beyond so, but the words got locked in my throat when Rafi's lips kissed a trail of fire over each knuckle and up to my wrist bones before flipping my hand, grazing his mouth against the sensitive tender skin on the inside. I gasped when I felt the point of his tongue. Heavens, I was ready to combust until I was nothing but a pile of ash in the immaculate foyer. Gracious, the *foyer*!

"Rafi, anyone could come in here and see us," I whispered, my other hand lifting to grip the lapels of his coat. I wasn't sure whether it was to push him away or pull him closer as my stare found the clock. "We only have three minutes left."

"Then let's make the most of it," he replied as that wicked mouth of his climbed its way up my forearm, chasing the gooseflesh peppering my skin.

"This is unseemly," I protested feebly as if any part of me

truly gave a whit about modesty. "You cannot be seen touching me like this unless your wish is a swift trip to the altar."

"And what if I do want that?" he murmured, pausing in his devastating ascent.

Everything stopped . . . my thoughts, my breath, my very heart. "I beg your pardon?" His hand released mine only to reach forward and tunnel its way into the curls at my nape, anchoring sweetly at the base of my skull. My pulse streamed.

"You asked me why before," he said quietly. "It was for you, Zia, surely you must know that. Your care and esteem for Miss Perkins at the Old Bailey could not have been more obvious. I knew it would make you happy if she was safe. I wanted— *want*—to make you happy."

My chest suddenly felt ten times too small. "Rafi."

"You see me like no one else ever has, Zia. I've never felt so comfortable to just let go and be who I am, unapologetically and enthusiastically, as I've been these past weeks when I'm with you." His other hand reached up to cup my chin, thumb brushing my jawline, the position so bold that it would be obvious to anyone what we were doing, but I no longer cared. I never wanted him to stop speaking. "You have a gift for bringing out the best in people," he whispered. "With Miss Perkins, with your friends, with anyone who is fortunate to know you."

My vision swam with unshed tears. "Truly, I don't think any of them are thinking that at the moment. I'm sure they are all wishing they'd never met me. Are you certain you don't wish to save yourself before you're swept away into the perilous whirlpool of Zia Osborn?"

"Too late." That smirk of his graced his lips for the barest of seconds. "And in case my meaning didn't penetrate that intrepid mind of yours, with your permission, I intend to speak to the duke." Vulnerability crept over his face. "I know my timing is ghastly, but say you'll marry me, Zia."

A silly part of me still wondered if this was some fever dream, but Rafi's hands around me were real. His sincerity was real. *This* was real. But I could not drag him further into this mess until I was sure I wasn't going to be accused and sentenced. He did not deserve that or any of the ensuing scandal. The viscount would not be satisfied until someone bled, and I could see on his face that he wouldn't let this go. My mother had told him to declare his grievances, and I'd no doubt he would.

"Promise you'll ask me again when this has all been settled," I whispered, curling my fingers into a fist and dragging him even closer.

Though disappointment flashed briefly in his stare, he nodded after a beat. "I'll wait for as long as you need, Firefly."

God. This. Man. My throat tightened. "Will you please kiss me now?"

His eyes shone, turning to molten silver, but before he could acquiesce to my rather impulsive request, an obnoxious cough popped our tiny bubble, making us leap apart. Heat rushed to my cheeks as I peered up to see my brother staring at us with a conflicted look on his face as his head swung between Rafi and me.

How much of that had he heard? Had he heard Rafi propose?

Heard me beg for a kiss? Mortification filled me, but I jutted my chin high, refusing to feel an ounce of guilt.

Keston ran a hand over his jaw. "Not to crash whatever this is, but Father is about to burn a hole in the carpets, and with the froth he's in, I don't know how much longer I can put him off from stalking out here to find out what's keeping you." That sharp gaze cut to Rafi. "Or better yet, *who* is keeping you."

"On a scale of one to ten, how furious is he?" I asked my brother, glad that he'd chosen to keep the peace for the moment. Which could only mean one thing . . . there was a much bigger threat on the horizon.

"Twenty."

I sighed. It was time to face the consequences of my actions. My parents would be the first hurdle. If I could convince them somehow of my good intentions, perhaps I had a chance of surviving this disaster unscathed. Or at least the others could. I'd take the fall gladly.

Rafi squeezed my hand as if he could read my thoughts. "Don't quit on me now, Firefly. I'm with you every step of the way."

"Me too, Zia," Keston said. "Even though I don't claim to understand what would drive you to fleece *me,* of all people. Was it because I forgot your birthday? I knew that would come back to bite me in the arse."

I couldn't help it; I laughed at his droll expression, aware he was trying to make light of what was to come. "Yes, Kes. That's exactly why. Everything is about you."

His arm looped over my shoulders. "Jokes aside, I'm always here for you." He glared at Rafi on my opposite side. "And if you survive Father, I'll give you a chance to save the life of my best friend before I trounce the daylights out of him for daring to flirt with my baby sister. Don't think I don't know what this is!"

I arched my brows. "You think a little flirtation is worse than fleecing the viscount at a gaming hell, racing in the Midnight Row, and fighting a duel for money in the West End?"

Keston blanched as his mouth dropped open. "What in the actual *hell*, Zia!"

"Honestly, Brother, think of the children," I said.

"Never mind. I shall send one of the footmen for a priest to read you your last rites." My brother shook his head in disbelief. "What were you thinking? Stealing? Illegal betting? Fighting?" His expression was censorious, though the light of admiration also burned in his gaze. "Please tell me you at least won."

I grinned at him. That was more like it. "Ask Rafi. It was him I beat both times."

Keston's brown skin darkened to purple, his fists balling. "You knew about *all* of this?" he ground out. "Why didn't you stop her?"

"What are the odds of preventing a storm?" Rafi said, unperturbed that his best mate was ready to wipe the floor with him. "She had to run her course. I was there to keep her as safe as I could."

Keston blinked, anger draining somewhat as his gaze cut from Rafi back to me. "Who even *are* you right now?"

"Your sister," I said softly. "Who needs you."

All the pent-up aggression bled from him as he dragged me into his arms for a hug, and I took enormous comfort in that. Whatever happened next, I wasn't alone, no matter how vexed he was with me.

When the door to the library closed behind us, my father saw Rafi behind me and opened his mouth to rail, but the duchess forestalled him with one fierce look.

"With all due respect, Your Grace, I'm not leaving her alone right now," Rafi said, and I swear I nearly swooned. No one willingly went up against the Duke of Harbridge . . . and Rafi was doing it for me.

A vein pulsed on my father's brow, but after a fraught handful of seconds, he nodded, though his eyes shot daggers at Rafi. To his credit, Rafi didn't shrink in the face of the duke's displeasure, and I reached back to find his hand. I squeezed and laced our fingers. He wasn't alone, either. We were in this together.

"Explain," my mother said to me.

I drew in a breath, taking strength from both Rafi and my brother. Ela offered me a reassuring nod from where she stood next to Keston, her face pale and tight. I only had one shot at this, at convincing my parents to put their collective influence behind me. Behind *all* of us.

"It's true that the Lady Knights exist, but we're not a gang," I said quietly but clearly enough to be heard. "It's simply a group of young women who formed a book club and then decided we wanted to do something productive and daring with our lives before we were put on display for the season and married off to someone not of our choosing. And before you instantly assign blame to Miss Perkins, she did not put me up to this."

"She facilitated it!" my father said.

I shook my head. "No, Papa. She simply opened my eyes to other women fighting for human rights, like Mary Wollstonecraft and Hannah More, and those daring to be different in fields not normally accommodating to women, like what Mary Anning is discovering in paleontology, despite being uncredited for her work, and what Caroline Herschel is doing in astronomy." I glanced at my father, whose face grew redder by the minute, knowing he was going to make some remark that none of those women were aristocrats . . . that that was not *my* place or duty. "And let's not forget our own Lady Hester Stanhope, who travels in the East wearing men's clothing and is a pioneer in archaeology." My gaze flicked to my mother, who was listening with avid interest. And did I detect a hint of pride in her expression? "Or Mama, who fights tirelessly for women's rights."

"That is not the same thing," the duke said with a dismissive sniff. "Can you imagine the scandal if word got out that our daughter was part of something so radical? No gentleman would want a bar of you." I warmed at the fact that Rafi certainly would, but then went cold as my father pointed out another hard-hitting fact. "Or any of your so-called friends for that matter. Their reputations would be ruined irreparably." His gaze flicked to Ela. "And we are all intimately familiar with the impact of the *ton*'s disdain."

Oh, we were.

Greer's engagement might be called off. Nori would be

shunned. And Lalita would never be able to make the match she needed to placate her aunt and uncle. Those two grasping wretches would certainly marry her off to whoever would take her. Bitterness filled me. Perhaps that would serve her right. If she hadn't told Sarah, then none of this would have happened. Sarah had to have told someone, otherwise why would her parents have taken her out of school? It was suspicious.

"Girl gangs!" my father growled. "The absurdity."

"A book club, Papa, not some nefarious gang. Viscount Hollis was stirring up trouble to make it seem worse than it was. We would never hurt anyone, and we only took money from those who we knew wouldn't miss it."

Livid blue eyes bored into mine as my father's jaw dropped at my inadvertent confession. "I beg your pardon? *Took money?*"

Heart sinking, my knees shook. "It's not as bad as it sounds, Papa. It was just from Keston and his mates. We had to save the orphans, and, well, the money was better to put food in their bellies than lost on the gambling tables," I blurted, knowing I was stretching the truth, and sent a pleading gaze to my mother. I had to redirect the conversation before my father expired from apoplexy. "And besides, it's obvious that the viscount is only going after Miss Perkins and Welton because he wants the building and the land for his gaming hell! He doesn't care about how many lives he will destroy."

Silence descended. "Is that so?" my mother asked softly. "How do you know this?"

"Sister Mary told us. We were just trying to help save the orphanage, our school, the church." My voice wobbled, but if anyone could salvage any of this, it would be my mother. "Mama, please believe me. We didn't rob anyone of great importance, just Keston and his mates."

And the viscount . . . though I'd rather not mention him.

Keston belted out a chuckle in the wake of that. "And you didn't think to ask, Sister?"

What could I say? That it wouldn't have been as fun? That the act in itself was as much of a rebellious stand against our pretty cages? "It would not have been enough. And since then, the property owner has tripled their rent, from three to nine hundred pounds, under duress from Mr. Atkins and the viscount. Outrageous."

Risking a glance at my father, whose face was bright red, I braced myself for his eruption. I could sense the silent throttling of his ire. Being part of a group of young ladies pushing decorum was one thing, but admitting to robbing people, even if it was my own brother, was much worse. Though his lips were a translucent line and that vein was staking a claim on his temple, my mother's hand on his arm kept his temper at bay.

The duchess drew in a clipped breath. "He might not have actual proof, as Mr. Kaneko said, and surely your brother and his friends wouldn't press charges against you, but Viscount Hollis's claims of hysteria could make things quite difficult for you girls as well as your teacher."

Mama was right. The allegation of hysteria could be a serious concern. Men had committed women to asylums for less. My stomach soured. We might be safe with the weight of our families behind us, but Miss Perkins would not be.

The duke cleared his throat, fighting for composure. "Zenobia, how could you have been so reckless?"

I hung my head. "It was foolish of me, Papa. I understand that now. My heart was in the right place, I promise."

He let out a breath and closed his eyes. "I believe you," he said with a sigh. "Where's my little girl who was always the soul of civility and decorum? Who never set one toe out of line? Who always did as she was told?"

I sniffed wryly. "She grew up, Papa. She got tired of letting life just happen to her. It's meant to be lived, isn't it?" I bit my lip. "You and Mama always told us to remember who we are, and to think for ourselves, and that's what I'm doing. You named me after a queen. What kind of queen would I be if I willfully ignored injustice and suffering?"

"There are other ways to fight against those things, my darling," my mother said gently.

"Like what?" I burst out in frustration. "We are forbidden to own property of our own. We cannot work to earn money, lest we reduce our chances of making an advantageous match. We are only expected to sit and look pretty, and let our minds languish from disuse, while the men in our society tell us what to think and what opinions we should have."

"Your father doesn't do that, and neither does your brother," Mama said.

"Isn't that what Papa is doing right now?" I asked resentfully. "Trying to corral me and control me?"

"You're my daughter!" he roared. "I care about your safety, girl. If you want to save the children, save the children! But don't put yourself in danger and think you're battling for the greater good." He paced again before stopping and grasping the bridge of his nose with his thumb and forefinger. "Don't knowingly break the law and try to explain it away with respectable intentions, Zenobia. That is privilege. Consider if someone less fortunate than you had done the same. What do you think would happen then?"

My spirits deflated as I thought about the fourteen-year-old boy and the nineteen-year-old girl who had been sentenced to transportation and death, respectively. They had not been lucky. Neither of them had had parents who had stared down the Lord Mayor and took their daughter home. Or even a proper barrister. If I'd been a commoner and Viscount Hollis had brought his accusations about me to his friend Atkins, I would have had no chance.

"You're right, it was wrong of me. I'm sorry," I said, dejected.

The duke crossed the room and kissed my brow in a rare show of emotion. "I know you are. But for now, you are confined to your quarters. I forbid you to leave this house and to see those friends of yours." He lifted his gaze to Rafi. "Or him, for that matter. Though I applaud his courage for standing his ground to support you."

Horrified, I stared at him. "But, Papa—"

"It's for your own good, Zenobia." He gave me a fond if regretful smile. "Sometimes even queens, as clever as they are, need to be protected from themselves."

CHAPTER TWENTY

The most holy band of society is friendship. It has been well said, by a shrewd satirist, "that rare as true love is, true friendship is still rarer."

—Mary Wollstonecraft

I was about ready to scale the walls or yank my hair out by the roots, whichever came first. I'd been confined to the house for the better part of a fortnight, and even though Keston and Ela had been here, it wasn't the same. I missed my friends. I missed Rafi. Despite his gallant promises of rescue, there was only so much he could antagonize my father. When he'd climbed the trellis outside my room a couple of days in, he'd only made it halfway before being discovered. The duke had then stationed men around the house. A second rescue attempt via the scullery had earned poor Rafi a thwack with a broom from the house-keeper. After that, we both agreed that I'd serve out my sentence alone.

Flowers and notes from each of my friends had been delivered, but it only made the forced separation harder to endure. Even playing my pianoforte hadn't brought the comfort it usually did.

What also made things exponentially worse were the headlines in the gossip rags that hinted of scandal.

WHERE ON EARTH IS LADY Z _____?

IS LONDON'S JEWEL PART OF THE ONGOING
HYSTERIA INVESTIGATION AT THE WELTON
HOUSE SCHOOL FOR ELEGANT YOUNG LADIES?

DO TELL, WHAT SKELETONS IS OUR DIAMOND
HIDING?

WHAT DO THE DUKE AND DUCHESS OF
H_____ HAVE TO SAY?

My absence from the *ton* was conspicuous in the extreme, though my parents had explained to our circles that I was recovering from illness. The family physician had recommended staying in bed and lots of rest. From the bits and pieces of information I could glean from Ela, Viscount Hollis had launched his official grievances against the Perkins sisters, and as expected, the two elder ones had hung their sister out to dry, renouncing all ties. True to his word, the vile man had also cut off his nephew quite publicly, stating that his behavior was unbecoming of their line. Total poppycock, of course.

Rafi had retaliated by scheduling an equally public presentation of his art at the British Institution's Pall Mall Picture

Galleries, and he'd invited the prince regent. The show would be in one week and I'd already received my invitation. Hopefully, my father's punishment would not last that long, but even if it did, I didn't care what I would have to do to be there. I would not miss Rafi's vernissage for the world.

While I resented my father's decree with every fiber of my being, I also saw the wisdom in it. Greer had written that her whole family had been interviewed. So had Nori's, and she, too, had been forbidden from leaving home for a week. All four of my friends, including Lalita and Blythe, had been asked to temporarily leave Welton, which I knew would not have gone over well with Lalita's aunt and uncle. She had been silent, though she'd sent baskets of baked goods in lieu of words. Had she been interrogated, too? I felt disconnected and cut off from my circle.

"Lady Zenobia," my lady's maid said, making me jump from where I sat idly holding some truly atrocious needlepoint, totally lost in my thoughts. I'd completely botched the roses, and now they looked like sad, crushed pink socks with green ears. Who embroidered socklike roses? Clearly a miserable, glum girl with nothing but time on her hands who couldn't stitch two threads together.

"What is it, Gemma?" I asked grouchily.

"This was delivered to you via urgent messenger." She handed me a sealed message, a bright smile on her face despite my rancid disposition. She'd had to bear my bad humor for almost two weeks. "You should get dressed and go for a walk in the gardens. The weather is lovely today."

I scowled and stared down at my stained dressing robe, which was covered in crumbs from my breakfast. "No thanks, I am a prisoner."

"This house is definitely a prison," Gemma agreed. "The horror of it, truly. Honestly, I do not know how you can possibly bear it."

I narrowed my eyes. Her face was arranged in a pleasant expression though her voice was sardonic in the extreme. "Are you being sarcastic, Gemma dear?"

"Goodness, it was rather on the nose, milady." She laughed. "And yes, you're acting like a very spoiled brat at the moment. Have a bath and get some fresh air."

"I should sack you," I said without any heat in it.

Gemma shrugged, her lined face crinkling. "You'd only hire me right back."

She wasn't wrong. As she bustled about my bedchamber, putting out my clothes for the day, I opened the message she'd brought. It was from Rafi. My heart skipped a silly beat at the sight of his plain, meticulous handwriting and then promptly skipped another at the address.

My ever beautiful Lady Knight,

Be ready for adventure at ten o'clock this evening. Dress in highwaywoman's clothing and arrive in your carriage house for further instructions. I urge your discretion in this matter, lest our efforts be for naught. I am counting the hours until you're back in my arms.

Yours in esteem,

R.

I let myself swoon for a full minute, maybe two, before rereading it once more. My curiosity was certainly piqued. *Highwaywoman's clothing?* I took that to mean gentlemen's trousers and a shirt, which made my eyebrows shoot to my hairline. What on earth did he have planned? It also said to be discreet, the words *urge your discretion* underlined. I didn't want to risk incurring any more of my father's wrath and have him extend my sentence, but I was very intrigued and also quite sick of my own company. What would it hurt to escape these walls for a few hours?

Putting the letter to the side, I sniffed my armpits and winced. Gemma was right—I was in dire need of a bath. And perhaps a walk. It would do me good to stretch my legs.

The hours passed by at a snail's pace as I waited for the time in Rafi's note to come around, and I was a vibrating mess of pins and needles when I heard the clock in the foyer strike ten times. I'd spent the day distracting myself with more terrible embroidery, working on the song I'd been composing, and harassing all the kitchen servants to the point that Cook had shooed me away with a frying pan.

Gingerly, careful not to make a sound, I tiptoed down the stairs. My parents were out, but I had no doubt that my every step would be reported back to the duke. I'd made a huge scene about turning in early because I was so tired. The house was quiet when I slid out the side door and hurried to my carriage house. Fingers fumbling with the lock, I unlatched the door and walked inside, only for my jaw to fall to the floor as the lamp illuminated.

My best friends faced me: Greer, Nori, and Lalita.

And Rafi, who stood to the side.

"What are you all doing here?" I breathed, and nearly crashed headfirst into their arms. I wanted to scream with joy, but I contented myself with muted sounds of delight. It was *so* good to see them!

Greer grinned. "What do you think? Breaking you out."

"But my father . . ."

"What the duke doesn't know won't hurt him, and we don't plan to be gone that long," Nori said with a gleeful grin.

Lalita gave me a hesitant smile. "It's good to see you, Zia."

"You, too." My acrimony had all but disappeared in the wake of a good few solitary days of reflection. I didn't care if Lalita had been the one to tell Sarah, which had started the ball rolling in the first place. In the end, I had to be responsible for my own actions. That had been a bitter pill to swallow, but swallow it I had.

"Where are we going?" I asked, sneaking a glance at Rafi, who hadn't said a word, only watched me with a smile hovering over his lips. I wanted to run over and embrace him just as I had the others, but a sudden bout of shyness gripped me.

Seeing Rafi in the flesh after his declaration two weeks ago felt monumental. And gracious, he looked delicious. His dark hair was windswept, brushed back from his face, and curling over his collar. Tendrils fell onto his angular face, highlighting the sharp lines of his cheekbones and jawline, and the full curve of his lips. . . . *Guh.* I dragged my gaze up with a gulp. Piercing gray eyes under thick brows glinted like silver pools of mercury, and when they met mine, it was all I could do to stay upright.

"Close your mouth, or you'll catch flies," Greer teased, and I instantly snapped my lips shut, feeling my cheeks flame at being caught.

Nori shoved me so hard I nearly stumbled. "Don't just stand there, you dunderhead!"

Face hot, I let my legs carry me across the room. It was a handful of steps at most, but it felt like a mile, each pounding heartbeat making my chest squeeze tighter and tighter. "Hullo," I said, my hoarse voice practically unrecognizable.

"Firefly," he said softly, warmth shimmering in those hypnotic eyes. Warmth and so much more that I could barely think. In my solitude, I'd almost convinced myself that I'd imagined Rafi's declaration and his proposal. But no. The truth was staring me right in the face. I drank him in and didn't even spare a thought to concealing any of my emotions. I might not have been able to articulate them aloud—*yet*—but I wanted him to see.

"You look good," I said dimly, and wanted to kick myself.

That treacherous smirk tugged at the corner of his lip. "You are exquisite."

Pinning my lips between my teeth, I fought the wave of

pleasure that engulfed me. I was dressed in a shirt and navy waistcoat with black breeches tucked into boots and a plain coat. My hair was braided into a sideways tail that crossed from one side of my scalp to go over my shoulder. It was free from jewels or flowers. My face was freshly scrubbed without a hint of lip stain or rouge.

And yet, I'd never felt more beautiful.

He lifted my hand to his lips, kissing my knuckles as he'd done before. Tingles spun through my bones like tiny bolts of lightning. My mouth dried, lungs shriveling to the size of peas as I recalled the kiss that had decimated me. From the gleam in his eyes, he did, too.

"Chop, chop, you two," Nori catcalled, making me snap out of my lustful trance, and I hopped back like a deranged bunny in utter mortification. "Unless you want us to wait outside and give you"—she cocked her head in deep thought—"say ten minutes to work whatever this is out of your systems? Or maybe twenty? You look . . . quite overcome."

"Nori!" I burst out, horrified.

But Rafi's smirk only transformed into a full, uninhibited grin, causing a dimple—*holy mind-smelting swoon*—to flash. "Come now, Miss Kaneko, I'd need at least a solid hour," he drawled with a wink. "To take my time and ensure total satisfaction."

Oh. Dear. Heavens. Above.

Was he talking about . . . ?

From the look on Nori's delighted face, she hadn't expected that response. Greer was grinning and Lalita had gone the color of a tomato. "Mr. Nasser, an unselfish lover," Nori commented. "Color me pleasantly surprised."

Ears burning hot, my mouth went slack. My poor heart didn't know what to do with itself. Trample its way through my rib cage and launch toward him, or drum itself to a beatific, glorious death. Rafi lifted his hand to my chin and gently eased my jaw up.

What was happening? I let out a breathless wheeze at the fantasies—no thanks to Nori's last comment—that suddenly invaded my vision. My ability to take a full breath fizzled. We'd all talked about coupling on the evenings spent in this very carriage house when we'd stolen Mama's ratafia and really gotten into our cups. But my imaginary lover had always been faceless. Now he had a face. *Rafi's* face.

"Cat snatched your tongue?" he teased, his thumb moving to trace over my bottom lip. He looked like *he* wanted to snatch said appendage. And I wanted to let him.

I moved backward, pulling myself out of his mesmeric orbit, and dragged a full breath of air into my aching lungs. Had he always been this tall? This commanding? This *delectable*?

"Come on, calf eyes," Greer said, yanking on the end of my braid. "Let's go before the two of you obliterate the place with all this tension."

I fought futilely for composure. "I have absolutely no idea what you're talking about."

"Sure," she said with a wink. "Oh, wait, I have something for you. I'm not certain if you saw these yet."

She handed me a set of trundled newssheets. I braced myself

for the contents as I unrolled them. The headlines in the *Times* were enough to cool the heat in my blood.

THE WELTON HOUSE SCHOOL FOR ELEGANT YOUNG LADIES TO CLOSE!

BUILDING LOT ON SHELTON STREET UP FOR AUCTION

My heart sank. Viscount Hollis had gotten exactly what he wanted. Quickly, I scanned the rest of the article, seeing that even though Welton was closing its doors, Miss Perkins's fate still remained undecided. The article accused Miss Ada Perkins of being a danger to the young ladies in her care and admonished the school for allowing questionable reading material. It went on to say that a small group of mothers, directed by Lady Joshi and Mrs. Peabody, had led the charge in the teacher's condemnation, after Lady Joshi had found a copy of *Frankenstein* in her daughter Petal's possession.

Lalita wrung her hands. "This was all my fault."

"No, it wasn't," I said. "Not yours, not ours. And I want to apologize for thinking that any of you might knowingly betray the code." It wasn't enough, I knew, so I forced myself to face Lalita. "I'm sorry that I was upset that you told Sarah about us. I should not have accused you of not caring about the Lady Knights." I expelled a hard breath. "The truth is, we all knew the consequences of what we were doing. We could have been found out any other way. I think when Miss Perkins told us *alis volat propriis,* she didn't mean committing any crimes by spreading our wings. So, that's on us."

"You were right, though," Lalita said in a small voice. "I think I confided in her because I wanted to get back at you. My feelings were hurt that everyone was moving on without me, and I wanted a *reaction.*"

"I'm sorry I made you feel that way," I said.

"It was an accident, you know," she said softly. "Petal's mother told the Peabodys, and Sarah's parents whisked her away to Bath for some special hospital for girls suffering from hysteria when she attempted to defend the book to them. She was locked in a padded room for a solid week. She wrote me that she didn't mean to expose the Lady Knights—she was explaining about the uncertain future of the orphanage, and it slipped out."

Suddenly, I regretted my uncharitable thoughts. That sounded absolutely horrid. "Is she well?"

"She is, I believe, but she has completely capitulated to her parents' demands and won't return to London this season. She's at their country house in Reading, but she's afraid to be banished back to Bath."

Nori shook her head. "I don't blame her. Those kinds of hospitals are a nightmare."

We all stared at each other on the brink of tears. I was so grateful for their friendship, even through all the ups and downs. At least we had each other, and that had to count for something.

"Group hug!" Nori announced, and I felt myself suffocated by three half-crying, half-laughing girls.

I met Rafi's admiring stare over their shoulders and warmed at the approval in his eyes. It wasn't easy admitting to my friends that I'd been wrong, but it definitely erased the burden I'd been carrying.

"Enough of this dramatic caterwauling," Greer said after planting a loud kiss on my forehead. "Let's get down to business, shall we?"

"Wait, what are we doing?" I asked, and then froze, staring down at the telltale clothing I'd been asked to wear. "Not another heist, are we? Because I'm quite certain that the duke and duchess will have words for me about that, or worse. And I do value not being locked away until I'm old and wretched."

"No." She grinned. "Nothing so criminal." She made a small space between her thumb and forefinger. "But maybe courting a wee bit of trouble in Covent Garden. Don't worry, we have the big bad Mr. Nasser to protect us. Anyway, if you're worried, it's your decision."

Trouble? I could not deny the bubble of excitement that expanded inside me at the thought of visiting the thrilling West End of London. Not even the thought of bearing the brunt of my father's displeasure or Mama's disappointment could curb my enthusiasm. Having been cooped up for days on end, I was chomping at the bit. And I trusted my friends not to push things too far. Besides, Rafi would never let anything untoward happen to me.

"To Valhalla!" I whisper-yelled to Greer, who gave a soft whoop.

We left the carriage house silently and piled into Rafi's waiting carriage at the far end of the mews. It was a tight squeeze with the five of us, but I certainly wasn't going to complain. I was sandwiched between Rafi and Nori, while Lalita and Greer took up the opposite bench. I tried not to inhale Rafi's warm scent of sandalwood and fresh rain, but it was nearly impossible. It was also impossible not to be aware of the hard muscles pressing into my right side or the fact that only two layers of fabric separated our legs. He was a veritable furnace. Or perhaps that was me, immolating from the inside.

I gulped and made the mistake of looking over at Greer, who waggled her eyebrows in the most obnoxious manner. I had to stop being so transparent when it came to the gentleman next to me.

"Might I remind you that I know one Lars Nielsen's address by heart," I mock threatened, and then watched in satisfaction as her leer vanished.

Greer's eyes widened. "You wouldn't!"

"Turnabout is fair play, don't you think? What would sweet Mr. Nielsen think of his betrothed gallivanting across London?"

Her grin returned. "He would tell me to be safe and have fun."

My eyes narrowed. "What about keeping boiled sweets in your cleavage?"

Her cheeks went pink, but she tossed her head. "Who do you think came up with the idea so I don't get rage-hungry? He's saving lives, and you don't even know it."

My revenge plan deflated. Lars was clearly above my petty attempts to get even.

"He sounds like a good one," Rafi said, his deep voice tumbling over me.

"I'm not keeping sweets in my décolletage, so don't get any ideas," I said under my breath, earning myself a smirk from Rafi that should not have been as wicked as it was.

"He's my best friend," Greer said. "Well, outside of this lot, that is. But we grew up together, and Lars gets me in a way that no one else does, just as I get him." She hesitated, then nodded as if to herself. "We're both a bit different to everyone else in how we feel about each other. It's not sensual." She jabbed her pointer finger at us and waved it in a circle. "Not like the two of you. We care for each other deeply, and we are both pleased with the betrothal."

I was shocked that she was disclosing anything about her intended to Rafi when she'd taken months to open up to me that she even had a fiancé. Much less one who mirrored her own ambivalent thoughts on attraction and intimacy. It was rare to be accepted so unconditionally, especially if one didn't adhere to traditional standards. I was happy for my friend.

"That's good," Rafi said. "It doesn't always happen that way. True matches in our world are unusual. I'm glad you found that."

I knew he was talking about his own parents. When his father died, his mother had returned to the man she'd loved. I had no idea how she could share him with other wives or so many concubines, but I also understood that love came in many forms and relationships could take different, fluid shapes. Case in point was Nori and Blythe. Or my brother's friend Blake, who seemed to have a different flavor of the week, no matter their sex. Or even Greer and Lars, who both didn't experience sexual attraction at all. Love made space for all of us.

As if he could hear that last thought, I felt Rafi's gaze flutter to me.

I have no idea how I managed to hold it together until we got to where we were going, somewhere near Drury Lane in Covent Garden, but I did. The inside of me, however, was a melty, puddly mess. As the coach slowed, I glanced down the street to where Rafi's place was. That reminded me. "Is Miss Perkins still at your studio?" I asked him.

"She is."

Perturbed, I glanced at my friends. "What will happen now that Welton has been closed? Will her sisters take her in?"

Lalita's face crumpled. "No, they've kicked her out, and she hasn't been able to find a new position since."

"They can't just abandon her. That's wrong." I scowled in disgust, filled with a need to check in on her or at least show her that she had our support. "Do we have time to stop by since we're so close?"

Rafi checked his pocket watch and nodded. "We do."

It didn't take us long to arrive at Rafi's studio, and we all crammed inside when a smiling Miss Perkins welcomed us in for a cup of tea. Despite it being his residence, Rafi remained in the small receiving salon where Gemma used to sit. Miss Perkins seemed sprightly enough, though she had dark shadows under her eyes. "What a pleasure it is to see you, girls. I trust none of the recent happenings have stopped you from reading?"

Everyone laughed. Of course, she would be concerned that we had slacked off. "No, Miss Perkins," we chorused, though that was a bit of a fib on my part. In my misery at being punished, I'd scoured my parents' library, but nothing had held my interest, not even the stack of deliciously gothic penny romance novels I'd discovered on the topmost shelves. Those had only made me yearn for Rafi . . . and that in itself had been pure torture.

"We heard about your sisters," Greer said, setting her teacup and saucer down. The mood quickly sobered. "What are you going to do?"

A defeated sigh left Miss Perkins. "Keep trying to find employment, I suppose, but no one in the *ton* will hire me as a governess because of the scandal. I might have to leave London, or even England."

I gasped. "You can't."

"I might not have a choice, my lady," she said sadly, and my heart sank. There was no solid connection between the Lady Knights and Viscount Hollis's plan to discredit the school, but I couldn't help feeling guilty that we had made a bad situation worse for poor Miss Perkins. Any whisper of gossip and her chances of working as a teacher or governess would be greatly reduced. Add hysteria into the mix and parents would balk. I balled my fists but kept my smile up for my teacher's sake.

After we finished our tea, said our goodbyes, and were once more in the carriage, I cursed under my breath, drawing the attention of my friends. "We need to do something."

"We could write to the *Times,*" Lalita suggested. "Express our outrage."

"Or have all our horses defecate on Lady Joshi's and Mrs. Peabody's doorsteps," Nori muttered, and we stared at her in shock until she raised her hands. "I'm jesting. Mostly."

I suppressed my laughter at her fierce expression. "What if we could find her a position or confront her sisters or do a petition to save Welton?"

"Count me in," Greer said, and the other two nodded emphatically.

I mulled the ideas over in my head. Collective pressure was a tool that could be used to make things happen. I'd seen my mother use it in her appeals to her various groups. Perhaps she'd be able to offer some advice.

My mind was whirling by the time the coach stopped in front of a well-lit private house. Over the doorway was a sign that read QUEEN'S ROSE with a dented wrought-iron rose and vine that reminded me of my sock embroidery. I bit back a chuckle. Perhaps it was a sign. Impatience filled me at whatever surprise was in store.

Was it some kind of gentlemen's club, hence the clothing I'd been directed to wear? Would it be like the one with the fighting? But when we entered the club behind Rafi, who handed over some kind of card to the director, I noticed that it was much more spacious than it appeared from the outside. Then the music was the next thing to hit me. That along with the fact that both men and women crammed its walls. It was bright and boisterous and fairly crackling with energy. I loved it!

The space was some kind of tavern or maybe theater or maybe both, though there was no big stage as far as I could see. Tables were strewn about the cramped place, occupied by entertained patrons who were in the middle of eating a meal. There was a dance floor where couples were swinging each other to the fiddlers standing at the edge. I couldn't help the grin that broke across my face. It felt like supper and a show.

"Shall we ask to be shown to a table?" I asked loudly, though there didn't seem to be a free seat in the space.

"Your friends will go to my box," Rafi said, and then I realized that there were upper supper boxes around the sides, very much akin to a fancy theater. I registered his words a second late. "But you and I will go over here."

His box? I stumbled in confusion as my friends grinned with some secret they all knew. "Have fun!" Greer said.

"Don't swoon," Nori chirped, while Lalita shot me an enthusiastic grin.

"Don't swoon?" I repeated in confusion while Rafi led me away. "Why in the world would she say such a thing?" Was I actually going to do something that I would need to fear for my sensibilities?

Rafi chuckled. "I'm sure she meant it in the best possible way. Some people can get nervous for a performance."

Oh. I stumbled. Wait. What *performance*?

We stopped at the stage, where Rafi spoke with the manager. And then he was grinning and shoving a sheaf of papers—sheet music from my studio—into my hands. Bewildered, I stared at him as I heard the stage manager announce a special treat for their audience featuring a new kind of music. The crowd broke into cheers.

"And without further ado, I present Mistress Knight."

My soles were glued to the floor and Rafi gave me a little nudge. He held out his palm, and in it were three pairs of screws of varying sizes, two bolts, and a chunk of rubber. "You're on. Show them what you're made of."

I could barely think after he smashed his mouth to mine, kissed me absolutely senseless, and propelled me onto the stage toward the pianoforte illuminated by gaslight. The panic didn't come until I was in front of the instrument with my music in place, but as I ran my fingers over the keys, I felt at home. In this tavern in the middle of nowhere with all these faceless people eagerly waiting. I was terrified, but I'd never felt more alive in my life.

I would play my music for these people. I approached the edge of the small dais, my voice ringing clear. "My name is Knight. I'm a pianist, but not one that you've ever heard. Some may find it strange, and others off-putting. Some may think it monstrous, but at the very core of ourselves where our inner strings are broken or worn, where the very imperfect soul of us resides, we find that a flawed harmony can be beautiful, too."

With that, I arranged the screws and the bolts along with the rubber and the last sheet of my music over the strings. I could feel the curious gazes of the other musicians, and my nerves went taut. I glanced over to the side where Rafi stood, his gaze ever so proud. His belief in me was everything. "Bring down the house," he yelled.

Grinning, I intended to do just that.

By the time I was finished with the piece I'd composed for *Frankenstein,* its powerful notes soul jarring and life-giving, my body was humming and my fingers were numb. Dead silence preceded the thunderous applause that I stood for to take my bow. People crowded me as I stepped off the stage, asking what type of music that was and how I'd come up with it.

"I don't know what it's called," I replied in a daze. "I use parchment on the strings to get that bassoon-buzzing type of sound, and the rest is experimental. Some pianofortes have special damper pedals that do the same. I certainly did not invent it, but music is like a language, one that's ever evolving."

"Astonishing," someone told me, patting me on the back, and I warmed at the praise that was echoed by many others.

By the end of it all, I was breathless with exhilaration as I threw myself into Rafi's waiting arms.

"You were magnificent, love," he said, spinning me in a circle.

"Thank you for doing this." He'd given me the one thing I'd said I wanted if I could choose—to play my music in front of hundreds of people. Brimming with joy, I gazed at him, and the world revolved around us like he was the sun. "Rafi?"

"Yes, Firefly?"

I let him see it all . . . every last emotion I'd hoarded for years. "I am positively, absurdly, *wildly* in love with you."

CHAPTER
TWENTY-ONE

True beauty and grace must arise from the play of the mind.

—MARY WOLLSTONECRAFT

Thank every star in the sky that my house arrest had finally been revoked. My father had relented once the scandal had died down, but I knew the reprieve was mostly thanks to my mother, who was of the firm opinion that action was the seed to absolution. One had to make the effort to make amends, not just suffer the consequences. I was grateful and relieved. After all, a girl had important things to do—art shows to attend, petitions to get signed, and sisters to convince. I had to start righting my wrongs.

It had taken several days of work to track down every girl at Welton, the fourteen outside our book club group, but with Greer at the helm, we were quite successful. Only Petal and Sarah's signatures were missing, for obvious reasons, but we took a vote amongst ourselves and decided to forego getting theirs. The last thing we needed was for their parents to spread poisonous gossip to the others.

But this was it. A last-ditch effort to save the most remarkable teacher I'd ever had. I inhaled and exhaled, holding the paper with all the signatures, and knocked on the door.

"Enter," someone said, the eldest Perkins sister, I presumed.

Flinching from the weight of their stares, I made my way to the seat in front of the large desk. As expected, Mrs. Perkins occupied the one, while her younger sister sat to the side. Both wore pinched expressions as if they could guess what was coming.

"Good morning, Mrs. Perkins, Miss Perkins," I said firmly and clearly.

"Lady Zenobia," the elder woman said. "Why have you come?"

Though I bristled at her patronizing tone, I stayed outwardly calm. Per my mother, the key here was to be both respectful and confident. Respect was valued no matter the situation, and an inherent sense of confidence bolstered any message, especially if it was controversial in nature. It also made rebuttals less likely.

I pushed the folded parchment across the mahogany surface of the desk. "I have come here with a signed petition to solicit your compassion and reinstate Miss Perkins, your sister, to her duties at Welton, wherever that may be. She is truly—"

"Miss Perkins is no sister of ours, Lady Zenobia," Mrs. Perkins interrupted.

I stared, my heart hollowing.

"She does not conform to the values of this hallowed institution," the second sister said on the heels of the first. "And thus, if Welton House is to continue, she will no longer be a part of it."

My gaze narrowed. "She's your sibling. How could you just cast her aside because she encouraged us to read?"

"Blood, alas, is no guarantor of piety," Mrs. Perkins said in a tone so arctic I could swear I felt frostbite on my face. "What Miss Perkins has done is an insult and a sacrilege to our good name. Those books are blasphemous, and our sister is a blight upon this school that must be expunged."

"How so?" I asked in as calm a tone as I could manage, despite wincing at the depth of her hate. "It's just a story, a cautionary tale. Isn't the Bible one as well? Surely, that, too, is a social commentary of sorts on the acts of men."

"Do not seek to lecture us on theology, young lady," Miss Perkins snapped.

"I do beg your pardon," I said with forced sweetness, widening my eyes. "It was not my intent to lecture or cause offense. I simply meant it to say that a novel like that simply allows us to recognize the evil that exists in the world and warns us to be vigilant and keep our distance. Surely Miss Perkins should be lauded for that? For her foresight and cleverness?"

If the eldest sister's face could cool any more, she would literally turn into a block of ice. I suspected she could see right through me and my tongue-in-cheek criticism. With the tip of one finger, she pushed the petition back in my direction. "Thank you for coming, but I assure you, we are quite firm in our decision."

"But—"

"Good *day,* Lady Zenobia."

That was a dismissal if I'd heard one, and I would not

get much by arguing further, not when they had clearly made up their minds to excoriate their sister. It was dreadfully unfair! Channeling my mother, I canted my head as haughtily as I could manage and took my leave. This wasn't over by any means. The two people who should suffer the most were those hateful women!

By the time I made it back home to Mayfair, I was seething with rage.

I would buy that whole damn school if I had to!

I'd use my dowry. That was worth something instead of being promised to some gentleman. Would Rafi care if I came to him without one? Many aristocrats depended on their wives' dowries to help save deteriorating estates, but I knew that Rafi wasn't lacking for coin. He didn't seem like that kind of man, but then again, people's motivations baffled me sometimes. A woman's dowry in our world was like a scepter being handed off from one male to another—payment for goods and services.

But the real question was, if for some reason he did care about my reduced circumstances and his reputation by default, could I sacrifice my future happiness for another woman's? For Miss Perkins, I absolutely would.

When I arrived home, I handed my cloak, bonnet, and gloves to Forsythe. I was determined to see this through, but as always, the impediment to my success and the chains over my dowry was my father. At this point, it was beyond understood that he'd had enough of Welton for a lifetime.

"Forsythe, are the duke and duchess home?" I asked, feeling my resolve settle.

"Yes, my lady," the butler said. "His Grace is in his study and Her Grace is in the gardens, I believe."

"Thank you. Could you send a footman asking her to meet me in my father's study, please?"

He bowed. "Of course, my lady."

I smoothed my skirts, strode to the duke's study, and rapped on the heavy oak door before I could lose my nerve. I cracked the door and popped my head around to make sure that he was alone. "Hullo, Papa," I said when I saw that he was. "Might I have a word?"

Serious blue eyes met mine as I crossed the expanse of carpet to his desk. He wasn't in a bad mood, though I could tell he was cross about something, which wasn't in my favor. "What is it, Zenobia? I'm quite busy."

I flinched at his brusque tone but trudged forward. "I need to discuss something with you, but I've requested Mama's presence as well. Can we wait for her?"

His eyes narrowed at that, but before he could demand for me to tell him, my mother swept into the study, smelling of the outdoors and ruddy cheeked, with smudges of dirt on her hems from the garden. She was still beautiful. Clearly my father thought so, too, because that frigid countenance softened considerably as he came around the desk to greet her with a kiss. When I was a girl, I'd always hoped that one day someone would look at me the way he looked at her.

Rafi does.

Heart swelling, I pushed the thought of him away, lest it distract me from my mission.

"You're back," my mother said. "How did it go?"

"Abysmally so," I replied. "They were horrid and rude." When my father cocked his head, my mother briefly explained my idea with the petition and what I'd hoped to accomplish.

"I could have told you that would be a waste of time," he said, leaning back to prop his hips against the desk. "Though rather admirable and resourceful on your part. Unfortunately, bigotry is alive and thriving, even within families, and intolerance is rampant, especially toward progressive views and modern literature."

If my eyes could widen any further, they'd pop out of my head and roll over the floor like a pair of marbles. "So, you *don't* think Miss Perkins was in the wrong?" I ventured carefully.

To my surprise, my father laughed, reaching for my mother and drawing her into his side. "I married one of the most unconventional, outspoken, intrepid women in the world. Why would you ever think I would think Miss Perkins was at fault?"

"But you were so angry . . . ," I mumbled.

"Yes, at you, for putting yourself in danger," he said.

I frowned. "And the scandal?"

"Zenobia, I do not relish toeing the lines of decorum, but it behooves us to understand how aristocratic society works. There is a structure in place. I don't care for scandal in itself. I would have you do whatever makes you happy in this world. But because the world isn't made up of people like us, we have to tread very carefully amongst our peers so that we can be voices for those who have none." He pointed at the papers on his desk. "Take this bill I've been working with your mother on, for example. If

I didn't have the influence I do, my odds of success of getting it through the House of Lords with support would be much less."

My frown deepened in confusion. "You're saying I need to appease people? Awful people?"

He shook his head. "Not at all, but I would caution that any interaction could benefit from pausing and speaking with wisdom. Your mother has a favorite adage about flies, vinegar, and honey."

I nodded, knowing that one well. "We have to pick and choose our battles, as well as the hills upon which we fight," I said.

"Correct." The duke laughed and nuzzled my mother. "Though I am rather impatient when I run out of honey and vinegar both. But luckily, I am saved by my beautiful duchess's skills of charm, wit, and persuasion."

Smiling, I stared at my parents, each of them so different—my father's pale skin and my mother's deep brown complexion, his bright blue eyes and hers dark as night, her tumbling wealth of inky braids and his wispy blond hair. And yet, they fit together as if they'd been born to be. Keston and I were amalgamations of them . . . their looks, their intelligence, their compassion, their will, their stubbornness, and their sheer mettle.

"Papa, Mama," I said with a deep breath, straightening my spine. "I wish to buy Welton with my dowry. I want to be the change that needs to happen."

They both stared at me. "Your dowry is meant for your wedding, Zia," my mother said.

"It's an archaic custom," I protested. "Like you're paying for some man to accept responsibility and care of me. If someone truly wanted my hand in marriage, they would not care whether I came with a penny or pound."

"A betrothal arrangement in the aristocracy is a transaction," my father said. "Regardless of how unpalatable it might be to you, that is the way it has been done for centuries."

"Then maybe things need to be different," I said fiercely.

My father nodded. "I don't doubt that they do, my girl."

Emboldened, I went on. "Teachers like Miss Perkins are rare. Women who run local circulating libraries and reading rooms are rare. They should not be punished for encouraging young ladies to think for themselves and hoping for a better future." I paused. "Will you approve my request, Papa?"

The duchess disentangled herself from my father's embrace. "No need for that." My heart dropped. I'd expected resistance from him, not her. But my spirits were instantly buoyed by her next words. "I'll buy the school."

"Darling," Papa began, but my mother stopped him with a sidelong glance.

"You did not marry a milksop, and you did not raise one, either," she said. "Zia is right. We need to protect our teachers and educators, particularly women. They are the best hope of every new generation. Lady Felicity has said that owning Hinley is quite a rewarding experience."

My father smiled and then shook his head at me. "A brain like a vise. You two likely have that quality in common. Very well, buy your school."

The duchess winked. "Thank you, my darling, but I wasn't asking."

Staring at the building hosting Rafi's exhibition at No. 52 Pall Mall, I held my breath at the entrance as I descended from my father's coach. Guests were still lined up, waiting to enter the vestibule, and the inside North, South, and Middle Rooms would be teeming with wall-to-wall art connoisseurs. Tonight was Rafi's night, and I couldn't be prouder that he was showcasing his art to the world. From all accounts, his uncle had been livid, but Rafi had not cared for the man's approval. His art meant something. Even his mother had returned to England from Persia for her son's artistic debut. I'd meet her tonight—yet another reason for my jangled nerves.

Followed by my faithful Gemma, I approached the line, wondering if I should wait, but the gentleman of the hour saw me arrive and hurried down the stairs. "You came."

I smiled at Rafi, his expression uncharacteristically harried and much too adorable as he led me inside the gallery to the end of the North Room and the start of his exhibit. "Of course, I did. Nothing could have kept me away."

"Who knew it would be such a crush?" he muttered. "I thought only Kes, Ansel, and Blake would be here, but it seems like all of the *ton* showed up."

"Everyone loves a handsome, artistic, reformed rakehell," I

teased. "Should I be worried about any of these ladies stealing your affections?"

"You never have to worry about that." He pulled me scandalously close, drawing avid attention from those around us, including my brother, Ela, and the rest of their friends, but for once, I didn't mind. Let them all stare.

I smiled and peered up at him. "Good, because I can't get rowdy in this dress."

"In case I forget to tell you later, you are breathtaking, Zia," Rafi told me, his gray eyes gleaming at the Grecian gown that left one shoulder daringly bare. I'd chosen to wear a moonlit silver tonight, a shade that matched his eyes when he painted. "Come. I have someone I wish for you to meet."

I gulped as a very beautiful woman wearing a jeweled headpiece and sheer veil, whose son favored her looks, including her thick dark hair and sparkling gray eyes, approached. Her floral-embroidered jacket with gem-crusted cuffs was layered over a navy silk shift with flowing bell sleeves and wide trousers, and the sumptuous clothing only heightened her stunning appearance.

"Mother," Rafi said. "This is Lady Zenobia, the girl I wrote to you about."

I blinked. He'd written to her about me? Inexplicably tongue-tied, I curtsied. "My lady, er, Empress . . ."

Her laugh sounded like bells. "I am not empress, but you may call me Lady Farah. It's a true pleasure to meet the young lady who has tamed my ungovernable son."

"Oh, I don't know about that, Mother," Rafi teased with

a twinkle in his eye. "Once you get to know Zia, you might change your mind about who tamed whom."

"Rafi!" I exclaimed, blushing.

Lady Farah laughed. "I am thrilled I could meet you in person. When my son wrote about a girl who turned him inside out, I knew she had to be special."

"He probably meant that I make him want to tear his hair out." My gaze flicked to Rafi, and I nearly swooned. At the utter softness in his eyes, I wanted to kiss him so badly, but we were in public and in front of his *mother,* so decorum had to be maintained.

I squeezed his hand instead when someone drew Lady Farah away for an introduction, and then more of his admirers descended upon him, which left me free to wander the exhibit. The pieces were quintessential Rafi, all bold strokes of color and deft texture. But what had me blushing was the centerpiece of the show . . . the one of me.

And the bloody prince regent and his entire entourage stood in front of it!

"He has captured the lady's expression so marvelously," I heard the prince say. "It's a remarkable portrait. Is it for sale?"

"Regrettably, Your Highness, not this one," the owner of the gallery said. "But shall I show you his other works? Perhaps one will suit you."

"Very well," the prince said with obvious disappointment. "Inform Mr. Nasser that I intend to commission him for a private piece."

Heavens, my heart nearly came apart at the seams with pride.

Seeing my painting under bright gas lamps on an entire wall of its own made my breath catch. To the casual observer, it was an enormous canvas of a woman's body in repose, holding a half-eaten pear while reclining on a chaise longue. Her expression was half-lidded and deeply sensual, as if she shared a secret with the painter. Rafi had titled the piece *Muse.* Deep down, I rather liked being his secret catalyst . . . and his muse.

Because in truth, he was mine, too.

I turned, and as if we were two things dragged by gravity, I saw him thread his way through the crowd back to me, and I basked in his magnetic presence. "The prince loved this one," I told him over my shoulder. "He wanted to buy it."

Rafi lifted the knuckles of my right hand to his lips. "No one else gets to keep you but me."

My heart threatened to crash its way through my rib cage, and I was sure everyone in this gallery could see my feelings for this gentleman written all over me. I peered up at him, seeing nothing but sincerity in those gleaming gray eyes. "And do I get to keep you?"

"I thought you already knew, Zia. I'm yours."

CHAPTER
TWENTY-TWO

It is far better to be often deceived than never to trust; to be
disappointed in love, than never to love.

—Mary Wollstonecraft

The art show was a smashing success, and by the end of the evening and in the days following, Rafi had earned a dozen new
commissions, including a royal one. Viscount Hollis had been
effectively silenced by all the praise his nephew received. I had
laughed quietly with Ela—who had learned in a very circuitous
way that joy and success would always make for the best revenge.

Rafi wasn't the only one making important life changes. In
addition to composing my music, I hadn't had a full sleep in
nearly a week, considering how hard I'd been working to buy
all of Welton before the official auction. My mother had assured
me that the purchase was going through despite how long it was
taking even with Mr. Kaneko's excellent skills.

I was impatient. I wanted Miss Perkins to be back where
she belonged, enriching young, hungry minds. I consoled myself

with the fact that she would now be the headmistress of a brand-new school—the Osborn School—where anyone was welcome, even those in need of funding. The curriculum would still include the fundamentals of propriety and politesse, but girls would also have access to other subjects like mathematics, philosophy, science, and astronomy to name a few. The languages would expand from French and Italian to several others including Latin, Japanese, Hindi, and even some Creole options. There would also be musical instruction with a variety of instruments and styles, both classical and modern, to choose from. And students were welcome to read whatever they pleased, with the approval of their parents, of course.

Humming under my breath, I performed my morning ablutions and wondered whether today was the day Mama would tell me Miss Perkins could finally return. I was also curious as to what, if anything, had happened with Rafi's uncle and my father's very diligent barrister. I'd learned via very careful eavesdropping that Mr. Kaneko had filed on behalf of Sister Mary a bill of complaint with the Court of Chancery, which was an equity court led by the lord chancellor. It wouldn't stop the auction, but a suit would delay it.

I gritted my teeth. No doubt Viscount Hollis would be able to weasel his way out of it somehow. The man was like a roach. As if my thoughts had summoned the cad, when I heard the butler announcing the arrival of Viscount Hollis as well as Mr. Kaneko, every sense in my body perked up. What was the viscount doing here?

With a glance at a narrow-eyed Gemma, I tiptoed down the stairs to the landing and peered over the railing to the foyer. Sure enough, the slimy, smug-faced rotter was being shown to Papa's study while Nori's father followed, his face unusually grim. My heart sank. Had their efforts failed?

I had to get closer.

"Lady Zia, no," Gemma hissed, but I ignored her. This was much too important. I made my way down to the foyer, my lungs constricting with unnecessary panic. As I approached the open door, the footmen in the hallway frowned, but I placed a finger to my lips and scowled. I wasn't above pulling rank to get what I wanted.

Viscount Hollis's smarmy voice filtered through. "You think you can stop me with this puny suit?"

"No," I heard my father say. "But Mr. Kaneko here can bury you in paperwork if the title deeds and documents for the tenement aren't up to scratch. The lord chancellor, Baron Eldon, is a personal friend of his."

"You only delay the inevitable," the viscount crowed, and my palms itched to punch something. He sounded much too confident. Would we lose Welton after all?

There was quiet before anyone spoke, and in the silence, my nerves spiked. "That may be so, Hollis," my mother's musical voice chimed in. "Which is why we have proof that you have been illegally draining the accounts of the inheritance left to your nephew by your brother, the terms of which are extremely specific."

A gasp was followed by loud spluttering. "I beg your pardon! How dare you—"

"I don't have to dare, sir. The evidence is right in front of you."

The sound of a file hitting the top of a desk made me jump, and I could almost imagine the viscount's expression at whatever he was facing. The proof would not be pretty, knowing my parents. They went for the jugular, especially when our family was threatened.

"Where did you get this?" Viscount Hollis demanded, though the smug bluster from earlier had drained out of his voice.

"We have friends in powerful places," my father said calmly. "Now, let me be very clear to you, Hollis. If you attempt anything with your nephew, this file and all its contents will be delivered to the authorities. I'm sure they will be very interested to see how you have been misappropriating his inheritance for years."

"How dare you . . . ," the viscount began again. "This is *my* father's money. I have every right to spend it as I see fit."

"No, this was your brother's last will and testament." My father tutted, his voice dangerously low. "Transportation will be the least of your worries, if you are convicted of larceny and embezzlement."

For a moment, there was no sound, and then a chair slammed into a wall or the floor. I pressed into the wainscoting as a furious viscount came storming out of the study, his eyes wild. Clearly, I hadn't flattened myself enough as his gaze found me. "You!" He advanced swiftly in my direction. "You and that good-for-nothing boy are the bane of my existence."

I could smell his fetid, whisky-infused breath, and I braced for contact, even as I saw the footmen moving in slow motion out of the corner of my eye to stop him and my parents bursting into the foyer. An unexpected blast of cool morning wind from outside kissed my overheated skin as the front door blew open.

"Touch one hair on her head, Uncle, and it will be the last thing that you ever do."

Rafi's deadly voice made us both swing toward him, and I saw the moment the viscount realized that it was over . . . and what else he stood to lose in plain view of many witnesses.

My veins bubbled with excess energy as he whirled with a curse and left. I nearly collapsed into Rafi's arms as he strode forward to catch me. "How did you know he was here?" I whispered.

He stroked my cheek. "He was fuming, muttering about your family. So, I followed him. Did he touch you? Hurt you?"

"No. You arrived just in time."

A throat cleared, and my eyes met my father's. His cold blue gaze slid to the boy who held me, warming slightly with relief. "Didn't I warn you to stay away?"

Rafi's shoulders firmed as he canted his head in a polite nod, as much deference as he could manage with a heap of boneless and completely besotted girl in his arms. "I believe I told you, Your Grace, I'm not going anywhere."

Four days later, Gemma popped her head into my carriage house, where I was working on a new piece. Encouraged by the reaction to my own galvanizing performance at the Queen's Rose, the muse had been overflowing of late, and I'd spent many days composing into the wee hours. I glanced over at the easel in the corner near the large window that got the best light. The nicest part was that since Rafi didn't have a studio to paint in, with my mother's permission, he'd brought an easel here. As long as Gemma was around, he could paint to his heart's content.

And paint he did.

Though I had to admit that there might have been some frantic kissing in between painting sessions as well, whenever Gemma excused herself for a minute or two. I felt my cheeks heat at the memory of being pressed up against that very windowpane whereupon I'd been kissed within an inch of my life. It appeared that Rafi saving my neck in front of my parents had earned him their gratitude, if not their devotion. At least my mother's. My father was still an ice block, and who knew if he'd ever thaw, but Rafi was more than determined to chip away at him.

"Thought you might want to know that your father has a visitor," Gemma said, and winked. That was odd. I didn't really care who called upon the duke—they were usually all old peers who wanted something.

"And?" I asked glancing up.

"He's quite a brilliant young painter who is in every news-sheet and gossip rag today with more glowing accolades from the prince regent," she said, hand fluttering to her heart, her face bright with mischief. "He's here about a certain young lady, I suspect."

I blinked, wrinkling my nose as her words sank in.

Oh. *Oh.*

Standing so quickly I nearly knocked over my piano stool, I gathered my skirts and ran past her before halting and racing back into the cottage to check my face in the small looking glass. My hair was all over the place in a riot of curls, and there was an ink splotch on my cheek. Damn and blast! I licked my finger and scrubbed at the spot, but it was stubborn. At least my hair cooperated when I put two jeweled combs in on each side.

I was certainly *not* the epitome of a well-bred young lady, galloping like a runaway foal across the back courtyard to the kitchens. How long had he been here? Was he still in with my father? What were they discussing? Was it . . . ? My entire body shuddered at the thought of an official proposal. Would my father toss him out on his ear . . . or worse? He was certainly capable of that, and God knew he was taking an age to warm up to Rafi.

I nearly crashed into poor Forsythe as I barreled around the corner. I composed myself, though I could barely breathe. "Is Mr. Nasser here?"

"I was just coming to fetch you, my lady," Forsythe said, his dark eyes twinkling. "He's in the front parlor."

"Oh, he's not in with the duke?" I asked as my breathing slowed.

Forsythe shook his head. "Not yet, my lady. He asked to call upon you first, and depending on how that conversation went, he hoped to speak with the duke."

Goodness, if this breathlessness persisted, I was absolutely going to faint.

Taking measured inhales, I smoothed my trembling hands over my skirts and entered the room. I left the door open, though just a tad. Not that Rafi and I hadn't thoroughly trampled on the boundaries of respectability.

The visitor in question stood before the hearth, dressed to the nines in a smart black coat; a silvery waistcoat that matched his eyes; a snowy, perfectly tied cravat; snug breeches that I tried hard not to notice; and polished Hessians. I could stare at him forever.

"Special romantic encounter this evening, Mr. Nasser?"

He turned, and the view was even more spectacular from the front. That sinful smirk that did untoward things to me formed, making my mouth dry. "As a matter of fact, I do, Lady Zenobia."

"With whom, pray tell?" I asked, feeling rather frumpy in my nothing-special green-and-cream muslin dress.

"The most infuriating lady in London."

I grinned despite myself as he prowled toward me. "Oh, you must be at the wrong house. I have it on excellent authority that she lives down the road."

"The most marvelous lady in London, then."

I fluttered my eyelashes up at him as I found myself caught in his arms. "Well, now I would say, sir, that you are in the right place. Keep on with the compliments, if you please."

Brilliant, laughing gray eyes with gilded silver flecks peered down at me. "Smart, funny, feisty, incredibly talented. Shall I go on?"

"Please do, good sir."

"You are the most beautiful girl I have ever seen." His eyes memorized every inch of my face. "Even with ink on your cheek and your collarbone, you are exquisite."

Stupid splotches! I scrubbed at the spot on my cheek with my fingers and then ducked my chin to attempt to see the other offending spot. Alas, it was out of my range of vision.

"Allow me." Rafi pulled his glove off and lifted the pad of his thumb to my lips. Then he drew my lower lip down, gathering the moisture there. He moved his thumb to the mark on my cheek, rubbing gently, before descending to my collarbone.

"Thank you," I whispered.

His gossamer touch made shivers descend, knuckles moving back and forth upon my skin as though they were a brush and I was his canvas.

He shook his head as if to clear it and then, without ceremony, dropped to one knee. "You told me to ask you again when everything was settled. So, I am here." Rafi grasped my suddenly numb fingers as I stared astonished down at him and he pulled out his ring—*the* ring—the one I'd once stolen from him and thrown into his lap in the carriage after our duel. "You make me feel like I can do anything, Firefly, like I can reach the summit of every mountain. Like I can be anything and anyone my heart desires, and you will never fault me for it. You make me want to be a better man. As I got to know your heart, I realized more and more that I was falling in love with you."

"Rafi . . ."

"Marry me, Zia," he said huskily. "Make me the happiest man alive. I don't care that you don't have a dowry. None of that matters to me. I will take you with nothing but this dress. . . ." He grinned wickedly. "Or nothing at all if that is your wish. I only care about you."

"I have a dowry," I blurted. "Who told you that?"

"The girls." Red smudged over his golden cheeks. "I wanted to make sure I had their approval first. It wouldn't do if the people you love most in the world hated me. They said something about you buying Welton."

"My mama bought the school. I still have a dowry." I glanced down at his handsome face. "A sizable one."

"Then your dowry is yours," he declared. "Thanks to my late father and mother, I am not in a financially precarious position. You can use it however you see fit. Make your mark on the world however you wish, Zia. That money belongs to you." He stood and reached up to place his hand over my heart. "All I want is this. Us."

I smiled. "You have it."

"Is that a yes?"

Through tears, I dragged him up, giggling as he pushed his ring that was much too big but still so very perfect onto my third finger. "Yes! Yes, I'll marry you. Now kiss me before I get snot over both of us."

"I forgot how obnoxiously charming you are," Rafi said,

gaze glinting with amusement and so much affection it made me dizzy.

Sniffing, I pulled a face. "You love me with all my many flaws, don't deny it."

Rafi's hands wrapped around me. "You're right, Firefly. I treasure you just as you are."

CHAPTER TWENTY-THREE

I do not wish them [women] to have power over men; but over themselves.

—MARY WOLLSTONECRAFT

Watching my brother and the love of his life get married was one of the most beautiful things I had ever seen. There wasn't a single dry eye in the church nor at the wedding breakfast. Even my father's eyes had been glossy. My mother had daintily pressed a handkerchief to her eyes while Ela's old chaperone Lady Birdie had openly wept.

I was one of the bridal attendants in addition to Ela's best friend, Lady Rosalin, Lady Simone, and two of Ela's friends—a lovely couple Miss Justine Diaz and Miss Qadira Ali, who Ela affectionately called, J and Q, from her time at the Hinley Seminary for Girls in northern England. The fitting for our dresses had been relatively painless, and the champagne-colored gowns with scarlet chaconia brocade had been as stunning as Ela had described.

I'd never seen my brother look so happy, and Ela was a vision in her gorgeous gold-embroidered red sari, which had been designed and sewn in India. I sat in the church with my parents, knowing that Rafi was only a few rows behind. Soon that would be us. . . .

He'd approached my father formally for my hand in marriage, and Papa had put him through his paces. He'd even brought in Keston to speak to his character. Thankfully, my brother had come around. The interrogation, for lack of a better word, had lasted hours, but Rafi had persevered. My mother had been pleased to hear that it was a love match. That was all she had ever wanted for me. While our wedding wouldn't be for another year, the thought of it . . . of being Rafi's *wife* was beyond comprehension. It boggled the mind. I'd read in some penny romance novels that reformed rakes made the best husbands. I supposed that might be true if they met the right partner.

"Are you ready, my lady?" Gemma asked as I slipped on a pair of white gloves for the ball that evening, hosted by our family to celebrate my brother's nuptials as well as the formal announcement of my engagement.

"Is it too much?" I asked, studying my reflection in the mirror. The dress was a golden silk with an overlay of chiffon and seed pearl embroidery stitched at the bodice and hem. It left most of my shoulders bare, with a daring expanse of décolletage. My hair had been swept back from my forehead and weaved into tiny, intricate braids, forming a crown with the lower half left to fall in shiny, multicolored spirals. The gold of the dress picked up the golden and bronze lights in my brown hair.

"Not at all," she said, and then, "Mr. Nasser will be smitten."

"He'd better be." We both laughed. Pleasure coursed through me at the thought of seeing Rafi's reaction, and my cheeks flushed. I hadn't worn this dress just for him. It was for me, too. This was a special evening. Not just because our engagement would finally be announced, but also because everything had been finalized with the Osborn School, and it was a milestone that deserved celebrating.

Miss Perkins had gladly accepted my mother's offer to run the new school. Though Mama had also asked the two elder sisters—we had been at odds on that—whether they would like to stay, they had mercifully declined. Last I heard, from the sudden dearth of students, they'd decided to open a new finishing school in York. Miss Perkins, however, had stayed and would be here tonight at my special invitation.

"This is a new chapter, Zia," I told myself, somberly meeting my own serious-but-sparkling amber eyes in the looking glass. "Perhaps even an exciting new volume."

The last had been a challenging experience . . . but I'd also deepened friendships, found love, saved an orphanage, bought a school, and learned a bit more about who I was. Even though the Lady Knights had gone quiet for obvious reasons in the past few weeks, I would never cease feeding that fire in my heart.

After one last perusal, I thanked Gemma and walked to the balustrade overlooking the enormous ballroom. Feeling delightfully full of heart, I caught sight of my friends near the refreshments room, chatting animatedly with Miss Perkins as well as Sister Mary. I was so happy they had both come! Usually balls in the *ton* hosted by other aristocrats were exclusive events, but my mother's parties were known to have people from all walks of society. Sister Mary shifted, and my heart warmed at the sight of a little girl wearing a pretty pink ruffled dress hanging on to her dark robes. Oh, Beth looked darling! Normally children would not be allowed at balls, but my mother must have made yet another exception for me.

My gaze parsed the dancers, searching for the only gentleman I wished to see, but there was no sign of Rafi anywhere. Disappointment curdled in my gut. Was he not here? It wasn't like him to not send a note if he was ill or otherwise, especially for an event of such importance. Perhaps he was only late. Still, it rankled. Our engagement was going to be announced this evening, after all. I stifled the burst of frustration and calmed my rioting emotions—the Rafi I loved would surely have an excellent reason for it.

Holding my head high, I descended the staircase, feeling hundreds of eyes flock to my person. As a duke's daughter and a declared diamond of the season, I was used to the attention, and though it used to make me uncomfortable, I saw it now as opportunity. These women all had voices, and they needed to be heard, and these men who held the keys to the kingdom would have to learn to share. I felt my smile bloom as I made my way to my parents.

I curtsied. "Mama, Papa."

"You look lovely, darling," my mother said, and I returned the compliment. She practically glowed in a deep red gown that made her skin appear lustrous. Diamonds sparkled at her neck and threaded through her coiffure, the braids cascading down her back. She normally wore them up, but I liked this, too. Clearly, my father did as well, because he could not tear his eyes from her.

"Papa, you look handsome." My father was an intimidating figure most days, even more so when he was dressed in formal togs. Tall and debonair, he wore raven-black evening wear offset only by a white cravat, his hair slicked back with pomade. His blue eyes glittered with pride as that gaze fell on me.

"You look beautiful, my girl." His stare warmed. "I'm very proud of you, you know."

"Even after all my dreadful mistakes?"

He nodded. "Just so. Everyone stumbles from time to time. It's how we respond to those setbacks that shows the world who we are. You're an Osborn. We never choose the easiest path because that's not in our nature. But the reward is both the journey and the destination."

"You're quite philosophical tonight, dear," my mother murmured with a fond smile.

"I suppose I am," he said. He grinned at me and winked. "I have to keep impressing her somehow, or she'll throw me over for some young dandy. Now, excuse us, Zenobia love, while I escort my splendid wife for a dance."

Laughing, I watched in rapt wonder as they began the next waltz. Graceful, elegant, formidable. My mother laughed as my father twirled her, and I felt my heart lift. Their relationship wasn't an easy one. It took work, effort, and compromise. Strong opinions and stubborn natures weren't always conducive to smooth sailing, but my parents communicated, and even more, they respected one another.

With a last lingering glance, I made my way over to my friends, who all stunned in their gowns. Lalita wore a gorgeous royal blue sari, shot through with silver threads. A young man in modest clothing stood beside her, and I had to look twice before I recognized him as Brennan . . . as in my *coachman,* Brennan. I widened my eyes in shock, but she just smiled, reading my expression. "Life is much too short to be playing by someone else's rules."

"What about your aunt and uncle?" I asked.

"Let's just say a certain duchess with vast influence had a word or two for them," she said, making me gape anew. "They prefer not to be socially shunned forever."

Evidently, my thoughtful mother had intervened on Lalita's behalf as well. "That's good, no?"

My friend let out a soft laugh. "Let's just say the fear of being completely cut off from this world set my aunt and uncle on another course from using me or my sisters to improve their circumstances." She glanced at her companion, whose gaze was as adoring as ever. "Brennan, of course, you know Lady Zenobia."

"My lady," Brennan said with a bow and a cheeky grin.

I canted my head. "Brennan, I must say, I'm glad you finally took your shot."

"Me too, my lady."

Surprises were everywhere, it seemed. I had no idea that

Lalita would ever be so bold as to take her own happiness into her hands . . . and with a boy so far below her in station. Here was a spark of the old Lalita!

Nori and Blythe looked gorgeous in their gowns, which were on the simpler side but no less beautiful, and I was offered the sparest of greetings before Nori dragged a red-faced but clearly smitten Blythe toward the balcony leading to the arbor. I lifted my brows, and Greer chuckled.

"They're almost as bad as you and Nasser. Where is that devilish scoundrel anyway? I'm surprised he wouldn't be attached to your hip with you dressed like *that*."

I snorted but blushed. "Thank you. And late, it seems." I took in the extraordinary ensemble of charcoal coat, gray and silver waistcoat, and black trousers that she was wearing. It suited her so well. "This outfit is amazing!"

"Thanks. I want you to meet someone." Greer gestured to the tallest boy I'd ever seen, who was in conversation with Miss Perkins. Pale blond hair flowed past his shoulders, and wide ice-blue eyes met mine. He resembled some kind of Viking angel. I stared unabashedly. "May I present my fiancé, Lars Nielsen," Greer said. "Lars, this is Lady Zenobia."

My eyes nearly popped out of their sockets. "I have to admit, Mr. Nielsen, a part of me thought she'd made you up and wrote letters to herself." I dodged a playful cuff from Greer. "But I am glad to see that you are indeed a real boy. Please, call me Zia."

"Zia," he said with a mischievous grin. "You are everything she described, except for the warts, the witch hat, and the broom."

Mouth agape, I shot Greer a look of fake outrage. "What kind of best friend are you? You told him I was a witch?"

"Of course, I didn't," she shot back, arching a pale brow. "I told him that you were a *soulless* witch."

We dissolved into laughter before I could gasp out a "nice to meet you" to Lars.

Miss Perkins was taking in the exchange with her usual pleasant smile. Her gown was a bold statement of midnight black, setting off her red hair perfectly. But then again, I expected nothing less from a woman who took pride in standing out.

"I'm so glad you came," I greeted her warmly.

"Thank you for inviting me," she said. "This is incredible."

I nodded and let out a breath. "Miss Perkins, I know the last month has been hard, and I want to apologize for any part I played in that."

"You have nothing to apologize for," she said.

"I do," I said. "I made choices that put us in danger. You lost your job . . . and your sisters."

She placed a hand on my shoulder. "I got a better job, and as far as my sisters, we've never seen eye to eye. I suspect a break has been long in the making, but I do wish them well wherever they are." A smile curved her lips. "And I accept your apology, though it's not necessary. I hope you'll stop by from time to time. To say hullo to Beth, who asks about you daily. And to teach. I already have requests for your very unique kind of music. Organized piano?"

I frowned in surprise, both at her knowledge and the description, but the latter was apt.

Pleasure filled me at the idea that someone wanted to learn *my* musical style. "I'd be happy to. Enjoy the ball, Miss Perkins."

Before I could move, a small tulle-clad body collided with mine. "Zia!" Beth cried, and then blushed, her eyes rounding. "Cor, you look like a princess."

Her mouth·was covered in blue icing and her eyes sparkled with joy. "So do you, Honey B."

"That's not my name!" she said with an adorable pout. "It's Lady Beth . . . andralissa."

I laughed. "That's very pretty."

"Mind your manners, Beth," Sister Mary scolded gently before greeting me with a warm smile. "We've just been to the refreshments room, and I had to pry her away from the desserts. She's vibrating like a tuning fork."

"What's·a party without sweets?" I said, crouching down to envelop the sticky child in my arms. When it came to hugs, I didn't care about a bit of sugar. "Eat whatever you want, love."

"I shall," she said brightly, and then made a show of looking around. "But first, where's your beau? That scallywag promised he would show me how to dance a Scotch reel."

So, Rafi was here, then? I bit back my laughter. "I'll be sure to remind him."

"Tell him I am waiting forthwith to bestow my favor," she said, nose high.

"Beth," Sister Mary chided again, though her mouth twitched with amusement, and then leaned in, her face going solemn. "Lady Zenobia, I wanted to thank you for everything you and your family have done for Bellevue and Little Hands. I shudder to think of what might have happened had that dreadful viscount succeeded in his plans. Bless you, child."

"You're welcome, Sister Mary, but I didn't do it alone." Uncomfortable with the praise, considering some of my own controversial actions, I gave her a small smile. "I'm simply glad Beth"—I broke off at the sharp poke in my side—"forgive me, Lady *Bethandralissa,* is safe."

After that, I couldn't help my grin as I made my way around the periphery, and wondered again where Rafi was. Our ballroom wasn't *that* big. I accepted a glass of champagne from a footman and watched the dancers begin a new set, this time a quadrille. Only a handful of minutes had passed before a shiver of awareness passed over my skin. Glancing up, I searched the room for the only person who could cause that feeling, but there was no sign of him. Perhaps I'd been mistaken.

"Looking for me?" a deep voice said from behind me.

As Rafi's familiar woodsy scent surrounded me, I took a second to bask in the rich baritone that never failed to make every part of me shiver with want. "You're late."

"For good reason, I promise. *God,*" he whispered. "Zia, you undo me. You're a vision."

"Thank you," I said, mesmerized by him in much the same way that my powers of speech deserted me.

"I cannot believe I get to love you," he murmured, and the heartfelt words nearly made me melt.

"Rafi."

"I need to . . ." He shifted us so we were in the shadow of a marble pillar, and his lips met mine in the softest of brushes. His tongue danced over my bottom lip with a groan before he pulled away. "That's better." I instantly craved more, but this had to do for now. "I have something for you."

"Give it to me later," I said fervently. "Let's go to the arbor this minute."

He laughed. "Zia, your parents, not to mention your brother, would throttle me if we disappeared in the gardens." His hands cupped my face. "And besides, I cannot be held responsible for my actions if I get you alone in this dress."

Before I could open my mouth to say I wasn't going to complain about a deuced thing, he reached into his pocket and placed a packet in my hands. Momentarily distracted, I felt the thin oblong shape. "What is this?"

"Open it."

Curious, I untied the string and pulled open the paper. It was a book, a very familiar red-leather-bound book with gold writing that resembled the ones we had returned to Miss Perkins. "You got me a copy of *Frankenstein*?" I asked.

"Peer inside," he said.

With careful reverence, I cracked open the spine. There was something written there. *To Lady Zenobia from the author. With affection, M.*

Wait. *M* as in *Mary*? I blinked in disbelief and read the inscription again, feeling goose bumps break out over my skin. "You got this signed to me? From Mary Shelley? *How?*"

"Lord Byron owed me a favor," Rafi said. "It's an important day, and I wanted to get you something special. I'm sorry it took so long, but he was on his way to Bologna, having stopped in England for a short visit from Venice."

Tears of joy brimmed. "Rafi, I don't know what to say."

His finger tipped up my chin, those eyes of his so full of love that I was happy to drown in them. "Yes, you do. *Alis volat propriis,*" he whispered. "Now, soar high, Lady Knight of my heart. Show the world how bloody brilliant you are."

With a tiny sigh, I bit my lip. He was talking about my music. Mary Shelley was iconic; I was just me. "What if I fail at being a composer or make the wrong choices? *Again?*"

Those dimples appeared as a true smile erupted on his face, one that not many people ever got to see. "You won't, but I will always be here to catch you, Firefly." He grinned. "And if you ever want to try another heist or two, I've got your back."

"My criminal days are over," I said with a laugh. "But I'll take the first offer."

Gray eyes full of sincerity met mine. "Forever and always, my love."

My heart was going to cleave past my ribs and burrow into his chest where it belonged. Not caring who was watching, I rose to my tiptoes and kissed him, not holding back for a single second. I would do it—I would fly with my own wings.

Without fear. Without reservation.

And I would scorch the heavens.

BEWARE; FOR I AM FEARLESS, AND THEREFORE POWERFUL.

—MARY SHELLEY, *Frankenstein; or, The Modern Prometheus*

AUTHOR'S NOTE

This book was a wild ride! Research is so fascinating to me when writing in any historical era, and the people I researched for this particular story certainly did not disappoint. A quick note of reference on time period: This story takes place at the tail end of the Regency era in England, which was from 1811 to 1820. Also, this is an antihistorical novel, mostly because it features an entirely diverse and inclusive cast of characters. We never want to erase or sanitize the ills of history—and the books that center those stories and narratives are so important—but as a person of color myself, sometimes you just want to celebrate the joy in finding love and being loved while dancing a waltz in a glittering ballroom. That's the beauty of fiction . . . stories have power and hold unlimited possibility.

Quotes from Mary Wollstonecraft's *A Vindication of the Rights of Woman: With Strictures on Political and Moral Subjects* were used at the start of each chapter. My intent here was to use her quotes to serve as a reminder that women have been fighting for equality and fair opportunity for centuries. Arguably the mother of modern feminism, Wollstonecraft was ardent about education and the fact that women's brains were just as capable as men's. She viewed men and women as members of an equal partnership, believing that women weren't simply performative objects for the good of men but human beings working for the collective benefit of society. I wanted the quotes to provide insight into Zia's thinking and why she chooses to do certain things the way she does, especially after having studied Wollstonecraft's work.

Mary Shelley, the iconic eighteen-year-old who wrote *Frankenstein* and the daughter of Mary Wollstonecraft, was a trailblazer in her own right. To pen such a compelling piece of fiction at such a young age is an unbelievable accomplishment; that the work has endured for more than two hundred years is proof of its significance. She wrote *Frankenstein* in 1816 when she was on holiday in Geneva with her husband, Percy Shelley, her stepsister Claire Clairmont, Lord Byron, and John Polidori. It was then published anonymously in 1818 and became an instant sensation. Mary Shelley has said that the idea for the novel was inspired by a nightmare after a competition was set by the group to pen the best ghost story. *Frankenstein; or, The Modern Prometheus* is often considered the first science fiction novel. How cool is that?

The Bluestocking movement, featured in the novel, started as a group of women sharing literary interests in the mid-eighteenth century. A few men were also invited. Some say that the movement got its name when one male invitee declined to attend, saying he wasn't dressed for the occasion, and he was told to come in his ordinary "blue stockings." The nickname stuck. The participants focused on intellectual pursuits and literary discussions, including the impactful works written by writers like Mary Wollstonecraft and Hannah More.

In this period, most aristocratic young girls were educated

at home by governesses and private tutors. Women were not allowed to attend university, and some subjects, like philosophy and science, were considered much too advanced for their sex. Both Wollstonecraft and More vehemently disputed that kind of thinking. However, for young girls in the gentry or daughters of poorer peers, seminaries or finishing schools like Welton usually provided instruction on feminine accomplishments like singing, dancing, drawing, embroidery, and languages like French or Italian, and classes were geared toward social skills and finding suitable husbands. Many of these schools focused on religious education as well.

Women who wanted to step out of socially designated roles to learn complex subjects or read controversial materials were viewed as radical, which brings us to *hysteria,* an important element of *Lady Knight.* Zia is not a girl who likes being told what to do. She is trying to find her place and her voice as she navigates the many limiting social rules of her station, and she has to make sure that she doesn't lose the little power she has by finding herself sent away to an asylum. Hysteria was first recorded as an affliction caused by movement of the uterus in ancient Egypt as far back as 1900 BCE but became more commonly attributed to women and girls when they acted out or stepped out of line in the nineteenth century. *Hysteria* comes from the Greek word *hystera,* which means *uterus.*

Several French physicians in the late 1700s had theories that hysteria was a physical ailment that led to emotional instability and that women were predisposed to it. Playwright Henry Fielding wrote in his novel *Amelia* in 1751 that women were subject to extreme emotions—*"A Disorder very common among the Ladies . . . Some call it Fever on the Spirits, some a nervous Fever, some the Vapours, and some the hysterics."* I found it fascinating that many women were condemned to private and public asylums if their conduct or modesty was called into question or if their behavior was deemed irrational. Many men used the excuse of hysteria as a way to control their "difficult" wives, mothers, and daughters, much in the same way as the men in power in this novel attempt (*unsuccessfully,* I might add) to do.

In this era, music was a male-dominated art, especially since some instruments were deemed gender specific. It wasn't ladylike for a woman to play the cello, for example, because of the position of the instrument, or the violin, because the "arm movements" would do "unfailing harm to femininity," according to Karl Heinrich Heydenreich in his book *Der Privaterzieher.* In the nineteenth century, playing the piano was a sign of wealth, grace, and accomplishment for young women. However, this meant playing only compositions that were appropriate, especially according to pastors and writers (most assuredly men) of the time, and certainly not the kind of music that our heroine, Zia, favors.

Later on, in the second half of the century, as the middle class grew, more and more women took to the stage as musical performers, playing previously male-dominated instruments. By the turn of the century, they were allowed to attend conservatories and play in orchestras. Composing, too, was considered a male domain. Unsurprisingly, given patriarchal standards, male composers were viewed as more skilled or proficient when women were equally competent.

Zia's special way of playing the piano is known in modern musical circles as prepared piano. The term *prepared piano* comes from actually preparing the piano with elements like bolts, screws, rubber, and paper that are placed on or between the strings to create percussion-like sounds before playing. Though it wasn't called prepared piano during the Regency era, it was a method practiced by creative musicians even before that time. Kelly Moran's "Limonium" and "Halogen" are extraordinary contemporary pieces to listen to if you're interested in how I imagine Zia's music.

I had a challenging time in my research finding aristocratic women like Zia who composed music and were well received by society. I did find two, though. Interestingly enough, one was named Amalie and the other Amalia. Imagine my surprise, considering my own name! Duchess Anna Amalia of Saxe-Weimar (1739–1807) was a German composer. Born a princess, she was a pioneer of music in her court, known throughout Europe as a center of cultural influence. She composed several symphonies as well as an opera. Princess Amalie of Saxony (1794–1870) was another German composer, harpsichord player, author, and singer. She composed operas and chamber music and wrote comedies under a pen name. Despite her royal duties, she was passionate about her music. She was a philanthropist and devoted supporter of the arts.

A little bit about Persian history since my hero is Persian: Rafi's family was part of the Qājār dynasty. The Qājārs ruled from 1779 to 1924. In the nineteenth century, Persia was the epicenter of political, cultural, and economic development. It was a patriarchal society: A woman's world was the home, and in all social classes, women devoted their lives to household activities. In wealthier families, girls were educated by private tutors in reading and writing in Persian, Arabic, and French, in addition to receiving religious instruction. As in England, they pursued interests like embroidery and music. During the Qājār dynasty, women were noted as some of the most skilled poets, writers, religious leaders, and artists. Wealthy female patrons found ways to empower each other through art, music, and poetry.

On the subject of Rafi's stepfather, I drew inspiration from a real historical figure, Fath-Alī Shāh, who was the second king of the Qājār dynasty. According to *Persia: Ancient & Modern,* written in 1874 by John Piggot, he supposedly had four wives and close to a thousand women in his harem, and he fathered hundreds of children who survived him.

One last research tidbit—the two criminal cases Zia overhears at the Old Bailey were *actual* cases! The Right Honorable John Atkins, Lord Mayor of the City of London, mentioned in the novel, presided over these cases. I was horrified to find notes in the official records of the Old Bailey for Wednesday, January 13, 1819, that a fourteen-year-old boy, Thomas Brown, was indeed found guilty and sentenced to being transported for stealing a handkerchief. A nineteen-year-old, John Dowding, was found guilty of breaking and entering, and stealing several rings and brooches. He was sentenced to *death.* No wonder Zia is so terrified when she overhears the verdicts. However, it's important to note that during this time period, such consequences were primarily reserved for commoners. Aristocrats would not have been punished so severely.

The true message of *Lady Knight* is not about breaking the law . . . it's about breaking invisible boundaries. It's about how to be smart, resilient, and compassionate and how to have agency while constantly advocating for yourself in a world where everything might not always be on your side. It's about not losing sight of who you are and never giving up on yourself or your dreams. At the end of the day, you cannot control other people or how the world sees you. The only thing you can control is yourself—how you think, how you act, and how you respond. And know that no matter what . . . you are, and will always be, enough.

Hope you enjoyed reading *Lady Knight*!

XO,

ACKNOWLEDGMENTS

To my editor, Bria Ragin, who is the absolute diamond of the season, thank you so much for believing in me as an author and allowing me to share my stories with the world. It is such a joy (pun intended) to work on these books with you. In truth, I see a lot of you in Zia, in her absolute fearlessness, creativity, and passion.

To my hands-down superstar agent, Thao Le, who has always been in my corner, cheering me on, giving me advice, and pushing both me and my career to the next level, I have so much gratitude for you. You're also a diamond . . . *the* diamond . . . ALL THE DIAMONDS. Thank you, thank you, thank you.

To Nicola and David Yoon, I'm so thrilled and honored to have a second book with Joy Revolution. Thank you for letting me be a part of such a monumental imprint. Enormous thanks to Wendy Loggia, Beverly Horowitz, and Barbara Marcus! To the incredible designer Trisha Previte and artist Fatima Baig, you absolutely smashed it yet again. I'm so in awe of your talent. Huge thanks to the production, design, sales, and publicity teams at Joy Revolution/Penguin Random House for all your efforts behind the scenes—I'm beyond thankful for your support.

To my assistant, Karen Delabar—you have saved me more

than once these past few months—I am so grateful we connected. Thank you for all you do. To my brother, Givan Kyle, thanks for all the lunches and brewery dates and for listening to me vent about all the things. To my ladies, Katie McGarry, Angie Frazier, Aliza Mann, Brigid Kemmerer, Wendy Higgins, Vonetta Young, and Suzanne Hammers, I have so much love for you. Thank you for always checking in on me (and especially Suzie for making me go to the gym). Your friendship means the world. To all the readers, reviewers, booksellers, librarians, educators, extended family, and friends who support me and spread the word about my books, I appreciate you so very much.

Finally, to my amazing husband, Cameron, who always encourages me to spread my wings, thank you for being there no matter what. And to our three beautiful children, Connor, Noah, and Olivia, how I love seeing you figure out who you are and who you want to be in this world . . . I hope you'll never be afraid to fly.

ABOUT THE AUTHOR

AMALIE HOWARD is a bestselling, critically acclaimed author of several novels for teens, adults, and young readers. *Booklist* called her young adult historical romance *Queen Bee* "a true diamond of the first water." Her books have been featured in *Entertainment Weekly, Cosmopolitan, Oprah Daily,* and *Seventeen.* When she's not writing, she can usually be found reading, being the president of her one-woman Harley-Davidson motorcycle club, or power-napping. Originally from Trinidad, she lives in Colorado with her family.

amaliehoward.com

Revenge is her
opening move.
Love might be
the endgame.

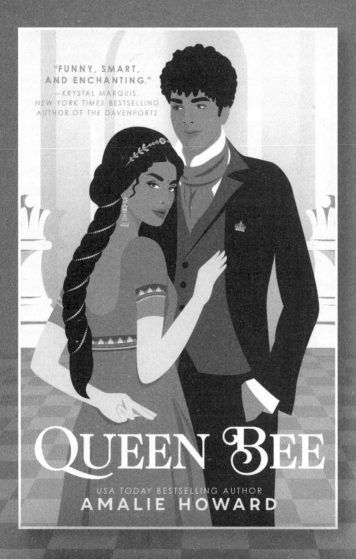

Lyra

Everyone sees what you appear to be, few feel
what you are, and those few do not dare to oppose
themselves to the opinion of the many.
—NICCOLÒ MACHIAVELLI

London, March 1817

Wincing at the ache in my ribs—I could have sworn I'd
heard one of them creak—I sucked in a shallow breath, my
fingers white-knuckling the chair as Sally, my lady's maid
and friend, pulled the laces of my stays. Traditional long
stays weren't ever truly laced *tight,* just enough to under-
score the lines of the gown, but I could barely breathe as
the stiffly woven twill fabric pinched my upper torso. The
pressure in my chest was most likely due to nerves.

I was about to take down the reigning queen and king of
this year's social season, which meant the evening had to be
perfect . . . *everything* had to be perfect. First impressions
were a valuable tool, and a person usually had only one
chance at them.

"A bit looser, Sally," I said through my teeth.

She met my gaze in the mirror, her green eyes calm. "Breathe in, count to five, and then release."

Listening to her sage counsel, I inhaled and exhaled. Panic prickled beneath my skin, but with each gentle tug, I felt it start to ease. Stays were a lady's battle armor—after all, I was going to war, the glittering ballrooms of London my battlefield.

Tonight wasn't about finding a match from the marriage mart. Tonight was about claiming what was mine—position, influence, power. Those things had been taken from me without my consent . . . things that were my right as the daughter of a peer.

A splendid come-out. A glittering social season. An impressive suitor.

All *stolen*.

And I intended to take them back.

It was my very first season . . . my ticket into the *ton*, the crème de la crème of British high society. From February to midsummer, the elite left their grand country estates and flocked to town for countless balls, dinner parties, and entertainments while parliament was in session. Arguably it was the best time to launch a son or daughter of marriageable age into society and make an excellent match.

Nostalgia gripped me. It would have been nice to come out under the name my parents had given me, but that chance was lost forever now.

My nemesis had taken that from me, too.

The basic tenet of revenge was simple. Niccolò Machiavelli, author of *The Prince,* had the right of it: If an injury has to be done to a man, it should be so severe that his vengeance need not be feared. In other words, crush or be crushed. Revenge was much like chess—a game of positioning and strategy. A game of patience. A game of power.

A game I intended to win.

Poppy Landers was going down.

Breathe. You've got this.

Reaching for equanimity, I focused on my plan to take down the queen and checkmate the king. As with any round of chess, the first move would set the tone for an entire game.

The season's opening ball at Almack's Assembly Rooms, the so-called seventh heaven of the fashionable world, would be vital to my success. Receiving an invitation voucher to Almack's was a rite of passage, and one I intended to savor. Luckily for me, my companion and chaperone, Lady Birdie, was dear friends with Lady Sefton, one of the esteemed patronesses of the institution, and once Lady Sefton had confirmed that I was suitably wellborn and in possession of an obscene fortune that would make the eligible gentlemen sit up and take notice, my voucher had been approved.

I sucked in another quick breath as Sally and the other maids lifted over my head the delicate ivory gown that was adorned with fine chikankari embroidery of lotus flowers and vines. For jewelry, I wore my late mama's nine-strand pearl necklace, which fell in luminous tiers. When she'd been alive, she always used to say that nine was an auspicious number, and that the pearl gemstone ruled by Chandra, the power of the moon, would imbue fearlessness and emotional balance.

I needed both in spades tonight.

The maids cooed and made clucking noises of admiration when the buttons were hooked and my gloves and slippers were fastened into place.

Even Lady Birdie, who was sitting in the corner on a chaise, sniffed, her eyes going glossy. "Goodness, I've never seen a prettier girl."

"Thank you, my lady," I said. "However, I am sure there will be many lovely young women in attendance tonight."

"You will outshine them all, my dear, I'm sure of it."

When Sally and the girls were finished, I walked over to the mirror and stared at my reflection. Every raven-black lock of glossy, freshly dyed hair was in place, coiled around the crown of my head and wound into intricate loops. My brown skin glowed, thanks to my mother's skin care regimen of sandalwood paste, almond oil, turmeric powder, and rose water. Hazel eyes sparkled from beneath a heavy fringe of thick eyelashes, and my lips were soft and plump.

The image was a far cry from the plain, acne-prone child I used to be.

This girl was older, beautiful, and unnervingly confident.

They won't see you coming.

"You are a vision," Sally whispered from behind as she

handed me a matching satin reticule that was to be attached to my wrist.

"Come along, dear," Lady Birdie said, as impatient as ever, her eyes narrowing on the clock. "Or we shall be late. You know how the patronesses are with their rules. They're rather ridiculous, I must admit, but I shouldn't want us to be locked out if we aren't there by eleven. Lady Sefton and Lady Jersey are not so bad, but the other ladies are ghastly. Don't tell them I said that."

"Of course not, Lady Birdie." I stifled my giggle at her peeved expression and followed her downstairs. On occasion, she reminded me of my mother. Before her illness, my mother had been a force of nature, bright-eyed, kind, and always wearing her heart on her sleeve.

You used to be like that, too.

I shoved that voice away—being sweet and naïve had won me no favors.

Lady Birdie was correct about the patronesses and their asinine rules. The doors were shut at eleven, and *no one* was let in after the doors had been closed. As if that weren't rigid enough, there were also the comportment rules and the dress requirements. Even the most distinguished of dukes had been refused admission upon occasion when they'd arrived late or without the proper wear. I fought an eye roll. God forbid a gentleman wear trousers instead of breeches, or tie his cravat without the required number of starched points.

The tiniest of snickers emerged as I smoothed my palms

down the front of my dress. I glowered with envy at Lady Birdie's choice of clothing—a gorgeous sari made of loose but extravagantly threaded fuchsia silk that left me with longing. I would have loved to don that! Instead I was stuck in this frothy concoction of a gown fit for a doll, although I recognized that looking the part was as critical as playing it.

I was no longer Lady Ela Dalvi, but Miss Lyra Whitley, the enigmatic heiress about to own this season and deliver justice to her enemies.

"Are you nervous?" Lady Birdie asked when we were finally ensconced in the carriage and it lurched into motion.

I shook my head with forced optimism. "Not really. I am merely interested to see what all the fuss is about. Lady Felicity told me that her come-out was a bit uninspiring."

"She would say that, though she was declared an Original—the season's loveliest lady—before the end of the ball. It was such a pity she quit London thereafter and never returned." She sniffled as if the recollection were painful. "Never mind that. It will be a wonderful evening, and you will have a smashing time. There will be tea and lemonade, bread and butter, and cake."

I knew what to expect from tonight's event, thanks to my mentor, Lady Felicity—or as she was known to me, Church. *Stale* cake, *weak* tea, and *warm* lemonade.

"I cannot wait."

Lady Birdie peered at me, her eyes growing more resolute, as if she was determined that I succeed where her previous charge might have failed. "Remember your manners and conduct yourself like a lady. No outward displays of temper or enthusiasm." I gave a dutiful nod. She didn't have to worry—I had no intention of failing—but it didn't hurt to have the reminders.

"Stand straight and tall," she went on. "If a gentleman asks you to dance after an introduction is made, you may accept, but no more than two times and *only* if you have a particular interest in said gentleman. Above all, do not find yourself alone with any gentleman, or you will see your reputation shredded to tatters before you can say a single word."

Good God, the irony was enough to make me huff a suffocated laugh.

I was well acquainted with the kiss of ruination. My reputation had already been exposed to the brutal touch of it and *hadn't* survived. Ergo the name change and my current machinations. My younger self, the gullible, green Lady Ela wouldn't have had a beggar's hope of taking on the filthy rich and lofty *ton*.

Or Poppy Landers.

Hence my elaborate and entirely Machiavellian plot for revenge.

In which the first and most crucial step would be to infiltrate Poppy's circle of friends. Once that was done, I intended to dismantle her inner court, become a diamond of the first water and charm away her suitors—one in particular—then sully her reputation as she'd sullied mine. The fifth and final step would be to have Poppy removed from the *ton* for good.

There was room for only one queen.

And that would be me.

"I understand, Lady Birdie," I murmured. "I will not disappoint you."

Too much was hinging on this—my past, my present, my future. The familiar bubble of resentment and bitterness formed inside me, and I shoved it down. I could not afford to be distracted by *feelings*. This come-out was my *due*.

When we arrived at the address on King Street and the liveried groom opened the carriage door, we descended the steps and entered the building. Introductions were made to Lady Sefton—a pale but pretty brunette—and Lady Jersey, with her impeccable coiffure, porcelain skin, and intense stare. Lady Birdie greeted the latter as Silence—a nickname, perhaps—and embraced her warmly before we found our way into the crowded hall.

I took a moment to discreetly gawk at the enormous ballroom, with its huge marble columns and gilded mirrors, already filled with people dressed to the nines. It was a feast for the senses. Elaborate gas lamps illuminated the sprawling space, and clusters of fresh flowers added lovely splashes of color. A small orchestra sat at one end on a balcony, and what looked to be a rousing quadrille was already in progress.

Heart humming with delight, I let my eyes sweep the crowd. It wasn't long before they stopped and swiveled, and my lungs seized as though grasped by a giant fist. Goose pimples prickled every inch of my skin.

He was here.

Lord Keston Osborn, the Marquess of Ridley, was still the only boy who could make my heart feel like it was caught in a stampede. Though he wasn't a boy anymore. He was a *gentleman* now . . . nearly nineteen. Fit, dashing, and sickeningly handsome.

He's part of the plan, he's part of the plan, he's part of the plan.

The chant was pointless—I could barely focus, much less look away.

A broad brow beneath beautifully chaotic dark brown curls led to a strong nose, bold cheekbones, and wide, quirked lips. Even from a distance, his rich brown skin gleamed with health, and that chiseled jaw could have cut glass. He was surrounded by a small group of other young men, but they paled in comparison, especially when those lips parted in a grin.

Sweet merciful heavens . . .

This—my unexpected and entirely *too* visceral reaction to him—was going to be a problem. I knew it as well as I knew my own heart. I'd foolishly been hoping that time had dimmed my memories of him, but three years had hardly reduced those gut-punching good looks or the effect of that smile. If anything, he was even more magnetic.

I should have hated him. But hate was a useless emotion . . . unless properly directed. Despite the muddle of yearning and nostalgia swirling in my belly, I had *purpose,* and I gave myself the stern reminder that he was merely one piece in this game. My principal foe—the queen—was somewhere else in this enormous ballroom.

"So what do you think of London, Miss Whitley?" Lady Jersey asked, peering at me down the length of her patrician nose.

Moistening my lips, I looked at her and smiled as though the floor hadn't been pulled from under my feet. "I love it so far, my lady."

"A far cry from Cumbria, isn't it?"

I nodded, casting my eyes down demurely. These patronesses loved flattery. My tone held just the right amount of protracted awe—it wasn't hard to do. London was in a class of its own. To many of the *ton,* it was the center of the universe, and Almack's was its glowing jewel. "Cumbria is certainly not anything like this!"

"Yes, well, we try." She smiled as she canvassed the room, her mood brightening. "Follow me. I've just had the most marvelous idea of introducing your charming ward to my nephew," Lady Jersey said to Lady Birdie, her calculating stare returning to me. "You're around the same age, and his set will take you under their wing, I'm sure of it. You seem like the right sort of girl."

And by "the right sort," she meant that I had an excellent dowry, which was already a topic of fervent gossip, according to Lady Birdie. Money had a way of opening the tightest, most elite circles. Fortune, connections, beauty, and virtue—the recipe for female accomplishment in the *ton.* One didn't even need to be beautiful if one had coin.

To Lady Jersey, I was a fortune with legs.

She cut briskly through the crowd, and we followed. One did not insult a patroness with a refusal, after all. We came to an abrupt stop, and I barely had time to take in my surroundings near the refreshments table before Lady Jersey tugged on my arm. "Here we are," she said. "Ridley dearest, may I present to you Miss Lyra Whitley. She is Lady Birdie's ward and new to town. Miss Whitley, this is my nephew, Lord Keston Osborn, the Marquess of Ridley and heir to the Duke of Harbridge."

Time slowed, my pulse rushed in my ears as conversation stopped, and I *felt* a handful of curious stares flock to my person. Good gracious, I *wasn't* ready to meet him face to face so soon. Still . . . I looked. I couldn't help it.

My word, he was tall! I'd grown, too, but I had to be at least half a foot shorter than his strapping six-foot frame. Up close, I saw tawny hints of bronze and russet chasing through the dark brown curls that had been seared into my memory. My gaze traveled over the fitted black coat and pristine white shirt to his cravat, arranged just so, topped by a square jaw that my fingers itched to trace. A pair of brown eyes flecked with topaz and gold, and filled with amusement, met mine.

Could lungs fail? Simply cease working?

Because, sweet baby bunnies in a basket . . . air was in scarce supply.

"A pleasure to make your acquaintance, Miss Whitley," his deep voice said, drizzling over my senses like warm honey on a hot scone.

Dear God, why was I thinking about honey and scones?

Because now my mouth was watering like a leaky pipe. *Pull yourself together, for God's sake!*

"And you, Lord Ridley." At least I had the wherewithal to curtsy and address him formally . . . not by his given name which sat on the tip of my tongue. Calling him Keston aloud would be the ghastliest faux pas.

I was barely paying attention as he introduced the three other boys around him—Lord Ansel Chen, Lord Blake Castleton, and Mr. Rafi Nasser—when Lady Jersey and Lady Birdie turned to greet a couple who had stopped to speak to them. At the moment, I was trying to act like my insides weren't dissolving into lava and setting everything on fire.

The marquess's eyes crinkled at the corners as he studied me, a slight frown marring the perfection of his face, as if something had troubled him for an instant. Coldness gripped my stomach in a fist. Would he recognize me? Was my plan doomed before it started? But then he only smirked as one of the boys behind him said, "Welcome to London, new girl."

Irritated with my fears, I reached for the sangfroid I'd practiced for hours. I was Lyra Whitley . . . and Lyra Whitley meant to dance on the bones of her enemies. Lyra Whitley was a force of nature . . . a soldier armed to the teeth for battle and a phoenix rising from the ashes of her past. Lyra Whitley was everything Ela Dalvi needed to be in this moment.

An opposing *queen* about to take control of the board.

I turned to the one who had spoken. Rafi, he was called.

Rakishly handsome with a pair of dark gray eyes that twin-
kled with interest in his golden-brown face, he oozed en-
titlement. I had to emulate that. *Embody* it.

Batting my eyelashes, I grinned and put the slightest bit
of flirtation into my voice. "So, what's a girl got to do to get
some lemonade around here?"

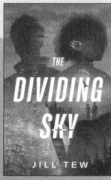

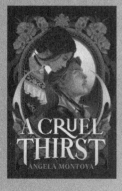